MARCH IN TIME

MARCH IN TIME

MEL MCNULTY

Melissa McNulty

For R.P

I

Hither & thither, her eyes darted. Ears cocked for the slightest crunch of leaf underfoot. With one final glance, she slipped the trowel from her jacket, and jabbed at the base of the headstone. The scrape of metal on sodden earth obscene in the silence of the Kirkyard.

"I think this belongs to you."

She kissed the roll of paper and buried it.

Five months earlier

13th February 1928

Dearest Reader,

> *If you have found this letter, then I am long gone.*
> *I realise this might seem a touch ghoulish, this strange*

voice from beyond the grave, but I canna deny the thought gives me a tickle.

I've no idea why I'm writing this. But then, how I spend most nights doesn't make much sense. Frozen, moth-eaten blanket wrapped about my shoulders, I've become a sort of ghost, haunting this once fine house. But sitting at this desk in a vain attempt to keep my mind occupied is better than lying in bed staring at the ceiling with sea of a thousand drowned faces behind my eyes until I blink and stretch and greet the dawn. My one comfort is in imagining my own darling wife might still sleep sound in our bed.

On a side note, if said bed is still here... well, let us say, I hope you are not newlyweds. And I suspect the native woodworm, perturbed at our invasion, have taken to sabotaging the floorboards, so for God's sake, mind where you put your feet.

Her spine prickled.

Laura shoved the delicate leaves of paper back into their envelope, returned it to the solid oak trunk from whence it came, and slammed the lid.

Her morning had been spent scrubbing lurid red spray paint from the living room brickwork. Tired of wire brushes and buckets of icy water, the rickety ladder up the loft had seemed a more tempting prospect.

"Just too damn creepy!" she said, though no one was there to answer. "Though I'm not so surenow." The rafters creaked beneath her weight. "Damn place might well be haunted, for all I know." She shivered and recalled the rickety bed her and Jim had launched into a skip the week before. *What bloody nonsense. Give yourself a shake, woman!*

With a scowl, she brushed back a handful of mousey

brown strands which had fallen into her face and hoisted herself to her feet. Her foot caught on a patch of rotted wood which crumbled under her toe. "Honestly, it's a miracle the ceiling's never caved in."

Having achieved almost a full three centuries, she doubted the dilapidated farmhouse would stand many more a Sutherland winter. *I'm sure it has its charm but seriously? He couldn't have picked a nice little cottage? One with a proper roof? Or would that have just been too sensible?* She grunted, lifted herself over the hatch lip and back down the ladder. *This place was cheap for a reason!*

*

"You are such a wuss! Spooky voices, wooh!" Jim wiggled his fingers in Laura's face. He dropped deadweight onto the sofa, which answered with a crack and a giant puff of dust plumed into the air.

"Careful, you great bampot! You should know by now, there's nothing in this house that isn't condemned or on its last legs and will you stop trying to scare me. My day's been weird enough, thank you very much!"

"All right, all right. So, the place is full of old tat. Bin the lot if you like. Start fresh."

She crossed her arms about her midriff and his scruffy face crinkled. "Stop acting like a toddler and drink your wine."

Laura frowned and lifted her glass. Still, she took pleasure in noting a few extra crows' feet spreading out from his eyes. It had been a while since she had last properly inspected her husband and she noted the tatty woollen jumper dotted with moth holes and the subtle greying at his temples, though at thirty-four he was still only a young man. Perhaps a touch less svelte than he might have been at one time. No longer the same cock-of-the-walk but quietly endearing lad she had met on a weekend bender under the glitzy designer lights of George Street. *Letting yourself go a little, my darling?* "Well, I suppose at least you'll be here to scare any ghosties away while you help me clear out some more junk this weekend."

"Erm, aye. I maybe forgot to mention that Geordie might have asked me to work overtime this weekend, and I might have said yes."

The Tick-Tock of the mantle clock with the filigree waggedy wa' swung in a precise, deafening rhythm. Her gaze remained fixed ahead.

"How much overtime?"

The tune to Top Gun popped into his head only he was a Maverick with no Goose and he scrambled for the right response. Any excuse that would wash. He could cope with Laura's displays of sound & fury. They would eventually burn themselves out and often led to more interesting outcomes, but this deceptive calm required the same deft light of foot as a minefield. "Uh, upuntilsundayafternoon."

"So, near enough the whole weekend then. I see."

"Laura, I'-"

But she had already risen and her determined stride towards the stairs told him this was not an occasion to follow. He slumped back into to sofa which let out another dismayed creak and he swallowed the last of his own glass

*

The spray paint kids hadn't managed to crack the lock on this one. For some mysterious reason, this room required its very own key alongside the front and back doors. An unventured dank space full of even more grimy things in need of gutting. Back in Edinburgh, it was so easy to fling rubbish into the back of a car and drive it to the nearest of many local tips. *But no. Instead, we had to move to the middle of nowhere because **he** had this vision of some perfect sodding countryside idyll.* She had done her best to enlighten him. Several times.

She wiped some excess WD40 on her jeans then smoothed a finger over a dado rail which separated wood panelling from wallpaper and held a poof of thick dust bunnies up to the light. "How long's it been since anyone last threatened this place with a duster?" A lump rose in Laura's throat. "I wonder if you ever got lonely. Jesus Laura, you're not getting sentimental, are you?"

She spun on her heel towards the open doorway.

What the hell was that?

"Come on, where are you? I can hear you laughing. How did you get in here?"

Nothing.

She pulled her grey woollen cardigan tighter about her shoulders and puffed the remaining air from her lungs. *There's no one there. And exactly why are we our own again? Because your donut of a husband would rather be at work than help.*

She stomped over to the double-aspect windows and thrust open the threadbare curtains to let the March sunshine into the stale room. A group of school kids played in a field over the road. "See, you're not going mad."

Under sunlight, a faded floral pattern poked out from the yellowed walls and particles floated in the haze. *It really is like a film set in here. A very sad, abandoned film set.*

Piled high by a stately mahogany desk was a stack of brittle newspapers. Laura lifted them one by one and brushed away years of dirt. "The ERA? I'm sure I've seen these before in a second-hand bookshop." Having removed the papers, her eyes lit upon a pair of posters which had lain beneath; illustrations of fanciful ladies with secretive smiles, in still-vibrant hues of yellow and red with the name *Mr George Edwardes Esq.* clearly legible in the lower right corner. These, she set aside with a newfound respect. *Stuff like this is worth a fortune. And they're in decent nick.*

Shrouded under the posters was a box of records. 78s, and most of them still in their original paper covers. She flipped through a few.

> *A Little of what You Fancy Does You Good*- Marie Lloyd
> *If you were the Only Girl in the World*- George Robey & Violet Loraine
> *The Boy I Love is up in the Gallery*- Katie Day

Someone had annotated this last one. **'Katie's first pressing- so proud!'**

"I wonder who Katie was." Laura asked the empty room and cringed. "Are you really expecting an answer, girl?" She was a woman of science and tended towards the rational, but an atmosphere threaded through this house, tangible as drifting smoke.

"I need air."

*

Typical Scottish weather trying to trip you up. Looks sunny but soon as you're over the doorstep, it's bloody baltic! The brass knocker juddered and clunked as she jammed the sticky door back in its frame. *That'll be another thing to add to the list, then.*

Rogart was not so much a place as a collective smatter of mainly post-clearance hamlets. The largest of these was the village of Pittentrail, through which trains rumbled either north to Thurso and Wick or south to Inverness. Laura's new home was at Blairmore, the oldest of these settlements, bordered by hills where houses were sparse and presided over by the white-harled Saint Callan's Kirk, lovechild of an eighteenth-century madman. In fact, the whole area was apparently littered with historical gems, but Laura had yet to cultivate an interest in any of them

Out of a customary stubborn disregard for gloves, she shoved her hands deep into her pockets. Her wellie-booted feet schlooped down the steep track towards the clamour of the children. She'd barely rested her elbows upon the drystone wall which bordered off the field, when an overly cheery voice and a mop of blonde curls sprung up from the other side.

"Hello, I'm Mhairi!" A knitted mitt, all fingerless and bobbled in lurid colours, presented itself under Laura's nose. "You moved in to the Begg Hoose!"

"Oh, hi." She took the proffered hand, willing her heart rate to return to normal. "Sorry, what? I was off in a wee world of my own there."

"The house on the hill? You live there now, don't you?" Mhairi pointed over Laura's shoulder. "It's known as *The Begg Hoose*. The women who used to live there, that was their name, I think. The kids at the school did a project on the village last year. She's my wee one. Izzy." She nodded to a child bouncing about on the grass who sported the same curls and wide-eyed expression.

"So, you know a bit about the house then?"

"Och, not really. Nobody's lived in it for years, but Mrs Matheson would. She lives just down the road there. Come on, we'll go and drop in on her. Izzy, come find me at Mrs Matheson's when you and your pals decide you're hungry!"

"Oh, but-."

"Nonsense!" Mhairi reached over the wall and grabbed her arm. "You must know there's not a village in the Highlands which disnae have its local auld besom. You'd have to meet her at some time or other at any rate, you're as well to get it over with. Never a soul passes through here without catching the eye o' Mrs Matheson!"

*

"And what brought you to Rogart then, Laura?" asked Mhairi while the hunched and pink-bedecked form of Mrs

Matheson fussed with the tea things in the kitchen. "Are you sure I can't help you there, Mrs Matheson?"

Mrs Matheson lived in a tiny croft right next to the signpost at the northern entrance to the strath, so she was quite literally the village gatekeeper. No one ventured in or out without the old woman casting her beady gaze over them. While the cottage carried a certain 'old lady musk,' it was immaculate and comforting. Like going to tea at your aunties.' In one corner sat a short bookcase filled with Mills & Boone and Catherine Cookson paperbacks and in another was a hunk of metal with a wire loop poking from the top. All mod cons.

"No m'dear, you're grand, it's just about ready, you two carry on!" Mrs Matheson called back to the clatter of teaspoons.

"Sorry Laura, you were saying?"

"It's alright. There's not much to tell. I, well my husband, saw the house, and we moved. That's about it."

"And you came all the way here from Edinburgh?" Mrs Matheson placed a final tray onto a coffee table already groaning with cakes and biscuits. "But that's not an Edinburgh accent."

"You've a good ear, Mrs Matheson." Laura fidgeted with her fingers. *Just open that particular can of worms right off the bat, why don't you?* Folk in Edinburgh didn't notice her odd little inflections here and there or if they did, they usually mistook her for the 'fur coat, nae knickers' Morningsider type- which suited her fine. "My husband is. I'm originally from Skye. I left at eighteen to study at Napier." she said and accepted a tea-filled cup and saucer. "It was Jim's idea to come north."

"Agus a bheil na Gàidhlig agad?"

"I did." Laura answered in English. "When I was young. Think I've forgotten most of it now. Haven't had much use for the Gaelic since I left."

Mrs Matheson made a small *hmm* in the back of her throat as she pushed a pair of round spectacles further up her nose. Laura sunk deeper into her chair and took a sip of tea. The old woman had the disturbing air of a headmistress, though her owlish eyes twinkled.

"We were wondering if you could tell us about the Begg Hoose, Mrs Matheson."

"Mhairi, I keep telling ye, it's Aileen now, lass. You're not a child now. So, you've taken on that old place, have you? Been empty and falling to bits these last 60 years syne. It'd be nice to see it lived in again. Lot of elbow grease, though. I hate to think what like it is inside."

"It's... a challenge. Do you remember the people who lived there? Some of the things I've found, they're over a hundred years old."

"Now do I really look that old?" Aileen gave her swishes of white hair a playful coif and the other two shared a smirk. "A wee bit, Mrs Begg, herself. Though I was only barely at school when she passed. I've no memory at all of her *companion*." she said with a curious expression. "I don't believe Mrs Begg ever married, mind you, but in them days it was polite to call the auld dears Missus."

"She had a companion though?" asked Mhairi.

"Well back in those days, companion could mean many things. Neither of them was local, mind. Mrs Begg was from away up in Caithness if I remember right. For whatever reason, she'd left when she was younger and never went back. Bit like yourself, lass." Aileen eyed Laura over the lip of her teacup. "*Flora!* That was her name, now. Flora Begg. As I say, I was too young to remember her very well, but she was a kind soul, always had a sweetie to hand for the bairns who passed by. A touch sad. I think she missed her friend. A southerner, she was."

"From Edinburgh?" asked Mhairi.

"No, no! Flora brought her up from London!" said Aileen with great mirth, as if the poor woman had been a rickety tea chest lugged to Scotland on a horse and cart. "Very glamorous in her day, so I gather and a fine singer, aye. She used to hum away to the plants in the garden, so said my ma. Lovely woman. For a Sassenach."

"I found the name Katie Day on some old records today. They looked quite early. One of them said 'Katie's first pressing.' No chance that could've been her?"

"No lass, I wouldn't have thought so. I mean to say, what would such a woman be doing up here?"

"But d'you think that was her name, at least?"

"Could have been. But then could just as well have been Smith or Jones. Now, I'll tell you something interesting about Flora Begg. Folk say she was a soldier."

"A what?" Mhairi blinked.

"Aye." said Aileen, drawing out the word the way busybodies do when they've some secret knowledge worth imparting. "How true this is, I don't know, but somebody told my mither Mrs Begg had lied to get into the army, and they came here because she had a friend in the area, auld man MacKechnie- the doctor an' his wife. He knew the secret, having been in the army himself.' Of course, it's probably all nonsense. Village gossip. A bit different, was Flora, and folk will make up their stories. Not that I ever pay any mind to such things."

*

"Do you think it's true? What she said about Katie and Flora?" Mhairi asked as the two women crunched along the pathway towards their respective homes. Izzy bounced along beside them, having indulged in far too much tea and cake for her mother's liking, of course at the behest of incorrigible Aileen Matheson.

Laura hugged her chest. *Why didn't I at least bring a scarf? Mind you, I wasn't exactly expecting an ambush.* Though she couldn't deny, the afternoon had been a pleasant one, if a touch awkward in spots. *I know it's only natural. New place, unfamiliar face, everyone wanting to know your life history, but it was so different in Edinburgh.* Sure, people had asked questions in a general chitchat sort of way, but it was easier to put people off in the city. *No inquisition by wee old wifies with too much time on their hands.* "Who knows? Does it matter now? We don't even know if the names are right."

"Aren't you even in the least bit curious? Your house could have been owned by two..." She paused and reached forward to cover Izzy's ears. "Two badarse women and you don't care?"

"Not particularly. It's in the past. Someone else's past. Other people's lives, not mine. Why don't you get into it if you're so interested? Can be your next school project."

"A project about two *lesbians*? One of whom pretends to

be a man and the other, probably went about strutting her stuff on the stage? Practically harlots, m'dear! Nah, wee place like this, if the parents didn't have a purple fit, that auld goat of a minister would. I could lose my job."

"So, you're denying The Gospel of Matheson instead, eh? Blasphemer! Something tells me that'd be a far deadlier course of action."

Mhairi shook her head. "Think about it. Mrs Matheson only knew Mrs Begg as an older woman. But old folk weren't always old. Did you spend much time wondering what your own granny was when she was young?"

Laura frowned.

"Exactly. Nope, it's your house, it's definitely our special project." She winked. "Listen, Izzy's off to her dad's next weekend, why don't you and Jim come to the pub? Meet some of your new neighbours."

"Alright. You're on."

*

Later in the evening, Laura watched the dance of the fiery fairies up the sides of the inglenook fireplace. Her socked feet toasted pleasantly on a footstool, big toe toying idly with a loose thread.

"Here you go." Jim handed her a mug of something warm as he slid *gently* onto the couch beside her. "Time for some new socks?"

"You're a good chap. Yeah, not had time to pop down to Inverness in a while. Should really get around to doing a bit of shopping." She snuggled into his side, curling her legs beside her.

"True. On both counts." He kissed the top of her head and slid a heavy arm about her shoulders.

"I met some of the neighbours today."

"Yeah?"

"Yeah, Mhairi lives further up the Strath. She teaches at the primary school. She has a daughter. Izzy." Laura left the statement hanging in the air. "And a Mrs Matheson. They were kind. Think they thought they were rescuing a wee lost sheep." She chuckled and scraped her cheek against the rough wool of his jumper.

"I wonder if Mhairi'll be teaching our own wee bairn someday."

The hopeful note in her husband's voice was almost enough to make Laura crack. Almost.

"See, you might get to like it here after all."

"Maybe." But Laura's mind was already somewhere far off, in a world of unpalatable possibilities, the crackle of the fire long forgotten.

*

Morning brought with it a new resolve. Laura took a deep breath and eyed the trapdoor to the loft. "Face it, it's this, or ripping out the kitchen."

Balanced on her tippy toes, she pressed the ceiling panel with outstretched fingertips and allowed the hinged set of ladders to pivot towards her. She flipped the catch on the bottom rung and the final set of treads rushed towards her.

She sat upon one of the sturdier looking rafters and took a second to reverently stroke the seasoned oak timbers which made up the lid of the sea chest in which she'd found the letter the day before. Her fingertips bumped over the natural knots in the wood which rest beneath a layer of silky varnish.

Laura tucked her middle three fingers under the rough iron handle and pulled hard. The letter, she set aside for a moment and sifted through a mound of photographs and magazines. There were more fragile issues of The ERA which showed theatre listings, adverts, and articles like modern day 'what's hot' lists, as far back as 1884.

A small hardback was tucked into one corner. 'The South Seas and other Adventures' by Robert Louis Stevenson. She remembered being made to read Treasure Island at school. "At least it was more interesting than Hamlet. Someone liked a good yarn."

She gave passing attention to some of the illustrations for a while then set it to the side and brought a handful of photographs onto her lap. A few of the postcards had faded writing on the back, others not. Mostly the same two faces throughout. "I wonder if this is Mrs-not-Mrs Begg and her friend."

One picture stood out above the other. The same women again, but younger, with illicit smiles and what looked like an ancient wooden rollercoaster in the background. As she examined the outfits, one of them did appear to be in costume although what exactly, she couldn't tell. Age had blurred the image and an inept attempt by the original developer of the photograph had left the corners flaking away. She had seen this sort of thing before as a curious child and her grandfather had explained it as having something to do with the chemicals being poorly mixed by the original developer.

"You look happy."

She turned the postcard over to see if the back would give her a clue as to the sitters' identities, but all it said was *'From the face on the other side of this picture.'*

"Wonderful."

She sighed and took one last look at the image before placing it with the rest of the paraphernalia. When she delved back into the chest again, her touch found fabric. What came away in her hands was the most beautiful mint green silken dress wrapped in delicate tissue paper. The material slipped through her fingers and pooled into her lap like mercury. Pearls, dotted about the lacework, still shimmered, even in the few dusty streaks which broke through the grimy skylight, as though they'd just been plucked fresh from the sea. The waist was tiny, topped with a rather fuller bosom. The full skirt flowed like a river to the floor. *Mrs Begg, if Mrs Matheson's story was true then you were one lucky girl.*

Though beguiled by the splendour of the garment, the laced hem was getting dirty where it trailed the mucky floor. With regret, she refolded it, noting the discreet brown paper label which attributed this wondrous creation to **John Redfern & Sons. Paris, New York, London.**

Next, she followed a mischievous glint in the blackness and met the coarse texture of embroidery. She inhaled sharply and tugged on a heavy heap of cloth, bringing it into the light. It was a tailored bodice-cut jacket of unadulterated sumptuousness.

Striking gold embellishments strode boldly from the cuffs

and a matching row of splendid silk buttons fastened all the way from hem to collar. An over layer of decorated panels in a beautiful, soft Hunters Green French serge formed the outer coat which split up the centre to reveal a malachite under layer. The inner lining was a decorative oyster shell pattern in black & white satins. It was the most marvellous work of fabric in the world. "I thought the dress was spectacular, but this is exquisite." She bounced the jacket up and down a few times. "How the hell did anyone manage to wear this thing?"

But the casket held yet more secrets. Beneath the jacket lay a trunk. Thinner. Blackened tin and battered. "This thing's seen some action." The catches were stiff, and the hinges squeaked in protest. What lay inside looked like something straight out of a comic opera- an ornate military doublet in bright red Melton wool with white & yellow collar and cuffs. *The costume in the picture! So much for the army, Mrs Begg. Village gossip, indeed. Ha! I'm on to you, Flora. I've seen Tipping the Velvet.*

In another thick layer beneath the jacket, was a pile of green & blue tartan with a red stripe, bound altogether with a huge, tarnished plate buckle. "Crest's definitely regimental but I don't recognise it. Some serious kit, though Flora. It must have cost you a bloody fortune."

A flat jewellery box lay in the corner of the trunk, a touch moth eaten, but the catch lifted easily enough. What she saw inside gave her much pause. A set of medals, none of which she had any hope of recognising, inscribed with the name **3492 Sgt. Sinclair Patterson Begg.** They looked antique. "Who the hell is Sinclair now? Whoever you were, you were clearly a brave old boy."

A further, smaller box revealed even more medals. She'd

seen these ones often enough on *Roadshow* to recognise 'Pip, Squeak & Wilfred' but that was where her knowledge ended. Looking at the inscription, however, this time Sinclair was a Major. *Is that even possible? Sinclair's son, maybe? Sergeants don't suddenly become majors.*

She furrowed her brow. "The letter." *Begg isn't that common a name. Could this have been written by Flora's brother, maybe? Has Mrs Begg had it wrong all these years? Was he the soldier? Were Sinclair and Flora married? Or even Sinclair and Katie? If Katie even existed. God, this is so confusing.*

The note was an inch thick, the handwriting faded and minuscule, but nosiness got the better of her.

I hope by the time you move in the place won't be in too bad a state. When we first bought it, it was nothing more than a crumbling ruin with a handful of decrepit fireplaces and the walls barely standing. It took some work, but we built a home here. Know one thing. This house has been a happy one.

Sleep is uneasy quarry for me, tired as I am. It is strange how much more difficult it becomes, the older you get. I can remember laughing at an ancient aunt when I was still only a chiel' myself. She wouldn't go to bed until many hours after the moon had risen and still be up and about well afore the lark. Little did I know! But then, my own weary eyes have seen such things my aunt could never have dreamt of.

2

With its heather-swept hills, jagged cliffs and unending horizons, Caithness is a land of shadows and shifting lights.

In the winter, daylight's barely broken through the clouds by mid-morning. By late afternoon the darkness returns, but instead, across those most northerly skies, vivid greens and blues and purples shoot through the twilight skies.

In summer, when the herring boats set again to sea and the women return to the fields for the cutting of the peat, the sun shines on past Midnight.

To those who know the all the local legends like the Selkie of St Trothan and the faerie hills, it is a magical place but barren and unforgiving to anyone daring enough to try scratching out a living from its unyielding soil. It amazes me, still, how my family clung on for as long as they did after over a century of clearance, sheep & famine.

I left at sixteen. Sturdy from tilling the earth and eager for adventure beyond my father's lime-washed longhouse with its one chimney instead of the usual two. Nobody could remember why we were missing a lum. The house was already generations old by the time I came along. Just another of those long-forgotten oddities.

There is nothing like those violent gales which whip from North to East with no mountain to slow their path. Your own hair slashes *at the skin on your cheeks, 'til you're convinced they'll bleed. In the village of Badbea, mothers would tie their children to rocks to prevent them from being blown into the sea while they scraped away at the meagre spots of cliff-side scrub their laird had cast them away to. Their raw, weather-beaten faces bundled behind tattered shawls whose hems had ripped away to ragged tassels.*

I couldn't stay. I would hear stories from the local men who had sailed on great hulking ships to the Crimea, or whose fathers had battled with Wellington in Flanders, Portugal, or Spain. Even the sons of Sinclair themselves, had fought at Quatre Bras. Most of them came back with missing limbs or eyes, and barely a beggar's penny to keep body & soul thegither. I paid no heed to their warning scars.

Worse, I lied...

London, February 1899

Bang!

And out went all the lights.

In fairness, it's probably knackered my hand more than his head. State that arse's in, he's feeling no pain. The man shook his bruising knuckles in the frigid air and huffed on them. "Sorry about that, Missus...?"

"It's Miss Vaughan. Katie Vaughan. And I should be thanking you."

"S'alright. I was passing and heard the scuffle." said the stranger, in a lilt unfamiliar to Katie's ears. "But you're welcome."

"I'm grateful to you, sir. Not many gentlemen would have stopped to help."

"Oh. That's a sad thing to say."

"You're very kind. Mr-?"

A sudden qualm struck the young woman. She peered deeper into the gloom and could just make out a flash of scarlet red and the tell-tale nipped in silhouette of a uniform. Sick fear lanced through her gut.

"Flora."

"I beg your pardon?" Katie blinked and backed away.

The man's warm chuckle slashed through the icy air to tickle about her ears. He stepped into the narrow glow afforded by a lantern above the stage door, removed the Glengarry cap from atop his head and held out a set of swollen fingers.

Katie regarded the stranger's ready smile and her heart beat a little louder in her ears. Once, when she had been a young chorus girl on a helter-skelter tour around England's provincial theatres, she'd had the misery of having to share a stage each night with one permanently inebriated Glaswegian. The voice of this so-called comedian had grated in her ears and his choice language was worse. She took his fingers in a tentative grasp and stared harder, examining the play of the lamplight on the man's cheeks and the cast of his eyelashes.

"I swear, I'm exactly as I say." The soldier hissed through gritted teeth and Katie jerked her hand away.

"I'm sorry. But you really are a girl!"

A terrific gust of belly-laughter was Flora's only reply, but a flush darkened the other woman's cheeks and she reached out to grasp Katie's wrist again before she could bolt. "Apologies, Miss Vaughan. What gave the game away?"

"Your eyes. There's sincerity in them. Even if you did laugh at me." A groan brought both of their attentions back to the ground where the drunken dolt from earlier stirred on the frost-bitten cobblestones. "Friend of yours?"

"Never seen him afore. But I doubt he'll stay that way much longer." She prodded his ribs with the toe of one boot, buffed to a mirror-shine. "Perhaps we should..."

"Yes." Katie wrapped her fingers tightly around Flora's wrist, but instead of leading them into bracing late-night chill, she brought Flora back through the stage door of the Gaiety Theatre.

South Sudan, September 1898

Private Begg stood to attention before Major Stockwell, pith helmet under one arm, and body so stiff her spine might snap. Her bones trembled beneath a layer of khaki and the sweat which lashed down her back had little to do with the blistering desert heat.

"Precisely what the hell am I to do with you, Begg?" Stockwell slammed the flat of his palm on his desk from where he stood behind his chair. His generous height loomed over her beneath the low canvas ceiling. His ruddy face seethed with barely contained fury.

"I don't know, sir"

"You don't know. Indeed. You saved an officer's life, for which we must all be grateful and in the ordinary course of events, your actions would require some kind of reward, perhaps a promotion. But there's just one tiny problem with that."

"Yes, sir"

"Explain to me two things, Private. One; how is it, one of my most promising men suddenly sprung a pair of tits this afternoon and Two; why I shouldn't administer punishment myself or else send you home and let the War Office deal with you."

"Sir!" Her mind scrambled for anything that would help her, wondering exactly what said punishment would mean, though she had a rough idea. *All I wanted was a bit of adventure.*

"How in the blazes did you make it past the medical?" Stockwell blustered on. "On second thoughts, it's better I don't know. You, we can do without, but we can't afford to lose a doctor."

"If I may, Sir?" said Captain MacKenzie who, until now had remained a figure of silent observation in the corner. "I wonder is this worth the humiliation? The Seaforths are a young regiment. If news of this got out, that we'd let a farmer's daughter dupe us into recruiting her, we'd be a laughingstock. You recall that damn Bulkley woman a few years ago? And the embarrassment it caused for the entire army when that got out. Besides, much as it pains me to admit it, Begg has proven herself to be an effective soldier. Up until now." He cast her a sharp glance. "Might it not be more prudent to hush things up for the time-being?"

"You mean let her stay rather than admit some damned girl has given us the slip?"

"Much as we might wish otherwise, we can't throw her out in the middle of the desert. Questions would be asked and even if we could, supplies are having enough trouble reaching us as it is. We've no horse to spare and leaving her to die does seem a little excessive for the crime. This girl wants to play soldier, I say we let her. For a while."

Stockwell eyed Flora with something suspiciously like a twinkle in his level gaze. "You may have a point, MacKenzie." He scratched his chin for a moment then leant forward, his voice a low growl. "You might be a damn silly bitch thinking she can come out here and play at men's work, but you're also a damn brave one. Soldier, eh? Well, soldier you shall be."

Flora swallowed against a dry throat as the major continued.

"Whether your actions were courageous or just damned foolish, I haven't decided. In your favour, you have the respect of the men. And you did save an officer from an untimely meeting with his maker, so you will get your promotion. If only for appearances' sake. A step up the ladder should afford you some level of protection, should the unfortunate necessity arise." He nodded at MacKenzie who flicked a pair of cloth strips in Flora's general direction as if swatting away an irksome wasp. "Carry on Corporal and be grateful I like you otherwise I'd be having you dragged out of here by your hair and lashed to the nearest gun carriage like we did in my day, understood?"

"Yes, sir. Thank you, sir."

"Don't thank me, Begg. And don't go expecting any favours, either. When you get yourself killed, it'll be on your own head and no one else's. I only pray you don't take any good men with you when you do." Stockwell side-stepped into his chair and reached for a pipe which lay on a dish full of ash, tooth dents visible in its wooden mouthpiece. He gave it a solid couple of taps before striking a match to a fresh pinch of tobacco. "What's your name? Your proper name."

"Flora, sir. Flora Paterson Begg"

"Good. Now I know what name to give when the day comes I have to write your parents. You are dismissed, Corporal. And Begg? You breathe a word of this to another living soul and I will not be responsible for whatever occurs. Understood"

"Understood, sir. But what about the men who saw-"

"The men saw bugger all. An aberration of the heat. Dismissed. Get those stripes sewn on by morning."

Corporal Sinclair Begg saluted then turned smartly to take 'his' leave. As Flora disappeared into the blazing afternoon, Captain MacKenzie turned to the Major. "Strong words, sir, but she took 'em well, I thought."

Stockwell grunted and lifted himself off his chair to perch on the edge of the desk and took a few pensive puffs before replying. "You have to be tough on 'em sometimes to get the best out of them, Mac. I've seen a lot of excellent soldiers over the years, and I've seen some bad ones too. She might well be a woman and she might well find herself on the wrong end of some braggart's prick one day, but I hope for her sake, not. There's some spunk in there."

"I've never considered you much of a feminist."

"I'm not. I despise it. My wife is a marvellous woman. Keeps a fine home, but a woman she is, nonetheless. I'm not quite sure what Begg is, but the fact remains, she's a capable

NCO. Doesn't flinch under fire, has a strong enough back too. We can't afford for this incident to make a mockery of us. Better we extract some use from the girl before we move her on. Pragmatism, Mac! While you're at it, have a quiet word with the surgeon, Doctor MacKechnie. Best to apprise him of the situation." He frowned. "Though I suspect he already knows."

"What about the rest of the lads?"

"I'm not too concerned. I meant what I said earlier. Most of the lads like her. The rest? They'll keep their mouths shut if they know what's good for them. They'll simply have to lump it. We'll keep a half-eye on her for now. I'm tempted to say let's just drop her off at the first available opportunity, but let's just watch and wait, shall we?"

*

"I don't know if I believe you!" Katie smacked Flora's arm.

For a split-second, she regarded the practicality of Flora's outfit with envy. Flora had produced a box of matches from one of her cartridge pouches and the two women sat companionably in the warm glow of a pair of footlights. Their legs dangled off the edge of the stage, their feet vanished in the blackness below, although Flora's tanned knees keeked out from beneath the hem of her kilt. Everyone else had long since left. Aside from having to hide behind a costume rail from the whistling caretaker on his night-time rounds. The whole theatre was theirs.

"It's true! I saw a poster for the Seaforths at the post office in Thurso on my way to the market, and I reckoned it looked a bit of a lark. I fancied myself strutting about in the uniform, and maybe seeing a bit of the world. So, I cut my hair just short enough to hide under a hat, lifted some of the money from the back of the hearth and paid a drayman to take me to the nearest depot. Took a bit of arm-twisting with the company surgeon."

"And you've never been back home?"

"I couldna turn up looking like this, could I?"

"I suppose not. Have you been enjoying London? It must be very different to home."

Flora's mouth made a funny shape. "Aye, it's, err, aye. Fine. Dirty, smelly place that it is. It's fine."

"So not a fan?"

"No, not really. No offence."

"None taken. I'm not a Londoner either. It does require some getting used to."

"I thought you were London through-and-through. The smart end, of course. Where do you call home then?"

Katie's face froze for a second then looked away. "How did you get these to look so real?" She held the bristles of Flora's fake moustache up to the light.

Flora raised a brow. "Not so clever as any manner of trickery you might conjure here. I chopped up my da's shaving brush. It's as well I left when I did. He'd have gone dafter over that than my disappearance. Anyway, I used a rock to rough up the rest of my face and smeared dirt over it. Didn't fool the doc for a minute, but he took pity on me. No idea why, I'm just grateful he did. Anyway, he signed me fit, helped me disguise myself a bit better and I've never looked back."

"Is it exciting, like you imagined? Or is it awful living with a lot of crude men?"

"Bit of both, but it's home now. What about you?"

"Oh, my story's nothing so interesting as yours. I've been on stage since I was a child."

"It's interesting to me. I've never met an actress before. Well, not a real one. Met a few fakers over the years."

"I'm just part of a chorus line, really. I'm what they call a Gaiety Girl. Nothing so grand as an actress. We're supposed to be the perfect young society ladies, the kind any gentleman would be pleased to introduce to mother over tea and scones."

"You look like you're dressed for a party." Flora nodded to the ruffle of deep blue chiffon which peeked out from beneath Katie's heavy black overcoat. "Am I keeping you?"

"No." All the while Flora had been telling her story, Katie had found herself unwilling to let go of the other woman's injured fingers. At first, she had passed off her tender caress of the roughened skin as gratitude for Flora's aid. But her presence was comforting. "Jennie picked herself up a Johnnie for the night so some of the girls were going to dinner at Romano's. Mr. Edwardes arranges for us to dine there at half price, but I wasn't in the mood. I've had a much more pleasant evening here. With you."

"Well, I've had passed a very *pleasant* evening with you too, Katie. But I can't be staying out too late. I have to be on parade first thing tomorrow morning."

Katie's cheeks darkened as she watched Flora stretch out her limbs. "Will you visit again, Corporal Begg?" The two women regained their feet, their bodies coming scandalously close. Her mouth twitched. "If you really were a man this would be most improper."

"Well, you know what they say about soldiers." Flora gave her a wink. "I'll be back as soon as I can." Katie's eyes were the most intense ice blue, even in the limited stage light and she found herself mesmerised by the widows peak, strong brow line and the fine wisps of black hair which swept back from her temples. *No good will come of this, Flo.'* "I promise."

"You never told me what brought you to London, Miss Corporal."

"No, I didn't, did I? Turns out, if you're going to be a Corporal you have to know your letters and numbers… they never knew until after they'd promoted me that I'd never learnt. I'd done a crafty job at hiding it, for a while. So, while the rest of the lads headed south, they shipped me off here. Get my A, B, C's sorted. God-knows why but Stocker's taken a liking to like me. Lucky or I'd be gone altogether."

Flora turned towards the blackness of backstage. Several moments passed before she realised the only steps she could hear were her own. She turned back just in time to catch a look of consternation on the other woman's face before a proprietary mask of polite indifference covered over it. "Are you alright? Have I done something wrong?"

"No, don't be silly." said Katie, who closed the gap between them again and looped her arm around Flora's elbow.

Flora paused. "Come on lass," she said finally. "Let's see you home."

3

"God, I swear Mhairi, it's like they're in the bloody house!"

Laura scraped her fingernails over her scalp. The splintering wood in the hearth crackled and threw out a fierce heat which stung the women's knees beneath their jeans while they blethered over a hot chocolate. *Ye'll be getting the fireside tartan, lass!* her grandmother would say. She picked at a loose thread on the tweed wingback. "This chair's seen better days."

"Came with the house."

"I thought you'd always lived in Rogart?"

"I have. More or less. But when Izzy came along, I needed somewhere for the two us. This place felt homey. And the furnishings weren't too bad. Just old."

"It suits you. And that sounded an awful lot more patronising than I intended, sorry."

"I'm homey?"

"I didn't mean it like that. But you belong here. I meant to say before, it's been nice having someone to talk to."

"What about your husband?"

Laura took another sip of tepid chocolate then pulled the 'I've-made-it-to-the-gritty-stuff-at-the-bottom' face. "Jim's not so much of a rock in a storm these days.

"Oh?"

"Let's just say, he hid his sadness at my redundancy admirably."

"I know you were a nurse, but you've never actually told me what you did."

"I was a trauma specialist." She thumbed the rim of her now empty mug. "I had the perfect job in a hospital on the outskirts of town. It was my life. I loved my patients, watching their achievements. Even just a simple thing like being able to stick the kettle on. I couldn't imagine ever doing anything else."

"What happened?"

"The hospital closed. My patients who couldn't be discharged were all transferred to the new Royal. Now Jim has me hidden away up here where he thinks he can wear me down into starting a family."

"Is that true or just what resentment's telling you?"

"God, you really just cut straight to it, don't you? I don't know. Sometimes. It's not like he's a bad guy but by god, he has tunnel vision and this way of making me feel like such a failure as a wife. I lie awake at nights, just staring at the ceiling. Then I'm tired, so I snap, and hate myself for it so I snap even more."

"Sounds like a vicious cycle. Surely there's other jobs out there, though?"

"Nearest proper hospital's in Inverness. It'd be a hell of a commute. I'd do it, but it's like dead man's shoes. I haven't told Jim, but I already sent off some enquires a few weeks ago."

"And?"

"Nothing. Said they'd 'let me know'. I won't be holding my breath."

"You're in a hell of a position."

"Yeah."

"Side note," said Mhairi after a quiet minute or two, "I wish I could've seen those clothes, they sound amazing."

"Come over tomorrow and have a look for yourself."

"Really? I'd love to!" Mhairi's eyes glowed.

Is this what happens when you spend every day with bairns? Laura wondered.

"You weren't tempted to try one on?"

Laura shook her head, discovering an intense interest in the flames which licked up the sides of the hearth.

"You sure? I mean, you find a boxful of fabulous, genuine vintage costumes and you didn't even contemplate playing a wee bit dress-up?"

"No, that's ghoulish!" Laura shivered. "Besides, nothing would've fitted me. Well, the uniform maybe, but no!"

"Uh huh."

"Seriously. The waist on these things were teeny, I'd be lucky if I got a leg in!"

"Tight-lacing."

"What?"

"Women in the Victorian and Edwardian eras." Mhairi spread her fingers and leant forward. "They would train their waists from a young age to fit into the tiniest corsets they could, especially women who were supposed to be, like, beauty icons."

Laura scrunched her face. "I suppose this was another school project? I thought you were meant to be teaching these kids something useful like Beginners Guide to Atom-Splitting? Or Tax Evasion 101?"

"Oi! Cheeky. I'm a brilliant teacher, thank you very much and no. This was some private research."

"Oh?"

"Yes, but that's another story." Mhairi bit her lip to disguise her grin. "The point I was trying to make before I was so rudely interrupted, is someone like Katie would have been well cinched in by the time she was dancing about on-stage."

"But that sounds painful. Why the hell would anyone do that to themselves?"

"Every era has its standards of beauty. Y'know Dita Von-Teese is famous for it and her waist is microscopic. Are you going to sit there and tell me you've never dressed in anything totally impractical just because you thought Jim would fancy you in it?"

Laura buried herself deeper into her chair and hid her face behind her mug. "We're not talking about me. I just can't believe Flora would have liked seeing her in those things if it was hurting her. She might have kidded on as a man, but she was still a woman."

"People thought differently back then, but who knows? Maybe Flora didn't like it? It's not like we're ever going to get to ask her. Besides, if Flora was in the army, she probably never considered it."

"It's just so barbaric. She must have seen the marks, surely?"

"And what if she did like it?" Mhairi's eyes twinkled. "Some ladies do, I hear."

*

Throughout the rest of the evening, Laura's discomfort grew arms and legs. Once she had gotten over the initial 'creep factor' and started reading further into Flora's letter, she'd developed a burgeoning affection for the woman. Here was a girl who had broken convention to pursue a career denied to women of her time, and largely made a success of herself, if the medals were anything to go by. Laura respected that.

Then came Katie Vaughan, the opposite of everything Flora stood for, yet it seemed they had fallen in love regardless. Perhaps it was unreasonable, but the idea of Flora tolerating the infliction of such a torturous and controlling device on someone she loved, just didn't sit right. *Did it make her feel powerful seeing Katie constrained like that?* The worst of it was, Laura hadn't a clue as to why this rattled her so much. She didn't even know if any of it was true, or a fantastical narrative her wild and unruly imagination had concocted to irritate her.

It was these bizarre thoughts which plagued her sleep. Tossing and turning in dreamy wakefulness; the two states splashed and collided until in sweat-drenched delirium, they were indistinguishable. Motion pictures inspired by photographs of times well beyond living memory flickered behind her eyelids in a restless jumble.

It's like that Scalextric set dad bought me for Christmas one year, only I hardly ever got to play with it.

This constant churning of irrelevant minutiae was hardly an aberrant disturbance. *Face it Laura, in the space of three months your entire life's been turned inside out. You've been stripped bare. The man who says he loves you has shut you away in this Highland hideaway like a latter-day 'Rebecca.'*

Once this frenzy reached its crescendo, she would descend again into reason and remember the picture her twisted dreams painted bore no resemblance to the man she had married. Jim hadn't conspired with NHS Scotland officials to have her nursing unit close. She had agreed to move to Rogart by her own absence of action to the contrary. Sin of omission. She had docilely gone along with the plan, deciding it was easier to just resent him later.

That job at Achnagarron was made for him. You couldn't hold him back from that. He's a talented engineer and this is his first real shot for him. He's earned this.

The house might be shoddy but it's a roof. Our roof. Apart from the bit that's caved in thanks to bloody kamikaze seagulls.

But that's what all this is about, isn't it? You're powerless. For the first time since... the last time. Only you vowed you'd never feel that way again.

And just like that, her mental slot cars would go whizzing round the next hairpin bend. An endless peak and trough of blame & shame which left her drained and exhausted.

Laura pulled a face as she took a healthy glug of the day's first black coffee while her slippers swept along the floorboards from the kitchen into living room.

The steaming bitter liquid soothed her gently back to Earth, tiny molecules of caffeine suffusing her with quiet clarity. Jim had gone off to work early doors, so the house was peaceful.

A disgustingly cheery knock rapped at the door.

Don't scream, Laura. Do. Not. Scream.

*

"You weren't kidding. These are exquisite!" said Mhairi over the rustling and shushing of a dozen different fabrics.

Laura smiled and sipped at her second coffee. Its warmth permeated through the last vestiges of the previous evening's turmoil. They were balanced on opposite rafters in the attic. The dusty timber gave the odd squeak of protest every time one of them moved, but it was pleasantly snug. The dreich morning clouds provided minimal light through the skylight, so an underpowered torch provided a warm, yellow glow.

Despite her misgivings, she'd instantly brightened when Mhairi had come bustling through the front door with her infectious energy. It was the school's Easter break and Izzy had been packed off to her dad's in Helmsdale to spend the day on his boat.

"I still can't believe they've just been sat here all these years."

"Have you thought about sticking them in a museum? I'm sure somewhere like Historylinks in Dornoch would be thrilled to have something like these. Mind you, you'd have to do a bit more research on them first." Mhairi turned away for a slurp of tea, leaving the implied question hanging in the air.

"I guess I should really look at that."

"Resistance is futile." Mhairi put her mug back down and held up one cuff of the green bodice-cut jacket until the embroidery scraped her nose. The tip of her tongue poked out between her two front teeth, her features crinkled in intent scrutiny.

Laura laughed. "You ken if the wind changes, ye'll stay that way!"

"Why don't we bring these downstairs so we can see them properly in the light?"

"I suppose we could."

"Good. Then you can try them on!" Mhairi bolted down the ladder with the jacket flung over her arm, leaving Laura to swat at the air behind her.

*

Five minutes and much cajoling later, Laura stood in front of the full-length Edwardian mirror in the master bedroom, examining herself in the green coat she had fallen so much in love with.

Never normally one to gawk at herself, she couldn't help admiring the way the smooth tailored cloth made her appear at once svelte yet also 'womanlier'.

The short-cut corselet nipped in snugly at the waist, then rounded over her hips to a V-point at the front, granting her the illusion of an hourglass which her naturally pencil-straight runner's physique did not possess.

"Wow, look at you." Mhairi stood behind Laura's shoulder and met her friend's eye in the glass. "It really suits you."

"You think so? Not gonna lie, it feels amazing." She swished back and forth like a waltzer in front of the mirror, one arm covering her midsection as she dipped into a sweeping bow. "You've seen Katie's picture. Can you imagine the reaction if she'd walked into a room wearing this? A thousand heads turned just for a glimpse of her."

"They made quite the handsome couple. Mind you, so do you and Jim from the pictures I've seen."

"I'm not so sure about that." Laura sighed and wrestled off the jacket, tossing it in the vague direction of a chair and lolloped on to the bed. "I feel like I've lost all the control in my life. And there's just something about those pictures of Katie & Flora that... I dunno, they looked so happy. I remember when me and Jim looked like them. Now, after what we talked about last night, I can't help wondering if Katie ever felt like I do? If Flora ever made her feel..."

"Feel what?"

"Constricted." Laura choked as one brick of her meticulously constructed wall wriggled loose. "I know it sounds dramatic. I know I'm being ridiculous. But my head went on a total bender last night about corsets and feeling so confined you can hardly breathe. I feel like I'm in one of those things. Everything's so tight around me, my ribs could burst." She swiped at her eyes. "This is so embarrassing."

Mhairi dropped to the bed beside her and slipped an arm about Laura's shoulders. "Talk to me."

"I don't know what else to say. It's like the calm *after* the storm where all the raging thunder's died away and what's left is ragged silence. Or the sadness after you've been front row at the most amazing concert. You come away and your ears are ringing. White noise. Hollow. How do you explain emptiness?"

"I think you just did. Quite eloquently too. There's a gap in your life, a very profound gap. It just sounds like you don't quite know what to fill it with yet."

"Jim thinks it should be a baby. He's been hectoring on at me for years but now, it's like, time's up. The last few weeks, my world's been spiralling. I'm not even sure who I am anymore. I feel so trapped, like I've been stolen away in the night. And he won't listen. I'm starting to feel like a thing. Like I'm not real, anymore. Just an ornament on the fireplace. Or worse, some sort of machine on his damned wind farm."

Mhairi lifted her chin with a single finger. "Like a paper doll. And you can't keep going on like this. Listen, I didn't know the old you, but this one's still pretty awesome. What can I do to help?"

"I only wish I knew."

"Well, we can make a start tonight. You still coming to the pub?"

"Wouldn't miss it."

*

The general chatter in *The Drookit Dug* faded just long enough to give the strangers the up and down, then resumed. Various strains of Scots with the occasional word of the Gàidhlig filled the beer-soaked atmosphere. The dim lighting, the off-angle stone walls, walking sticks and wellie boots by the door lent an intimate feel. The band's jigs and reels buoyed the evening cheer, although the frontwoman seemed to be trying out her best cat-murdering impersonation.

"Annie Huntley." said Mhairi. "She's delusions of grandeur."

"Evening lass, what're you in the mood for tonight? I've a fresh bottle of Bunnahabhain with your name on it." said the barman, whose bald head gleamed in the warm glow of several well-stocked cabinets.

"Whisky for me, please." said Laura.

"Same. I'll get them, though." said Jim.

"Put your money away! Make it three doubles, please Tam, but in honour of our new neighbours, let's make it a Talisker."

"Thank you." said Laura, accepting the ten-year-old Skye malt.

"Here's to you, Mhairi." said Jim.

"Och, away. Here's to you two and your new home. Slàinte!"

"Ah, so you'll be the young folk moved into the Begg Hoose, then?" said Tam, loud enough to be heard above the clamour, and slung an off-white cloth over his tweed-clad shoulder.

The general chatter faded to a curious murmur.

Then a scrape of wood and a big, burly man, well over six foot tall, raised his pint in the air. "It's a braver soul than I'd take on that auld place. Tam, their next drink's on me!"

Applause rippled through the pub with several patrons toasting the newcomers.

"See, your house is legendary round these parts." Mhairi

raised her tumbler in the tall man's direction. "That's Callum, the village bobby."

"Aye, new chap. Only been here eight years but he seems decent enough." said Tam as he poured three more Taliskers. "Be needing another bottle of this, I think."

"So, if the copper's in the pub..." said Jim.

"Who's minding the sheep?" Mhairi laughed.

"Point taken. Here's cheers!"

Frost lay thick on the ground by the time Laura, Jim and Mhairi slid up the Strath towards home in a mishmash of limbs. The couple dropped Mhairi off en-route and fell into bed, fully clothed. The drink flowed something fierce at *The Dug*, with seemingly every generous local intent on plying them with all the booze in Tam's cellar. Jim flopped onto his side and made a clumsy grab for one of Laura's breasts, but she pushed his hand away. He groaned and she pressed a kiss to his forehead.

"Sorry babe. Think I'm too blitzed."

"Mmph." He was already passed out.

Won't be doing that again in a hurry. Oof.

*

Two days post-hangover-from-hell, Laura looked on in dismay as a cascade of self-help guides and CDs tumbled into her lap. *I should've known better, asking Clara out of the blue for help. A couple of rough 'how to' guides would have sufficed. Does the path to inner peace really require so much paper?*

Clara Fotheringhay-Bell was, as her name would suggest, a tad on the posh side. She had moved to Scotland from some Berkshire backwater where her father owned a large estate. Clara, herself, held no pretensions of being the next Lady of the Manor. One of those real 'go-getter' types, she knew what she wanted and more-or-less always got it, whether it be a new job, car, or the latest model of boyfriend.

She also had a wicked sense of humour. Laura had taken to her straight away.

They'd met while Laura was doing a brief stint covering a shortfall at the Edinburgh Royal Infirmary. Clara had come to Laura's rescue after she had gotten turned around in one of the hospital's warren-like corridors. They'd become fast friends on a hastily arranged night out, hitting the Grassmarket pubs before staggering into Espionage A.K.A meatmarket central. They made it home after a few questionable dances and not too many bruised male egos, to spill out of a black cab, collapsing, utterly kaylied, on Laura's living room floor on Clermiston Road.

The only thing about Clara was, she was something of a self-styled 'guru' and belonged to what Laura secretly referred to as the 'happy-clappy brigade.' All hippy and New-Age-y.

"You'll never be one of goodie-two-shoes-with-bandanas, Laura, but anything's worth a try."

So she'd picked up the phone.

Now, two days after a somewhat vague and awkward conversation over the phone, a scornful Laura sifted through the pile of booklets and recordings that had arrived in the post.

Manifest Your Dreams!

Cosmic Ordering: What You Want is Already Yours!
Don't Seek the Change- Be the change!

That last one sounds more like something for middle-aged women. Or a one-armed bandit machine with an identity crisis. She sighed. The irony of the titles not lost on her. "If I knew what I wanted I wouldn't be making such a prat of myself."

Listlessly, she tossed one item aside after another until a single pamphlet caught her eye. A short meditation guide- in bullet points. '**Clear your mind in the place you were happiest**' it said. "Not sure I have one of those." She twisted her fingers. *Not quite true though, is it.*

There was one. Long-since banished to the deepest recesses of her mind. She glanced back at the molehill of discarded incense-snorting guffery behind her.

She uncrossed her legs, moved through to the kitchen, and flicked the switch on the kettle. Placing the oily leaflet on the countertop, she grabbed her favourite mug from the draining board. Wonder Woman in a nurse's uniform. The girls at work had each been presented with a little gift after a particularly harrowing incident back when she'd been breaking rocks in A&E. Foul weather had caused a major pile-up on the M90 heading towards the Forth Road Bridge. Her team had been sent out with the Incident Response Unit. The weather was still wild when they got there and the work arduous. The mug was a symbol of the bond that had formed that dreadful evening. *Shame what happened afterwards. How arrogant can you get?*

A sad smile crossed her features at the memory then lifted

her gaze to the view outside the window. The skies were a cloudless blue, the temperature having lifted just enough to make sitting outside a pleasant prospect. *Spooks in the attic aside, the land is beautiful here.*

Outdoor space was at a premium in Edinburgh. If you wanted a garden, it was going to cost you and even if you were lucky enough to snag yourself a small patch of precious turf to call your own, it always came with the accompanying thunder of endless buses and screaming kids. *Funny, I never realised how much I'd missed the peace and quiet until I came here.*

She pulled open the back door and breathed in the fresh scent of morning. Taking a seat on the wooden bench which stretched along the white-washed wall beneath the kitchen window, Laura sipped the delicate citrus blend of Lady Grey whilst the buzzing bees zipped diligently by, their fat, fuzzy bodies ladened with lumps of yellow pollen. She allowed her eyes to close and filled her lungs which made her a touch giddy. The smells and sounds of her surroundings cuddled around her insides and weaved themselves into a blissful fantasy.

It was so easy, after all that. A contented place where time had been meaningless in the enchanted ignorance of youth. No longer did she rest on a bench in an unnamed garden in Rogart. Instead, she sat in the doorway of her Uncle Iain's croft on the Isle of Harris. There was a touch of heat in the sun, but enough of a breeze to rustle the leaves of the large oak tree, towering over the corner of the small garden plot.

Nearby, an iron gate, badly in need of oiling, occasionally squeaked and clattered. Old Mrs Duffy's daughter would be hanging out her mother's washing down the road to the left and in the other direction, Sandy and Jaisie's wee paper wind-mills stirred in the warm gusts.

The sweet perfume of fresh grass and ancient roses washed over her from a small, oval island in the middle of the lush lawn, and if she were to raise her head and peek over the hedge top, she'd see whooshing breakers, restless against the icing sugar sands of the beach below.

A flash of deep pink came strong into focus, and she remembered her great-grandfather's fuchsia bush with its drooping narrow bells which provided just enough canopy for a tiny Laura to hide under as a child. As family tradition dictated, in this working croft passed through generations of fathers and sons, this one small patch of greenery at the front of the house would ever be laid to the incumbent lady of the house to potter with as she pleased.

In her mind's eye, she gazed at the stone step beneath her feet, scraping her teenage trainers over the rough pebbled concrete in front of the doorway where she sat. It glowed white in the sun. Her bum was made numb by the unforgiving tattered red carpet of her uncle's hallway and if she listened, she could make out the ever-present battle between the Bakelite radio stuck on the horse racing results and the television blaring a John Wayne film at full blast.

This was far and beyond where she wanted to go but a pair of sun-dappled legs appeared to her right, accompanied by the metallic squeak of a 70s deck chair. She couldn't make out a face, but she recognised the dainty bare feet. Just beyond the edge of the doorway, her grandmother basked in the sunlight, a pair of knitting needles and the Saturday crossword discarded casually on her lap in favour of an afternoon snooze.

All long-lost days carry a twinge of hurt. An ache for the things that can no longer be, but beyond the sting, therein can be found contentment. *It's a strange, bittersweet...*

"COO-EE!"

4

Surprising was the pang of guilt when Mrs Matheson came 'coo-ee-ing' into her garden to ask if she'd done anymore investigating into the mysterious Mrs Begg. But still, Laura reciprocated Aileen's hospitality as Highland tradition dictated. She hid her embarrassment at being caught short well by arranging her single packet of broken custard creams on a side plate. She was still emptying the boxes of supplies from her and Jim's old flat. But biscuits are surely a priority in anyone's book.

The matriarch who kept a steadfast eye on the comings and goings of Strath Rogart was far more interesting than Laura have given her credit for, although she had been right about one thing. Aileen Matheson was a retired headmistress, spending most of her career teaching at the same school which Mhairi now taught at. But it was her youth spent in service at nearby Dunrobin Castle which Laura found really fascinating.

Aileen's obvious delight was charming, and it made Laura glad to indulge the old woman as she regaled her with the many adventures she and her best pal Lily shared on rare days off, as well as local legends such as the tragedy of the Edwardian servants who mysteriously drowned one night while returning home from an impromptu party on a nearby island surrounded by quicksand. Laura didn't doubt every village resident had already heard these stories a dozen times or more, but she was glad to provide a captive audience and displayed an appropriate measure of awe in all the correct places.

Back in the attic, she settled herself on her favourite joist, prepared this time with an overstuffed fluffy cushion and a large glass of red wine.

The evening sun was fading and so two tapered candles she had found in a drawer gave the perfect glow. Laura checked her watch. *Another couple of hours yet until Jim'll be home. Dinner can wait.*

She searched the faded lettering for her place in the story. *Remember now, not too keen. You're only doing this for the neighbours.*

*

Did I dare show my face at the Gaiety again? I wasn't sure if I'd be welcome. Katie's eyes, when we parted, told me I'd said something wrong, but pride & shame kept me from going back to ask.

Yet each night, with the wrought iron bedstead pressed against my head in thae jeelit barracks, my mind drifted back to the crisp air and the icy ache in my bruised knuckles. The rough blanket clumped in my fist, a poor substitute for the gentle grasp of her fingers.

She was exactly as every Gaiety Girl was supposed to be. Perfect feminine elegance. She was pretty at that time. She hadn't yet grown into the confident beauty I knew much later. Dainty too, but I was sure there was more to her than what she showed on the surface. I'd seen cavalcades off empty-headed adornments with their fawning smiles and ridiculous giggles with their petty crushes. Flimsy things that hung on troopers arms. Katie would never have been one of those.

The other reason I had not returned was due to circumstance.

After our chance meeting, I walked Katie all the way home to Delancey Street, where she shared rooms with four other girls and a housekeeper employed by Mr. Edwardes as a sort of chaperone. Once I dropped her home, I still needed to double back the full distance then about half again to make it back to barracks at Windsor. Neither was Katie the fastest walker. Like many women, she had a love of the most impractical shoes. Ne'er she changed, either. Always had to look her best, even if her only audience was me and the chickens in the hen hoose. She certainly provided her share of village amusement.

Anyway,

I strolled into Victoria Barracks in the wee hours. The lads standing guard tipped me the wink- it was only a couple of hours before the first bugle blast.

I was dead on my feet at parade. It became clear on the Present Arms, I hadn't re-secured the bolt properly on my Lee-Metford last time I cleaned it, which Captain Cosworth found out to his cost when it landed on his foot. Got two weeks in the cells and loss of privileges.

And so it was nearly a whole month before I was able to get another weekend pass.

Gaiety Theatre, London, March 1899

Flora gave a light tap on the door from where a dozen powdered dolls came flurrying out in a great whoosh of ruffles and crinolettes. Aside from a few catty shrieks of scandalised laughter and maybe a favourable glance, they paid *Sinclair* little more mind. She stalled at the threshold of the large communal dressing room.

Katie had her back to the door, a silhouette in the moonlight. There was no inkling she'd heard Flora's knock above the high-spirited clamour of escaping females, her body clad in nothing more than a black chemise, and her hair piled high in an intricate pattern of delicate curls which left her shoulders bare and a long sweep of exposed neckline.

Katie reached for the key on a fluted paraffin lamp which sat on the dresser. Tiny muscles in her back glowed in the firelight and flittered in a mesmerising staccato.

Flora's gaze drifted to the lacework of ebony hair at the base of Katie's neck. Her fingertips tingled as she tried to follow all the little loops and swirls.

Living among her fellow Tommies, experiencing the way a man stands in the world and takes his pleasures so freely, her horizons had been considerably broadened. Still, she'd noticed her own quiet curiosity with the female form differed from the gruff manner of her comrades. Tavern-dwelling whores were there for the taking- a quick but satisfying tumble for a fair price. Yes, she had taken lovers when the need arose. Paid and unpaid. She enjoyed their company.

Having performed heavy labour from a young age, Flora had developed a powerful physique which made her masculine disguise convincing enough, in spite of the company surgeon having categorised her diet as 'poor' on enlisting. *Poor, indeed. I told him us crofters were just used to living on less!*

The expected womanly curves had never made an appearance. Her hips were poker-straight and, she flattened a palm to her breast, yes, her bosoms negligible.

Far from gracious, she was roguish with the humour to match, unafraid of mischief, and she'd never be caught dead swooning. *Travelled half the world where I belong and mebbe I have, but I'm still walking a' tween swan and cock.*

She cleared her throat.

Katie jumped and grabbed at a curtain, clutching the heavy drape to her breast, oblivious to the fact she was now exposing the generous curve of her posterior to the alleyway outside. It took her a few seconds to recognise the figure who was now biting their own knuckle. Katie frowned. "It's you."

"Aye, I suppose it must be." Flora ignored the other woman's accusatory tone. She leant on the back of a convenient chair and tried her best not to smile.

"I had quite believed you vanished, *Miss* Begg, and now here you appear, unannounced, in my dressing room."

"Ah, well, I can explain."

Katie stared at her, hands perched atop hips while her jaw edged its way further and further away from the rest of her face. "I'm waiting Corporal."

It took all of Flora's considerable willpower not to laugh.

If Flora had behaved this way in front of her father, she would have met with a swift clout about the lug. Although the way Katie had leaned on the word '*Corporal*' sent fire up the back of her neck. "I wanted to come back before now, but I got into a wee bit o' bother."

"What sort of 'bother'?"

"Well, there may have been a slight accident with a rifle."

"Good god, you didn't shoot someone, did you?"

"No! No, I dinnae think they'd let me out after two weeks if I done that!" Flora chuckled. Katie made a hmph-ing noise in the back of her nose, though by the time Flora had related the debacle with Captain Cosworth and the bolt she was laughing too.

"He's a crabbit sod, anyway. The lads thought it was funny. They snuck me extra rations those two weeks I got locked in." said Flora. Her laughter trailed away. "So, do you believe me?" She took a chance and stepped further into the room until she was only a few inches from where Katie remained in front of the window, the curtain fallen away.

"I don't know why I should. I don't know you at all well, but I don't believe you would lie to me."

"I'm glad." Flora reached out for a discarded taffeta sheathe slung over the back of a chair. It didn't matter if it was Katie's or not, she draped it about her shoulders and allowed her fingers to rest at the top of her arms for a brief second or two before dropping them altogether to clench at the small patch of air which remained between them. "Then I should be honest again. Truth is, even if I wasn't confined to barracks, I didn't know if you wanted me to come back."

"What? Why? I told you I wanted you to see you again."

"The look on your face. The one you got when I told you why I was here, in London."

"Oh." Katie's gaze dropped to the Flora's fidgety fingers.

"Oh? What does 'oh' mean? Were you embarrassed? Was that it? Ashamed because I'm just a glaikit crofter's daughter, not fit to be seen with?"

"Flora, I don't even know what that means." Katie lifted her fingers to Flora's cheek. "But no, no, none of that. Not at all."

"Then what? Because you barely broke breath to me when I walked you home."

"I'm not entirely certain." Her voice was so quiet, it drew Flora even nearer until the satin of Katie's slip brushed the hairs on Flora's scarlet coat. They matched each other breath for breath in the dim lamplight. Katie stroked back the odd strand of hair that had strayed out from beneath Flora's Glengarry. "It's just in that moment I realised how very different you and I are. We come from very different places. I've never met anyone like you. It's not a bad thing. It was a moment. Just one moment."

"Are we too different?"

Katie shook her head. "Perhaps."

Flora's face fell.

"But I don't wish to believe so."

*

Flora and Katie walked arm-in-arm, setting a slow pace

towards Delancey Street. Katie snuck a glance at Flora. *It's like a game, this. Hiding in plain sight. Never in all my days did I ever have the desire to walk out with a man. Never wanted to be so conventional. Yet look at us.* There were no raised eyebrows from passers-by, no shocked glances of disgust. All the world saw was a Tommy and his sweetheart. *I'm not sure if I like this or not. It is rather daring. Provocative in a way that gives the most delightful sensations. Down there. And it's freeing. But it's all pretend. An illusion. A respectability I've never wanted.*

She allowed their fingers to intertwine but frowned when, through her velveteen glove, her thumb detected a cruel deep-set dent that ran all the way from Flora's index knuckle to her wrist. *Why didn't I notice this before?* She curled her fingertips into Flora's palm and allowed herself to be held.

They walked in a peaceful silence for a while. Katie's lip curled at the clip of Flora's tackety boots skimming the cobbles. "Did you see the show tonight?"

"I saw your bit towards the end. I'm no expert but I thought it was grand."

"The whole show is 'my bit' but thank you. One always loves to hear an excellent review of one's performance."

Flora laughed. "Was that a joke, Miss Vaughan?"

"Perhaps."

"Not half-bad, I'm impressed." She brought them to a halt and sniffed the air. She grinned, tugged on Katie's hand, and drew her down an alley.

"Flora, what-"

"It's alright. This way."

They emerged onto an open broadway. Flora pulled her towards a steaming cart on the street corner.

Katie's eyes widened and her belly rumbled. "Chestnuts!"

"That's right, Miss! Chestnuts so 'ot, they'll melt the knac-. Begging your pardon, Miss. Warm your cockles, they will. That'll be a round dozen, then sir?"

Flora tipped a couple of coins into the man's mitt and handed Katie a newspaper poke.

"I haven't had these in years. Thank you." The first chestnut hopped about between Katie's fingers. "Toastie!"

"You're welcome. Careful while you're peeling them, though, the shells can be sharp. We heat these over campfires."

"It's so romantic to me, your life out there. Friends, comrades, breaking bread under the stars, singing songs of home."

"Hmph. It might sound romantic, but the truth... ain't. You've got a dozen or more filthy blokes all crowded together in cramped tents snoring their heads off and creating the ungodliest stink."

They wandered some more, both women dragging their heels just a bit more until they arrived at the corner of Delancey Street. Katie stopped and turned to face Flora, bringing the other woman's hands between them. Flora tilted her head. Katie only lived a few doors down.

"Mrs Hegarty had about a thousand fits when she saw me come home with you last time."

"Ah. Aye, she didn't look too chuffed, right enough."

Katie lifted Flora's chin. "Let's make this abundantly clear. I am not ashamed of you Corporal Begg. And I only live just there." She pointed towards a blue painted door, barely visible beyond the edge of a bank of mist which Flora had decided was a permanent fixture in this city. "I promise I will be quite alright for the last few feet."

Flora watched Katie's face for any waver in her sincerity. *Don't be stupid, Flora. Course she can walk the last few bloody feet by herself.* "I'll stand here until I see the door close."

Katie smiled, but it was tinged with something Flora couldn't pinpoint.

"You are a one-of-a-kind, Flora Begg."

"It has been mentioned once or twice." Her eyes crinkled in that smirk she invariably wore. It was so obvious when Flora's mood fell. She always had this look like she was in on the joke. When it went missing...

Before she was aware of what she was doing, Katie peeled the fake 'tache from Flora's upper lip and brushed her own over her cheek. When Flora didn't back away or move to the contrary, she lowered her face to kiss at the corner of her mouth. When Flora still showed no reaction, however, Katie pulled away and pressed her hand flat against Flora's scarlet-clad chest. "Well, it was lovely to see you this evening Flora, I do hope you'll come again." She turned away but she had only made it a step or two when Flora reached out and grabbed Katie's wrist. Her thumb skimmed the bare skin where Katie's midnight blue sleeve and matching glove had separated. The contact sent tiny sparks into Flora's hand, all the way up her arm, into her back and spread throughout her body.

"No, wait, Katie. I'm sorry, I wasn't... can we try that goodnight again?"

Katie hesitated but relented at the soft tug on her wrist.

"I'm sorry." said Flora again. Their eyes locked. Mrs Hegarty would no-doubt be twitching at her net curtains, but it didn't matter. The entire world had distilled to this one corner of Delancey Street.

Flora smoothed her fingers through Katie's hair. Her other hand o Katie's hip urged her closer until their mingled breaths twisted and danced in the frozen air.

The anticipation was interminable, as millimetre by millimetre passed before Flora's lips were on her own. Katie took Flora's chapped bottom lip between her own two fuller ones and licked a warm trail along its breadth. Flora's hands trailed towards her spine before her two solid arms encircled her, squeezing with just the right amount of pressure. *It's so wonderful and warm here*, thought Katie and wrapped her own arms about Flora's neck as the taller woman toyed with her top lip. There was a mutual pulling back before Flora rest her forehead against Katie's and rubbed the tips of their noses together.

"I noticed last time, but this street of yours is a bit on the well-to-do side, is it no?

"Well, Mr Edwardes likes us to have somewhere suitable, should the occasion arise."

"Oh. I see."

"Don't worry. I'm not interested in anything like that. I much prefer penniless corporals."

"In which case I should be alright then."

"You are decidedly more than alright."

"Hmm, I should also be saying goodnight Miss Vaughan."

"And I should say goodnight Corporal Begg."

Neither made any effort to move.

"You smell like fresh cut heather."

Katie grinned and pushed her nose into Flora's chest. "Mm hmm, it's my perfume. And you smell like... like," she sniffed harder. Truthfully, it was like metal and... *rotten egg?* She hadn't been aware of it before now. She wrinkled her nose and opted to rest her cheek on Flora's shoulder instead.

"Gunpowder. It's the sulphur you can smell. Not the nicest, sorry. I stopped smelling it ages ago."

Katie didn't need to answer, content being rocked steadily from side to side. They stayed that way for a little while until Flora became aware of the dropping temperature. "May I see you tomorrow?"

"I suppose you may."

Flora lowered her mouth to the corner of Katie's jaw and placed one last kiss to her pulse point. "You suppose?"

"Oh, didn't you know? A lady should never appear too keen."

"No, I did not know. Not being acquaint wi' many respectable ladies. In which case, you'd best go, or I'll never let you. Goodnight lass."

Katie smiled, closing her eyes and hugged Flora harder. She had to almost push herself away. "Goodnight Soldier."

Flora looked on. As promised, she waited until the house door was firmly shut before turning on her heel and disappearing into the fog.

5

"And you just left it like that? How can you possibly have zero interest in what happened next? I like this by-the-way."

Laura slid a dinner plate to where her neighbour caressed the smooth finish of the long oak table. "A good sanding and a couple of coats of Danish oil. It's come up grand though. And it's proved to him I'm not entirely useless at the old DIY."

"I never said you were useless. Just a tad less than enthusiastic." Across the kitchen Jim stood by the open dresser, a pair of wineglasses raised in question, his eyes flitted between the two women.

"Please, love." said Laura while Mhairi shook her head. He pulled out a bottle of Merlot from a wire rack under the countertop and filled two glasses.

"Mhairi, I forgot to ask you the other night, what do you teach?" He laid a hand on the chair to Mhairi's right and took a sip.

"Erm, children I think."

Jim laughed. "I meant 'what subject'?"

"I gathered." Mhairi smirked. "I don't really have a specialist subject, it's just primary kids so bit of everything, really."

"Enjoy it?"

"I do. It's like any job, there's good days and bad but the kids are bright as new pins."

"Excellent. You'll be teaching our wee one soon. In fact-"

A clatter of plates from the sink interrupted him, and Mhairi looked between Jim and Laura. "You're not...?"

"No, I'm not." Laura slapped a damp dish cloth onto the drainer and turned to face them both.

"Well, not yet." said Jim, as he swilled the wine about in his glass.

"Not ever!"

She hadn't intended it. Not so bluntly, anyway, and not in front of company. It just slipped out. But there it was. The scrape of chair on flagstone brought both their attentions back to Mhairi, who was valiantly trying her best to sneak away.

"Sorry Mhairi. Please forgive us." said Laura. "Come on and sit yourself back down, we'll have a nice meal."

"Only if you're sure." Mhairi slid back into the narrow gap between chair and table. "If you two have things to discuss then I'll just as easy go home."

"Don't be daft. Now sit." said Laura and glared at Jim as she grabbed a pair of oven mitts. "I'm just about to dish the dinner, anyway and there's too much for two people."

"You could always freeze what's left?"

"Laura doesn't believe in freezers except for ice cream. But we'd no hear o' it." Jim took a seat beside her and offered a winning smile that was only a little forced. "Laura tells me you've a wee one yourself?"

Laura gritted her teeth as she continued with the dinner and attempted to tune out the conversation.

"Yeah, I've a daughter. She's staying round at her pal's tonight, hence my landing on your doorstep. I'm sorry I walked in on your dinner plans, though."

"Nonsense! We're glad of your company. Laura talks about you a lot, in-between paranoia about the spooks in the attic. Although I've not made much of a listener lately."

Poor man thought Mhairi. *He is trying, bless him, but he's on a bit of a hiding to nothing.* She also noticed something Laura had mentioned to her the other day. A false air of the 'Highland' in his speech. Laura found it annoying, but Mhairi had to stop herself from giggling every time he opened his mouth. Townies who moved up and tried to be more native than the natives were an endless source of humour. A large steaming bowl of slow-cooked stew was pushed under her nose. "This smells amazing."

"Best fill your boots then, there's loads left."

Mhairi dipped her fork into the splodge of stew. The New Zealand lamb Laura had bought especially for this evening was rich and so well-cooked it was falling to bits. "I'd have been round long before now if I'd kent you could cook like this."

"I'm no chef. Just browned off with 'ping' dinners and salads, so I raked through the boxes and dug out the slow cooker. Fancied something nice tonight."

Mhairi caught the wince that flitted across Jim's face. His recent absences due to all his, entirely optional, overtime had meant the renovation work needed to bring the house up to snuff had less stalled than never got going. *Another landmine trodden, well done girl.* "What else was Flora saying to it then?"

"Just what I mentioned earlier. They had their first kiss. Very 'Brief Encounter,' snog-in-the-fog kinda thing."

"But it's exciting, don't you think? I mean, it's a classic romance!"

Laura chuckled. "It's not a book, Mhairi!"

"It might as well be. Have you decided what you're going to do about it?"

"Nothing. I'm going to do exactly nothing about it. What's the point?"

"Then why are you still reading it? Jim? What do you think?"

Jim, who believed Mhairi very brave, leant back in his chair with his hands linked across his middle and shrugged. "Everyone needs a project, hon."

"Not you too. You weren't even interested until now."

"No, but you are. It might do you some good."

Laura threw him one of her favourites from her arsenal of hard stares.

Mhairi dragged her fork through her dinner. *It's going to be a long evening.*

*

The narrow torch sparkled off the soggy gravel and their shoes scrunched along in the still night.

"Have you any idea what's going on with her?"

Mhairi took a breath. *I was enjoying that silence.* She wasn't sure why, but she had expected to dislike Jim. Instead, she had found him a ruggedly charming and decent man. Yes, perhaps he was working far too hard and yes, he was making a bit of an arse of things, but he wasn't a bad bloke. He wasn't the most sensitive soul, but it was hardly a hanging offence.

She couldn't have pinned her expectation on any one thing Laura had said, either. It was more a sense of apathy she seemed to have towards him. *Or maybe you should just stop always expecting the man to be at fault. I should show Laura that meme I saw the other day; Confucius say, woman who wear wonder-bra make melons out of beestings! Either way, it's their mess.*

"Really Jim, I don't. I know she isn't especially happy and if it were her choice, the two of you wouldn't be here."

"She told you that?"

"She didn't have to. You can't see it?"

Jim looked to his feet. "Subtlety's not my forte."

Mhairi frowned. *Alright, so he is thick as bloody mince.* "Have you ever actually tried, you know, asking her?"

Jim mumbled something Mhairi couldn't make out.

"I'll take that as a no. Why the hell not?"

If her vehemence surprised him, he didn't show it. In fact, he showed little to no reaction at all and Mhairi understood something of Laura's frustration with the man. *How the heck did he ever manage to get married in the first place?* She sighed as they finally reached her house. "If you want my advice, you'll talk to her before it's too late. Thank you for walking me home."

Mhairi unlatched the garden gate and turned up the garden path when she heard Jim's voice behind her.

"You think it's gotten that bad?"

Mhairi blew away a stray curl tickling her nose. "Why don't you try opening your eyes? Look, you're not a bad guy. I find it hard to believe you're this daft. I think you set out with the best of intentions, but she's going through something. Something huge. I'm not even sure what, exactly. But it's not your money she needs. You want this marriage to work Jim, you need to be present. Do you remember when you two first met?"

"Why d'you ask?"

"Just indulge me a second. What was she like? Back then?"

"Beautiful." he said, and his eyes glazed. "We met at The Dome. We were both on our Christmas nights out. I was absolutely plastered. My mates dared me to go over and ask her out, but I couldn't do it. In the end, I reckon she got so fed up with me goggling at her all night that she came over, howked me up on to the dance floor and demanded I stop staring and get on with it."

The two of them shared a smirk.

"She sounds forthright."

"She was." said Jim. "It doesn't take long to fall for Laura. I remember one time I tried to impress her in Prince's Street Gardens. Some guy tossed his Frisbee way off course. I made this crazy dive, not paying a blind bit of attention where I was. I tripped, went arse over head over the top of a bench and my foot knocked out some old boy's falsers. He got a face full of ice cream and I cracked my wrist. She wasn't impressed. In fact, she was downright brutal. Typical nurse. She patched me up only after I found the dude's gnashers in the hedge. I went home that night and told my mum I'd met the girl I was gonna marry." He dipped his face. "She's brave, and altruistic under the sarcasm. She helps people. She's someone you never want to hurt. But I keep seeming to do it anyway only I don't know how."

"She once said something about you which, I probably shouldn't be telling you, but I think you need to hear, regardless. She said 'Jim's your stereotypical engineer. If it doesn't have whirring cogs or can be fixed with a quick dash of oil, he doesn't understand it. He only understands the things that make sense.' I hate to break it to you, but human beings aren't machines. They're scary and messy. I get that this is hard, and I really do believe you're one of the good ones, but you need to open your ears. Night, Jim."

She stepped inside and left the man to his thoughts. Jim continued staring into space long after Mhairi's words had faded.

*

An hour later, Jim found Laura drying dishes.

"You were a while."

"Aye, I headed for a dander after I dropped Mhairi home."

"Should've said. I'd have come for the walk."

"Nah, it's okay." Jim stretched out his back and rubbed his eyes. "Needed to clear my head."

"I see." Laura flipped the switch on the kettle. "Which way did you go?"

"Up the strath towards Blairmore. Listen Laura, can we talk?"

Laura nodded and poured herself an Earl Grey. De-caffeinated.

He bought himself a bit of time by faffing about with his coat and scarf. "I know there's something going on."

"You do?"

He sighed. "Well, all right, I haven't a scooby. But I talked to Mhairi, and she said there is."

"You talked to Mhairi about this?" Laura slammed her cup onto the table, barely noticing the hot tea that sploshed over her fingers. "You went to my friend to complain about our marriage? You haven't got balls to talk to me yourself, so you go behind my back instead? What the hell did she say, anyway?"

"No I didn't. She barely said anything but for the record, this is why you are so impossible to talk to. You fly off the handle at the slightest thing and I'm left feeling like the arsehole."

Laura bit her lip and took a few deep breaths. "You're right. I'm sorry." She paused and glanced at her toying hands. "You ever notice this? How much of our life together rests on a knife's edge? It was exciting when we were too young and stupid to not enjoy it. But what's that a basis for now?"

"I dunno, it's not been all bad."

"Course it's not. But I have a problem. Things from my past. I've no idea why they've started bothering me now. Maybe it's because up here I've got too much time to think. Or it's this digging back through history malarkey. I don't know. But I'm changing in ways I don't like."

"Then you need to deal with it." he said softly. "But I've no idea how to help you. You don't talk to me."

"I know."

He took the chair beside her and covered her hand with his own. "Whatever it is Laura, I'm here. I'd do anything to make things okay for you again. But I don't have the answers. I wouldn't even know where to look."

"That's the thing though, isn't it? I don't remember when things were ever okay. Not for a long time, at least. Maybe it's time I went back to the scene of the crime."

"Crime?"

"Yeah. I even the thought of it makes me feel like throwing up, but I think I need to go home to Skye."

"Alright. What do you think you'll find there?"

"God-knows. But one way or the other, I have to know."

*

Midday the following afternoon, a naked engine grunted outside the living room window and Laura popped her head out the front door. Her eyes widened at the sight of Mhairi sat astride a bonafide crotch-rocket. Mhairi twisted the throttle and let out a couple of revs in greeting, grinning from ear to ear, her blonde curls poking out from under her helmet.

"I didn't know you could ride one of those!"

"Well, I just thought, if we're heading to Skye we might as

well have a wee bit fun while we're at it! Poor Midnight Meg here has been cooped up in the garage the last few months-time to let her stretch her wheels." Mhairi patted the fuel tank of the black Triumph Bonneville T120 thrumming between her thighs.

"Meg?"

"Aye, after Tam o' Shanter's horse. She goes like whip when you open her up. Go get your bag." She shoogled a spare helmet at her. "Want to make the most of the daylight."

Laura dived back inside, slung her rucksack over her shoulder and swung her leg over the back of the hog.

"You've done that before!"

"Never!" Laura yelled back over the thump-thump-thump of the engine.

"Ah well, it'll be an experience for ye. Always let me set the lean of the bike and go with it. Ready?"

"Go!"

And Midnight Meg ripped away as promised.

6

The worst of winter had faded and coming to meet Katie backstage to walk her home was a much pleasanter affair on the rare nights I could get away. Years later, Kate let slip that she could have hailed a carriage anytime she wanted- on Mr Edwardes' expense. To which I demanded an apology for my poor battered feet.

Most days I finished school at around four or five. Madame Pettershall was far easier going than any sergeant. After class, I'd spend a few hours on guard duty. If I was lucky, I might have an hour or two free to run to the Strand and wish my lass well. As the weeks wore on, I grew painfully aware our time was running short. My CO only expected me to be in London for six months before I'd have to re-join my regiment. Trouble was, I didn't have the same appetite for it. My patience was at its thinnest when I managed to beg one last weekend pass.

The first time I saw 'A Runaway Girl' I didn't know where to look first, sat up in the gods as I was.

The dancing, the colours...ladies dressed in harlequins and giant headdresses leaping about the stage. The nearest thing I'd seen of the like was among the bazaars of India. The 'Soldiers in the Park' finale was the most wonderful. There were girls dressed up as soldiers in plain sight! Even now, I can still hear the orchestra and the cho-

rus line telling us to come, listen to the band. I could barely sit still until some grumpy bastards in the row behind telt me to shush.

When Katie waltzed on the stage, my heart thundered in my ears. There was not a part of me that didn't burn. I could scarce breathe as some nameless actor swept her from her feet and twirled her round and round. She was as I had never seen her afore. Her hair left long with a gypsy scarf tied in a simple knot. Her costume a loose skirt and blouse which flowed to the music as she danced. So free.

Flora knocked on the open dressing room door. Katie was in an intent conversation with a girl of rather ample and overt proportions.

"Look, Katie Day! Your bonny soldier laddie has come calling."

While the words were friendly, her demeanour, Flora didn't much care for as she glanced between them. "Who's Katie Day?"

"Just an idea our manager has. Nothing important, darling."

"Nothing important, says she!" said the woman. "Why-"

"No." said Katie. "I'm certain we can discuss this later."

"I see. And who is this tall, dark, handsome stranger? You've been remiss in introducing us, dear."

"Fl-"

"Sinclair!" Flora shot Katie a glance and stuck out her hand. "Sinclair Begg."

"Yes, Sinclair, may I introduce Miss Evelyn Grayson."

"Perfectly charmed, I'm sure." Evelyn offered her cheek.

After the most stilted press of lips Flora could muster,

Evelyn sauntered back towards Katie, the enormous bustle covering her beam end sashaying exaggeratedly as she went. Flora's face twisted. *Bloody awful things.*

"Let me know when you're done with this one, I want my turn with him." Evelyn muttered into Katie's ear. "Lovely to meet you Mr Begg. I'm certain we'll be seeing a lot of each other in the future."

Flora waited until Evelyn had taken her leave before an eyebrow. "What the hell was that?"

"Evelyn expects every man she meets to be instantly inflamed with passion for her."

"Huh. It's as well I'm not 'every man' then, isn't it?"

"Hmm, you're not any man. A fact of which I am very, very grateful. Now come kiss me hello."

"I don't need telling twice." One kiss led to a second and a third. Flora slipped her arms about Katie's waist and nudged her nose.

"Hmm, no, you're very well trained these days. Much better." They remained there for several minutes, eyes closed and swaying, Katie resting her head on Flora's shoulder. "What are you thinking?"

"You're wonderful. And you were right, the show was magic."

Katie laughed and kissed her cheek before she pulled away and returned to the dresser. "I guessed it might appeal to you, somehow."

"I canna get over it. My head still feels like it's floating about."

"That was just my kiss." Katie grinned.

Flora shook her head and folded her arms. "You really belong up there."

"It's not forever."

"No?"

"I've been a chorus girl since I was seven years old. The theatre is fine for a while, but it's all I've ever known. I want more. I want to be a couturier, that's my dream. I love fashion. I always have, but I've never been able to afford it on my own. I wear what Mr Edwardes provides for me, but it's a means to an end. Then there's the movement to consider."

"Movement?"

"The Suffrage movement."

Flora scrunched her forehead.

"I go to meetings at my local chapter. We only began two years ago, but we've done great things so far. Though Mrs Pankhurst disagrees."

"You might as well be speaking Dutch, I'm afraid. I dinnae ken anything about suffrage. Don't think Caithness has ever heard of it. The army definitely hasn't. Only suffrage I ken of is when you try and take your boots off after a twenty-mile march."

"Who's Ken?"

"No one important. Sorry."

"I wish you'd stop apologising all the time."

Flora bit down on her initial response. "You just got that look on your face again. Like you don't quite know what to do with me. And sometimes I don't know how I'm supposed to act around you. I don't get to meet many women like you. I've never met a woman like you."

"Makes two of us."

"I hope it's a good thing."

"Flora Begg, you are without doubt the most unexpected, but most welcome surprise. If I look as though I don't know what to do with you, it's because I honestly don't. I never believed a woman like you could exist. But you do. And I couldn't be happier. It's only that now and then, you baffle me. It's not a bad thing, my love."

"Well that's good to know. I do have one question."

"Anything."

"What's a cutch-ooh-re-yay?"

*

By the time they reached Delancey Street, Katie had learned another half-dozen Scots words. Several of these, she was convinced were unrepeatable in polite conversation, despite Flora's assurances to the contrary. That was the trouble. Despite her lack of schooling, Flora was clever. She was quick. Katie was never sure whether she was being serious or poking fun and it left her with a constant sensation of being caught napping.

Flora paused at the corner as usual, but this time there was no kiss goodnight and no lingering look as Katie took her leave. Instead, Katie merely gave her a brief glance then led her along the street towards the blue-painted door and pulled Flora inside just as she had at the theatre the first night they met.

"Won't Mrs Hegarty go daft if she catches me in here?"

"Yes. So, we'd best not let her catch you. Now step exactly where I do."

Flora did as she was told. Wherever Katie would lift her foot, one of hers would follow until they made it to the third-floor landing. Katie closed the bedroom door behind them.

"You've done this before."

"Those stairs creak something awful. After too many late nights at Romano's, I learned which bits were safe."

"I admire this side of you, Katie Vaughan."

Katie made a brief sound of tacit agreement while she cast off her coat and hat. Flora took the opportunity to have a nose around. The room was basic but comfortable. The nearest streetlamp was two doors away and offered a faint but warm glow. *Hell of a lot nicer than the barracks anyway.* She sniffed the air; something floral and heady.

Flora turned around when she reached the window. She hadn't realised she'd been followed and found herself nose-to-nose with Katie. Then Katie's mouth was on hers, her fuller lips a delightful warmth. A frenzy of ripples broke out all over her body at the sounds of their kiss, centring upon one or two very specific areas.

Her hand found its way to Katie's lower back and pressed her close while her other hand let loose the curls clasped at her neck. But as their kisses grew more passionate, Flora urged Katie's shoulder away, their breathing obscene in the silent house.

"We should stop."

"I don't want to."

Katie pressed herself tight against Flora's body, wrapped

her arms about the taller woman's neck and her fingers fiddled with the gold buttons along the front of Flora's tunic. Her lips trailed from her jaw to the base of her neck, and she kissed her way down the line of freshly exposed chest, but Flora eased her back again.

"You're sure this is what you want?"

Katie took Flora's face in her hands, rubbing her thumbs across the black powder stains under her eyes. "Our time is short and therefore precious. I may play the perfect innocent young lady, but I am not blind to the ways of the world, Flora. I can't keep you here forever, so I refuse to waste another minute. I don't pretend to understand why, but this feels right. You feel right."

Flora took Katie's fingers in her own and kissed each tip. "Slowly." Lips met while Flora fumbled about at the lacework of Katie's corset. Katie let out a hiss. "Are you alright? What did I do?"

"No, darling. It's alright. You just tightened it by accident."

"I think you might need to give me some direction."

Katie bit her lip. She lifted Flora's hands and guided them along the silver clasps at the front. "See, like this."

The restrictive garment to fell away and her face dropped into a grimace as she felt her way along the bumps and ridges left by cords. "Kate, what-"

"Shh." Katie pressed a finger to Flora's lips. "It's alright."

"Doesn't it hurt?"

"Only when I was a child. Not anymore. Now for god's sake, kiss me."

*

Daylight keeked past the curtains, which nobody had bothered to draw, as Katie stroked the scar tissue which ran along the back of Flora's hand. Their joined fingers at rest between them on the blanket. "You've never told me where you got this."

"You've never asked."

Katie heard the mirth in her lover's voice and gave her a poke in the ribs.

"Happened at Omdurman last year. It's how I got caught. Spotted a sniper behind a rock about to take a shot at this Lieutenant Harley fella. Dervish rifles were ancient, but any bullet will put a dent in you, maybe even somewhere important if you're unlucky. I knocked Harley out of the way, but the bullet nicked my hand on the way past. Anyway, my tunic buttons got stuck on his cross belt and, well you've heard the rest."

"They hurt you." She buried her nose into Flora's shoulder.

"It's nothing. Got mentioned in despatches for it, though. Now if you want to see hurt." She slid her foot out from beneath the covers and wafted it in the air. From ankle to pinkie toe ran a line of mangled flesh with a single slice of bone jutting out from the base of said toe.

"Dear god." Something unpleasant rose in Katie's throat and she swallowed hard.

"Ploughing accident when I was eight. Never did heal right."

"You were ploughing when you were *eight*? Why on Earth weren't you in school?"

"Hmm, it's normal in the north. Da' was at sea. No mother at home so I got left to tend the croft. I'd borrowed a neighbour's cuddy to drive the plough thinking da' would be chuffed I'd got it done twice as quick, but the blade got stuck. I forget what on. When I tried to free it, the horse bolted, and my foot got trapped in the rig and the blade sliced right across it. Was stuck in bed for a week afterwards. Da' was furious when he got home."

Her tone, she kept light, but the memory of her father's reaction and subsequent belting while she lay with her foot stuck up in the air still stung.

Katie pressed a kiss to the skin under her cheek. "Well, no more accidents now."

"That's going to be a bit difficult."

"Tough. Because I intend to keep you around for a very long time, Soldier."

And nothing more was said. For a while.

"May I ask you something?"

"Hmm?"

"When did you know?"

"Know?"

"When did you *know*?"

Flora pretended to consider the question. "Oh, about thirty seconds after you kissed me the first time." Katie slapped her shoulder and Flora laughed. "I was seventeen. Some of the lads had dragged me into a tavern. I wasn't in the mood for boozing, but they wouldn't take 'no' for an answer. So, there we were on our first round and yin o' the hoors took a bit of a shine to me. She must've known, but she never let on. Maybe she just fancied an easier night. She led me upstairs. Soon as she took her dress off, I knew."

"You have loved other women."

"Loved? No. Cared, aye, but not in the way you're meaning."

"I'm not sure whether to be comforted by that or not. But you have known physical intimacy before."

"It... served a purpose, and the girls were discrete as long as they were paid well enough. That sounds all wrong."

"No, I think I understand. It's just I have little experience. There was one girl, two years ago. I believed I loved her. We were part of a touring company together."

"And now?"

"Now what?"

"You said you believed you loved her. Sounds like something changed. I'm wondering what."

"She did. Or at least, that's what I told myself. When she left me to marry. It was the practical thing but knowing that doesn't make it hurt any less, does it? And now I've changed too."

Flora smoothed her fingers about Katie's shoulder. "Well, if nothing else, there's no chance of this girl getting married."

Katie nuzzled in further. "I have known you a mere fraction of the time I knew her, yet the feelings are so much more intense. I have no idea what any of this means, Flora. I don't know if it's just because our time is limited. But if I'm not with you, then I am constantly thinking about you."

"I've never felt this way, either. It's a good thing, I think."

"Yes, it's a good thing, Flora." But the conversation had drained the last of their energies, both women sinking deeper into the bed and fighting the urge to yawn. "Would it be entirely unacceptable if we were to spend the day in bed?"

"Entirely. Let us be unacceptable and get the sleep we never had last night."

"Yes please. Goodnight sweet girl."

"Night, my darlin' lass."

7

Laura folded the crinkled pages with care and tucked them away in an inside pocket of her rucksack.

"Well, that was something."

"What was?"

Mhairi appeared from the tiny kitchen area at the back of the house, brandishing two toasting forks and a large bloomer.

"I was reading." Laura took a fork and speared a slice from the bloomer. "Things got steamy."

"That was quick!"

"Nah. It's jumped forward a bit. Just as well. You seen the size of it?"

"As the actress said to the bishop." Mhairi curled her lip. "Sounds like Flora had a lot to say."

"She did but, y'know, I get it. I mean, you and I get married, or have kids... or get divorced, and there's paperwork, certificates. What did they get to even say they were here? They lived a life."

"Sounds like you're warming to them." Mhairi stared at the bread browning in the fire. "On that note."

"I suppose I should be telling you stuff. S'why we're here, isn't it?"

"I was just going to ask if this is where you lived?" Mhairi glanced at the whitewashed walls and chintzy curtains of the rental cottage.

"Not in this house, but Dunvegan, yes."

"What was it like? It's not exactly the big city life you're so keen on." Mhairi leaned back in her chair and munched.

Laura fought a smile. *Does she realise how cute it is when she forces herself to be patient like that?* Patience was not one of Mhairi's many natural talents. In fact, a very naughty part of Laura sometimes kept her waiting deliberately just to watch her squirm. "It was okay. I never knew any different."

"What about your family? D'you still talk to them?"

"Nope."

"Nope, you don't talk to them or...?"

"Never seen much point in talking to gravestones." Laura looked at her shoes, bread abandoned to crumble into soot.

"I'm sorry"

"Everyone's always sorry. That's why I never talk about the past. They wouldn't be if they knew the truth."

"Anyone ever tell you you're way too hard on yourself?"

"You don't know."

"Because you won't say."

"Think I'm just gonna go to bed. It's been a long day." said Laura after a pause.

"Laura, I didn't meant to push."

"It's fine. Really, I'm just tired." She rose out of her chair but turned back as she reached the doorway of her bedroom. "Listen, why don't we go a wee saunter tomorrow? I can show you some places."

"I'd love to."

Mhairi continued to stare long after Laura's bedroom door had closed. "How the hell am I supposed to help you?"

*

The following morning, Laura was awake and dressed well before Mhairi shuffled in the vague direction of the kettle, scratching her arse.

"Thought you were set to lie there all day, dosser!"

Mhairi stared at her and mentally debated the rifling of Laura's bag for contraband while the woman in question handed her a black coffee. She squinted through bleary eyes. "I mean, you look like Laura but..."

"What, I can't wake up in a good mood? No? Not allowed?"

"It's allowed. Just unlikely."

"Well, get a shifty on then. Today, I showcase to you the highlights of Skye! C'mon, goonie off, claes on."

*

"Am I meant to plant a flag or hunt for the oxygen tent?"

It was only a three and a half hour walk to the top of Neist Point, but Mhairi's lungs burned with each inward breath. "Too much time in the classroom. Not enough walks up Ben Bhraggie."

Laura chuckled, hands on knees and a tad lacking in puff herself. "It's been a while for me too. We could have stuck to the path, but I wanted to bring you all the way to the top. Bad idea. However, I give you An t-Aigeach."

The entire day had been like a sort of forced march, though Laura had selected some truly spectacular spots. Their journey had started by the dramatic cliff side Dunvegan Castle, and Neist was their final stop. And the best bit was Laura knew all the stories to accompany every single stop along the way.

"A wee bit puggled there, hen?"

Mhairi smacked after her, her wobbly legs barely carting her up the last two or three steps. She halted, hands on knees and attempted to breathe. Once she'd regained some semblance of equilibrium, her eyes opened wide, and took in the frigid oceanic expanse ahead.

Beneath their noses was one of the many Stevenson lighthouses which dotted the Scottish coastline, gleaming white with yellow accents and a black conical roof the shape of a witch's hat.

"This is the point. Over the way there are Ramasaig and Waterstein." said Laura and pointed to another line of cliffs that stretched far away to their left. She had to yell over the shriek of the gulls above and the roaring waves below. Spits of white froth sprayed their faces, high as they were, testament to the raw power of these Atlantic waters.

"It's stunning. But why are we here?" Mhairi shielded her eyes from the reflection of the sun still sparkling off the water despite the thunderous clouds in the distance.

Laura looked away, the breeze ruffling her hair. *Time to come clean. There's no running here.* "This is where my father died. The tide was well in like it is now. It was a youngster bringing the boat in and he got caught. The Selkie. Her keel ran straight up over the ridge of one of those stacks down there. The collision pushed her vertical. It wasn't a big crash, though, and they were all strong swimmers. They should have all made it to shore no bother. But one of the boys got dragged under. Dad went back to get him. His pal made it up to the surface, thought my dad was right behind him, but he never came back. Salvagers brought him ashore a day later. They said a bit o' the mast had fallen and clocked him on the head. Knocked him unconscious. There's still a smear of red paint on the rock." The words were mechanical. She swallowed against a throat that was dry and tight.

"How old were you?"

"Twelve." A single tear trickled down her cheek. "It happened." Laura snorted, scrubbed at her face with her sleeve and turned back for the path.

Mhairi trailed after her, unsure of exactly what was happening but willing to go along with it for the time being.

She took them a different direction, bringing them to a rough vehicle track around twenty minutes later. Laura followed it, her head swivelling back and forth, back, and forth, searching. She came to an abrupt stop at a point where the road hit a bend close to the cliff's edge.

"Laura, be careful!"

Laura was wandering dangerously close to the precipice. She glanced over the side and her stomach lurched. It was a sheer drop with nothing but the churning sea below. "I'm fine." She said quietly. "This is where it all started. It's where she died." she tapped her toes on the ground.

"Your mum?"

Laura nodded.

"What happened?"

"I did."

"I don't understand."

"I mean, I killed her. Or might as well have." Laura paused. "Mum was a district nurse. I was fourteen and being a brat. Mum and I were supposed to be heading to her best pal's wedding in Drumnadrochit, but I didn't want to go. I started acting up and was driving her crazy. I pushed her too far, and she dropped me off at my grandmother's. But I guess that wasn't enough for me because I spent the whole night kicking off at her until Gran gave in and phoned the hotel. Mum decided to come back and get me, but Gran begged her not to drive. There was a squall threatening to blow in and the hotel at Drumnadrochit was a good two hours away, at least. But she did it anyway. She made it as far as the island too, although the rain would have been pouring through the soft top by then. She had one of those ancient Sunbeams. Baby blue and white. Used to say it made her feel like Grace Kelly. Bloody thing leaked to hell, but she point-blank refused to sell the damn thing.

This was as far as she got. See that stump over there? It used to be a sycamore. Not big, but it was enough for her to lose control when it blew over. The wreckage was scattered down the bottom there, but they never found her. They reckoned she was swept out to sea."

"God, Laura."

"I think I need to walk."

"Where are we going?"

"No. I think I want to be alone for a while."

"Honey, I'm not sure that's such a good idea right now."

"I'm fine. I'll see you back at the house. Please don't follow me."

"Laura-"

"Go back to the house, Mhairi. I'll be alright."

*

Laura hadn't a clue where she was going but the groundskeeper assured her it was ten rows along the centre aisle then three in on the right. The dark clouds which had been threatening since midday were now overhead, and the breeze had picked up.

She found the headstone just as heavy drops began to splosh onto her head and shoulders. Her knees buckled and she sunk into the ground, the soil already turning to a thick, sludgy mud. Wet earth filled her nostrils and the birds above turned silent. Her fingers traced grey stone lettering.

JACOBINA STEWART

Her cries rivalled the wind. Mingled rain and tears streamed between the tendrils of hair now plastered to her face. She bent forward, her hands and forehead braced against the rough surface as she wept.

*

Mhairi's stomach sunk at the gathering storm. *Where the fuck are you? What the hell can you possibly be doing out in this?*

She glanced out the window at Meg, all forlorn on her kickstand. The Bonny was a potential death trap in conditions like these. *But what choice has she left me?*

She grabbed her helmet.

Pelting rain battered her visor. *Seriously, when is someone going to invent wee window-wipers for these things? And I haven't the slightest scooby how to go about finding her.*

After about an hour of driving about with side winds continually trying to swipe her off the road altogether, she saw a gate and a sign half swinging from its post and rolled off the throttle. By the thinnest stroke of luck, she clocked sight of Laura in Dunvegan Cemetery.

The storm masked her approach and gave her a valuable minute to figure out her best approach. "You ran away, didn't you?"

"I was an adult and chose to leave. There's a difference."

"You chose to run away. And now you regret it."

"Yes, I regret it! What do you care?"

"Of course I damn-well care!" Mhairi dropped to her knees and gripped Laura's shoulders, forcing her to turn around. She frowned at the tiny droplets of blood which dripped down her friend's forehead. "Why the hell do you think I came here? Whatever you think, whatever this crap you've mythologised about yourself is, it's not true. None of it. None of this is your fault, Laura."

"But it is! I left her. Don't you get it? I left my Grandmother all alone, and she died by herself. I should have been there. I should have stuck it out, and now I'm all that's left. I'm the one alone. That's my punishment."

"Now you listen to me." Mhairi stared unblinking into Laura's face, their noses almost touching. "You are not alone. I know you feel like it. And yes, you're allowed to feel lonely. But whether it's me, or Jim or hell, Aileen Matheson thinks the world of you. And wee Izzy loves her Auntie Laura. We've all got you. You just refuse to let any of us in."

"They left me behind."

Mhairi's chest tightened, and she eased her grip. "None of this is anyone's fault, least of all yours and I'm positive your granny would be so hurt to see you like this."

"I can't stop it. I've tried. Everything just hurts so much"

"Then we need to find a different way."

"How?" Laura shivered under her coat, the saturated lining sticking to her bare arms.

"I don't know but we'll find a way." Mhairi rubbed her hands briskly up and down her shoulders. "Come on, let's get back. It's freezing and you're soaked through." She hoisted Laura to her feet and dragged her back to the bike.

With less haste, she got them back on the road, zipping through the winding roads with as much care as she could while still keeping a respectable speed. Then it happened.

The landslip collided with the front wheel before either of them saw it, and Meg spun from Mhairi's control. In pure human reaction, she slammed on the front brake and sent herself flying. The bike flipped and crash-landed on top of her while Laura flew off the back and skidded halfway back along from where they'd just come. Then the world went black.

8

The more our relationship deepened, the more I was troubled. I had lost my heart to Katie already. But I was worried I might just break hers.

The Powers that Be had granted us extra time and lulled into a false sense of hope.

4th October 1899

"It's time then?"

"Had to happen." said Flora, crumpled papers clutched between her fingers. "I'm bound for Fort George to meet up with my old CO. He's taken over the second battalion. Might even get to see some of my old pals. There's always a few get transferred across."

"How long will you be gone?"

"I don't know. A few months. Likely more."

"Very well. I shall wait."

"I don't think that's such a good idea. You've a life to be

living, Kate. It's a noble thought, but you daren't put yourself on hold because of me. I'd never ask such a thing of you."

"You are not asking, I am telling, and it is no use trying to dissuade me otherwise, Flora Begg."

Flora shook her head. "I'm sorry. But that's not going to happen."

Katie forced herself to take a deep breath and clasped her hands in front of her face. "Don't treat me like a child. I may not be as worldly as you, but I am a grown woman and I know my own mind. I will decide what is best for myself, not you or anyone else."

"And you won't change my mind."

"Then we're at an impasse."

"Seems so."

For several moments, they stared at one another. But the silent battle of wills gave way to resigned frustration and Katie flopped on to the bed with a grunt. "It's my fault. I knew I wouldn't be able to keep you and I made no attempt to stop myself from loving you."

Flora came around the bed to kneel in front of her. "You're hardly the only one guilty of that. Just the opposite. I wish so much that things were different. But we must accept the things which cannot be changed. I canna tell the future. Only the present. Which is to say, I love you very much and it breaks my heart to leave you. But go, I must. I've stood on the battle line before. There are no guarantees. No promises I can offer. Remember these past months fondly if you must. But better continue as if we never were."

She cupped the other woman's cheek in her palm and Katie turned her face to kiss the calloused skin.

"When?"

"Hmm?"

"You haven't told me when you're leaving."

"Tomorrow."

"Tomorrow! How could you-"

"There was a delay. I didn't receive the order until yesterday afternoon. I swear, I wouldn't have kept this from you." Sweat prickled beneath her hairline as she breathed hard. "I swear."

"If I truly cannot change your mind, then you must do one thing I ask."

"Name it."

"Come to the Gaiety tonight."

*

Flora fidgeted through the first act of *A Runaway Girl*, both frustration and curiosity growing with each interminable second. Everything was as she remembered. Leading lay, Ellaline Terriss, was just as glittering. The sets and costumes as spectacular, the dancing as hypnotic. The bold, brassy music still soared. Then at last the Master of Ceremonies appeared and thwacked his gavel against a convenient bit of proscenium.

"Ladies & Gentlemen! Ladies & Gentlemen! Mr George Edwardes wishes to bestow upon you a most magnificent treat. For tonight, we have a solo performance by one of the truly great rising

stars of the era. May I introduce, for your pleasure and mine our
very own, Miss Katie Day!"

Flora's head snapped as she bolted upright in her chair and
her heart threatened to batter its way out of her chest.

Katie stood alone on the darkened stage, her virginal lace
skirts illuminated by a single lantern. The entire theatre had
come to a standstill as her song caught on the smoky air and
rose higher and higher up to the rafters. It was already a classic, one everyone knew the words to, but they didn't sing
along. Katie's voice was too pure. Entirely too sweet.

Flora thought back over the times she had lain back in
Katie's bed, content in the cheerful hum that escaped as she
washed or pottered about her room. It was always pretty but
unremarkable. Now, among the cheapest seats in the house,
the rest of the world had fallen away.

Katie gazed up through the dusty lamplight toward the
balconies. To the casual onlooker it was all part of the act as
she sang to her boy up in the gallery, but her eyes remained
fixed on the slip of scarlet visible through the glare. As the final note drifted away, she blew a kiss in Flora's direction.

There was a momentary stunned silence between the end
of the song and rapturous applause which followed, then the
houselights were raised, and the second act erupted onto the
stage in a series of flashes, and tumbles, and whirls.

Flora shut her gaping jaw and stumbled past several disgruntled patrons. It was far too early to head backstage but
the excitement bubbling through her body would not allow
her to sit still.

She burst through the swing doors at the entrance and cut

a dash round to the side alley, her tackety boots skidding on the cobbles. She bounced around outside the stage door and shivered. A single dong from St. Martin's clanged through the night. *Only half-past. You've another two acts to wait, you damn fool. Damn and blasted fool in love. What have you gone and done, Flora.*

*

Katie's eyes searched about the dim, empty house. *Of course she's gone you little fool. What did you think was going to happen.*

Footsteps clipped on the floorboards behind her and for a second... she sighed. *It's not her, stupid girl.* A slow clap joined in with each step.

"Soldier boy didn't hang around then? Looks like he doesn't love you like you thought, Katie Day. Perhaps your little ditty was all just too much."

Katie resisted the urge to turn around. *Yes Flora has abandoned you, but you are not going to give her the satisfaction.*

"Evelyn! Are you coming? Oh, Katie, there you are!"

Katie tilted her face towards the chandelier closed her eyes. *Don, your timing is impeccable.*

The director reached out his arms and pressed a theatrical kiss to her cheek. "Well done, you darling girl! What did I tell you? You're going to be my perfect star. Don't you think, Evelyn?"

Evelyn flitted a half-glance in their general direction and feigned interest in her fingernails. "Perhaps. If she ever stops pining over her long-lost lover. Anyway Don, I've been meaning to ask you-"

"What's this?" Don lifted a hand. "Has our Katie finally lowered the drawbridge?"

"You didn't know? He's all she's talked about for months now. Sinclair this, Corporal Blah, that. It's embarrassing. Though I'll admit he is a handsome beast. If one goes for that sort of thing."

"It's nothing." Katie shook her head and looked to her shoes. "He's not here, anyway. He was in the balcony when I did my song, but then he disappeared. I... I wanted to show, him, how much I... Maybe it really was all too much. And now he's gone. Maybe I'm too much."

"Don't say that sweet girl." He handed her an only slightly soiled handkerchief from his trouser pocket.

"You don't understand. He always comes for me after the show. Always. I've looked everywhere." She dabbed at her eyes. "Sh-he's leaving tomorrow for Africa. He warned me earlier not to wait for him, he said it wouldn't be fair to me. But I asked him to come here tonight. I thought perhaps, if he heard me sing for him, it might change his mind. What if he truly does mean to make a clean break of it?"

Don flashed his eyes at Evelyn, who did her best to appear oblivious under the giant plume of pink feathers on her head. "*He* sounds a very honourable sort of chap, Kate. And he might be right. You, my dear, are going to be a West End smash. A bonafide hit! Besides? Him only a corporal? My darling, I have a list of European crowned heads and American tycoons who'd court you tomorrow if you'd only allow it. Look in the mirror once in a blue moon, for Heaven's sake! Look at old Connie Gilchrist, *she* became a countess and you're twice as pretty as her! Now, no buts. You're coming to dinner with us. We are going to cheer you up. You can forget any affair with Her Majesty's troops, leave him to play with his rifle! We're going to snag you, at the very least a viscount, but we'll try for an earl."

"But-"

"I said no buts." He grabbed Katie's elbow, then one of Evelyn's and frog-marched them offstage.

*

Flora shoved her hands deep into her trouser pockets. *Christ, it's a beezer the night.* In retrospect, it may have been a touch rash to come out here and wait in the freezing cold instead of sitting through the rest of the play and meeting Katie in her dressing room like she normally would. *What the hell's keeping her this long?*

Everyone else, including the stagehands who were usually the last to leave, had already gone. *The manager's probably congratulating her on a job well done. Canna say as I blame him.* Her teeth were chittering by the time the door opened, and three figures bumbled into straight into her.

"Fl- Sinclair!"

Her lover was an intriguing shade of blue.

"Why, Corporal, so lovely to see you again. And such a great relief, too. Our dear Katherine, here, has been quite disconsolate by your absence, but here you are."

Flora cocked her head at Evelyn.

Two years prior, she and another private had been walking the streets of Crete when McCreary stepped on a Cat Snake. Neither of them had seen one before, but Flora would always remember the look on her pal's face when the damn thing bit him on the arse. Those vile, poisonous reptile eyes had gleamed with predatory intent as it sunk its teeth home. *That's where I've seen you before, lady.*

An unfamiliar man made a grab for Flora's hand. "You're the chap we've been hearing so much about. Quite cast your charms over our girl."

Flora looked over at a red-cheeked Katie. *This fella needs to stop flapping his jaws.*

"Evelyn and I were just taking Katie for a late supper; I don't suppose you'd care to join us? She tells me you're leaving tomorrow. Such a shame! Oh, I didn't introduce myself, I'm. Don, how do you do?"

Jesus, man talks faster than a charging bull. And bangs out as much shite as well.

"Thanks Don, but no. No thank you. It's kind of you to offer, but I've no right to disturb your evening. I should head back to barracks, anyway. I just wanted to tell Kate how," she paused, silently begging Katie to meet her gaze. "How stirred I was by her singing and-." She broke off. *This prick needs to take his smarmy puss elsewhere before I deck him. And that sour-faced...* It was no use. Her throat seized and the right words just wouldn't come.

Katie stepped towards her until her body was a mere breath away and the saltwater which twinkled on her eyelids held every ounce of meaning her the polite words could not.

"You were right. I see that now. It was stupid of me to think otherwise. Goodbye Sinclair."

Don slipped his arm about her shoulders and stole her away from the glow of the stage door.

"Bye, Katie."

*

Tap.
 Tap.
 Crack.

Rough hands tore the window open so hard a shower of paint flakes scattered into the chilly night.

"Who the bloody hell's down there?"

"Please! I'm looking for Corporal Begg, it's imperative I speak with him!"

"You know what time it is, Miss?"

"Yes and I'm sorry but please! Tell him it's Kate."

"Alright, alright, give's a minute and keep your bloody voice down, woman!"

The window slammed shut.

Lance-Corporal Micklethwaite tip-toed across the barrack floor to find Flora's bunk. His toe caught a nail, and it took all his willpower not to yell, hopping about on one foot for several agonising seconds before the tapping started at the window again.

'Alright, keep yer 'air on!' He muttered.

He found Flora and tried a gruff whisper in her ear but that didn't work so he grabbed her shoulder instead and shook hard.

"What the fuck are you doing?" Flora's arms flailed.

"Some bloody bird's been tap-tap-tapping for you at the bloomin' window! Says her name's Katie. Flippin' 'eck, Corp, you don't half like them posh! You ain't got her into trouble, have you?"

Flora thumped his chest and he let out a satisfying yowl which prompted a series of grunts & groans from the surrounding bedsteads.

She slid her woolly socked feet across the room and peered through the mucky glass. Three floors below, wearing the same midnight blue velvet coat she had left her in hours earlier, stood Katie in the ankle-height grass. With a grumble, Flora threw on the khaki jacket and kilt she had laid out for her travels and hot-footed it downstairs.

As soon as the ground floor door opened, Katie cantered over to her, but Flora shushed her and led her off into the woods outside the encampment walls. "It's two in the morning."

"I know, I know, and I'm sorry. I'm so sorry, Flora."

"Not that I'm not happy to see you, but what on Earth are you doing here so late?"

"I had to see you. I couldn't let you go like that. Not like that."

Flora led them under a towering oak tree. Katie brushed her fingers over the other woman's cheeks. Flora leant to kiss her, drawing her close. "I can't stay out here too long."

"I understand, but I have to say this. Flora, I've thought

about it, and I've decided. I can't give you up and it's no use trying to change my mind. I'm going to write to you every week until you come back. However long it takes. I can't lose you."

Flora smirked at her. "You're fairly sure about this, then?"

"Yes. No arguments. So, we're agreed?"

"I think."

"Good. Now then Soldier, I'm not leaving this spot until you've made love to me. Understood?"

"Understood. You're far bossier than any general, you know that?"

"Oh, just do as you're told."

*

"Kate?"

"Hmm?" Katie's mind struggled up through the most pleasant fog.

"Can I ask you something?"

"Right now?"

Flora raised her face from Katie's neck. "Right now."

Katie frowned and lifted herself into a sitting position, the warm nest of leaves crackling under her hands. "What's wrong?"

"Are you embarrassed by me?"

Katie paused. "Why do you ask?"

"Your friends tonight. They gave me a good once over. And you said nothing. In fact, you looked shamefaced. It's not the first time, either. And considering everything that happened today, you changed your tune pretty damned quick after you'd been with 'em."

"And I didn't kiss you goodbye. Flo, I don't know how to answer this without sounding... churlish."

"Hoi! Who's there?" The click of a rifle bolt and the two of them sprung apart. "Who's there, I said!"

"Private Cottard, what the hell do you think you're playing at?" Flora pulled her tunic shut and rose to her feet.

"Begging your pardon, Corp. Miss." Cottard lowered the tip of rifle and tugged his cap. "Just off out on patrol."

"Your patrols bring you out to the woods now, do they?"

"Er, no. Sorry Corp. Micklethwaite said you 'ad a girl out here. Nice. Very nice indeed."

"Christ's sake, away with you, man!" She pushed at his shoulder and turned back to face Katie who was still on the ground, propped on her elbow. She wore a sly smile, and her eyes were creased at the corners. Flora recognised the look.

She sunk to their makeshift mattress, water droplets from the ground cover cold on her bare knees. She leant forward until she had a fist either side of Katie's head supporting her weight. She edged further and further, closing the distance, their eyes never breaking contact until the very last moment when their lips made contact. They kissed for several minutes, each lost in the other. Then Flora pulled away.

"You're not getting away with it, y'ken."

"What?"

"Not answering my question."

Katie grasped Flora's shoulders. "You gave me a fright."

"I what?"

"You disappeared!"

"No I didn't I was waiting for you. For two whole acts!"

"Well I didn't know that did I? I finished my song, looked up and you'd vanished. Then I couldn't find you backstage. And I suppose I let my fears get the better of me. I let Don and awful Evelyn convince me I was right to let you go. Then when you turned up outside, my stupid pride stopped me from saying all the things I'd meant to. But the second I walked away from you, I realised I couldn't have been more wrong. I couldn't let you leave believing I'd given you up so easily. I have no intention of ever giving you up, Flo'. You're mine. I don't ever want you to be anyone else's."

"I still don't think you could've looked very hard. But yours, eh? I like the way that sounds. Not my father's. Not the army's. Yours." Flora lowered herself back to Katie's waiting mouth. Their joint breaths grew heavier, and hands began to stray. "By the way, was that what you were hiding from me?"

"Hiding what from you?" asked Katie, dazed. *So much for my powers of distraction.*

"This Katie Day bit? Why wouldn't you tell me?"

"I don't know. I didn't really believe it would ever happen. I never banked on becoming a star. I thought you'd find it ridiculous. I do."

"Kate, you have a gift. I never knew you could sing! Not like that. When you sang tonight, I felt as though you were singing straight at me."

"To you. And I was."

"I hoped so." Flora traced the line of Katie's lips with her finger. "But if you made me feel like that, you likely made everyone else feel the same way. Why would you think I wouldn't be happy for you?"

"When you put it like that." Katie raised her face, her lips parted. "Now, where were we?"

"What if I don't come back?" Flora cocked her head.

"Flora, I'm not even going to contemplate such a thing." Katie sighed, bracing her fingers against the other woman's chest.

"Kate, we have to 'contemplate' it. I'm going to war, not a picnic in the park like in your show. I've stood on the line before, I've seen what happens when the bullets fly."

"I'm never going to win with you, am I?"

"Not in this, no."

"Very well. If you don't make it back, then you shall meet your end knowing you were loved. Very much. But it's not going to happen. You are going to come home hearty and healthy, and you will find me, right here, waiting for you."

Flora looked at the woodland floor and smirked.

Katie smacked her arm. "You knew what I meant!"

Flora laughed. "Love you."

"And I love you. Can we stay here for a while? I want to keep hold of you as long as I can before the army reclaims you."

"Aren't you getting cold?"

"Hmm, a little. But I have learned you are nothing if not resourceful, Flora Begg."

**

A solid month and a half went by before Mrs Hegarty called up the stairs to announce that the second post had arrived with a letter addressed to a **Miss K. Day**. Of course, could have been another note of appreciation from a well-wisher, one of the more surprising aspects of her recent acclaim.

She had expected it to take months before gaining any sort of notoriety, and quietly hoped the whole cockeyed scheme would fizzle out before it ever got off the ground. But thanks to Don and Mr. Edwardes' expert marketing, she was rapidly gaining celebrity.

Don had shrugged away her concerns and said, *'enjoy it, darling!'*

Well, that might have been fine for some, but it wasn't the theatre which filled her dreams at night.

As soon as she spotted the BFPO postmark, Katie snatched the letter out of Mrs Hegarty's fingers, tossed a haphazard apology over her shoulder and tore back upstairs.

She took care to arrange herself on the bed; pillows stacked behind her, a fresh glass of water on the bedside table.

With deft fingers, she lifted away the transparent sticky wafer, determined not to tear it any more than necessary and sniffed at the single page note, desperate to catch any hint of Flora's scent. Nothing.

My Darling Kate,

This is the first chance I have had to write you. The voyage here was rough, then as soon as I got here, they sent us to relief a town by the name of Kimberley, only when we got within about fifteen miles we had to stop and make repairs on the railway line. Sergeant Gunn tells me the Boers wrecked it some time back.

He's helping me write this, by the way, as I'm still none too confident. He was a man of letters before he enlisted. Now he's company clerk.

You mind me telling you about Lt. Harley? (Why is lefftennant-spelt like that? Makes no sense.) Well, he came here with Major Stockwell and looked none too pleased when I turned up. Stockwell favours me though, and it's good to be back with some of the other lads from my old unit. Turns out the rest of them have been sent to India on peacekeeping duties. Sounds dull to me. At least here, there's sure to be plenty action.

Anyway, that's it for now. We're going to be stuck here for a while, I think, and as ever, supplies are thin so hopefully get a chance to write again soon. It's lunchtime here and you have to be quick getting to Mess.

Bye for now,
Love,
Fl Sinclair

Katie dropped the letter onto her lap and stared at it. "That's it?" She picked the letter up again and turned it over and over in her hands. "Damn you, Flora Begg."

She dumped the letter into a drawer and rushed down the stairs and out the door, leaving a bemused Mrs Hegarty in her wake.

Grateful to find the building quiet but for a few stage-hands, she headed for her private dressing room- one privilege of her newfound fame she rather appreciated and sealed the door behind her.

Knock! Knock!

Katie groaned.

"Who is it?"

"Ellaline!" Came the sing-song response.

"Just a minute!" Katie called back but she needn't have bothered for Ellaline let herself in anyway.

"I thought that was you, rushing about like a banshee." Ellaline took a seat on the chaise. "Do tell."

"It's nothing."

"Oh, come on! A problem halved and all that?"

Katie hesitated. Ever since the tragic murder of her father two years earlier followed by the sudden death of her mother, everyone treated 'Lady Hicks' with kid gloves. Although, to Katie's mind, Ellaline was a formidable woman of indomitable character. She rolled with the punches and had a knack for turning the worst of situations around to her advantage. "It's not important. I received a disappointing letter this afternoon."

Ellaline tilted her head. "That's a funny word."

"What is?"

"Disappointed. Customarily, letters are either glad tidings or bad news. Which was yours?"

"Neither I suppose." Katie rest her chin on her hand. "It was the content."

"I don't follow."

"Hardly surprising. I don't follow me, either."

"Forgive me for saying this, Kate, but you haven't seemed too thrilled of late. Shouldn't you be excited? You're the critics' flavour of the month."

"Yes, but what good is it when it's something I never wanted in the first place?"

Ellaline regarded her. "Is that really what's bothering you?"

"It's part of it."

"And the other part?"

Katie toyed with one of the cords hanging from her waist and debated the merits of telling the truth about her situation with Flora.

She opted for the half-truth. She told Ellaline that she had met a man. She told her of their whirlwind romance, but he had gone off to war. She told her about Flora's- Sinclair's-background; her family, the army and the illiteracy which had brought her to the big smoke in the first place. She told her about the awkward encounter with Don & Evelyn and the fact that Flora still believed she was embarrassed by their relationship. Last, she told her about the letter and it's disheartening lack of content.

Ella listened, nodding where appropriate and injecting an occasional pertinent question.

"You know, Kate, I think you're a terrific girl with a very dear heart, but I just don't understand you."

Katie stared at her. "How so?"

"You meet this remarkable young man who is nothing but

kind. He's brave, handsome, and clearly worships the very ground you walk upon. Have you any idea how rare such a man is? His first attempt and writing to you wasn't so great. He's trying, despite everything else you've told me. Why be so quick to discount that? Are you afraid of what others will say?"

Katie dipped her head. "Perhaps. Things feel so right when we're together, but when we're apart, I have doubts. After reading his letter, I can't help but question whether what we had was real. We're such different people. I believed us too different. Though the longer we were together, the less I found I cared."

"We all have doubts, my dear. As for those two, damn them. Damn the lot of them!" She smacked a hand over Katie's dressing table.

"Ella!"

"All Don is interested in is finding his next young starlet. If you were spotted on the arm of some dashing lord, that would suit his purposes. As for that trollop, she'd have her wicked way with anything in trousers. You stick to your guns, Katie Day. Write back, explain everything to him like you did with me just now. If he's the man you believe him to be, he'll understand. And if you're so uncertain, then send him something of yours, a picture. It'll remind him of what's waiting for him."

"You're right. I've been a fool. A silly little fool."

"No. Foolish possibly, but never a fool. It's no wonder your head is in a spin. But please do yourself this favour and write back." She placed a hand on the other woman's knee. "Don't give up just yet. You'll feel better for it."

"Ella, there's something else. Something I dare not tell anyone. Even you when you've been so good to me. And not just today. I don't know how I would have managed these past months without your support."

"Well, I hope someday you'll be able to tell me. In the meantime..."

"Yes, in the meantime. Best get ready. Friday night's always a busy one."

"I'll leave you to get dressed." Ellaline rose from the couch, "If you should need anything."

"You will be the first person I call upon. And thank you again."

*

Magersfontein, South Africa, December 1899

"Begg! Letter for you!"

A stained envelope sailed through the air onto her lap. The needle she was using to stitch a hole in her jacket nearly flew straight up her nose. She twirled the paper over in her grasp. Sitting more upright, she tore open the envelope, sputtering at the dust the sudden movement had kicked up.

"Hello my love,

I've missed you..."

9

Laura stretched and stared at the ceiling, the paper rough between her forefinger and thumb. As ceilings went, it was uninspiring. *Typical '60s.* Not like she wasn't used to hospitals, but when you had the time to notice the crumbling plaster and stench of disinfectant, there was an understandable air of the depressing about them.

I hate this sprawling about. She raised herself up on her elbows, but the throbbing in her head made her pinch her nose. *S'pose I got off lightly. Concussion and a few scrapes. Poor Mhairi. Bikers jeans don't protect you from a massive hunk of burning-hot metal landing on you.*

"You're a Donoghue now?"

In the doorway stood a tall, matronly woman with honeycomb hair held back in a French twist, and a clipboard in her hand. "I almost didn't recognise you under all those lumps and bumps. How're you feeling?"

"A tad heady and achy, but I s'pose I'll live."

"You will, by the grace of god. What on Earth were you thinking, being on a bike in such foul weather? And not a helmet!"

"Wasn't exactly planned."

"I should say not. Your mother would be furious."

"Would she really?"

"Laura MacInnes, what a terrible thing to say! Of course, she would. The very idea, risking your neck for no good reason."

"I'm not so sure."

"And just what do you mean by that?"

Beth's question was simple enough, but Laura's pause was long and her gaze downcast. Beth moved closer to the bed.

"It was my fault."

"How? You were a bit stupid being sat on the back, but as far as I'm aware, you weren't actually driving the bike."

"I don't mean the bike."

"Then what?"

"Because most things are my fault."

"Honestly, I've rarely heard such self-pitying claiver."

The clipboard clattered on the bedside cabinet.

"It's true. Everything is. Ever since Mum."

"You must've cracked your head harder than I realised. Laura, you were fourteen and your mother had an accident. Tragic as it was."

"You remember when mum left your wedding? Because of me. I was meant to come with her, but I didn't want to go. So, I kicked my heels until she went on her own. Then I kept phoning the hotel and being a little brat because I didn't want to stay at Granny's either. Eventually she gave in. Granny begged her not to drive in that storm. If I'd just done as I was told..."

"Rubbish. I loved your mother well, but by god, she could be pig-headed. She was a grown woman who made her own decisions. Your grandmother wasn't the only one who warned her not to drive that night. Both me and Steve did too. You can't go through life blaming yourself for what other people choose to do, you'll drive yourself insane."

"I'm already there. I don't sleep, my life's in tatters, my marriage is in shambles. Take your pick."

"You always did have a flair for the dramatic, Laura. Your life's not in tatters, you've a bump on the heid. And if your marriage is in shambles, then either unshamble it or remove the ring. The only person who can fix your problems is you."

"Do you offer all your patients this much TLC or am I special?"

"Only the ones that deserve it. Some of them, I give a real boot up the bahookie."

"That's comforting."

"I'm not here to sugar coat. I get my patients better. Sometimes that means reading them the riot act. I remember those years. You were no picnic. But you were a teenager. Helen was a young widow. You'd both been through something terrible. If your mother had lived, bless her, the two of you would have come out the other side and been best pals. This isn't what brought you back here, surely to goodness?"

"It is. Mum. And gran. Dad too, I suppose but, mainly mum and gran."

"You were trying to make your peace with them. But it's been nearly twenty years. Why now?"

"Because I'm struggling to work out who I am. And I'm tired of fighting fires."

"You put one out and another starts." said Beth, her tone much mellowed as she took a seat on the edge of the bed.

"I was at the cemetery. Mhairi was worried and she came to find me. None of this was her fault."

"I don't doubt it, but she's still going to have to answer some tough questions."

"She's in trouble because of me."

"She allowed a passenger on her bike without a helmet. I doubt they'll chuck the book at her, but there'll be a nice wee fine and a good talking to coming her way."

"I feel terrible."

"Should think so. And you're still avoiding my question."

"I don't like the person I'm becoming. I lost my job and now I'm a terrible wife too. I can't give Jim what he wants."

"And what's that?"

"A child."

Laura's quiet reply was a far cry from the brassy youth Beth remembered and had begrudgingly admired. That kid was ready to grab the world and crack its neck. This Laura was an overstretched elastic band.

"When you say you can't...?"

"I'm not sure I'm able to. And to be honest, it doesn't bother me. Kids were never on the agenda as far as I was concerned." Her skin burned like it had that stupid night her colleagues had made her do the Ice Bucket Challenge, but lodged in her chest was a dead weight, solid and immovable. "Jim's wanted us to start a family for years. Whenever he brought it up, I would talk about my career, and how I didn't want to mess things up. I was doing too much good."

"And now?"

"Now I've nothing to hide behind anymore. My career's

been stolen away, and it's left a giant hole in my gut. But I'm not looking for a baby to fill it."

"Do you have a good reason for not wanting children?"

"Do I need one?"

"Precisely! So why aren't you telling him that?"

"Because I doubt he'd accept it. He's hell bent on the white picket fence thing. Just because I'm the last one standing in our family, my mind hasn't changed. Quite the opposite. It's pressure I don't need. I hate being this way. I hate the loneliness. I'm thirty-one years old and everyone I ever loved is in the ground. And I know that starting a family is what I'm supposed to want. But there's been a mistake. Do you have any idea what it's like to wake up each morning and wonder what is so wrong with you, you deserve to be punished this way? I don't want to live like this anymore, but I don't know how to change it. And even if I did, I doubt my equipment's in full working order, so it's all moot anyway."

For long moments Beth contemplated the battered young woman with her listless fingers curled on her lap atop the knitted blanket. "I remember when you were a child, you were so precious, so loved, and you knew it. You were fearless. Then after all those terrible things happened, it was so damned impossible to push you on anything. And you never pushed yourself. You've always been bright, but you coasted all through school. When you left the island, I thought finally you might have found that spark again, but I never understood why you left the way you did. Did you ever ask yourself what made you pick nursing?"

"Mum was a nurse."

"No. Try again."

"I wanted to help people."

"Closer, but it goes deeper than that. What do you feel when you help someone get better, Laura?"

"Relief? Happiness? Pride?" She sighed.

"Come on. What's the real hard truth here?"

"I do it because I feel better, alright? Because it makes me less of a fucking shit head." Laura's outburst rattled about the walls for several moments. "Sorry."

"Don't be. We're getting somewhere."

"It won't solve anything."

"Won't it? You've just admitted you're entire career has been based on trying to salve your conscience. That's huge."

"Oh god, when you put it like that, it sounds so awful, so-"

"Naked?"

"Yeah."

"Excellent. Now move forward."

"I don't know how."

"Course you don't. If you did, you'd have done it years ago and I wouldn't be having to listen to you whinge."

"What happens now then, oh wise one?"

"You do the work."

"What the hell does that even mean? I don't speak Yoda. I was hoping you'd help me here."

"I just did. My mother claimed she had the second sight but I'm no mind reader. Only you know what you want. If your career is so important to you, why haven't you found yourself another posting yet?"

"It's not that easy!"

"Laura, if you were all that determined, you would have done it by now."

"Why are you being like this?"

"Because I've known you since you were born. And because what you need is a damn good kick. Your father, god rest him, was a kind man, but you are your grandmother's and your mother's daughter. They were the strong ones in their marriages. They had to be. Your father wouldn't have made anything of himself if it hadn't been Helen, pushing him to do better. You've the same spirit, but you're not embracing it. You're letting everything happen to you. It's not how you were raised, and it's not what I expect from you. I suggest you make your peace with the past. Do it soon. Then go home and face the present. You've a lot of years ahead of you. Too many to grow bitter for things which can't be undone."

Laura's lip curled.

"What?"

"Nothing. You just reminded me of someone I've been reading about."

"Yes, well." Beth rose and headed to the door. "I have real patients to see to."

"Thank you, Beth."

"Don't go thanking me yet. Sergeant Anderson will be outside waiting to have a word with you. I expect he's finished with your friend by now. In the meantime, you'll be staying here an extra night for observation. You'll be heading home tomorrow morning."

The door clicked shut and Laura threw her head back into the pillows. "Christ."

*

The waggy-finger treatment from Sergeant Anderson was embarrassing, but he was at least kindlier and less abrasive than Beth. *Never fun getting your knuckles rapped aged thirty-two!*

"Knock! Knock!"

"At last, a friendly face! What are you doing hopping about? Should you be up so soon?"

"Nurse Cadwell's just been showing me how to use my crutches so be-warned, missy, I am mobile and deadly!" Mhairi waved one crutch in the air.

Laura couldn't help but laugh. "I'm sorry." She winced as her friend hobbled over to the seat the sergeant had not-long vacated.

"Ach, what for? Not your fault." But she was puffing with the exertion, and Laura's stomach twisted.

"Kinda is. It's my fault you had to come after me. I'll go half-ers on the fine. And the damage."

"Dinnae be daft. That's what friends do. I'm not angry, Laura, although I'd like to understand what drove you to that place. You were a mess when I picked you up."

"Yeah. There's a lot of that going about." Laura snorted and glanced at the plaster cast coating Mhairi's leg. "Speaking of messes. What's the prognosis?"

"They're going to let me go with you tomorrow. There's not a lot more they can do for me here, so they've booked me in to see the surgeon at Raigmore. Pins and a plate job."

"Oh god, I really am sorry!"

"Laura." Mhairi tried to pull the other woman's hands from

her face, not quite reaching. "It's one of those things. It's a miracle I've beaten the odds this long. Was bound to come fleeing off eventually."

"I feel rotten."

"Well, don't. But seriously, I want to know."

Laura closed her eyes and recounted her conversation with Beth.

"And now my head's all foggy."

Mhairi watched her for a moment, chin perched on hand. "Do you know why Dave and I broke up?"

"I remember the way you talked about his boat and figured it was a lifestyle thing."

"Partially. Mainly it was Izzy. I mean, I wouldn't be without her now, but god-knows, we'd never have made a family. There were so many things I loved about him; his energy, his optimism, but he wanted to stay a kid for the rest of his life, and I couldn't afford to. I wasn't ready to be a mum, either, but I also couldn't bare the idea of getting rid of her. So, we split. And you know what? He's a great dad. On the weekends. Never in a million years, would he cope with the day-to-day rubbish. He lives in the tiniest cottage because he's permanently skint which, fair play, never bothers him. He's living the freedom dream. Izzy loves going to stay with him, but there's no stability there. No substance. If we'd not been so careless one drunken night, we'd have parted company eventually and moved on. Our relationship was never on what you'd call solid ground. You have something solid. But that's no good when you're bound for different things. You either have to meet in the middle or..."

"Or we go our separate ways."

"I know one thing. You shouldn't have children for the wrong reasons. If you do, you'll only resent it later. Then everyone suffers. The both of you need to be clear on that."

"Thanks."

"You're welcome. Now, how's the story going? Any juicy developments?"

Laura laughed and filled her in on the most recent 'episode' of the *Flora and Katie Chronicles*.

"Aww, melt." Mhairi patted her chest.

"I know, it's like something out of Mills & Boone."

"Wait, do you think she'll come back?"

Laura gave her a blank look. "I guess she must do." She waved the papers in front of Mhairi's face.

"At least you have something decent to read. Was good of the owner to bring our bags over."

"I somehow think it had more to do with making sure the house is empty now he can squeeze in another paying guest."

"Are you always such a pessimist?"

"I'm a realist."

"You've just no romance in that soul, have you?"

Laura glanced at the sheets of paper on her lap. "Would be kinda nice. Having a wee bit of faith. You could almost believe love can conquer all."

"Funny when you think about it. In a way, Flora and Kate had much more freedom than you and me."

"How d'you mean?"

"Well consider this for a second. Women like us meet someone and that relationship conforms to a certain 'ideal'. We want the hunk, or the one with the piercing blue eyes and abs of steel. Alright, maybe that's a slight exaggeration."

"Erm, yeah."

"But we meet what we think is the perfect guy. He pursues us, we bring him home to meet the family or our friends, you get engaged, get married and knock out a couple of kids and that's what society tells us is 'the norm'. Right?"

"Sort of." Laura frowned.

"I'm not saying that's what always happens. Hello. But Flora and Kate didn't have any of those expectations on their relationship. They got to concentrate on just being themselves."

"True, I see what you're saying but don't forget, they were only able to do that because folk took Flora for a man. I mean, they couldn't have gone out in public together as a couple otherwise. Not like us if we went for a date with a boyfriend."

"True, but it's a thought. They didn't have to conform to some predetermined plan because one didn't exist."

"You're right. In fact, that's pretty much exactly what I was just saying to Beth. Thank god times have changed."

"But have they? Out of curiosity, when was that last time you and Jim went out?"

"Not that long. A few weeks. Maybe more."

Mhairi gave her an imperious look.

"Gloating's not attractive, Mhairi."

"I'm just saying, maybe it's about time you two concentrated on something other than your unhappiness and remember why you got married in the first place."

"You think Jim's unhappy too?"

"You don't?"

"I've never asked. S'pose I figured that saying as we're doing everything he wants, I didn't need to. Maybe I should."

"Maybe. And now in this great spirit of openness, there's something else that's been niggling away at me. Something you said, on that road. You said that's where it all started. Where what started?"

Laura picked at her blanket. "I don't think I've told you how grateful I am that you came here with me."

"You're welcome. Didn't Jim think it was a bit weird you didn't want him instead?"

"I never stopped to ask that either. Having him here would've just muddied things."

"Do you think you found what you came here for, at least?"

"No. Not yet. There's something I need to do. And I need you to come with."

10

Magersfontein, South Africa, December 1899

Rain hammered on the bivouac roof. Stray globs blew in and splattered the paper under Flora's wrist as she fought to keep the damn thing from flapping about, pencil growing slippery in her fingers where an incessant stream of water dripped from the peak of her helmet. The shivering didn't help either.

"Blasted thing!"

"Trouble?"

"It's this bloody weather, can't get my pencil to stay on the paper. Or the paper to stay under the pencil, whichever way round it is."

"Does it need doing right now?" Sergeant Gunn removed his glasses. It was no use trying to glower at someone if you couldn't see them.

"Yes! Katie said my last letter wasn't good enough. I haven't had time to write back. She'll be thinking I've taken umbrage an' gone off her. I need to make a decent effort of it this time."

"I doubt lack of effort was the problem, you were sweating

bullets over that last one. Besides, I'm sure she didn't put it like that."

"Might as well have."

Gunn closed his eyes. "God, grant me patience. What was wrong with it?"

"It didna say enough. Not enough lovey-dovey stuff. I'm no good at that sort of thing."

"Course you're no. None of us are. But we have to keep them happy. So what have you got scribbled this time?"

"Nothing yet. I canna get the damn paper ae keep still!"

"Right, over here. Now. Christ almighty." He dragged out his chair and pushed her into it. "What do you want to say?"

"I'd like to tell her about what's been happening here, but it'll only come out wrong."

"Depends on how it's put. War's not usually deemed suitable conversation for a lady."

"I have to say something. What else can I talk about? Besides, she's tougher than most."

"Oh, that, I believe. She'd have to be to put up with you." He grinned.

"So, what do I do, clever dick?"

"Gie's it here." He grabbed the paper and swept off the surface water, reading the few words Flora had managed to scrawl. "This'll no do it, Sink. Pass me yer pencil."

Dear Kate

"It's a lesson in the art of women, you're needing, son. Now, you talk, I'll write."

*

My dearest love,

We've taken a bit of a beating the last few days. I wasn't sure whether to tell you all, but I reckon you can handle it.

Perhaps it was retribution for desecrating the holy day. I don't know how much faith I have in acts of the divine, but after what I witnessed on Sunday there, it was almost enough to convince me.

The weather was much like today; a wild storm that made the air stink like iron. We advanced in quarter form, but it was pitch black and we had to huddle tight to not lose each other. Our boots were no match for the rivers of rusty rain pouring down the hillsides and we kept slipping on the rocks, cursing when our kilts caught on the thorns the whole climb. My knees are skint to hell. Then some damned...someone, let slip to the enemy we were coming.

All hell broke loose. The Boers opened fire on us, and we got stuck. Wauchope & Goff fell. No one was giving orders. Some of the Watch boys broke through but got cut up by our own shells. They pinned us down 'til near enough dawn until an officer somehow brought up one of our guns. Most of us that had survived up 'til then, got away, but we left a lot of good men behind on that hill. Reinforcements from the Coldstreams and Gordons did their best to get to us, but we got blocked off at the rear by a bunch of Scandies and they cut us up bad.

We got away by the skin of our teeth, but they reckon about 800 are dead or missing. Now we're being swept by typhoid and a lot of the lads are going doolally, myself among them.

We were cannon fodder that night. Not one amongst us escaped wound or death. I thought the days of building piles of bodies in a

Forlorn Hope were long past, but it seems not so. There'll be hell to pay once the dispatches reach home.

I'm sorry my last letter was a disappointment. I never want to disappoint you. It's your face I see each night before I rest my eyes, even better now, thanks to the picture you sent me. I mind that day and your face that first turn about the carousel. I'd never tried fudge before, either- I don't know what I imagined, but it was very sweet! It's a bon thing to remember and smile each night. The thought of you waiting keeps me strong. I am glad, now, that you're every bit as stubborn as me.

Sleep sound tonight, my darling.

Your Sinclair

Flo

London, January 1900

Katie pressed the note to her lips and closed pictured Flora's scraped knees. She scanned Flora's words again. *I doubt I should want to contemplate whatever was missing from that story. She was right about one thing, though; the outcry once the news broke. The papers have been having a field day and the Scots are about ready to riot.*

She'd barely the stomach for the numerous articles which described, in horrid detail, what had occurred at Magersfontein, and the senseless waste of life suffered by the Highland Division.

She eyed the diary on her dresser, then looked at the clock. Flora's letter had delayed her. The branch meeting was half an hour away. *That only leaves me ten minutes! I should take Flora's letter.*

It wasn't what Katie had had in mind when she'd suggested that Flora write something more detailed, but it was still an improvement. "Hardly romantic, but Ellaline was right. Flora would do anything I ask. Perhaps I should give her an example." A tingle shot down her spine.

The idea of unburdening her soul had been a good one, but when it came to putting pen to paper, she found she hadn't the heart. The discussion would keep until Flora came home and they could deal with it together. If it was even still relevant by then.

Katie had taken care in distancing herself from the West End crowd and devoting herself to the causes which mattered. "Maybe Flora's been rubbing off on me more than I realised."

She blushed at her own words.

"And until she comes home, I shall just have to spend every syllable of every letter showing her how much I love and miss her." She flicked a half-eye at the clock and grabbed her things. "Damn. I'll have to miss her later."

*

Breathless and red faced with a most unladylike sheen across her brow, she made it to Gower Street in gentrified Bloomsbury, with mere minutes to spare. Shrieks of laughter passed her by as she guzzled glass over glass of ice-cold water before making her way to the meeting room, A.K.A the Living Room, just as Mrs Millicent Garrett Fawcett was preparing to chair.

However many gatherings she attended, Katie remained in awe of the unassailable Mrs Fawcett. A handsome woman in her youth, she was respected across the country for her remarkable academic achievements.

Beyond the opening remarks, the meeting dragged while members squabbled among themselves until the floor was opened for Any Other Business.

After casting a nervous glance about the room, Katie stuck up her hand.

"The chair recognises Miss Day" said Mrs Fawcett. "The floor is yours."

Katie came to her feet, her entire body cringing. She was used to people gazing at her from afar, but the scrutiny of a dozen or more respectable ladies was a different animal. Her grip tightened on Flora's letter. "Ladies and-" Her eyes flitted about the room. *What in God's name is wrong with me.*

A murmur rippled through the crowd *'when did you last see that much rouge!'* said one woman. *'on a Whitechapel tart. Pity they never caught that Ripper fellow!'* replied another.

"I'm a performer." said Katie, aiming a scowl at the area from where the snide remarks had issued.

'We're not arguing with that, dear!'

She searched for at least semi-friendly face. Mrs Fawcett tapped a finger to her upper lip. Katie reached for her purse and screwed her eyes at her reflection in the silver clasp. Her stomach dropped through the floor. A red streak shot from the corner of her mouth, all the way up her cheek. "Oh no." The sniggering made sense now.

She groped around in her bag for a tissue, finding only a used one, but it had a clean corner. She dabbed at her cheek with sharp. She wished the ground would open and send her cursed self into Verne's subterranean ocean, whereby a passing plesiosaur might swallow her up and put her out of her misery. But Millicent's gentle face gave an encouraging nod.

"Ladies, my name is Miss Day. Miss Katie Day and I believe we must discuss this terrible war and the devastating effect it is having, not only on our great nation's morale but on our own brave boys. Is this war justified, I ask you? Can the imperialist elite of our government continue to sanctify such action when so many are suffering?" She trailed off, the words trapped under her breath, aware of a foreboding torrent of disapproval emanating from Mrs Pankhurst. *Why on earth, did I think this would be a clever idea?*

The image of Flora and her skint knees floated behind her eyes. "Ladies, I have brought with me a letter which I received today from my, my fiancé, Miss- that is, Mr Sinclair Begg. He's a Highlander." This drew another murmur, but this time it sounded almost sympathetic. "He writes of the appalling losses suffered by his regiment."

Katie recounted, word-for-word, Flora's letter, which garnered impassioned reactions from everyone in attendance, none more so than Mrs Fawcett, herself.

"Ladies, I ask you, though we seek equality for women, surely we must strive for true equality for all who are disenfranchised. Is it right that these poor men, with as limited access to education as many of our own girls, who serve this country so bravely, should suffer so needlessly at the hands of an ill-equipped patriarchal government? If women's voices echoed in the upper echelons of government, would these atrocities occur? We've all heard of the travesty that occurred at Magersfontein. This is man's foolhardiness, which causes men who are considered lesser, to be slaughtered by their hundreds out of ego. That innocent women and children should suffer so in the wake of such destruction. I ask you, is this right? Is the time not ripe to wrest the reins of power from those hands? Should we not stand with our fathers, our brothers, and our sweethearts? Surely, we should strive, not just for ourselves, but for every oppressed human who walks among us?"

*

Highland Brigade, Koedoesberg, South Africa, February 1900

The medical tent was in the furthest corner of the encampment. A reasonable quarter of a mile walk when one was fit. More of a challenge if one was suffering from a blitzed knee.

Captain Bill MacKechnie twisted Flora's leg from side-to-side. He was young for his rank and cut a dashing figure to boot. While a talented physician in his own right, there persisted a substantial quarter who refused to view his rapid rise as anything but nepotism; his father was Surgeon-General and held the corresponding influence.

"And you're still going to refuse a crutch?"

"I can't fight with a crutch. I can still walk."

"Aye, just." He made some notes, then leaned back against the next bed and folded his arms. "Truth be told, I'm amazed that wee twenty-mile saunter there, didn't kill you. When are you going to give up? Pack it in? Stockwell knows about you, you've the perfect get-out clause. What's more, he knows I helped you."

"It's not so simple, you know that." Flora gave her knee a speculative flex.

"But why not? Look, you've made your point. Dammit, I've had to patch you up so many times now, the men think you're indestructible. One of these days you won't be so lucky. Go home Flora."

"I signed on for the same duty as everyone else. I must see it through or what am I? Coward? This is my home."

"You're reckless. And it's not just me who sees it. You were fortunate, that's all. Another half-inch and that kneecap would've been beyond fixing. Be grateful you're not a horse. Those idiots might look on it as heroic, but I'm the one who has to pick up the pieces. By rights, I should never have helped you enlist. I thought you'd see for yourself what a daft idea this was eventually."

"So why did you, then?"

"Because I liked you. I wanted to help you. I was wrong. We weren't at war before. Not like this. It's all gone too far."

"Tell me something, Bill. Would you be giving me this lecture if I was just another of the boys?"

"Of course not."

"Save yourself the heartache." She patted his shoulder and swung herself off the bed, grunting as her foot contacted the ground. "I assume I'm fit to go?"

"I wouldn't go that far. But could I really stop you?"

"Strictly speaking, yes. You could pull rank on me. But in reality?"

"Indeed. Just look after yourself out there. Don't make me regret my own skulduggery even more than I already do."

"I'll try my best." she said over her shoulder, already hirpling off. From her breast pocket she drew the small packet that had arrived through the post that morning. She plonked herself on a handy stump and unfolded the note.

My darling,
Before I say any more, you must promise me that this letter is for your eyes only, my love. No one else must read it.

Flora glanced about her surroundings. She stalked off beyond the camp boundary into a neighbouring patch of scrubland, oblivious to the set of eyes that followed her.

*

The bark was rough on her tunic as she settled beneath the great forks of a Baobab tree, just deep enough into the scrub to obscure her presence, but not so far as to be challenged should someone chance upon her.

I miss you, Flora. I miss you lying next to me, your touch, your warmth. I unpin my hair- I know how much you love when it tumbles about my shoulders. Then I trace my finger across my lips and down the line of my neck. And it's no-longer my fingers, but your mouth I can feel.

"Christ, Katie." Flora couldn't help herself. With the page crumpled in one hand, her other grasped one meagre breast through its bindings and squeezed.

My hands run paisley patterns all over my body, touching me in all the most secret places that you have come to know so intimately. Places I didn't know could bring such pleasure until you showed me.

Flora's respiration came ragged and guttural. Her hand slipped beneath her tunic and clawed at her skin.

I whisper your name over and over as your mouth dips lower, praying no one hears. Even our breaths sound obscene in the night air. I often remember our last night together. You remember? In the woods.

Flora's hand faffed with her belt. The buckle rattled under

an uncertain grip. After an agonising struggle, she loosened the side straps and shoved her hand beneath her waistband.

My darling, the sensations you can elicit from me with only your lips! The way I'm helpless to the loving strokes of your tongue, but it's nothing to the communion I feel when you slip your fingers inside. I have experienced nothing so unfathomable, so cherished, as I do with you, Flora. My own fingers press deep inside me now. As long as I can keep the image of your face behind my eyes then I can believe it's real, believe in our intimacy. The way one corner of your mouth lifts in that half smile when you know I have given myself completely over to you. I cry out. I'm sure the others can hear, but I can't help it. I know I can lose the entirety of my being in your presence, Flora, and that I am safe. You'll bring me back to myself again when we're both ready, but there's never a rush. You tell me you love me, that we can stay in this secluded place that is only ours.

Flora's strokes grew harder, praying for her elusive peak to come quick. When it arrived, it wasn't graceful. The release shattered her senses.

Hours could have passed entirely unnoticed beneath that tree but for the orange glow in the sky, but every wisp of sweet erotic haze was driven from her body as she read the final paragraph.

I cannot wait for that day when you will come back to me, my love. Until that time arrives, my vow to you is simple. I will de-

vote each word of these letters to giving you every reason to fight on. Fight, Flora. Fight to come home. To me.

In the meantime, I took your last letter to our meeting this evening. All the ladies were appalled by the way in which your generals have behaved, and it has quite stirred them into action. Your words have become our rallying cry, darling. Mrs Fawcett is delighted. Isn't it wonderful? I've agreed to let her take your letter all the way to Whitehall!

Ever yours,
Kate

"Oh dear god. What the hell have you done to me, Kate? And who the bloody hell is Mrs Fawcett?"

*

Harley was a southerner with an air of the entitled about him. She glanced to the side. *Not a real soldier, just bloody-well fancies himself in the get-up.* She had despised him the second she had happened across him at Omdurman. Rumour had it, he'd been knocked back from a fancier uniform and he regarded his position in the Seaforths with resentment. What he hadn't banked on was the brutal, almost suicidal, fighting spirit of the Highlanders, which meant they had been at the forefront of the fiercest actions of the war and his bitterness had increased accordingly. He stood rigid next to her as they waited for Stockwell. *Can see this is going to be fun.*

"Ah, Lieutenant, Corporal, glad to see you both looking

fit." The Major took a seat at his desk. Behind him entered another man of imposing height, broad-shouldered and something of a legend. Major-General Sir Hector MacDonald or, 'Fighting Mac' as he was known to newspaper editors across Britain and beyond. The son of a humble crofter, just like Flora. He'd risen through the ranks, from lowly volunteer, off the back of his own grit and, on more than one occasion, had shown up that clot Kitchener for what he was. Flora couldn't help but goggle. She'd seen him in action at Omdurman. A lion in battle, yes, but he also radiated authority. A man who commanded loyalty and respect through the force of his deeds but his was a quiet power and his eyes carried a twinkle.

"You're no-doubt wondering why you've been summoned, so I shall cut to it."

Flora's attention snapped back to Major Stockwell.

"That little skirmish yesterday cost us. It's no one's blame. I don't know of any other fighting force which could've set to defence after a twenty mile march the way our lads did. But one of those taken prisoner yesterday was some distant relation of Wauchope's. Major-General MacDonald and I have received orders that we must retrieve him from the enemy at all costs." The two men shared a withering glance. "We have selected you both to lead a four-man detail to recover the Captain and however many men you can bring back with you before the enemy moves on to the Transvaal. We realise this is an onerous task and we do not ask it of you lightly. You will leave at nightfall. Take only volunteers. Two. Use this time to sort any personal arrangements. Understood? Dismissed."

Flora and Harley saluted, and heel turned.

"Just a minute. Begg, why are you hobbling?"

Flora swallowed. "Boots are pinching a wee bit, sir."

Stockwell narrowed his eyes, then nodded. "Very well. Carry on, Corporal."

"This the one you were telling me about?" said MacDonald once the canvas closed.

"It is."

"I see what you mean." He winked. "Though difficult to tell, at first, with the face furniture. Reckon they'll make it back?"

"One of them will but certainly not both."

"Care to wager?"

"You'll lose, Sir. My money's on Begg."

"I don't know, John. Harley was more than a wee bit humiliated after that fracas at Omdurman. Man has a score to settle. And you reckon your girl's up to it?"

"I do. And I take your point. He's had over a year to let his temper stew. But she's a scrapper and she's one of us. That bastard Harley's a southern namby-pamby with too big a chip on his shoulder. Tried for the Blues but someone at Whitehall turned him down. Let Begg hammer away at it. She'll do us all a favour."

"I hope she proves me wrong, then." MacDonald grunted and took his leave.

Outside, a few feet from the officer's tent, Harley came to an abrupt halt and whipped Flora around by the shoulders. She groaned as her knee jerked and buckled.

"You and I have a score to settle, Begg. If that's even your real name."

"I saved your life. Seems to me you owe me one."

"Let's get this straight. I am an officer of Her Majesty's

army. I didn't need saving from a... I don't know what you are. But you and your tits bursting out make a mockery of us all. You're a disgrace to the uniform." He spat, relinquishing his grip on her shoulders. "We'll see what happens tonight, shall we?"

"Aye," she said and shook him off, her tone a deadly chill. "We'll see. But you better hope and pray I don't see you first."

*

Nightfall approached and Flora hunkered behind a boulder, a short distance from Cronje's camp, between Harley and a Private who'd been introduced simply as Barclay. She didn't recognise him, but he looked a dour sod. Skinny with rapid ferret-like movements, he was sleekit. She could imagine him scurrying his way beneath the enemy's bullets. Not a useless skill. He was fidgety though, shifting his rifle from side to side and sending furtive glances her way.

"Easy, soldier." She breathed, and he muttered something she couldn't make out. "Problem, Barclay?"

"No, Corp." he said, but the use of her rank held an edge.

She opted to ignore the impertinence, choosing to believe the youngster was nervous. So young, in fact, that it was probably his first tour of duty, shipped off many thousands of miles away from Scotland. She'd been much the same. It either broke or emboldened you, and not everyone made it into the latter.

On his other side was Private Alexander. She liked him.

He was a cool hand and steady under fire. A fine choice for such a mission.

She fingered the outline of thin card tucked in her breast pocket and allowed Katie's presence, if only in spirit, to calm her nerves. Being wounded, or even killed in action was less worrisome than the prospect that that bastard, Harley, might make use of the opportunity to fill her back with lead. From the corner of her eye, she caught another disturbed expression on Barclay's face. *Am I gonna have to fight on three fronts tonight?*

Harley popped a pair of field binoculars from the leather case on his hip and scanned the terrain. "I see them." he said after a couple of lefts and rights, then centred in on their objective. The General's cousin and a further half-dozen or so Tommies were pinned to the ground a few yards away from the Boer's campfires.

"Left to freeze. Look, there's a path through that hillock there." said Flora. "It'd be treacherous underfoot, but I reckon we could manage it."

"When I want your opinion, *Corporal*." But he was already setting off in the direction Flora had indicated.

Flora and the two privates hefted their rifles to the clicks of bolts and webbing buckles and hustled after him with hushed footsteps.

The closer they edged towards the camp, the higher the sweet stench reached into air and the sick realisation of what must have been decomposing bodies below. The sloping rock face proved grip-less, and the foursome scrabbled down, smaller stones falling about their faces as their hands scraped for any kind of traction. They were too far away from the opposing army's encampment to turn any heads, but it wouldn't stay that way long if they didn't manage this with some speed.

As soon as they reached the ground, Barclay about-faced and threw up, dizzy from the fetid fumes. The other three ignored him, but his retching made Flora's gut twist.

"Come on!" Harley barked. "You two, get those ones." He shooed Alexander and Barclay to the right. "Begg, you're with me." Each pair disappeared into the rain that had started beating a steady tattoo on their helmets.

They found the Captain first and ripped apart his bindings, but he was too weak to make the climb by himself. Harley urged him to rest easy until some of the others could be freed first. They crept about in relative silence and got several men up the hill before Harley waved Barclay and Alexander over to help drag the Captain up the slope. Flora stayed behind to cut the ropes on as many of the remaining Tommies as she could. Given the state of most of them; half-starved and carrying any number of wounds, most of them wouldn't make the journey back to HQ, but at least they would have the chance. *Or else die as free men.*

An arm wrapped itself tight about her neck.

She must have cried out because all hell broke loose.

A strafe of shot from several Mausers joined the pelting rain while she struggled to break from Harley's grip. She gained enough momentum to lift her lower body and yank down on his arm, forcing him to break his hold. She turned, coughing, and whipped the back of her hand across his face, the force in the blow enough of a shock to make him stagger backwards until he lost his feet. She pounced, and the two grappled on the ground, Flora only just got the upper hand by slamming the butt of her rifle across his cheek when a stray bullet blasted through her shoulder, and she stumbled away from the prone man.

Barclay and Alexander watched on in horror as she one-handedly tried to find a hold on the slope. The pair of them reached for her arms and hauled her up, despite her yelps. Her nose scraped grit and came away bloody as all three glanced back to find the marauding Boers enclosing on the Lieutenant who had still not raised himself from the ground.

"I have to go back for him."

"You can't, it'd be suicide, Begg!" said Alexander.

She blanked him and brought her rifle round, ignoring the stabbing pain in her shoulder, and began picking off enemy troops.

"Help me." She yelled over the breaking storm.

Both men hoisted their weapons and started firing and even the rescued Captain, from his prone position at their feet, produced a tiny hidden pistol and managed to squeeze off a few rounds.

"Keep firing lads, then get the Captain out of here." said Flora, leaving her rifle where it was and sliding back towards the enemy guns.

A large, sticky red patch coated Harley's side and he was barely conscious. He tried to speak, but Flora was having none of it.

"Shut the fuck up... sir."

She gritted her teeth, hooked her good arm under his and dragged him bodily along the ground, faltering several times, praying the boys could keep up their covering fire long enough to let them all get out of there. She made it to the base of the small cliff when two sets of hands grabbed her tunic. It was an impossible task but somehow they hauled her and the Lieutenant together, up the cliff side, in time for her to pass out.

11

Her tongue caught the tang of salt and seaweed drifting in the breeze. Gentler today. A pleasant ruffle. A watery sun lay low in the sky, sparkling off the crests of foamy waves. She shielded her eyes. Deep turquoise stretched off into the distance. There were no clouds, no horizon, no boundary between sky and ocean, only that endless blue green.

Slick icing sugar shifted beneath her tan boots while the lapping waters cooled her toes. The beach was deserted except for the three of them. Few tourists would venture to the sparse island of Harris until Summer.

"Is that the house?" Mhairi pointed at a gleaming white stone cottage on the hillside.

Laura nodded.

"No use putting things off any longer." said Beth. "Time's long since passed."

"Yeah, you're right."

The trio headed over the machair and on to Seilebost.

The garden was a far cry from the patch of Eden she remembered. Rampant weeds swept across the lawn and neglected roses had rambled until their heads were all but rotted, leaving nothing but straggly thorn ropes. Iain had died shortly after Jacobina, and the dwelling had sat empty ever since.

The press of a single finger and the weather-beaten door creaked open to a welcome mat of grit and ground shells, blown in by years of Hebridean gales, which crunched under their feet.

Dank musk hung heavy in the air and flies buzzed about a mouldy plate of... *something.*

"S'pose at least the walls are still standing, and the windows look more or less watertight." A screech set Laura's teeth on edge as Beth shut the door.

"Sorry." said Beth as she ducked under cobwebs. "Not quite home-sweet-home, but the structure's still sound."

"Indeed." Laura ran her hand through a layer of gunk on a central table. "Uncle Tòrmod built this of out of railway sleepers as a wedding present."

"That's right. He worked on the railways."

"Aye, at Inversneckie. Until he got promoted and they moved him to Glasgow." Laura grinned. "Poor Uncle Tòrmod."

She stepped through to the kitchen, gave the cold water tap an experimental tug, and jumped at the gush which shot out. *A touch peaty, but the pressure's decent.* "It's funny how the wind sounds louder in here than outside."

"Think of it as atmospheric!" Mhairi's voice reverberated through the wall. "It's a shame to see it empty like this, it'd make a great wee holiday let."

"Och no, that'd be a waste of the land that comes with it." said Beth.

"Land?"

"A good bit of it. It was a working croft."

"Sheep or crops?"

"Wee bit o' both. Not what you'd call lucrative, but it kept body and soul together."

Laura caught dribs and drabs of the discussion as she continued to explore. On one worktop corner, poking out from the darkness, was a powder blue Bakelite radio. She smiled and brushed away the earthly remains of several spiders. *I wonder...*

She turned the wireless over in her hands, dismayed at the tacky substance smeared across the battery casing. *Guess not.*

"Who owns it now? This'd be a great business opportunity for somebody."

"No idea. You'd have to ask the council." said Beth.

Laura appeared in the doorway, her arms folded, bottom lip between her teeth.

"I do."

*

"Why didn't you tell me you owned a house?" Mhairi asked a few hours later. Beth had dropped them off at Kyle of Lochalsh to await the train back to Rogart, in plenty of time for a late lunch. Near the station was a place called Hector's Bothy. The soft brown leather and warm wooden tables provided a cosy shelter.

"It's not something I think about very often."

"Why not? In fact, why keep it if you're not going to do anything with it?"

"Well, *never's* a bit harsh. I just haven't yet." Laura shuffled her shoulders and spread her fingers around the mug of hot black coffee in front of her.

"Does Jim know?"

"No."

"There's hidden depths to you, girl." Mhairi flopped back on the booth bench. "You let your husband bring you up to Rogart when you didn't want to, not that you told him that. And all the while you've owned a property that could've solved your financial troubles before any of this happened."

"He was right. There's a whole big part of me he knows nothing about. On the plus side, what would you do without me? You'd be bored without us now." Laura flashed a winning smile.

"Which I still don't get. I don't get what you're so afraid of. I reckon he's got a pretty good grasp of your... quirks."

"I'm not sure I do anymore, either. I've lived like this so long. The secrets don't even feel like secrets anymore. There was that me and now there's this me."

"And never the twain shall mix? But there must be a reason. It had to start somewhere."

"Beth was right. I spent so many years running and hiding that it's part of my nature now. When things get tough, I walk away.

"Then you've no concept of where the line's drawn. Are you afraid that's what you'll do again? You'll end up walking away?"

"Maybe. I don't want to but when it comes to the crunch, I don't know that I'll be able to stop myself."

"What about before? Marriage isn't a picnic, you two must have had tough times in the past?"

"Not like this. And before, I always had my work. If things were difficult, I could hide myself away at the hospital. It never meant that much. We would fight and take our space. But we'd come back together. Now that option's gone."

"You were still running, Laura. It's only that before, you had somewhere convenient to run to."

"I guess so."

Lunch offered a welcome reprieve. Mhairi's innate talent for scrutiny and her ability to pick apart Laura's self-established mythology was something she could admire, even love, to an extent, but it was damned inconvenient too. She dug into her haddock & chips, scooping up forkfuls of luminous mushy peas with honest pleasure. *Diet schmiet!*

"What about this house then?" Mhairi mumbled around a mouthful of skin-on chips.

"Mmph, it came to me when Uncle Iain passed away, I was executor. God, that's hot!" She wafted her knife at her fish, squeezing the half-lemon over crispy batter. The sharp citrus fragrance mingled with the vinegar Mhairi had slathered across her meal tickled her nose. "Uncle Iain's wife, Chrissie, died when I was wee. They'd never had a family of their own, so they treated me like their own granddaughter. Long after Chrissie was gone, me and Gran would make the three-hour journey to visit every weekend. We'd hitch a ferry from one of the local boatmen on Skye. They always used to torment

me, saying we'd sink the boat with so many cakes and sandwiches."

"And you've never thought about selling it and making a
tidy wee profit? I mean, no offence, but I couldn't ever see you
living up there, Laura."

"No, me neither, but I knew it was there. It was the last
thing left."

"You couldn't bear the idea of someone else living there."

"Stop that!" Laura flung a chip at her.

"What?"

"It's not fair to read me like that."

"Aww, poor wee scone!" Mhairi laughed and fended off another potato missile.

*

"What's that?"

"It's another stack of letters I found when I was digging
back through the chest. They were tucked down the side."
Laura passed her the string-tied bundle across the table. The
steady chu-chud of the wheels beneath their seats, a soothing,
timeless rhythm. "It's letters Flora and Katie sent to each
other while Flora was away."

"Wow. Letters from the trenches are a hot topic right
now."

"These are earlier. Boer War, I think. That was South
Africa, right?"

"That's the one." Mhairi nodded and thumbed through grainy sheafs. "You been working your way through these?"

"I've read a few but, I dunno, it feels voyeuristic. These are personal. Intimate."

"Intimate?"

Laura flushed and found one of the earlier letters in the pile and handed it to her.

Mhairi skimmed through the first couple of passages. "I see what you mean. Ooh la la, Flora. Katie was a lot spicier than I'd have ever given her credit for. On yersel'!"

"Looks like. They certainly both had an appetite, that's for sure."

"It's funny, really. You don't think of Victorian folk as being overly sexual, but they were still human, same as us. Same base passions."

"True."

"What?"

"What, what?" Laura frowned.

"You." Mhairi pointed a finger. "Whenever anything the slightest bit naughty comes up, you get all shy and shrink away."

"Well, it's just not my thing."

"Christ, your honeymoon must've been a riot."

"Talking about it, I mean." *Thank God that lad over there has his headphones on. I hope it's Death Metal. I hope it's very loud Death Metal.*

"You are so repressed, you know that?"

"I'm not repressed, I just don't enjoy airing my dirty laundry in public, thank you very much."

"It's hardly public." Mhairi flitted her eyes about the

neighbouring empty seats. "What would you do if a patient came to you whose injuries were affecting their sex life? You would help them, yes?"

"As a clinical professional."

Mhairi sighed. "You can take the girl off the island."

"What's that supposed to mean?"

"It means you're not comfortable in your own skin."

"Yes, I am." The 'how dare you suggest otherwise' implied with an ominous glare. "Besides, I wouldn't describe Rogart as a hotbed of lust and sedition."

"You reckon? Auld Tom's had his eye on Aileen Matheson for ages. He took her bluebell-picking the other day."

"There aren't any bluebells this ti- oh."

"Bessie Docherty saw them walking out together on Sunday. The scandal!"

They shared a giggle.

"I didn't always live in Rogart."

"No? Thought you were born & bred?"

"I am but I left to study in Glasgow and then, I dunno. I had a wanderlust back then. Taught English in France and Italy for a few years. Had a lovely boyfriend in Florence. At least, I thought he was lovely until he suddenly remembered he'd already gotten engaged to someone else."

"Seems I'm not the only one with hidden depths."

"Not hidden so much. We all have a multitude of layers under the surface, Laura. Just some folk, you have to dig deeper." Mhairi gave Laura a pointed look. "Anyway, I had a hankering for home and then mum got sick. So I came back."

"I'm sorry."

"It's fine now. I've a good job. I have Izzy."

"Do you miss it? The wandering?"

"Sometimes. Sometimes I feel trapped. It wouldn't be so bad if her dad took a more active role. But then I look at that wee face. Things will change when she gets older. See. I do understand. More than you think. Just don't go running away anytime soon, okay?"

12

Koedoesberg, South Africa, February 1900

Flora's front teeth bit down on the tip of her tongue as she scratched pencil into paper with the hand that wasn't strapped into a sling.

Dearest Kate,
Trouble has stuck me in hospital this time but not to worry, they're not sending me home.

"Begg?"

The blood drained from her face.

"How are you feeling?" Bill MacKechnie folded his arms while casting surreptitious glances at Major Stockwell.

"Fine, doc. Better still if I was out of bed."

"Begg, Doctor MacKechnie and I have been discussing your case. I'm afraid there's no point flowering it up. There's no place for you on the front line. You'll remain here while the rest of us advance on Paardeberg."

"But sir-"

"No arguments. You're staying put. I know this comes as a disappointment. Doctor, be good enough to excuse us."

Bill raised his eyebrows at her from behind Stockwell's back but did as he was told.

"Though the injury to your shoulder was minor, I've been apprised of the injury you sustained at Magers'. I suppose the good doctor felt himself on thin ice with me already. And he was right. A fact for which you must bear some responsibility. Still, I expected better from the both of you. You should have been honest with me when I asked. In the usual course of things, I'd have you locked up, but I suppose your incarceration in this bed for the past week will have to do." A faint smirk made his pupils glitter, but it vanished as quickly as it had appeared. "Despite the good doctor's lack of judgement in certain areas, I do however share his concerns regarding your clarity of mind. You show great courage in the face of the enemy. It's a trait that makes the greatest of soldiers, like your hero there, MacDonald. But he'd tell you, himself, that bravery needs exercising with prudence. Harley was obsessed with proving himself because of a perceived snub, but you're just as bad. I don't know what haunts you Flora, but whatever it is, get rid of it. This army needs men like you. Men other men follow, to the ends of the earth, if necessary, but not blindly to a futile death. So, no arguments."

"Sir, I'm walking-wounded. I can travel."

"Only with the help of a crutch. I'll hear no more of this, Begg. Discussion over before I put you on a fizzer for rank insubordination. Clear?"

"Aye, sir."

Stockwell went to take his leave but halted in the doorway.

"By-the-way, you owe me a guinea, dragging that lanky bit of scrag-end back with you."

"Sir?"

"Nothing, Begg. Just a small wager I had with the General."

Flora flopped back onto the pillows. "Why did he have to call me Flora?"

She'd no idea how long she had wasted gazing at brown canvas before Bill reappeared by her bedside.

"What troubles you?"

"How do you know anything troubles me?"

"Experience."

"Don't get smug. It's love if you must know. And feeling like a fool."

"There's an adage says love makes us all fools."

Flora shook her head. "It was something Stockwell said."

"He read you the riot act."

"No. Aye. He called me Flora."

"Because that's your name."

"Not here, it's not. I don't know how to can explain it, but it's just something I know to be true. I don't feel like Flora out here. That's the name that my lover cries out in the middle of the night, but she doesn't exist in this place. Flora's weak."

MacKechnie cleared his throat. "Fl-Sinclair, I'm a Catholic and a doctor but choose not to view you from either a religious or a medical perspective, for I'm libel to fear what I might find. You're an odd duck. Unique, in fact. A one-off. But I can tell you, Flora isn't weak. Sinclair didn't leave home demanding the chance to make a better life for himself. Flora did."

"It's lonely. When you're the only one of anything."

"I don't think that needs to be true. You have a place here where, as Sinclair Begg, you are respected, even revered. Harley would never have made it, but your trying made it possible for him to dictate a last farewell to his mother & father. No one handed any of that to you, you did it yourself with a grace and humility that far outstrips where you've come from. Now don't go getting a colossal head, for by God, you've your faults. Faults which, I suspect, are going to land you in deep trouble one day. But you were borne to this existence for a reason, whatever you are. Now, anything else I can iron out for you?" He regained his feet, tucking his notes under his arm.

"I think that's all." Flora grinned. "Appreciate it. And not that I'm not grateful for the hospitality, but when d'you reckon I can make a break for it?"

"Not. Yet. You've still some more healing to do before I let you anywhere near a pair of peg legs."

"Fine. I'll just wither away in this bed, then."

"Hardly withering."

He stalked off in search of more grateful patients.

After he'd gone, she craned her neck to the gap where the edge of the tent didn't quite meet the ground and noted the fading daylight. *Don't think I'll be getting this letter written today.* Instead, she dumped her paper and pencil onto the bedside table and turned her attention to the tent flap, the way it played in the breeze.

"Corporal?"

Flora sighed. "Aye Private."

"I wondered if I might have a quick word if that's alright? It's Barclay, Corp. I was with you that night you got... this." The young man tapped his shoulder.

"I remember. What can I do for you?"

"The name's Drew, Corp." he said, removing his cap and taking her response as an invitation to sit. "I wanted to come talk to you only, I wasn't sure if it was right."

"Well, you're here now, so out with it, man." Flora said and forced her jaw open to stop her back teeth from grinding. "Say what you must and be on your way."

"I just wanted to say I was wrong about you. That day, that awful day, I saw something I shouldn't have. And I cast a judgment on you that was wrong. I've been wanting to apologise ever since."

Flora frowned. "What exactly did you see, Drew?"

"It's a bit indelicate but, well, it's my first tour. Not been joined up two minutes before they whisked me off out here and I was scared. Some of the lads talked about you. They said such unbelievable things, I didn't think any of it could be true, so I wanted to come talk to you. Get your advice. I went to find you. And I followed you. Out to the bushes."

For the second time that day, Flora blanched.

"I saw you in a, an improper position. I didn't know what to do or where to put myself, so I ran back to camp and told-"

"Lieutenant Harley."

"Aye, only he didn't seem surprised at all but told me not to worry, that he would take care of it. Said you were a disgust- well, I don't think I should repeat the words. Said I was a good soldier, and I was to follow his lead. Honest, Corp, I didn't know what he had planned. Then I watched what happened. I saw what he did and I what you did for him. He didn't deserve your kindness that night. Not only that, but you looked after us too and I saw for myself what the other boys had said was right. So, before I leave with the rest of them tomorrow, I wanted to come say my sorries, that I was wrong for the way I treated you and that your secret's safe with me. I swear."

Flora took time to absorb the young man's words. *No, not a man. He's a boy. What is he, fourteen?* "Where you from, lad?"

"Black Isle. Near Beauly."

"Beauly? Well, at least you had the sense to pick the Seaforths. Could've ended up in the Watch." Flora winked. "Alright Drew. Up you get. Attention." She barked with about half her usual strength, but still the lad snapped to it. "About Turn." Barclay swivelled smartly towards the door. "Aye, we'll just about make a Highlander of you yet, man."

"Thanks Corp. Er- ma'am?"

"Feck off, Drew, I'm not the bloody queen, you great gowk. My name's Sinclair."

"Alright, Sinky."

"Don't push your luck. See you in Paardeberg. Give the Boers Sinclair Begg's regards."

He grinned, clutching his cap with both hands. "Aye, Sink, will do."

She smiled after him, shaking her head. "What the hell have you gone and gotten yourself into now, Flora?"

*

It jolted her from her snooze. Screams and rifle fire. She bolted upright and swung her legs over the side of the bed, thrust back the flap, and stared at the chaos. All around, men were tumbled from beasts and carts, limbs hanging from their bodies by sinew. Horses and donkeys, set loose from their gigs, ran wild, dragged corpses through the dust.

Hobbling to a chair, she grabbed her jacket and slung it across her shoulders as Bill burst through the tent.

"I'm going out there, Doc."

"I know." he said, throwing a pair of wooden sticks at her. "Take your crutches and begone with you. I need the beds!"

She hopped into the maelstrom of muck, shouldering past innumerate dazed bodies until she spotted a familiar face and flagged him down.

"Alexander, over here man! What the hell's going on? It's like the end of days."

"It bloody is. Christ!"

"Steady." She grabbed him by the shoulders. "I'm not used to seeing big Ross-shire lads waving about. What's happened?"

"Enemy. Cronje had his boys dig in at the bottom of the hill and they waited. Let us think they weren't there. We must have gotten within about two hundred yards before they fired on us. By then it was too late. It's a bloody massacre! Men. Horses. All shot to pieces."

"What's the damage?"

"It's still going on. The Lieutenant only sent us back to fetch more ammo. They have us pinned."

"Who else is with you?"

"Barclay. He's loading up another carriage."

"I'm coming back with you."

"Should you be out of hospital?"

"Bugger that, Private. Now jump to it!"

An hour later, they made it to the frontline and Flora dropped beside Lieutenant MacPherson.

"Good God, Begg, can you walk without those things?" He motioned his head to the single stick she'd brought with her.

"I can hirple, Sir."

"Good enough. None of us are moving much anyway."

They crouched behind an upturned cart. It offered little protection from bullets, and would no doubt prove an inviting target, but it provided a sense of security.

"You have to admire the thinking Sir, digging in like that."

"It's downright sneaky if you ask me. No commander worth his salt would find that an honourable way of waging a war, Begg."

"I never said he was honourable, Sir."

"Indeed."

A friendly shell whipped past their ears.

"For fucks' sake, we're shooting at our own troops now. Blasted artillery, watch where you're pointing those damn things will you!" He screeched through the dim as those imperial shells began hitting home, exploding into the rock face above the enemy position. "Well done, lads. That's the way!"

Flora's eyes flickered. "I thought the plan was to avoid a frontal assault, Sir?"

"It was, Begg. At least as far as Roberts, Kelly-Kenny and MacDonald were concerned, but Roberts is sick, and Kitchener's taken his chance to overrule the lot of them. There'll be hell to pay in the coming days, I reckon."

"The light's dying, Sir. I doubt we'll be able to keep going much longer."

"There's the truth of it. All we can do for now is maintain our position until told otherwise. You never know, the Canadians could still break through."

"Aye, sir." But Flora's tone was doubtful. She stretched out her legs, back to the carriage, and raised her rifle so it pointed over her shoulder between the planks. An accurate aim was an impossibility at this range, anyway. Random shots were either lucky or unlucky.

Unknown hours passed and the moon already long risen before MacPherson had had enough and ordered his section to retreat. The entire brigade was scattered in the ill-conceived foray, and too many were visibly limping back to camp. In all this time, no orders had arrived. The troops were despondent. Exhaustion warred with dehydration and the shots exchanged trickled away to nothing.

"Time to go Corporal. Our duty is done. If little Lord Rumbledethump wants any more, he can damn-well do it himself. It's not up to us to hold this line any longer."

Never one to be found derelict, Flora found she couldn't help but agree. "I think you're right, Sir. No one's coming for us now."

"Indeed. Get the men together. We're marching to bed."

"Aye, sir. Come on, lads. Get moving! Watch your backs until we've reached a safe distance."

A series of tired and relieved grumbles sounded as the men dragged themselves to their feet. It was less a column and more of a loosely organised rabble back to camp, whereupon bedraggled souls dropped to their knees, eyes closing where they fell.

Flora trudged off to the farthest end of the encampment to collect the rest of her things from the hospital, her crutches having gotten lost somewhere along the road. What greeted her was open devastation. She found Bill leaning over a writhing man, his burnt skin indistinguishable from blackened khaki.

"Captain?"

"About three hundred dead or dying so far, we think. There's more still to come."

Flora eyes darted about the tent, one of many field dressing stations, but still, there wasn't enough room for every casualty to have a bed.

"Still think this was a good idea?"

Flora's face tightened. "I wouldn't be anywhere else."

The man, or what was left of him, on the bed between them sputtered and seized. Unthinking, Flora grabbed his rigid paw and held on, forcing herself to stare into the stark whites of eyes that now appeared to large for his head. She said nothing. Offered no words of comfort. Just stayed.

After several torturous moments, his body gave in.

"The more of them that die as quick as that, the more chance I have of treating the ones with a chance of surviving. That's the reality Begg."

Kit bag collected in silence, Flora drifted back to the main barracks. The campfires blurred and the everyday background noise of an army in the field sounded far away. Peripherally, she was aware of someone calling after her, but nothing was making any sense. A hand clutched at her shoulder, and she rushed round to grab the owner's neck.

"Corp! It's me Corp! It's Drew!"

She let go, staring at her own hand while Barclay doubled over and rubbed at his neck.

"Christ! You're strong for a- for a-. You alright, Sink?"

Flora nodded, transfixed by her own fingers, still flexed and rust red caked into the joints. "Sorry. I'm sorry. I'm fine, lad. What did you want?" She shook her head, willing the fog to dissipate.

"Did we do the right thing in coming back? Someone said Kitchener gave an order to dig in for the night. A few stayed, most didn't or worse ignored it. Doesna' sit right with me somehow."

"We did as bid by our commanding officer, Private. That's what obedient soldiers do." she said, but the pained look on the boy's face made her soften. "We did right. It wouldn't have done anyone any good if we'd stayed. Just the opposite. As the

Lieutenant said, if Kitchener wants any more, he can damn-well do it himself."

"MacPherson said that?"

"Indeed. We should get some rest. I doubt this'll be the end of it for us. Are you alright?"

"Aye. You caught me unawares, that's all." Barclay tipped his cap but before he'd gotten more than a foot or two away before she called out to him.

"Drew! What day's it today?"

"Sunday, Corp."

She nodded and told him goodnight before turning towards her own billet.

"Bloody Sunday."

*

London, July 1901

For about the hundredth time that morning Katie flipped through the newspapers strewn about the kitchen table. The reports coming back from South Africa were obscure and confused. Eyes stinging, she slammed her hand against the table and swiped the papers onto the floor.

A knock sounded at the door.

She made a grumbling noise at the back of her throat. "Who is it?"

"Only me."

Without waiting for further invitation, Millicent Fawcett swept through the narrow hall, lilac parasol hooked over her arm to match her hat.

"Still no word, I see." she said, noting the scatter.

"No. No word." Katie bent to gather the contemptible crumple of dishevelled papers and dumped them on the table. "I don't know what to think anymore. And I wouldn't put it past those wretched Fleet Street scandalmongers to be acting deliberately obtuse. They keep us hanging on and hanging on, desperate, until one day, a catastrophe breaks and there follow inquiries and sell-out stories and wailing mothers. And still they haven't had the decency to answer my last letter."

"Or the one before, or, indeed, the one before that. My dear, when will you learn, it's no good trying to sneak in through the letterbox. One must break down the door."

"And you such a moderate."

"I am, but the degradation of innocent women and children, regardless of creed is intolerable, and I am resolved to do something about it. Have you heard what is happening to those poor civilian families caught up in this fracas through no fault of their own? Concentration camps. Concentration camps! It's shameful the way our government has allowed, neigh, endorsed such cruelties. Miss Hobhouse has compiled a most damning report on the matter. Her findings are shocking. Now, after much lobbying, I have been granted permission to lead a small contingent of women to that continent to inspect conditions in the camps."

Katie sunk into one of the kitchen chairs.

"When would you leave?"

"As soon as possible, I should think. No time to lose."

"And where will you go?"

"Well, as far as we can, naturally. Miss Hobson has made it as far as Bloemfontein, wherever that is. Battling the military all the way, of course. They are doing the best to cover their tracks, as one would expect." She paused. "I'm sorry, that was insensitive of me."

"No, you are right in what you say. Believe me, I've more than enough cause to mistrust in how the army conducts itself."

"When did you last hear?"

"Three months ago. If Flora was more than a mere corporal, I'm sure I would have heard more by now. No one seems to care about the plight of the ordinary soldier."

"I confess I have little knowledge of such matters, but there is a truth in what you say. It's not ordinary soldiers like your girl who cause the trouble, but they bear the brunt."

"I am so grateful I have had you to confide in, Millicent. I don't know what I would have done without you these past months. And I still can't believe you took Flora's story to Whitehall."

"It needed to be done and to use a military term, it served as compelling ammunition to our cause. Naturally I did not reveal Flora's true identity. I doubt Mr Gascoyne-Cecil would approve."

"No, probably not. I'm still stunned that you do, in all honesty."

"I live in Bloomsbury." she said simply. "As do you now. Is it not well past time you broadened your own horizons?"

"Many would consider me a harlot by profession, and I'm

engaged in a forbidden romance. I'm not sure my horizons are allowed to be any broader."

"Nonsense. Face facts. At the rate things are moving, it could be many more months, years even, before Flora comes back. You are a young woman, not an old widow."

"Not that we know of."

"As far as we are aware, Flora remains hale & hearty. There is no reason to believe otherwise. No reason for you to shut yourself away. It's no crime to be alive."

"I know. I just feel so guilty."

"Piffle. Would she really wish you to be so miserable?"

"No."

"Well then. Now, I have passed on what I came to say and shall take my leave. I expect you'll be at work this evening?"

"Yes. We're performing *The Toreador*. I can't help but think how much Flora would love it." said Katie as she escorted Mrs Fawcett to the door.

"You mustn't think I am unsympathetic, Katherine. There are days I miss Henry very much, but I am fortunate. I see him each day in our daughter. And I have my work. Our endeavours give women like us purpose. Always strive for better. If not for yourself, then for those unable to do so for themselves."

"What if I can't? Each time I stand on that stage, I'm hollow. I can't bring myself to sing the way I used to."

"I have never been a performer, but one thing that has helped me whenever I've had to address a crowd is imagining that Henry is there, just beyond where my eyes can reach. He listens and cheers when I've won them over and tuts at my failures. He's with me in spirit. Flora's not dead, but that doesn't mean you can't call upon the memory of her."

"I'll try."

"Do. In the meantime, I shall host a little farewell soirée next Sunday. Elsie's coming down from Edinburgh to give a talk first then we'll share a few drinks and nibbles. Be sure to come."

"I will. Thank you so much for everything. You've been such a good friend when I was in dire need of one."

"Don't be silly, dear girl. You have enormous potential." Millicent cupped her cheek. "You could do remarkable things if you so choose, and not just within the movement. You're a career woman. I see your name at the top of the bill every time I walk past the Gaiety. You're already a success, but you aren't pushing yourself hard enough. Places for women like us do not exist by themselves. We must make them exist. You have that power, Katie. Which is why I am entrusting the branch to you while I am away."

"What? You can't! *I* can't. Mrs Pankhurst will spit feathers."

"I will help you in any way I can, but it's high time you trusted in your own abilities. I do. As for Emmeline, she hasn't the temperament for command. She's far too volatile. Besides which, I doubt she'll be with us very much longer. You break your own ground. Goodbye for now. Remember, I expect to see you next week."

"But Millicent? What am I going to do without you?"

"We shall find out, won't we?"

*

Highland Brigade, Eastern Transvaal, August 1901

Flora turned Katie's letter over and over in her hands. It was impossible to read in the night air, covered in mucky fingerprints, and several months old. A response was well overdue, but the wherewithal eluded her. Exhaustion was like a plague, infesting the encampment the same as lice and typhoid. She'd never caught a louse, mind you, but even just the thought of the wriggly wee bastards alone was enough to keep the itch constant.

"How are you, Begg? Still struggling on?" Sergeant Gunn removed his dripping helmet and squeezed under the meagre shelter of the tree.

"Same as everyone else, I expect."

"Aye, s'pect so. It's been a struggle ever since Paardeberg, and no point denying it. Pulled from pillar to post every five minutes. You planning on making an honest woman out of her when you get back then?" He pointed at the picture of Katie held between Flora's fingers. The edges were crumbling, and the image smeared reddish-brown, but Katie's face still glowed in the shine of a nearby lantern.

"I dunno, pal. Not sure I'm the marrying kind."

"Ach, you're mad, man. I would, like a shot."

"She's a beauty. More than that, I'm not sure who I am without her anymore."

"What's stopping you?"

"Woman like that shouldn't be tied down, that's all."

"Ha! Well, aren't you the modern man. S'pose the lassies go for that, eh? You'll forgive me if I disagree."

"Think what you like."

"When'd ye last hear from her?"

"March."

"March? Christ, Begg, sure she's not lost interest? Found herself a real man's man?"

"Careful Duncan." Flora's tone carried an edge.

"Hey, you don't have to convince me. You're the big hero round here, I just write the letters. I ken you're not a man to cross. And if she has got someone, you'll batter hell out of him."

"Damn, Gunn!" Flora rolled to her knees and straddled him. She grabbed the man's collar and raised a fist.

"Hey! Hey! Begg, I was just winding you up."

"Wrong time." She growled.

Two privates spotted the commotion and pelted over. The grabbed her by the arms and hauled her off before she had time to land the blow that would've broken his nose.

'Corp! Come on, now!'

'What the hell's the matter with you!'

Their voices echoed about the edges of a red mist. Hands dusted at her soggy uniform, but she shook them away and took off into the pitch-black downpour. She was well beyond the camp border before she cared enough to stop.

"Where the bloody hell am I?"

The glinting lamps of the camp had grown distant. Incessant rain kept the worst of the smoke down, but you could still smell the burning. The 'scorched earth' policy had proved controversial among the men, and Flora hated herself for being party to it. But orders were orders. "Maybe I should be more worried over the fact that I'm questioning which orders I want to follow and which ones I don't."

She knelt and rubbed her fingers over the charred remains of what had once been a fertile farm, its residents herded into one of the many so-called refugee camps which had sprung up everywhere. The stories abounded about these places.

Her mind travelled back to a land, very far away, where ancient crofts now lay ruined. Their roofs burnt away to cinders which had then shrivelled to nothing on dirt floors. Families decimated. Forced to flee. Hers had been one of the few to miraculously survive.

At first, Flora followed the company line, having witnessed for herself, the vile conditions in which the enemy had kept her comrades when the shoe was on the other foot.

"Am I any better? What the hell are we still doing here?"

She struggled to push these thoughts away.

"You swore to do a bloody job. Whatever else happens from now, you are not to go back on that. It's a blue funk. Nothing more."

Her fingers curled in the black soil and flicked it away before she lifted herself from her knees.

By the time she made it back to her bivouac, Gunn was waiting for her.

"I'm not here to cause trouble."

"Nor me. And I was wrong to act as I did."

"No, you weren't, Begg. I was out of line. I'd have deserved a good crack for what I said. It's this place."

"Well, dinnae encourage me, it could still happen." They shared a grin. "And you're right. It's getting to me too. We're all going mad. So, we'll say no more."

"You want a hand to write that letter?"

"Wouldn't mind. Don't think the last one was up to muster. And as we've already established, I've some making up to do."

*

London, September 1901

"*My Darling Kate,*

Whatever you must think of me, I canna even begin to contemplate. I wish for nothing more than to be able to share in your success. I've never even seen a 78 and further still cannot imagine what it would feel like to hear your sweet voice singing out at me from such a contraption.

This place is so very bleak, love. All fault of our own. I've no idea how much they report of our deeds back home, but I will live with the shame o' it the rest of my days.

We're still in the East Trans-vale. Botha continues his attacks on our column, and we continue our raids on his lands. It's likely traitorous of me to even say sic a thing but many of us are wondering what we're still doing here. The war seems to us to have ground to a halt and our losses feel hardly worth the little we've gained.

I'm sorry to sound so glum. It's difficult to write of love in such times. But know that I view your picture each night and tuck it beneath my pillow, so you are the first thing I see each morning. Gunn laughs and says I'm too modern a man. You and I know the truth o' it. He disnae ken I've written this last, though he's given me a hand with my spelling.

I wish I was better at this by now, so I didn't need his help. There are things I want to say to you without another's voice in my lug.

Also, I need to know what you and Mrs Fawcett mean by going to Whitehall. Please, whatever you've done, Kate, don't. I beg you. This could be the finish of me. The army'll go spare. Please, darling, you must keep my letters to yourself!

The new house sounds wonderful. It sounds as though Mrs Fawcett's friends have done right by you. I look forward to seeing it, if I am still welcome by the time I make it back. The parties sound great fun and it comforts me to know you've found good pals.

Whatever else, I am forever yours, however these words read. Know that I miss you, that the thought of you is what keeps me going.

I love you now and always,
Sending this letter with a kiss,
F."

Katie folded the page, held it to her chest and concentrated on breathing. She lifted it to her lips and sent a silent kiss back, praying that wherever Flora was, she would feel it.

In the two years she had been absent, Katie had never sensed such despondency. "She's changing so much. I don't know this Flora."

She read over the note again and a sickening qualm wormed its way into her stomach.

'Please, darling, you must keep my letters to yourself!'

Oh god, what have I done?

*

Kroonstad, Western Transvaal, May 1902

"I have heard through the jungle drums something rather disturbing."

"Sir?" Flora's ears flattened against her head. Her shirt clung to her back with sweat as she stood in front of Stockwell's desk.

"Yes. I have heard that you're intent on leaving us. Naturally, I've summoned you here to dissuade you. I'll be straight with you, Begg. I will not be returning to Fort George with the others. I haven't long left to retirement so instead, I am being posted to Edinburgh to take over the governorship of the Castle. It's a fine position and carries with it a promotion to lieutenant-colonel, a house... and I had intended on bringing you with me as my soldier-servant. The money's better, you'd have a permanent address for them to post your medals to and a promotion to sergeant. I understand you have a... a going concern, in London. I imagine that's your reason for choosing to leave us. But I would allow you most weekends off unless required for military duties. Take the evening to think about it and give me your answer in the morning. Incidentally, how are the repairs coming?"

Flora blinked and rocked back on her heels. "The lads are tired but they're doing their best. The chief trouble is the water supply's none too good, but I reckon they're glad for the peace."

"Yes, well repairing railways is heavy work. Unfortunately, we don't have navvies out here to do it for us. I hope you're doing the appropriate delegations."

"I'm managing, Sir."

"Not the point, Begg, you do as you're told. Delegate."

"Aye, Sir."

"Good. In gratitude for their service, the brass have invited our battalion to supply an honour guard for the Boer generals when the signing of the peace treaty takes place. That should raise the men's spirits. Right. You're dismissed."

Flora did as she was told but she stopped short of the exit. "Sir, if I may?"

After all the recent atrocities, Flora had experiences her fair share of doubts about a future in the army. But the one thing that hadn't altered was that the last five years, the men she had slept, eaten, and fought alongside had been her family. The only thing that had changed was now Flora wanted Katie as part of her family too. Now Stockwell was offering a chance at everything she'd ever wanted. *Mebbe be too good to be true*. But the words were out of her mouth before she realised. "I don't need to think about it. I'd like to accept your offer."

"Excellent, glad to hear it. But since you have, I should mention I have received several confidential communications from a friend in Westminster. Your 'going concern' could have done a great deal of damage with her recent flag-flying, bringing you and us into disrepute. I trust you know the matter of which I'm speaking."

The blood drained from Flora's face and her entire body prickled with a hot chill. "Yes, sir."

"Good. I'll say this to you and then a line drawn under the issue. I won't be able to cover up for you if this happens again. You'll be left to handle the consequences on your own. You're a good soldier with a promising career ahead of you if you keep your nose clean and don't draw too much attention to yourself. Don't let some bloody woman take that away from you. Keep her in line, Begg, that's all."

She swallowed, suddenly very thirsty.

"Aye, sir."

*

London, June 1902

The journey South was the final straw.

After three and a half weeks on the boat home to Scotland, Flora parted ways with the rest of the battalion in Edinburgh where she would remain with the newly promoted Lieutenant-Colonel Stockwell. Her leave would have to wait until after his installation as Castle Governor, a formal ceremony in front of a whole host of military officials and local dignitaries. The work was full-on, with neither Flora nor Stockwell having much chance to catch their breath.

Now, Stockers had his feet up in front of the fire while she trudged along an unfamiliar part of London, ignoring the glares of the well-heeled that passed her by. If she hadn't been so tired, she might have noticed just how leafy everything was. The gardens of Woburn Square were small but immaculate. Delancey Street had seemed posh to her eyes but at least there she hadn't felt *quite* such an interloper.

At last, she found the green door with the white pillars described in Kate's last note. By the time it'd arrived, there was no point in authoring a reply. Knowing the BFPO, she would be here well before the letter. *Just hope my knock's a surprise and not a shock.* A squirmy sound reverberated through her gut. *What if I don't like what I find? What if two years was too long to wait?*

The steps were the last straw. Her legs were dead, and she had to hang on to the metal railing. She chapped on the door in expectation.

No answer.

She tried again.

She'd been travelling all day. It was late. The theatre would have emptied long ago. It was too late to leave now. She could have always turned up at the nearest barracks, but she didn't think her feet would carry her there. She curled up on the steps, her long legs tucked up in front of her. The thread of her brand-new sergeants' stripes dug in where her arm pressed against the freezing ironwork.

She must have dozed off.

A distant voice brought her to wakefulness.

"Flora?"

Bleary eyes squinted in the dawn light. She could just make out Katie's delicate silhouette and relief washed over her until a second figure appeared at her side. The sun glinted off his top hat.

The aggravating announcement of their imminent arrival into Rogart sounded. Laura jumped and emitted an unholy sound deep in her throat as she shoved the letter back into its envelope.

13

A silver Skoda pulled up outside The Begg Hoose, and Laura pulled some cash from her pocket.

"You going to be alright tonight?"

"We'll soon find out. I'm more worried about you. How're you going to manage dinner on your peg legs?"

"Ach, I'll be fine. Aileen's daughter's keeping Izzy an extra few nights while I'm at Raigmore, so I've only myself to bother about tonight."

"Why don't you stay here? I'm sure Jim wouldn't mind dropping you down to Inverness tomorrow."

Mhairi gave her a wry smile. "Would it not be better to talk to the man first before you go volunteering his services?"

"Och no! That's what he's there for!"

Mhairi was about to comment but refrained when she caught the cabbie's ear cocked in their direction though his eyes remained trained on the empty field opposite.

Laura noticed and gave her a discreet dig in the ribs.

"Ow! Thou shalt not mock the afflicted!" The furrow that appeared on the man's brow only made Mhairi laugh harder. "Seriously now, away with you. I'm fine. I'll even give you a bell from the hospital once all's done and dusted."

"Fine. But you look after yourself, Missus, and if there's anything..."

"We're not having this conversation again. Now get in that house and at least make all this have been worth it."

The two shared an awkward hug before Laura retrieved her rucksack and made her way up the gravel path.

The first thing she noticed was the tinny scratch of a radio blaring coupled with a sort of scraping noise.

"Jim?"

She dropped her bag and sidled down the hall, the racket growing louder. *Is that Single Ladies playing?*

"Jim?"

She covered her mouth at the sight that greeted her through the kitchen doorway.

Her husband, man who couldn't carry a tune in a bucket, was bopping about in their kitchen, his thirty-four-year-old dad gut bare to the world, scraper in one hand with wallpaper peeling from every corner, shimmying his man-boobs along to Beyoncé's pop classic.

She let the scene unfold for as long as she could hold back the giant howl determined to rip from her chest. Jim let out a screech of his own, wrapping his arms about his torso in a frenzy. Laura had to grip the doorframe.

"You scared the shite out of me!"

"What on earth are you doing?" Laura stepped into the kitchen, her arms open but still brushing salty streaks from her face.

"Och, you know, just making a start." he said, forcing

his voice to a much more manly register, and accepted the hug. "Thought you might appreciate it."

"I do, I do. And that was certainly a sight! In fact, why don't you take this single lady off the market?" She kissed his neck and allowed her hands to roam the expanse of his back.

"What, you're not gonna buy me dinner first?" He returned Laura's interest, finding her lips, and running his fingers through her hair.

"Nah, you're a cheap date."

"Hmm, but will you put a ring on it?"

"Oh, I'm sure we can find something in my box of tricks to fit. Need to catch me first, though!"

*

Not long after her breathing returned to normal, Laura stared up at a single moon beam which streaked across the ceiling. She'd hoped the athletic encounter would settle her mind or, at the very least, exhaust her enough to sleep. Jim was already snoring. *Lucky sod. Tried his best, bless him.* A satisfied ache and the heady aroma of their exertions triggered a grin as she shifted beneath the sheets. *Mind you, it could be the bruises. Was a good idea to keep the lights off.*

She closed her eyes.

It wasn't long before her fist was battering the pillow. *It's no good.* She sighed and dragged herself from the oppressive heat of the bed. She tossed a resentful glance over her shoulder and padded down to the kitchen.

Coffee or tea. Coffee or tea.

"Coffee." She said and reached for a jar of instant.

The kettle whistled.

She took her coffee to the kitchen table and glanced about. *He's made a decent start, to be fair. Wallpaper's mostly off and those hideous tiles have gone.* "Sorry Flora."

The memory of how she'd found her husband made her grin. "Least I know he's still interested."

The coffee wasn't doing its usual trick of settling her mind, so she wandered through to what she had dubbed 'the music room' but had really just become a dumping ground. She *brr'd* at the frigid blast of air on opening the door. "Why's this room always so bloody baltic?"

She had a feel at the radiator. "That'll be another job on the list, then."

She stared at the disarray in dismay. "Bloody Jim's been in here. Can he not leave anything alone?" She popped the lid of a brass filigreed tin expecting to find... "Empty."

She rifled through the clutter spread across the desk. *Where the hell have they gone?*

It wasn't until she happened to glance up that she noticed the items she sought tucked into the frame of a fan shaped mirror which sat propped up against the wall at the rear of the desk. She took the pictures back through to the kitchen, stopping to re-boil the kettle.

The photographs were a few of the ones she had rescued from the loft right before she'd gone off on her Skye-ward adventure, but there was a specific one she was after. **'The face on the other side of this picture'**

"Well, you have a name now, Katie Vaughan."

Laura traced a series of russet streaks smeared over the woman's face. Just out of curiosity, she placed the three middle fingers of her right hand on top of the smudges. In an instant, images flashed through her mind, too quick for her to catch them. But the sounds of galloping horses rearing on gritty tracks and scent of copper rang hideously clear and a burst of hot grit stung her face. She dropped the picture on to the table. She blinked and shook her head before staring again at the red marks.

"If you could speak, eh?"

Her gaze wandered over the contours of the young woman's smile. "You could've only been about twenty here. So warm and full of life. Now you're lost to memory. But then that's what happens to us all, isn't it? When there's no one left to tell the stories."

"Who're you talking to?"

"Gah!" Laura jumped and grabbed at her chest.

"Sorry! But you ken it's daylight out there, you've not been up all night, have you?"

Laura stared at him before glancing out the window to where dusty purple clouds were giving way to the orange glow of morning.

"Guess so. Christ's sake, look what you made me do." She unclenched her fingers and tried to smooth out the image she'd just crumpled. "Over a hundred years this has survived."

"Sorry. What are you looking at, anyway?"

"Photographs."

"I can see that. Photos of what?"

"It's the pictures I brought down from the loft. You know, the ones you moved."

"Me? What you on about? I've never even laid eyes on them."

"But you must have done. I put them away in a tea tin before I went to Skye, but that's not where I found them."

"Well, I didn't touch them. Must have been your ghosties again."

"Don't say that."

"What? It's just a joke. This is becoming a bit of an obsession, isn't it?" Jim passed her by and helped himself to her coffee pot.

"It's not an obsession. You were the one who said I needed a hobby. I might not have been too keen at first but they're interesting. And they were real. People like you and me. They deserve to be remembered."

"True. I only wish they'd left the house in better nick."

"That's hardly fair. On that note, we really need to get the heating sorted before Winter comes back. I don't think the house would stand it otherwise. Neither would I, come to that."

"What do you suggest? I mean, we're not exactly flush with cash right now. My wages are about covering the bills and some of the maintenance, but I can't stretch to a new heating system. I know we agreed your redundancy package should sit in the bank, but I suppose if push comes to shove."

"Yeah, about that." Laura took a deep breath. "There is something I should tell you."

"You wanting to go back to work again?"

"Constantly, but that's not it."

"Good. It'd hardly be ideal if we're to be starting a family."

"Not this again." Laura's fingers scraped at her scalp. "Jim, we are not starting a family. We couldn't afford it anyway, even if I wanted to. Which I still don't, by the way."

"Ah, you say that. You're just scared. I understand, but y'know, neither of us are getting any younger and we have been married a few years. Mum's starting to ask questions."

"Your mum can mind her own. Look, I don't even think I can. Not biologically."

"What do you mean? You're not that old yet."

"That's not what I mean. I've had some concerns for a while and as it happens, I sort of, bumped into an old friend. She's a nurse too. Anyway, I had a chat with her about some symptoms I've been having, and she took some bloods. It'll be a while before I see any results, but she agreed that in all probability, conception could prove difficult to say the least."

"But that can't just be it. There's always options."

"No."

"What do you mean no? You can't just dismiss it like that."

"I can because I don't want to. Anyway, this isn't what I wanted to talk to you about. What would you say if I told you I own a property? Jim?"

"What do you mean, you own a property? Like a house?"

"Yeah. Like a house. It's a croft on Harris."

"How?" He ruffled a hand through his hair, then came to sit beside her. "More to the point, why the hell've you never said?"

"Because I haven't thought about it in long enough.

It's the old family home. I inherited it when Uncle Iain died. You know me, don't like living in the past."

"I dunno, seems like you do now." he said, and grabbed the postcards from the table. "Anything else you've been hiding from me?"

"No. And I wasn't hiding it. It just never came up."

"Laura, this could solve all our problems and you never said a word. D'you realise the stress I've been under since... Look, never mind. How much d'you think it's worth? If it's a croft, I'm guessing it has land."

"True. It'd make a great business."

"Right, so?"

"So what?"

"Let's put it on the market. Get the heating and the tiles on the roof fixed. We could do this place up nice."

"Jim, I don't know if I can bring myself to sell it. Not right now."

"I don't get you. These old crofts are a goldmine."

"Because that house... my family lived in it for generations. I can't give it up. Not just like that. I doubt I could ever picture myself living there, but I couldn't bear to see anyone else in it, either."

"Laura, you never talk about your family. You've not been back there since you were a kid and you've never mentioned any Uncle Iain. How attached can you be? You're not thinking practically. We can't afford to sit on two houses. One problem solves the other."

"How dare you? No, really, how *dare* you? I mean, I've never talked about parents with you, so I suppose you must think I wasn't 'attached' to them either! D'you not realise this is precisely why I can't talk to you about these things?"

"Oh, come on, Laura, you know I didn't mean it like that."

"No, I don't know that at all. Just because I haven't been back there in years doesn't mean I don't still love my family, don't think about them every day... don't still miss them. That house is all I've got left. You've no idea how hard it's been, these last few days. You don't understand what it means. Any of it."

"Because you won't tell me. I'm right here and you don't let me near anything that's important."

"Because I don't trust you!"

The statement hung in the air like smoke on a demolition site.

"And there's the truth of it. You don't trust me with your secrets. You don't dream of a life with me, Laura. If you ever did. You have a closer bond to these... these shadows who don't even belong to you, than you ever did to me." He threw the pictures at her. "Figure out what you do want. Then one day you might actually make a decision for once and stop silently hating me."

"Jim-"

"Save it."

He stomped upstairs. A few minutes later, the entire house rattled to the slam of the front door.

Whole body shaking, Laura began clearing surfaces, cleaning mugs, picking up piles of rubbish and dumping them into different corners. Anything to keep moving. Stop feeling.

A stack of unopened mail lay on the hallway table. Only one lacked a red **'URGENT'** stamp.

"Clara?"

The sight of her old friend's impeccable script eased the thudding of her heart.

Decision made, she swapped out her dirties from Skye and backpack slung, headed once more for the station.

Girls weekend in Edinburgh it is.

14

"Stand aside, Katherine, I'll deal with this ruffian."

But by the time the tip of his cane tapped Katie's elbow, she had already flung herself at Flora, who wasn't quick enough to catch her in time and they landed hard on the stone portico. Flora's breath expelled from her chest in an 'oof' while a gust blew up Katie's dress in a most unladylike fashion.

Katie her cheek to Flora's tunic, oblivious to the chaos ensuing on the lawn behind her back. An old man, one of two snuffer-outers who, at the sight of her billowing undergarments, clattered his stick into an inconsiderately planted tree. Several branches broke off and tumbled to the lawn. An innocuous occurrence in of itself, but a single splintered twig jabbed into the bum of a parked horse. The horse was attached to a funeral carriage. Flora cringed and pressed Katie's face to her chest.

A neigh of protest rung out in the crisp air, followed by the snap of leather, galloping hooves and the curses of the poor driver who careened off into the next street. The lamplighter held his flat cap to his face in horror, his snuffer still wedged in the tree.

"I hope it wasn't occupied." said Flora.

"I hope he makes it back in time for Mrs Fairweather's funeral."

With much floofing of skirts, they detangled themselves. Flora struggled to look at Katie as she helped her to her feet, her face tight and an intriguing shade of crimson.

Katie huffed, hands on hips. "Go on. Out with it."

Flora let out a great bray of laughter. She gripped her ribs while Katie looked on with feigned impatience.

Once she'd recovered, Flora hopped across to the green where the young apprentice lad was helping the old man retrieve his snuffer from it was still wedged among the tree canopy. From across the lawn, she could see a red-faced Katie speaking in hushed tones to the fop in the top hat.

"You know this man?" Fop asked in a voice which dripped with disdain as he stuck out his hand on Flora's return. She took it and he squinted at her the same way many had before him.

"Aye, she does. You're up awful early for your best bib and tucker."

"We never made it to bed." Fop looked entirely too smug.

"This is Mr Deacon Broderick, Sinclair. He's right, I'm afraid. He offered to see me home after a party last night. It ran on longer than we anticipated. He lives with his wife, across the square. Mr Broderick, this is my fiancé whom I was telling you about. He's just returned from South Africa. You didn't tell me you were coming home, darling."

"I wanted to surprise you. Reckon I did."

"You're home for the weekend?"

"Not quite. Me and Stockers have been granted a full two-week's leave."

"Two weeks?"

"If you'll have me?"

"Darling, that's the best news!"

Katie leaned into Flora's body and kissed her. Flora responded in-kind by snaking her arms about Katie's back, and swept her into the air, tiredness be damned.

"You've made me so happy." Katie cupped Flora's cheek. "The happiest of women."

"South Africa, eh?"

This fella doesn't take a hint. And he's a face like he's chewing a wasp. Flora grumbled and returned Katie's feet to the floor.

"Well, I suppose we all owe you a debt of thanks or whatever it is we're supposed to say under such circumstances. Give those Boers a good thrashing, did you?"

"Something like that."

"Mr Broderick's quite an intellectual."

"Is he?"

"Oh yes." he said. "Can't be doing with all that muck and bullets what have you. No, I'll leave that to you real chaps."

"I see. And what does an intellectual do?"

"Do?" Broderick laughed. "I don't *do* anything. Gentlemen have connections."

Flora yawned.

"Deacon, I think I need to put this one to bed. You look exhausted. Surely, you've not come here straight from Africa?"

"No, I had to go back to Scotland first. I've a lot to tell you."

"Come on, let's get some rest. Both of us. We've plenty of time."

"You'll be alright then, yes? Dear Katherine?"

Flora glowered at the man from over her shoulder but a smack to her gut turned her eyes front again.

"I'm fine, thank you Deacon. I had a wonderful evening. Until next time."

Flora's teeth crunched all the way up the stairs.

*

Katie woke first.

Neither had moved much at all during the several-hour sleep, though it was much bigger bed than the one they had shared on Delancey Street. *Strange.* She toyed with Flora's hair. *We've spent more time apart than we ever were together, and yet this feels so normal.*

But in observing her lover more closely, she noted the dark circles beneath Flora's eyes and traced furrows between her eyebrows which weren't there two years prior. *It's frightening. War must change a person. She looks ten years older.*

She placed the tiniest kiss to Flora's temple and left the warm bedding, tying her favourite silk butterfly robe about her waist.

She opened and closed each kitchen cupboard and sighed. She could go to the shops, but that would require dressing. Then again, Flora would still need feeding. *I can't leave her to starve.*

She crept back into the bedroom, knotted her hair into a semi-respectable bun and slipped on a pair of stockings and shoes. It was a belter of a day outside and the heavy coat she'd selected would no-doubt generate a few odd glances. *Mind you, why should that suddenly bother me now?* She had already developed something of a reputation, even by Bloomsbury standards. *Theatre people are meant to be eccentric.*

*

The smell of bacon was heavenly. She blinked against the daylight. Katie's tuneful hum was just audible over a chorus of pop and sizzle. *What a bon way to wake up.*

The sizzling stopped, replaced by the sticky shhtoop of bare feet on floorboards. Flora buried herself deeper into the blankets and feigned sleep. Maybe she should have gotten up and given her a hand. Instead, she bit her knuckles to stop herself from giggling at the juggling act going on beyond the covers, if the clanks of mugs and plates and bloops of sloshing tea were any indication.

Eventually, the bed dipped, and tender fingers slid beneath the blanket to stroke her ear. She made a show of yawning and stretched languidly. Katie narrowed her eyes.

"How long have you been awake?"

"Damn! How did you know?"

"Well, we know one thing. You'll never make an actor,

Flora Begg. I went to the butchers while you were sleeping. Eggs and bacon?"

Flora licked her lips, but it wasn't the food she eyed with hunger. "Sounds grand but you first." she said and straightened out her arm for Katie to slide back into her embrace. Flora's fingers slipped beneath the hem of Katie's stockings before reaching for the tie on her robe. "I hope you at least had the decency to get properly dressed before you ventured out, Miss Vaughan."

Katie pressed her lips to Flora's forehead. "Erm..." She hesitated. Flora's hands were doing the most wonderful things. "Perhaps not properly exactly."

"Strìopach!" said Flora, in mock scandal. Katie slapped her arm.

"Sergeant Begg!" She giggled as Flora's mouth attacked her neck. "Your bacon's going to get cold!"

"Don't care. I'm having a pre-breakfast first, you immodest woman, you."

"Oh, *you're* having?" Katie flipped the two of them over, and Flora's eyes widened. "I will show you immodest, Miss Begg."

The bacon was cold, but edible.

*

Flora rolled over. The lacework cushions scratched her nose. She pressed on her gut which clenched and roiled about the half-coo she'd not long demolished. *Need my eyes ayeways be sae bigger'n my belly? Need to teach Katie to think in army rations.*

Strange hissings and much shuffling emanated from the back of the room. She grinned and settled deeper into the cushions as Kate's soft voice floated through the air. Then Flora frowned. "She surely hasn't moved in an orchestra?"

As she tilted her head back on the arm of the couch, she was confronted by two mounds of most ample bosom. Katie leaned over her, her fingers stroking Flora's cheeks and temples.

"Hmm, that's nice. What's that music? Sounds like you."

"It is. It's my recording."

"How? I thought you needed one of those new gramophone thingies."

"You do. I bought one for when you came home. I wanted you to let you hear it." Katie dropped a kiss to Flora's hairline, revelling in the closeness. The warmth of their mingled breath tickled her chin.

"You bought it? You have gone up in the world, my lass. More to the point, why didn't I notice?"

"I have been keeping you rather distracted for most of the day, to be fair."

"This is true. How does it work? I mean how do they get the sound in there?"

"I'm not sure of the actual mechanics. I was only told to sing into this funny horn thing. The man did the rest."

"Interesting."

"You think so? I'm sure I could arrange a little tour of the studio."

"I'd like that."

"Consider it done. In case I've forgotten to say it, I'm so happy you're home."

They fell silent for a few moments, with only Katie's song filling the air, until the woman in question's chest grew heavier on Flora's forehead.

"Can't be very comfortable up there."

"Mm, no, I don't think I can stay this way much longer."

"It would feel just as good if you were down here."

And Flora was right. Although Katie's comfort was interrupted as Flora insisted on hearing both sides of the 78 at least twice more before she fell asleep on the couch. Not that she minded.

*

It wasn't until the following morning that Flora took proper notice of Katie's new abode. It was almost as salubrious as Stockwell's governors' residence at the foot of Edinburgh Castle. *How the hell does she afford all this? I know she said she was renting from a pal, but this isn't just a flat, it's a three-floor bloody palace.*

Through the sun-drenched double aspect windows, the area was très gentile with its tree-lined pavements. *And not a single doorstep with so much as a muddy toeprint.*

Her eyes fell on the table which separated her bare legs from the windowsill and the dozens of sheafs of paper scattered about the surface. On each one, a series of coloured triangles with lines sticking out and odd-shaped faces.

"Do I really get to keep you all to myself for a whole two weeks?Katie had appeared in the doorway, dressed for the day.

"You do. If you want me." Flora beamed at her, and Katie moved across the room to press her back to Flora's front. She pulled Flora's linen-clad arms about her waist and gazed at the world outside.

"I'll always want you. And your opinions. What do you think?" Katie reached for a couple of the drawings and shuffled through them.

"Err, they're good..."

"They're dresses."

"Oh. I see."

Katie slipped from Flora's arms.

"Kate?" Flora, totally bemused, clamoured for something to say.

She returned to the rustling of fabric. An exquisite garment was suspended from a hanger about her neck as she held the waist of the dress against her own.

"You made this?"

"Yes."

"It's beautiful. You really love green, don't you?" She said and walked towards her, tracing the ruched neckline with her fingers.

"You remember."

"I remember every single thing you've ever told me."

Her gaze travelled from Katie's eyes, all the way down the front of the embroidered hunter's green bodice, each silken ripple.

"It's corset-less."

"So how d'you make the shape?"

"These panels." Katie flexed the embroidered plates which ran up the sides and front of the bustier. "They're firm enough to create the illusion of a corset with no need for lacing."

"It's incredible, Katie. Truly. And very daring. What made you think of it?"

"You did."

Flora's brow creased for a moment, then she flushed at the memory. She bent forward for a kiss, mindful of the hanger still around Katie's neck.

Much as Flora's body may have felt so warm and receptive through the thin nightshirt she'd borrowed from her, when they broke for breath Flora's gaze turned towards the sunshine and the treetops which rustled in the breeze. Katie sighed.

"I've already kept you in here all to myself for far too long, haven't I, my love? Come on, why don't we go for a walk before you wilt through lack of fresh air?"

*

"Do you honestly believe that'll be it from now on?" Katie asked after they'd settled themselves on one of the many benches which bordered Regents Park's boating lake.

"There canna be any more wars to come now. Not after what happened out there. The terrible things we did. Never again."

"Under orders. None of what happened could possibly

be construed as your fault. Between your letters and what those... what the papers reported, it's abundantly clear whose fault it all was. You are not to blame."

"Maybe. But I was still a party to it. And that, I must live with. Kate, while we're speaking of letters."

"Yes?" Katie met her eyes.

Flora's chest tingled where Katie's hand pressed her, just the way she had pressed her to the bed that morning. She'd hesitated too long. "It's nothing. Nothing important. So when were you planning on telling me of our engagement?"

"I'm sorry. It was the only thing I could think of. I had to explain our relationship somehow when I read your letter at the meeting. Calling you my fiancé made us seem more serious. Flora, I want to talk to you about what I did."

Flora bristled. "It's alright, Kate. Let's not talk about this now. Let's not spoil the day."

"But-"

"Shh. Another time, alright?"

"Alright. I still can't believe I get to keep you for an entire fortnight. You really don't have to go anywhere?" She snuggled into Flora's side.

Flora gave her a squeeze. "Nope. All yours."

"It's the longest time we've ever had to spend with each other. Question is, will we survive it?"

"Aye, I reckon so. Or we'll kill each other."

"Or we'll kill each other. I hope not. Though you must admit, there is something wildly romantic about a crime of passion."

Flora snorted. "You are dramatic, alright. My money

would be on you, anyway. I've seen your feisty side. Now exactly how did I propose?"

"What?"

"In this fantasy engagement of yours. I need to know what to say to people. So how did I do it?"

"On bended knee, naturally."

"Naturally." Flora rolled her eyes.

"Well you are a romantic, after all."

"I am?"

"Yes!"

"First I've heard of it. And you said yes?"

"No."

"No? But how on earth could you refuse such a romantic beast?"

"Because I'm allowed to."

"Alright." Flora breathed deep. "When did you say yes?"

"When you asked the second time. It was here, in fact. On a day exactly like today. You found me sitting on a bench exactly like this, the light glinting off of your brass buttons. You picked up violet from that flowerbed over there and dropped to one knee. You said you could never be parted from me again." Katie looked up at Flora expectantly.

Flora's eyes twinkled with devilment. "You realise we'll still be living in sin. What will the neighbours say?"

Katie scowled and prodded her in the ribs. "Hang the neighbours. They already think I'm a tart, anyway. Gives them something to talk about."

"Why, Katherine Vaughan, I'd never have believed it less I'd heard it with my own ears."

"Too late to do anything about it now."

Flora chuckled and settled Katie's head back against her shoulder. "You were right about one thing. I am yours, and I'll stay as such. Until the final breath leaves my body."

*

For the next five years, there were no more wars to fight, but many more strolls in the park and nights spent wrapped about each other's bodies. We decided, for the sake of the liberty it granted us, that I should continue living as Sinclair in public. Katie even stitched me up some civilian weekend clothes from the theatre, for I had none. For the first time in my life, I was content to be home. A surprise to me as much as anyone else. I still loved the army, duty, and my comrades, but I had had enough of being shot at for no good reason.

Returning with Stockwell as his servant, with a promotion of my own, brought with it a new level of freedom. I spent the working week at the Colonel's disposal and my weekends were almost always clear to spend with Katie. The endless train journeys between Edinburgh and London were stuffy and uncomfortable, but the welcome at the other end was always worth it. A handful of times, she made the trip up to Edinburgh where we wandered the closes, and I scared her with spooky stories.

You've heard the adage about familiarity.

The year 1907 brought with it a tumble from our childish grace. Soon enough, my name was Mud.

9th February 1907

"Are you intending on getting up at any point to-day?" Katie shook the blankets. Flora shrunk away from the frigid air which blasted her nude form.

"What the hell for?" She grumbled and ripped the sheets from the other woman's fingers.

"The march! I've been telling you for weeks. Get a move on."

"And I've been telling you for weeks, I've no intention of going."

"Flora, it's important to me. Miss Strachey is counting on all our support. If everyone else can put aside their differences, then I don't see why it's so difficult for you." Katie made a grab for the covers but lost her balance and flattened Flora to the bed.

"Gracious speech, lady governor, but was this part of your strategy? If so, I don't think you'd make much o' a general."

Katie let out an odd sort of growl-huff and pushed herself off again, dusting down her skirt.

"You aren't coming."

"Now you're getting it." Said Flora but Katie did not look amused. "I daren't. Not like this. Besides, it's chucking it down out there. You'll get soaked, woman."

"I don't care. Can't you understand? If you didn't show yourself as you do, you'd be no different from the rest of us. Why won't you fight for that? For me? Wear a dress if you're so concerned."

"I'm not political like you, Kate."

"You are! You subvert convention every single day. Don't you see what someone like you could do for our cause?"

"Do you hear yourself? If I walked out in the open tomorrow, they'd haul me off and you'd never see me again. Unless that's what you're after. Is it?"

"How can you say that? How... God, I waited for you for two years, Flora. *Years.* And us only knowing each other a few months. How could you ever suggest such an awful thing?"

She was digging herself a hole, but it was too late to stop now. Never mind a roll, she was riding an avalanche. "How can I say that? You think I don't know how your fancy friends look on me? That I've forgotten all about what happened the night before I left?"

"Not this again. What more can I do to convince you, I am not ashamed of you? That I love you, for heaven's sake, you pig-headed, cantankerous..." Katie stomped and *eurgh*ed her way out of the bedroom

The slam of the door was the last thing Flora heard.

*

The march, planned for the opening day of parliament, was an utter washout. Hordes of women and sympathetic men swished to the tune of slopping cloth and waterlogged trumpets from Hyde Park to Trafalgar.

'*Mud Mud Mud Mud*' they chanted.

Her hem was a soggy mess and her umbrella had long

since given up the ghost, but Katie barely noticed. Still too busy trying to force the steam from her ears. Mrs Fawcett noticed something was wrong as soon as she had turned up at the meeting point, but a precious free moment proved elusive. A finger dinted her shoulder.

"Why, Miss Day! May I share my meagre shelter?"

"Mr Broderick." Katie smiled for the first time that day as Deacon Broderick lifted his brolly over her head.

"You are looking a trifle damp around the edges, my dear, if it's not impolite of a gentleman to say so."

"No, not at all Deacon, thank you."

"You're welcome. If I may make another observation, you seem preoccupied. Is everything alright?"

"Yes. Thank you. And you are quite right, as always. I am a little preoccupied but I'm not in a position to discuss it, sorry."

"Oh, so it's not trouble with your handsome sergeant, I hope?"

"No. Well, yes, it is, but I shouldn't be talking about this."

"Fair enough, though it's often beneficial to talk things through with an unbiased party."

"True, except you're not an unbiased party, are you?'

"Dear Katherine, I'm sure I don't know what you mean."

"And yet, I am perfectly sure that you do, Mr Broderick."

"Well alright, yes. Perhaps I am."

"And remind me, are you or are you not a married man? Sinclair and I may not be wedded, but I love him very much. We will work through our current disagreement."

"May I remind you my own marriage is not a happy one?"

"It makes no difference, for I am happy in mine."

"You don't seem it."

"Not today, perhaps, but tomorrow will be better. Sinclair and I are two opposites. Together we make a whole."

"Who are you attempting to convince? It's been such a long engagement, Katherine. Surely, if you were certain of the relationship, you'd have married him by now."

"I have no wish to be the legal possession of any man. Sinclair understands that. He's a modern man."

"Hmm, I must confess, I am uncertain I would ever agree to such a situation." He pulled her off to side, away from the main crowd, and held her by the elbow, a challenge implicit in his expression. "If you were mine, Kate, I would insist on possessing you."

Miss Day! Katie! A welcome voice called through the rain.

"It seems I have kept you from Mrs Fawcett too long, my dear. I look forward to our next meeting." He raised her gloved hand to his lips. Katie merely continued to stare at him.

"No doubt we'll see each other soon, Mr Broderick. Perhaps Sinclair and I shall meet your wife someday."

"I'm sure Mrs Broderick would enjoy that. She takes delight in colourful characters." His voice had stiffened, which, on another day, she may have stopped to remonstrate, but Millicent's voice drew closer and broke her from her stupor.

She took the opportunity to free herself from his grasp and turned back to torrential Trafalgar.

"Kate, we were wondering where you had gotten to, but I see Mr Broderick had so captivated your attention." Millicent quirked an eyebrow.

"Mr Broderick is... persistent."

"I see. More on that later, we don't have the time. Now, the northern districts are going to diverge here, the rest of us will continue to Exeter Hall. You, Pippa, and I will help organise. Alright?"

Katie did as she was told and lifted a placard, then heaved herself up on to one plinth corner of Nelson's Column, the weight of her soaked skirts dragging on her hips. *At least Flora's not here to say, 'I told you so'.* She used one hand to steady herself while the other nudged out the strip of 2x4 as far as it would go in an effort to direct the main column north towards The Strand.

"Job's a good 'un, I'd say."

Katie wobbled and held on for grim death as an attractive face floated up beside her. She darted a glance to the side with gritted teeth on her shallow perch. *Where do I know that face from?*

"It's Christabel but call me Chrissie."

"Oh, you're Mrs Pankhurst's daughter." Recognition dawned as she eyeballed Pankhurst, the Younger's outstretched hand. "I would take your hand, except... except- "

"Except you're desperately trying not to plunge off a plinth. I'm sorry, it's just I've been such an admirer of yours, Miss Day, have you ever considered touring the north?"

"I'm afraid not. My career's in London, but when I was

a chorus girl I travelled. Spent a season or two at the Alexandra."

"I used to go there as a child! I wonder if we were ever there at the same time? How funny."

"It is." Katie laughed. Or at least she hoped it looked that way as her face contorted with each skid of her court shoes on the marble.

"It's the Tivoli now, I doubt you'd recognise it." Pankhurst carried on, seemingly oblivious.

"Things move on. That's the way of it."

"How true. Do you think all this demonstrating is going to work? That it will 'move things on' in our favour?"

"None of us can be certain, but I believe in Mrs Fawcett."

"You believe her policy of moderation will win the day. Yet my mother speaks so highly of you."

"I very much doubt that. Your mother has made her dislike of me quite clear."

Christabel barked. "My mother gives that appearance to everyone. She is a kind woman underneath, but she's pragmatic. She understands the impact someone like you could have on our cause."

"Someone like me?"

"You're a household name, Miss Day. The Gaiety trained you to be the perfect genteel lady. Gentlemen follow you and women emulate you. Whether or not you realise it, you have a powerful voice. Why not use that power for the good of the movement? Do you not wonder why Mrs Fawcett has not suggested to you before? She fears it. She fears it would incite rabbles."

"And she's right."

"No. Miss Day, you can sound that rallying bugle and draw the sceptics to our side. Say you'll think on it, at least?"

"You make it sound like we're on a battlefield."

"Aren't we?"

"I'll think on it. That's all I can promise for now."

"That's all I ask."

"You are very loquacious, Miss Pankhurst."

"Oh, please! The women of Laconia were frightful harridans!" Christabel jumped back into the throng below and Katie concentrated hard on keeping the 'shoogle' from her placard. *God, I'm even thinking like Flora now.*

*

Despite the weather, the rest of the march went off without a hitch. The press turned out in full force at the meeting at Exeter Hall. The assembled crowd were treated to speeches by Eva McLaren and Keir Hardie, although they were frequently drowned out by the jeers of uppity hecklers.

"My, but haven't we done marvellous, all things considered?" said Mrs Fawcett as clumps of people broke up and filtered away.

"Agreed."

"Anything you'd like to talk about? You've looked pensive all day."

"Flora and I quarrelled before I left this morning." *Do I tell her about Christabel Pankhurst?*

"Over what? I thought you two were living in a permanent state of bliss?"

"We were. I think. I don't know."

"I don't like the sound of that, my dear."

My dear, the term made her skin crawl. Broderick's same words wriggled in her ear.

"I noticed that rattlesnake, Broderick was slithering about earlier, I hope he hasn't contributed to this malaise I sense in you. What's really wrong?"

"Nothing." Katie shook her head, "I'm fine, I promise. I should go, though. I have to work this evening."

"Very well, child. I know I needn't say if there's anything I can do-"

"You can't. That is, I don't believe there is anything. I just have to- Goodnight Millicent, I'll see you again soon."

Katie hurried off towards the Hicks Theatre, pushing her way past a barrage of well-wishers and autograph hunters. She stumbled and had to brace herself against a brick wall and sniffed hard. She lifted a finger to her nose, horrified when her velvet glove came away with a thick glob of blood. *Oh god, what is happening to me.*

A pair of feminine hands gripped her by the shoulders.

"Kate! What on God's green Earth's happened to you?"

"Ella! Am I glad."

"Let's get you inside."

Katie pinched her nose and slumped in her dressing room chair, while the rattle of China on a silver tea tray heralded Ellaline's return.

"I knew there was a reason I loved you."

"And there was me thinking it was just for getting you away from Edwardes."

"Ha, that too. Coming to work with you and Seymour has been the best thing. And the show is wonderful."

"You have the job, you needn't lay it on so thick. Even if I enjoy it."

"I know where my bread is buttered."

"You're avoiding the subject."

"I know."

"So?"

"Life isn't simple, but then what is nowadays? You caught me in a moment, that's all."

"It looked like a hell of a moment. Not trouble at home, I hope." Katie did her best to hide her flush behind the steam of the tea, but Ella was too wily for that. "I know that trick. Out with it."

"F-Sinclair and I quarrelled."

"About?"

"About the movement."

"I thought he supported it."

"He does. But he also doesn't want to be involved."

"Is that such a terrible thing? Seymour and I aren't the best example but even the most traditional of couples need their own interests."

"We're hardly traditional ourselves. But it's not just that. He's never said it out loud but, I'm aware that while Sinclair was away fighting the Boers, some of my thoughtless actions almost got him into serious trouble with his superiors. I don't know how he got out of it, other than his CO likes him. He's afraid that any involvement could jeopardise his prospects. Which I understand, I do. But he doesn't see how important it is to me. He says he does, but it doesn't feel that way. It feels as though it's an indulgence on his part. Like I were a child."

"Thoughtless actions?"

"Yes."

"Forgive me, but I can't immediately make the connection between how something you did here could ripple all the way to Africa."

"It's rather simple, really. And dreadfully stupid. I acted without consideration of the consequences. I wished, so desperately, to have my voice heard in the movement. To be taken seriously. I took one of Flora's letters to a meeting and read it aloud. Mrs Fawcett was so impassioned by the conditions and senseless slaughter that she took the letter all the way to Whitehall. Then I went to the papers. It caused quite the stir. I realise now that I shouldn't have done it. It was so foolish, putting him in that position. But I was lonely and desperate. I wanted so much to matter."

Ella handed her a clean hankie. "And have you told Flora any of this?"

"Certainly, I ha-" Katie's neck cracked with the sudden jerk. "How did you know?"

"I've felt there was something you weren't telling me since that first night we spoke all those years ago. To your credit, you hadn't slipped until now, although you've come close once or twice."

"You don't seem very shocked."

"We're in the theatre. Land of make-believe and endless possibility. Here, we may create whatever we wish the world to be. Do you really think you are the first creature of peculiar passions to grace the boards? That's the magic. Or have you forgotten?"

"I think I lost the magic long ago."

"Then, by God, find it again, Kate. You're too young and far too pretty to be so miserable. You're passionate and so in love, that much is obvious. This world we inhabit is a playground. If your heart is no longer in it, that's sad because you have a talent. You must, however, find something you *can* invest in. Do you have any idea where you want to go next?"

"Yes." She nodded. "I do. I know exactly what I want. And perhaps you're right after all. I can shape my better world from here."

"Wonderful. And whatever it is, if I can help you, you must ask."

"Thank you, Ella. I meant it. Your friendship these last years has meant the world. But there is one more thing. There is a man. His name is Deacon Broderick."

*

An incessant knock rasped at her ears until she

gave in, slammed an empty tumbler on the table and belly flopped from sofa to floor.

She scraped herself off the carpet and yanked on the door. Her eyelids were full of thorns. Slowly, the blurred mass of duck egg blue and feathers coalesced into something vaguely human-shaped.

"Mrs Fawcett, what I can-" Flora frowned. "What can I do for you? Katie's not home yet, she must've gone straight to work." She coughed. Even to her own ears, her voice was all chipped and splintered.

"Actually Flora, I was hoping I might be able to do something for you. May I come in?"

Flora staggered a bit to the side, keeping a grip on the door handle.

Millicent took a seat, pursing her lips at the empty whisky bottle. She waited until Flora slumped back onto the couch.

"How much do you know about our friend Mr Broderick?"

"Don't know I'd call him a friend. Not much. Don't like the man but he's done nothing wrong. Not that I know of, anyway. Why? D'you know something I don't?"

"No. That's what concerns me."

"He's not after you, is he, Mrs Fawcett? He says he's mairrit, although I've never seen his missus about." Flora chuckled.

"No. It's Katie he's after. Or seems to be, at least. He had her cornered at the march today."

"He what?"

"It's alright. She sent him away with a flea in his

ear, but the point is, he smelled an opportunity. I sense you two are at odds with each other and I don't like it."

"I don't like it much either but I'm in a no-win here. It's Kate or the army."

"Yes, and neither serves the other well. So, you have a decision to make. Which do you love more?"

Flora sat quiet for several minutes. She had been peripherally aware of the inevitability, but the dichotomy had never seemed so stark before.

"And whichever you choose, sort it now. There'll be no heading Mr Broderick off if he suspects the slightest chance of a rift between you. I have no evidence, of course, but he is not a man I would wish to see any woman I cared for attached to."

"You're point is a valid one, Mrs Fawcett, but at the moment my heid feels like it's been stuffed down a Pom Pom and blasted."

"Yes, I can see that. I'll leave you in peace but do pull yourself together. I realise your blood is 90% whisky, but alcohol is not usually an answer. For god's sake, sort this mess out before it gets any worse."

Katie found Flora in the same spot as Mrs Fawcett had left her, stretched out on the couch, snoring. A steady stream of drool leaked from the corner of her mouth and another half-gone bottle clutched under her arm.

"Wonderful."

*

She groaned and grabbed at her head. A sea of a thousand wee beasties writhed under her skin and her mouth was dry as blotting paper.

"Kate, will you please keep the noise down?" *'Damn woman'*, she added under her breath.

"No, shan't." Another door slammed, followed by a crash of plates and pans.

Flora hurled herself off the sofa and crawled to the kitchen. Her stomach lurched at the sight of eggs on the counter, and she hugged her middle.

"Don't worry, I wasn't making you any, anyway. God, you're just like him. And you stink."

"Uh, right. Huh?"

"When are you returning home?"

"Train's at seven."

"Good. Now if you'll excuse me." She brushed past Flora, knocking her straight into the worktop. "I have much to do."

"People to see?" Flora spat.

Katie turned on her heel. "Just what do you mean by that?"

"Nothing."

"No. Come on. If you have something to say, Flora, then say it."

"Deacon Broderick."

Katie's face fell but she covered it fast and assumed an air of scorn. "What of him?"

"What was he up to yesterday?"

"How did you- never mind, I can guess. What business is it of yours, anyway? At least he's supportive of the movement. You've made it pretty clear you're not interested what goes on in my life, but you're content to let me come home to find you passed out drunk. Was that to make you feel better or I worse?"

"I overindulged, you're browned off, I get it. But there's no need for all this caper. I asked a simple question." Katie had struck a cruel blow, even if there were some truth to it.

"You did. One that you're not getting an answer to. You can see yourself off. I have matters to attend to."

The next few days passed with no word from London. Her usual Monday call to the theatre had gone unanswered. She moped about the Governor's House, absent of all good humour. The first half of the week had proved busy, with herself and the Colonel engaged in arrangements for an official visit from renowned Polar explorer-turned-ambassador Fridtjof Nansen. It had been an interesting expression which crossed Stockwell's face when Sergeant Begg had produced a filled glass for the man with the words; '*God kveld, min herre. Vil du ha noe å drikke?*'

When quizzed much later, within the subdued red hazy coze of Stockwell's study, she had laughed and explained that Caithness folk spoke Norn which was similar enough to Norwegian that pleasantries were easily exchanged.

"I thought you were a Gael?"

"I am, Sir, but half the county are Norn and they're not always too friendly to the likes of us so it's handy to speak both, if you get my meaning."

"I see. Whisky?"

"Don't mind if- Actually, I'd better not, Sir, if it's all the same to you."

"Stuff and nonsense, man. Get that down you." he said, raising a crystal-cut decanter and pouring them each a large measure. "To Fighting Mac. Eachann MacDhòmhnaill gu bràth. Never a finer soldier."

"Or as fine a man. Slàinte." Flora tipped her glass in reply.

"Sit ye down, Begg. I wanted to ask you if all was well? Without sounding too much like a Dutch Uncle. Can't help noticing a certain change in your demeanour since you got back from your last venture south."

"Sorry, Sir, I don't mean it to. We had some crossed words. I think we might be on the way out if I'm honest."

"Because of a spat?"

"Because we're two very different people."

"Begg, I've been reluctant in the past to discuss your *relationship*. You're aware I don't approve of that sort of thing but your existence outside the uniform is your own affair, provided you're at least circumspect with it. It's unnatural. But then so are you. My advice to you is this. If you truly cannot resolve this conflict, then withdraw. Your conduct isn't in question, don't concern yourself with that. In fact, you've become a fine second. I'm not keen to lose you. Whatever it is, sort it now."

"Yes Sir." She rolled the smoky amber about her glass.

"Someone else said much the same thing before I left London. But I can't sort anything if she won't listen."

"Then you must make her! Blast it, Begg, get this woman under control or cut her loose. Are you man or mouse?"

Flora's teeth clattered on the rim of the tumbler, muffling her reply. "Neither. Simply good red herring, Sir. You don't really believe what they said about him, do you?"

"Mac? No. Just the bastards in that cesspit of so-called lords. It was a disgrace. I see they've erected another memorial up at Dingwall. All a bit late now. Whatever the man's private proclivities, true or no, it's no matter. That's not what makes a soldier. He was the best of us. You should know that Sergeant."

"Aye Sir, I do."

*

It was Friday afternoon and Flora had still received no word. Stockwell lost his patience with her evident distraction and ordered her to leave early. Even on the train, she was still in two minds whether turning up at Kate's was the best idea. But it didn't matter either way for the house was empty. Not unusual. *I could always turn up at the theatre. But what reception would I get?*

The mantle clock reminded her to yawn. She shucked off her kit and crawled into bed.

Flora screwed her eyes against the watery sun streaming through the curtains she'd been too tired to close. She reached out for the warm body beside her and hoped that Katie would still be asleep, but all her hand found was the chilly sheet.

"Kate? Kate?"

Nothing.

She bundled her goonie about herself and tip-toed through to the living room. Then the kitchen. She'd have tapped on the washroom door only it was already open and empty. *She can't have gotten up this early. It's only eight.* It was a lie-in for Flora but for Katie, this was still the middle of the night.

"Don't think I'll be bothering with a fire this morning, somehow."

Instead, she brewed herself up a quick tea, dressed in a rush, throwing on the uniform she'd discarded rather than hunting out a new outfit. She was rubbish at coordinating outfits anyway. That was Katie's job.

A sudden qualm struck.

What the hell do I do if... nope. Nope. Not going down that road.

She had no idea where she was going, but her feet landed on the doorstep of Mrs Fawcett. Millicent hadn't heard from Katie since the day of the march either. But at least she was up. She'd even offered Flora breakfast on seeing the woman's drawn features. It was a tempting offer, if only for the company, but time was ticking.

She was trotting back down the steps when Millicent called out after her.

"You might try Christabel."

"Who?"

"Christabel Pankhurst. She and Katherine were getting rather chummy during the parade. I'm afraid the WSPU may have gotten their hooks into her."

"So, you don't think there's any chance it's Broderick, then?"

"I am not a clairvoyant, but I don't believe so. And neither do you."

"I don't know what I believe anymore, Mrs Fawcett."

"Then that's a sad state of affairs, Sergeant. You'll find Miss Pankhurst staying with a friend on Duke Street. That's likely where you'll find Katie."

"Where on Duke Street?"

It was on the third knock, just as she was about to give up, when the black door rattled open.

"Yes?"

"I'm looking for Kate."

"Kate who?" The dark-haired young woman glanced over her shoulder.

"Kate Vaughan."

"Sorry, I don't know anyone by that name."

Flora stuck her foot in the doorway and growled. "Try Katie Day, then."

"Katie Day? The actress? Don't be ridiculous. You've come to the wrong house."

"It's alright." Came a faint voice from the other side of the door. "Christie, this is Sinclair."

"Pleasure, I'm sure."

"Aye, likewise."

Christabel stepped to the side. Katie remained in the shadows, her bottom lip caught between her teeth.

"Well, I shall leave you two to it. I'll be close by if you need me, Kate."

Flora jerked her head. "What the hell's that meant to mean?"

"How did you find me?"

"Mrs Fawcett telt me where I might find you. Now your turn. What did she mean by that? You need protecting from me now?"

"Don't be stupid. But you know things haven't been right between us. There're these things between us that just won't go away."

"So that makes me a monster?"

"No! You're getting this all wrong. God, you make me so angry sometimes."

"I'm getting it wrong. Course I am. It'd never be you, would it? You with your fancy friends and your fancy career. Christ, it's a wonder you've stuck with me this long! I came to bring you home but frankly, I reckon I should've stayed in Edinburgh. Seems my services are no-longer warranted."

The chain clattered in front of Katie's nose as Flora walloped the door shut.

It wasn't long before an arm slipped about Katie's shoulders.

"It's alright now. You've more important things to concern yourself with."

"Chrissie, I need to go after-."

"No, my love. You don't. You've done nothing wrong."

"It doesn't feel that way."

"No, I imagine not. Focussing on the task at hand will help. Let things go, at least for the time being. Is everything in place?"

"Yes. Yes, tonight. We'll organise ourselves at the Circus and march on from there."

*

The hammering was becoming incessant.

Flora! Flora Begg, I know you're in there. Open this door right now!

She nearly ripped the door from its hinges.

"What? Millicent, whatever it is, I'm not in the mood. I'm on my way to giving myself a damn good headache, in fact."

"Yes, but you're coming anyway." Millie yanked on Flora's arm and pulled her into the chilly stairwell, crisp to the scent of evening fires. "There is something you need to see."

Shaftesbury Avenue was absolute pandemonium. All around, coppers were pulling at women brandishing their fists in the air, using their truncheons to beat a path to the centre of the chaos. The entire street was a seething mass of heaving bodies in thick coats and elaborate hats, lit by the smoky orange glow of burning torches.

Yet a single voice soared above the clamour.

Remember our cause is just!

The horde bellowed back in delight.

For you and I fight for nothing more than the basic rights of man and woman. Whatever cost therein may lie! Let this be our battle cry!

More shouts followed.

It was late. Late enough that the evening's performance was due to empty shortly, but the innocent patrons would find themselves blockaded. The throng had swarmed the steps of the Hicks Theatre.

Flora tried to plough through the vast crowd, but Millicent grabbed her. "What do you think you're doing?"

"Kate's on stage tonight. I have to get to her, she's not safe!"

"Open your eyes, Flora!"

"What?" Her eyes darted desperately about the flood. All the blood drained to her boots, as she stood frozen to the spot. Her gaze fixed on the figure atop the steps, spouting the rhetoric and inciting the mob. "Christ. What the hell have you done, Katie?"

A flamethrower burst overhead, and Flora used her body to shield Millicent from the sparks.

The front rank of the crowd broke and rushed the theatre doors, smashing the patterned glass, shards showering the innocent patrons inside. Several others from further back, ran off in differing directions, throwing bricks at shops.

Katie could only look on in horror at the ensuing violence, powerless to stop the rampage which had taken on a life of its own. She didn't notice the hand making a grab for her arm.

Horses rallied on hind legs, custody wagons screeched by, and peelers began hauling people off, but there were too many. They battled to get to the ringleaders.

"Flora, no!" Millicent shouted, but it was too late. She'd spotted a gap and bolted straight into the throng.

Elbows and nightsticks flew at her, and her ribs took a sickening crack. A stray fist caught her in the eye. She barely had breath to clutch at it before she looked up in time to see Katie and her so-called friends being dragged off.

*

It was pitch black except for a narrow shaft of murky moonlight which broke through the bars. The grey bricks radiated ice and she was careful not to stray too close to the walls.

Katie curled her body tighter and rubbed at her wrists where the iron cuffs had bitten into her skin. She'd heard prison spoken of as a solitary experience Lonely. But since her arrival, Holloway seemed alive with women's screams, trolley carts and the brutal calls of the guards.

There came a series of thunks and strangled cries. It was close.

She hunkered against the edge of the bed and tried not to smell too deeply the filthy prison rags which they had made her don after stripping off and bearing her all to some despicable matron. They reeked of mould.

Tears welled as the thumps and screeches grew louder. *I'm not strong enough for this. I can't be like the others. Oh god, Flora, I know you're angry but, please. Please hear me!*

For the first time since she was a girl, Katie knew genuine fear and wept. She wept for Flora and for the happiness she had ruined. She wept for the career and no-doubt friendships which she had so arbitrarily destroyed. She wept for her foolishness.

Something heavy pounded at the door.

"Oi, keep the noise down in there!"

She gulped and did her best to push down the tears. *Oh, Flora, what have I done? I should have stopped all of this before it ever began.*

Now she could do nothing but wait her turn.

*

Three days later, the final giant set of doors clanked and squealed and an obnoxious stream of sunlight flooded her vision. Her head pounded in protest, and she shielded her eyes. She could just about make out a stern silhouette ahead, but the edges shimmered and blurred. As she shuffled closer, bumped along by the hand of a guard, the figure stomped closer, its folded arms uncrossing in a show of dominance.

"I'll take it from here, if you don't mind."

Flora's voice rang alien in her ears. The accent was the same, but her tone was strong. Gruff. *It's not Flora, though. This is Sinclair. Stepping in to claim his territory. And he's furious.* The realisation was at once thrilling and terrifying. She had never been exposed to this side of her lover's character, but it had the desired effect on the guard.

"Hmm, well, I suppose that's everything in order. You'd better keep this lady in line from now on."

"Yes, *thank you.* I'm sure you've a fine job to be doing elsewhere."

The daylight hurt and her uncertainty remained until the enormous blocks of wood and iron bolted back into place behind them. Frightened moments passed then Flora slipped her arm about her shoulders, and she sighed at last, burrowing her nose into the other woman's chest. *I won't cry. I will **not** cry.*

Tears spilled over and her body shook. Flora's arms wrapped tight around her, but they didn't stop. She half-carried her away until they were well out of sight of the prison gates, following a sign towards King's Cross which would lead them back home to Bloomsbury.

Copenhagen Fields with its grand clock tower lay just off the main road. Flora steered them towards a bench where she continued her quiet murmurings, smoothing her hand along the length of Katie's back.

'I'm sorry', she kept repeating.

Flora tilted Katie's chin, keeping their bodies close. "No. I'm the one who should be sorry. I should have been there to listen. Maybe if I wasn't so bloody hot-headed... I'm just sorry, lass."

"I can't believe you're not angry with me."

"Oh, I'm angry, don't worry. But mostly at myself. You tried to tell me how important all this was to you, and I refused to listen. I suppose because I couldn't see the problem for myself. You were right. I grew up far removed from city politics and I do lead a life of privilege. If they took that away from me tomorrow, I'd feel differently."

"I'm still sorry."

"As you should be." Flora chuckled and kissed the top of Katie's head. "You're not off the hook, but we can be sorry together. Are you alright? You sound a bit..."

"I'm fine. My throat's just a little sore, that's all."

Flora eyed her for long moments, scanning Katie's face and the bluish bruising about her neck.

"I can't believe you're here."

"There's an awful lot of disbelief in you today! Under the circumstances, Stockers gave me a few days compassionate. Needless to say I couldn't go into too many details."

They sat in silence for several minutes, content to let the world rumble on without them for a time.

"How did you get me out?" Katie lifted herself from Flora's chest.

"I called in a favour. Or rather, Stockwell's called in a favour and doesn't realise it yet."

"Oh. I got sucked in, didn't I?"

"You did a bit. You wanted to belong to something bigger than you. To feel you mattered. I can't help wondering, if I'd treated you better, if I had made it clearer just how very much you matter."

"Let's not, darling. There will be time for recriminations."

"I know. But if anyone could understand the need for belonging, to make a difference, it should have been me. I did have one thing I wanted to ask and if it's too much, you only need say. Something's been nagging at me. When I was drunk, the last time we were at home, you said I was just like 'him.' Who's him?"

"My father."

"Ah. You've never much talked about your family in all the time we've been together, and I've never wanted to press you on it."

"I never wanted you to pity me or think less of me."

"Kate, I'm a woman dressed as a man who cuts about as a soldier, and I've just broken you out of jail."

Kate smiled and dipped her head so that her face was partially hidden behind several loose tendrils of ebony hair. "True. It's just been buried for so long, I didn't want anything to poison us. Like something that's rotted beneath the earth. But it seems I managed that all by myself, anyway."

"Never. Nothing and no one could ever poison the way I feel for you, Kate. And when you're ready, you'll tell me. Anyway, speaking of favours," Flora sat up straight. "It's about time you called in one of your own."

"What do you mean?"

"There's many a true word spoken in anger. You were right when you said you waited for me while I was in Africa, not knowing if I'd ever come back. You did so because you loved me and because you kent it was important to me. Now it's time I did the same for you."

"What are you saying, Flo'?"

"I'm saying I'm leaving the army. I'm going to support you in all the things most important to you, as you have me."

"I don't know what to say."

"You needn't say anything." Flora sat back and lowered Katie's head to her shoulder. "I love you, Katherine Vaughan. In case I haven't said it enough lately."

"You haven't. But nor have I. I love you too, Sergeant Begg. Though I must confess, I will miss the uniform."

"I'd rather miss the uniform than miss you any more than I already have."

"But are you certain about this? The army's been everything to you."

"Not quite everything." Flora gave her shoulder a squeeze. "The army's been a family to me when I needed one. The posting with Stockwell's alright but it's no reason to stay. I'll do my time in the reserves but I canna see there'll ever be a need to fight again. I've thought long and hard. It's the right thing to do."

"But what *will* you do?"

228 · MEL MCNULTY

"Dunno. Maybe I'll just be a 'gentleman' and have connections." She raised a sardonic brow and stretched her long legs out in front of her. "Y'know, it's just as well I was only ever a sergeant."

Katie gave her a blank look.

"You'd never have made for an officer's wife." She winked and Katie smacked her. "Come on, let's get you home, and into a bath." Flora made a show of sniffing the air. Katie looked disgruntled but couldn't argue.

She toyed with Flora's belt, blancoed to within an inch of its life, though her eyes strayed to her own raw wrists. "Do you think we'll ever win?"

"Yes."

"You said that very assuredly."

"I did. Because I know you. And the others like you. You'll find a way, Katie. You always do. Your day isn't done yet."

The following June, I marched in a white shirt with a green and purple striped tie, next to Kate, who dressed that day in a gleaming white frock and sash she made herself. This time the sun shone, and we took turns carrying a pole of one giant banner which stretched the width of a single united column. We trooped along the embankment in a most audacious display of colour and music. It was truly a day of celebration and I had never been prouder.

15

"No way! A riot? Well done, Katie!"

"Right? I couldn't believe it either, but it's true. I googled!"

"I'm glad you stopped by." said Mhairi once the laughter had died down. "But why are you here?"

"I'm on my way to Edinburgh. My friend Clara asked me down for a girls' weekend. Thought I'd break the journey and come see you. I wanted to know you were alright."

"Uh Huh."

"What?"

"Nothing. Just seems strange, you taking off again straight after you got back."

Laura ran her finger along the neckline of her top. "Nah, not really."

"Laura."

"We disagreed on a few things, that's all. We both need some space."

"Uh Huh."

"Stop doing that."

"In the short time we've known each other, I've really come to love you, but I've also had a front seat to your relationship drama."

"It's not drama!"

"It absolutely is. Something happens you don't like and right away, you go into blame mode, whether it's of yourself or someone else. And then you do a runner."

"I do not."

"Oh? What's this then?" Mhairi glowered.

"Taking time."

"Time for... what?"

"Time to consider my options."

"Of course." Mhairi raised her eyes to the ceiling. "While conveniently hiding from the problem at the same time."

"It's a well-established fact that you can't deal with a problem if you're stuck in the middle of it."

"Oh, really?"

"Yes."

"And there was me thinking marriage was about working through troubles together."

"How would you know?"

"Excuse me? I might not have had the rings, the minister and the scrap of paper, but I'm not totally in the dark!"

"Pfft, you have no idea. You walked away from your last relationship when things got too hard, so don't tell me you're any better."

"Dave and I made a joint decision after a mature discussion and how dare you call judgement on me for that."

"Miss Thomson? It's that time, I'm afraid." A voice chimed from the doorway. "Are you ready?"

"As I'll ever be." said Mhairi with more cheer than appeared on her face.

"Mhairi-"

"Save it." She held up a hand as the nurse wheeled her bed towards the exit. "Sort your life out, Laura."

*

The journey south was an altogether miserable affair.

Torrential rain greyed out the scenery to a bleak blur. She wasn't in the mood to read and besides which, the heating had packed in, so Laura killed time by trying to blow her breath into shapes like some folk could do with cigar smoke.

By the time the train eased into Edinburgh Waverley, she had on the jumper she'd thrown on that morning plus one more and three pairs of socks.

She didn't so much step from the carriage as bounce and inhaled the familiar mix of diesel, rain and hops which flooded the city. *Locals never notice it. Damn, but I've been away too long.*

A bland feminine announcement offset the staccato clicks of dozens of heels and rumbling roller cases along the concourse as she approached the automated barriers.

Laura grinned.

Willowy with blonde hair, tie-dyed bandana and red beads which swung from her neck, Clara was an easy spot in a crowd. Even in Edinburgh. *Nothing like a good stereotype.*

"I'm so happy you called." said Clara as the two embraced. "Ugh, I've missed you."

"Believe me, you haven't a scooby what good timing you have."

"Tell me all, lady." Clara kept her arm about Laura's shoulders and led her to the escalators. "What's been happening?"

"Hmm, can I tell you later? My head's spinning."

"Of course, and I have just the thing to fix you too."

"What's that?"

"You, me and the girls are going clubbing. Sandy's getting married, so we're off to paint the town red. It'll give you a chance to catch up. I hope you've brought something nifty."

"Um, probably not. I packed in a hurry."

"So, Harvey Nicks first then dinner."

"I can't really run to Harvey Nicks these days."

"Nonsense. Tonight, you show these boys what they're missing, and I'll show them what they can't afford. It's gonna be fu-un."

Laura cast her a sly grin. "It would be nice to see everyone again."

"Ha! See. That's the Laura I know and love."

*

The rhythm of the bass pounded through the dance floor, ricocheted through her stilettos, and vibrated her bones. It was sex. A warm pulse that throbbed deep in her body and drove her on up to higher and higher planes. And alcohol. There'd been lots of that.

Clara was busy getting off with some random in

a darkened corner. Male or female, Laura wasn't sure. Sober Clara was straight as a die, but Clara on drink was unpredictable. Despite Laura's protestations, the other girls had long-since given in and headed home pleasantly merry.

Alone, she carried on throwing shapes with a queue of willing partners. The instant she felt anything suspicious prod into her crotch, she batted them away and either moved onto her next victim or danced solo for a while. Both perfectly fine options. Then a rather dishy example of the male animal swept her up in his arms. The clean aquatic scent of his aftershave wrapped around her senses, and she melted into him. Before long, he was grinding himself against her. She matched his movements.

"Jim?"

The man's laugh tingled in her ear. "I can be, babe." He gripped her hips and pressed harder.

"You haven't danced with me like this in ages. Why not?" She stamped her foot, or rather, tried to. Instead, her heel slipped, and she flopped into his body. She hung limp about his neck. The man reached into his pocket and flipped the lid on a tiny bottle and wafted it under her nose. Her eyes bolted open. Her body stiffened. "What the fuck was that?"

"Just something to liven you up a bit, sweetheart, that's all." He grinned.

Reality stung like a bitch, and she shoved on his chest as hard as she could. Propelled by the arms of a dozen strangers, she made it off the dance floor and fell headlong onto a manky couch. She had just about long enough to notice the questionable stains under her face before she blacked out.

*

"Morning!"

"Ugh. Way too chirpy. Go 'way."

"Aww but look! I brought coffee and croissants."

"Don't want." Laura grumbled and pulled the blanket up over her head.

"Come on, you can't lie there all day."

"Eurgh."

"What does that mean? Come on, now. Up! You'll not feel any better if you don't get moving." Clara grabbed a bare foot poking out from the blanket. "Raise yourself."

"Jesus-fucking-Christ, don't you have heating in this house?" Laura jolted upright and re-covered her legs. She pressed the top of her head with both hands for fear of it flying off.

"It's a beautiful day out there!" Clara swished open the curtains then narrowed her eyes at the lump still under the covers. "You look like shit."

"Cheers pal."

"No, really. What happened? I had to peel you off some rancid sofa. Did you get spiked?"

"I don't know. Yeah, maybe. Who did you cop off with last night? I didn't see you after about midnight."

"Erm, not sure. Cool couple, though. Ben and Gary, maybe? Can't remember. Very nice guys. Very nice, erm..."

Laura blinked. *That's Clara. That's also what you get for going dancing at CC's.*

"I saw you partying pretty hard, yourself. Looked like you needed to cut loose."

"I did."

"Care to share?"

"Pass me that coffee."

"Seriously? I gave up my morning salutations for this?"

"Wait, what?"

"Your life's turned to shit. Guess what, that's what happens when you lose your job and refuse to deal with stuff. I thought, I really did, when you asked me for help, that you were finally taking back some control, but all you've done is whinge on about how crap things are. Yes, some terrible things have happened to you. Things I can't even imagine. But it's long past time you pulled on your big girl pants."

"Okay, safe to say that wasn't what I was expecting."

"I'm sure it's not. But it is for your own good. Stop wallowing, Laura. Take a few days down here to chill if you need to but after that, you're going back up there again and making things right."

"What if I don't want to?"

"Even if that were true, my advice still stands. Make a decision and stick with it."

"Make a decision, Laura. Stop running away, Laura.

You're all singing the same bloody song and it's getting boring." Laura jumped from the bed and made a grab for her clothes, the movement sent a hot stab through her temples.

"Did it ever occur to you that we're all saying the same thing for a reason? Look at you. This is what you do. Worse, you refuse to listen to anyone."

Laura spun, jeans in one hand, doorframe gripped in the other. "That is not true." Bile rose hard in her throat. She didn't know whether to try and swallow or just let it come up.

"On the contrary. It's just that the truth hurts. Feeling a touch laid bare, are we?"

"Laid bare like you do with strangers every night of the week."

"Oh no, you are not turning this around on me. Your new friend might have given in, but I won't be so easy. I know you. And I know I'm getting under that thick hide of yours, so go on. I want to hear it. Does she know the real reason all this started? Does Jim? Or is it all *too hard*?"

"You. Shut up. Right now. Shut the fuck up."

"Oh, now we're getting to it, aren't we?"

"I told you that when I was drunk, and you swore you'd never mention it again. Don't you fucking dare!"

"Does his face still haunt your dreams? You're losing it, Laura but you won't help yourself. I think you enjoy being stuck in that darkness, getting to play the martyr and no one ever gets to know why. You seriously think you're the only one who's ever felt like you do?'

"Stop it!" Laura thrust her legs into her jeans and

hopped towards the door, not bothering to check if it shut behind her.

She steered clear of Clara for the rest of the day. Her wanderings took her through Greyfriars, the across the Mile, over The Mound and down through Prince's Street Gardens where she stopped for a coffee at the pavilion. The place was heaving. *Clara was right. Beautiful day it is. I was lucky to nab a seat when I did.*

The trickling waters of the Ross Fountain were always soothing. It was one of her traditional haunts. Pick up a new book and a latte from Waterstones across the road, then come here and read intermittently with people-watching.

"Sorry, do you mind if I sit here?"

Laura scrunched her eyes at the intrusive silhouette. "No, please, go ahead."

The girl, a student by the look of her, with her glasses, stripy top and mis-matched socks, heaved a sigh and plopped on to the bench. Her shoulders relaxed as she unburdened them of a heavy-looking rucksack.

Laura sipped her coffee and turned her attention back to the fountain. She glanced about at the immaculate lawns. *I wonder when all this gets done. You never actually see any groundskeepers. Are there wee gnomes that come out at night and mow the grass?*

"Are you alright?"

"Why do people keep asking me that?"

"Sorry, didn't mean to offend. You just looked upset." The girl held up her hand.

"No, I shouldn't have snapped. I'm fine. Rough day, that's all."

"Guessed as much. Didn't mean to pry."

"It's alright. I came here to just sit and be for a while. It was one of my favourite places back when I was a student."

"Me too. Look, I can be somewhere else-"

"No, no. I wouldn't hear of it. Sorry I bit your head off. Seems to be my go-to reaction these days." She nodded to the book bag by the girl's feet. "What are you studying?"

"Nursing. Though sometimes I wonder why."

Despite the heat, the hairs on the back of Laura's neck prickled. "How so?"

"You must have seen what's been happening on the news. The NHS is being stripped to the bone. Makes me wonder if it's worth it."

A spike of ice shot through Laura's spine. "It's *always* worth it."

"Talking from experience?"

"I was a nurse."

"Was?"

"Yeah. I was part of the stripping to the bone thing. I got laid off at New Year. Haven't been able to find anything since. Jobs are scarce now."

"Do you miss it?"

"Yes. Very much. I miss my patients. I miss seeing them outgrow their injuries to lead happy and rewarding lives again. I was a trauma nurse. Helping people walk or just being able to stick the kettle on again. Veterans, most of them."

"Can I ask what made you pick that route?"

"Because I am one." She glanced at the girl. "I've only ever told one other person. I was in the TA for a few years, just after I qualified. The Alexandra's."

"Wow. I've thought about the army but there's no way I could hack it. What was it like? Did you see anything scary?"

"Oh yes." Laura's gaze grew distant. "At first it was just good craic. But then, in my third year, I got sent to Afghan. I saw things. I've never talked about it much since. Just one night when I blurted everything out to a friend after a night out. I've never even told my husband. Now I've fallen out with them both and I don't know what to do. Whether to go back to Clara's or head home. Neither sounds like a great option right this minute."

"Look, we can talk about something else if you like?" The girl shifted in her seat.

"It's okay. It's not the kind of thing you should ramble on to some poor, unsuspecting stranger about, that's for sure. But that's why, when I came back, I trained as a trauma specialist. Help these boys and girls in ways I couldn't out in the field."

The girl stared straight ahead and gathered her nerve. "How long were you over there?"

"Six months. Then I got medically discharged. Me."

"What happened?"

Laura bit her lip and took a deep breath.

"I was... on an emergency extraction. You know those scenes you see in movies where the chopper touches down and there's dust flying everywhere and the troops jump out shouting things like 'ooh yah', all dramatically? Kinda like that. Anyway, it was touch-and-go, but we got the casualties on-board, still under heavy fire, but the infantry boys kept us covered. Then the pilot lifted off, but we'd barely got thirty feet in the air before a rocket went straight through blade mount and knocked them clean off. Came back to Earth with a bump. The crash killed my CO outright. My mate and I tried to pull out the surviving casualties before the carcass of the chopper blew. Still, the Taliban kept firing only the smoke was burning our eyes. We couldn't tell which direction it was coming from. We only had one choice. We found cover behind a blown-out jeep, but we hadn't managed to drag the wounded with us. I was just about to order Ray to cover me when an explosion hit. It knocked us both out. When I woke up, my ears were ringing, fragments of metal scattered all over my body. I was lucky. But something sticky weighed down my legs as I tried to move. When I lifted it..."

An image flashed in Laura's mind. A severed head cradled in her hands. It was hardly a face at all in the dust, but for the teeth pegged into the mandible and hollows where eyes had once been only moments before.

"It's okay. You don't have to do this."

"Ray was a combat medic. Good guy, trying to get into medical school. Just married with a wee one on the way. I was so confused, and the air was dry and rank. And everywhere this awful red mist steamed up from the bodies. To this day, I've no idea how long I sat with that head in my lap, just staring into space. I know the sun had gone down by the time a second rescue chopper came. They called out for survivors, but my voice wouldn't work. I'd

have still been there now. But someone saw my boot sticking out past the jeep and found me. And I just left them all lying there. My patients. Colleagues."

"I don't know you, of course, but I don't know of anyone who'd have done any different. Why would you blame yourself for that? What were you supposed to do? You're not Superwoman."

"That's not the point. I should've tried harder. I was arrogant, you see. Back when I was working in A&E I got sent out to deal with a pretty serious accident. More than an accident. It was a small disaster on the motorway. I got a pat on the back and thought I was some hot shit, great in a crisis. That's why I joined up. Turned out I just wasn't made of the right stuff."

"You survived."

"And they didn't."

"That's not your fault."

"But I shouldn't be here."

"Who says? I'm a firm believer that things happen as they're supposed to. You survived so you could come back and help others. Why they didn't, I don't know. Sounds like you're having a hard time right now, but I think you'll help a lot more people in the future."

Laura stared at her. "I never asked you your name."

"No." The girl winked. "Isn't it easier to talk to a poor unsuspecting stranger?"

"You've been the right stranger at the right time."

"Glad I could help. If I can suggest? Try talking to your husband. I've never been married, but it can't be healthy. Damn, I really need to get going. I have a class."

"Good luck with your studies. It'll be worth it, I promise. Best thing you'll ever do."

*

With no reason to stay in bed, Laura swung out her legs and got dressed. Clara was no-doubt already up and off for the early shift. She hadn't seen her since their set-to the morning before. *Avoiding me, no-doubt. Can't say as I blame her.*

The kitchen cupboards were uninspiring.
Breakfast out, it is.

She was off for another aimless wander through the city. This time, her meanderings landed her on George IV Bridge. *So, I could go to Surgeon's Hall and have a gander at the deid bodies. Possibly not. Or I could go get lost in the museum for a few... waitaminute, that's the library. I've never been in there before. They have archives in there, don't they?*

The National Library of Scotland is an austere building. On the outside, it melts into the sea of yellow Edinburgh sandstone. Inside were hallowed halls of dark wood with books, both ancient and new, from floor to elaborate domed ceilings. For a moment or two, Laura could only gape.

Cough.

'Lockers on the left. Do you have your card?'

She turned to see a squat figure peering at her from behind a high mahogany desk. She eyed the union flag sticking out of a small mount with a quirk of her brow.

"Yes. Had to remove the Saltire after complaints. Can I help you?"

"I'm not sure. I think I'd like to look up some records. And I don't have a card."

"I see. Well, in that case, you'll want the reading rooms. You will need to take out a card, though. I can arrange that for you here. In the normal course of things, we ask that you book a session twenty-four hours in advance so we can have everything ready for your visit."

"But that's just it. I don't know which records I want to look up. Please, I'm not here long. I go back home to Sutherland tomorrow."

"I suppose exceptions *can* be made. You'll need to head to the first floor and go through security. That handbag will have to go in a locker. May I suggest you begin in the multimedia room? You'll find computers with our digital archives. Likely a good place to start."

"Thank you, I will." Laura started for the stairs.

"*Ahem*! Credentials first before you go wandering off."

After the 'ordeal of the card,' Laura plonked herself in

front of a machine and logged on with her brand-new pass-word.

This is kinda cool. Like one of those mystery movies where the nerdy hero goes digging through archives and it turns out the murderer's great-great granny was a member of some secret clandestine organisation...maybe you're getting a little carried away, Laura.

The first screen booted up in flickering blue text with white boxes ready to be typed in.

What the heck do I look for? Births? Marriages? Deaths?

She continued her scrolling.

Digital galleries, no. Think Laura, what do you know? You know that Flora joined the army when she was sixteen, but you don't know when. You know that she was born in Caithness, though, and that'd have to be in, what, the 1880s?

It wasn't a birth record, but there was a record of baptism. It gave Flora's father's name only and otherwise didn't say very much.

It's just a list, dammit. Doesn't tell me anything. But then, what were you expecting? You can't look up Katie, you don't know when she was born either, never-mind where. You're not even sure what it is you want to know!

Hours passed. Laura's fingernails scraped against her scalp, her forehead pressed to the desk.

"What the hell was I thinking? This is the bit they don't show you in the films."

Her eyes felt scratchy. Probably bloodshot. She had found several records, more via happenstance than skill, but all they recorded were the same old factoids: place of birth, time of birth, father's name, etc.

A cartoon lightbulb may as well have pinged above her head.

"Maybe it's not Flora's records I need to be looking up at all."

Was it the purple cardigan or the jaw length perm, half falling out, which made the thin woman behind the desk appear so forbidding?

"Yes?" She pushed a pair of chain link spectacles further up her nose.

"Erm, hello. I wondered if you might help me. I've been trying to look up some records, army records, and I'm afraid I've not been able to find much."

"Perhaps. Do you know when this person served?"

"Er, yes. Sh-he, was in the Boer War first, then later in the First World War, I think."

"I'm afraid our records don't go as far back as the Boer War although you would find medal cards, enlistment papers etc. for 14-18. Have you tried looking those up?"

"I found a medal card, but it's not really what I was hoping for. I wanted to find out more about his actual service. Where he fought, mentions in dispatches, that sort of thing."

"Did this man survive the war?"

"Yes." She prickled in slight indignation.

"Ah, well, you see that always makes things trickier. One less record to look up. Always easier to find someone if they were killed."

Laura's throat tightened and her stomach dropped. "Is there nothing else I could try? Please, it's important."

"Well, I suppose if you know the regiment in which this man served, you could always get in-touch with the keepers of their archives and put in a research request, but that can be expensive."

"I don't care." The words rushed out. "I mean, I need to do this."

The woman stared at her.

"Very well. You can use your desktop here to rattle off an e-mail."

Laura returned to her borrowed workstation and googled the Seaforth Highlanders. *There we go. Highlanders Museum.* She clicked on the top result. *Research takes up to eight weeks. Well, I'm here anyway.*

'Dear Sir/Madame...

*

"You were right."

"Yes."

Laura dipped her fingers in the sink and flicked a few drops of soapy water at her friend. "Wouldn't you like to know which bit?"

"All of it."

"Alright, I'll give you that. But I finally got round to talking about it."

"With whom?" Clara carried on scrubbing at a stubborn patch of grease.

"No idea. Just a random I met in the gardens. But it wasn't so bad. And I've decided to head home in the morning."

"Probably best."

"Clara? Please." Laura cooried her head into her friend's shoulder. "I can't leave with us like this."

Clara huffed and dropped the wire brush into the water, splattering fluffs of white foam onto Laura's face. "No. So what will you do?"

"I don't know yet." Laura went to wipe her face over with a tea towel, but the oniony whiff of it gave her second thoughts and she flung it through the open door of the washing machine. "I can't give Jim what he wants. Some couples might be able to work through it but, I'm not sure we've enough reason to keep us together."

"Not being funny but haven't you got bigger problems? When was the last time you had a decent night's kip?"

"Pfft."

"Precisely. You can't take care of a marriage if you've nothing left in the tank. But it's hardly fair if one of you doesn't know the full truth. Look, I know I've been hard on you..."

"You were right to be. I haven't been fair. I honestly never set out to hurt anyone. I really believed I could just bury everything, and it would all be dead and gone. I was stupid. And I've ended up hurting so many people. Now there's no way to fix any of it without causing even more pain. But I have to face this, don't I?"

"It's always been your problem. Time for some self-growth, honey. But don't think this means I don't still love you."

"I know. If anything, it means you do all the more. Only a real friend would brave my particular brand of arseholery to try and help me. That's why I love you. You make me face up to reality when it's the last thing I want."

"So long as you do. You are a pain at times. But luckily for you, I'm awesome."

16

London, August 1913

I felt at a bit of a loose end, for a while at least. Drifting along with no real purpose. I was so used to being told when to get up, when to wash, when to eat. It was a trying adjustment. It took some time, but eventually things fell into place. Sounds strange, but I craved sweat and toil. I eventually found it, with a camaraderie like the army and a home life which meant weekends were for cooked breakfasts and lying in. I would still be bound to the reserves for a further six years, but all that meant was turning up at the nearest depot on the occasional weekend for a bit of drilling and shouting. Hardly laborious.

Their white skirts danced in the crisp afternoon air. The girls giggled at the shining bodies toiling on the floating platforms below.

"Yours for tuppenny-ha'penny, I reckon, lad." The words came with a hearty thunk on her back.

"Aye, you're no wrong, pal." Flora grinned and heaved her barrow up the sharp slope to the quay. "Ah, c'mon, it's lunchtime. Send the boys off for their pieces." She puffed and swiped at her brow.

"Righto, boss. No arguments there."

Flora staggered off, filled her canteen with tea and brought her sandwiches to the riverbank. The stone was cold and soggy on her bum as she swung her legs over the side. Her eyes fell shut upon the first bite.

"You're not much of a one for company, are you?"

"Not necessarily." She half-turned and indicated the empty air beside her. The girl flopped down next to her. "You'll ruin your dress."

"Not much to ruin." she said and picked at the frilly hem. "Nicest one I've got, though."

"Nah, it's pretty. What's your name?"

"Sarah. Sarah Flynn."

"You're Irish?"

"Dad was."

"Was?"

"He died. He was a docker too. When he wasn't drunk."

"I'm sorry. What about your mum?"

"She died as well. When I was twelve. Left me with my nine-year-old sister to take care of."

"That's rough. Don't suppose you'd like a sandwich? Nothing fancy, it's cheese & pickle."

"I really shouldn't." said the girl, but her eyes kept straying to Flora's lunchbox. "I like pickle."

"Go on." Sarah made a rodent-like snatch at the bread and flushed as she nibbled on the crust. Flora bit down on her laughter. "I'm Sinclair."

They ate in companionable silence, watching the boats and listening to the shouts of the longshoremen beneath layers of funnel fog. There'd been an acrid stench that had Flora near-retching when she'd first started, but amazingly no-longer tainted the taste of her cheese pieces. Katie had initially protested at the smell when Flora came home in the evenings but couldn't argue when Flora, quite logically, pointed out that it surely wasn't any worse than the eggy stink of gunpowder.

"Do you ever look at the ships and wonder where they've been? Sometimes I dream of stowing away and having adventures in wild, foreign places. I imagine tribesmen with great big spears and giant cooking pots."

"You've been reading too many stories." Flora smirked. "There's certainly a lot of world out there to be seen."

"It's nice to dream."

"Of course. And you must promise me you'll never stop. So did you grow up round here?"

"Never been anywhere else. Mind you, all the sailors I... meet, I feel like I travel the world just by staying here. Where are you from?"

"Scotland. All the way up as far as you can go without getting your feet wet."

"Is it like here?"

"Oh, no. Very different."

"Different how?"

"Quieter." Flora's gaze grew distant. "It's country-side, mostly. We have harbours, but not like this. In our harbours, the men bring big nets full of herring. We call them 'Silver Darlings' and the women gut them fresh at the water's edge and send them off in great barrels."

"I've never had a herring that wasn't pickled. What are they like?"

"Smelly."

Sarah laughed. "Where do you live now?"

"Bloomsbury."

"No really, where do you live?"

"Bloomsbury. Woburn Square, to be precise."

"That's not possible. Dockers don't live in fancy places like that. Besides, I hear there're some funny goings on up that way."

"Well, this one does. When he's in a fancy mar-riage-not-marriage."

"What do you mean?"

"My fiancée. She used to be on the stage. We've raised a few eyebrows in our time."

"You're not kidding! Who is she, then? Would I know her?"

"Mebbe, aye. Her name's Katie Day."

"I've heard of her! She's the one who got arrested for starting that riot a few years ago. I'm not surprised you're not married."

Flora shot her a sharp glance.

"I mean, she just doesn't sound the marrying type. I've heard she's a real firecracker. But you live together? In sin."

"Aye, we do. And she is. A firecracker. She's not on the stage anymore, anyway."

"That's a shame. One of the landlords over on Commercial Street there used to play her record. Lovely voice. What's she doing now?"

"I dunno. Draws triangles with stick arms and legs and calls it 'design.' She works for some fashion house or other and comes up with dresses."

"You don't sound happy about it."

"It's not that. I'm pleased for her. It's just well beyond me. You'd think after thirteen years together I'd get over this fear that one day she's going to wake up and realise she deserves someone much cleverer."

"You are far too sweet a chap. I don't usually get to talk to the men here. Not more than giving them a price, anyway. I think she's a very lucky girl."

"I bet they don't usually offer you lunch, either."

"No."

"She had a rough start in life too, y'know. Dad was drunk just about all the time, like yours. Knocked her mum about right afore her eyes. So, her mother ran off in secret. Passed Katie over to a travelling troupe. Begged them to take her before the husband started on her. Took her years to tell me that. But she's done alright for herself. More than alright." Flora stretched under the sun. "Damn. I'd best be getting back to the grindstone. Same time tomorrow?"

"I'd like that." The girl offered a gentle smile and danced off into the afternoon sun.

*

Katie smiled as a pair of arms slipped about her chest and a kiss was pressed to her temple. "Hello, my love."

"Good evening, my darling. Still hard at it?"

"Yes." She arched against the rickety chair. "But Millie went out of her way to get me this job-"

"You might as well do it properly." Flora finished for her.

"Have I said that before?" Kate stroked Flora's arm.

"Only once or twice. To be fair, you did keep shoving your drawings under her nose until she caved and introduced the two of you. I doubt she's ever recovered."

"Funny. But it's all good experience."

"I'm not sure it was for Mrs Fawcett." Flora smirked.

"Go and do something useful while I finish up and I might think about making us some dinner."

"Dinnae be daft, I can cook."

"No, darling, you can't. Besides, I like making you dinner. Makes me feel all 'little-wife-like.'" She raised her face for a kiss.

Flora frowned but complied. "Not my fault I've only ever cooked over fire. And you've never been the little wifey type."

"True, but I like playing the role occasionally."

"I'm not entirely averse to that." Flora nuzzled into Katie's neck.

"Nope, nope. Begone with you! I have work to finish." Katie pushed her away, giggling.

A few hours later, curled up on the couch, Flora stared into the fireplace. A lady on the gramophone was singing a song about a bull and a bush while Katie read, the clatter of a Summer storm brewing outside.

"Do you miss it?" asked Flora, tuning her ears to the music.

"Sometimes. In the same way that I know you secretly miss the army. But I look at our life and... I'm happy."

Flora *hmphed* through her nose. "What about the movement?"

"It'll always be there." Katie stretched and cuddled closer. "I felt they had given me meaning. A purpose. But that was wrong. I still dream of the day when you and I will achieve parity with the men of this world. Mind you, look who I'm taking to." She prodded Flora's side. "I'll never again let it blind me, though. Doing so cost me the friendship of woman I truly cared for and respected."

"Ellaline never did forgive you, did she."

"No and I honestly can't say as I blame her. I don't think using the theatre as a rallying point for civil unrest was quite what she meant when she talked about shaping the world. I never meant for things to get so out of control. But they did. Anyway, I don't need some separate identity anymore. I belong to nothing and no one anymore unless I choose that they should have me. That's true freedom."

"Aye, it is at that. You're a revolutionary, Katie Vaughan."

A rumble of thunder made Kate shudder and Flora gave

her a squeeze. "Wouldn't worry about that, love. Nothing to the storms we had in the north."

Katie lifted her face from Flora's chest and scratched her fingernails over the cotton of her shirt. "Why don't you ever talk about home?"

"I am home."

"Hmm, your heart is with me, but not your soul. I know you better than that, Flora Begg. Please tell me something?"

Flora's lip twitched. "Have you ever been by the sea in the whip of a storm?"

"I've barely been by the sea at all."

"Really? Not all those years of touring about as a bedraggled wee urchin?"

"Hoi! I was not. And no, we weren't really allowed out much, even if there was the time."

"Well, can you imagine the rattle of a bell that clangs in the harbour? Your father's boat's getting battered by gale force winds and all you can do is pray it survives the night. The rain comes in great sheets that tumble through the thatch and hiss in the hearth then turn to tiny puffs of steam. Windows, nothing as strong as the ones you have here, threaten to shatter.

It's both thrilling and terrifying to a wean tucked up in straw. But the best thing about a storm is the morning after. The still of bold, blue waters reflecting the sweetest sun. The air is clearer, and you've endured again. The men will hoist their nets and the metal scent of fired earth comes strong as you till it wi' the how.

You look up, and in the distance, cloud lingers atop the sleeping giants of Scarabens, Morven and off towards Assynt.

You remember this ancient land is not just yours. It belongs to both the generations beneath your feet and the bairns at play."

"I've never heard you talk that way. It was quite poetic."

"I can be poetic! Nah. Truthfully, I haven't thought like that in a while."

"It was beautiful, thank you. Must be hard to be so far away."

"Maybe at times, but the pay-off is more than worth it." Flora winked and did her best to stifle a yawn.

"Well, this revolutionary says it's time for bed."

"As you say, my wee radical."

*

The next day, Flora didn't bother to look up. She simply passed Sarah her own wrapped sandwiches when the girl plopped down next to her.

"Looks like a huge shipment today. That's not good." Sarah huffed.

"Tobacco, sugar and rum. Lots of it. What's so bad? More work to go around suits everyone."

"Suits you maybe, but not me. If the men are too tired, it's not good for my business. They either go straight home to their wives or into the pub and get legless."

"I see what you mean. I'm afraid I can't much help

you there, m'dear. It's not like I can go about ordering my lads to go- well..."

"It's alright, I know. And you do help. You talk to me. You don't treat me like just another whore, even if that's exactly what I am."

"You're not *just a whore*, Sarah. And mebbe, I've come across my fair share of... ladies of your profession. I was in the army. And I've seen what girls like you put up with. I didn't use their services too often but when I did, I always left them a bit extra."

"So, you wouldn't be tempted to 'use my services,' then?" Sarah asked and snuggled into Flora's shoulder.

"No, I wouldn't." Flora eased her away. "I'm very happy with Kate. How old are you if you don't mind me asking?"

"Sixteen."

"Jesus."

"I started selling myself when I was fourteen. Had to leave school when mum died. I skivvied a bit for a while, but the head housekeeper was a right bitch. Said I was after the master. It was all rubbish. But the man had a wandering eye. I reckon she was just jealous as his eye wandered on me. But I wasn't no whore then, not for any man. I fell into this when I couldn't get work elsewhere. You must think I'm rotten."

"No, I don't think that at all." Flora tilted the girl's face towards her. "Only that you're so very young. But you're doing what you must, and I canna find it in me to condemn you. Besides, you're one up on me. I never went to school at all."

"Really? But I've watched you work. You know how to read and write."

"Not 'til long after I'd joined the army. I got made up to Corporal, so they sent me here to learn my letters and numbers. If I didn't, I'd have lost my promotion. That's how I met Katie."

"Do you like it?"

"I like the fact I'm able to. Still not great at it, though. Never sat down to read a book."

"I'm jealous, Sinclair. You're a real adventurer. The places you must have seen."

"Indeed. D'you... are you employed by someone, or do you work alone?"

"Alone. There is a so-called gentleman, who's been pestering me to join him for ages, but I won't. You hear things about the way he treats his girls. It's alright though, I'm well shot of him. And most of my customers are decent enough. A few are a bit rough at times, but nothing too bad."

Flora grimaced, both at the mention of 'so-called gentleman' and the knowledge of the hardships this child had endured. For years, she had watched her comrades with honest curiosity, not always considering the backgrounds which must have driven these women to where they were.

"What's wrong?"

"Oh, nothing." She forced a smile and rose to her feet, offering Sarah and hand. "Just thinking, you're far too bright."

"Well, we are where we are."

The bell rang out for home time and weary bodies dragged themselves from bobbling pontoons and clambered down from mountains of scratchy sacks for their beds.

It had been a punishing day. Flora tried to arch her back but had to give in midway with a snap. Her shirt stuck to her, but for the sake of decency, she pulled on her jacket before she turned onto the first major public street.

"Sinclair!" Sarah came barrelling up towards her, brandishing something thick and red. "I was hoping to catch you before you went. I brought you this." She pushed the book into Flora's grasp.

"Treasure Island?"

"It's an adventure. I think you'll enjoy it."

"How did you- do I want to know?"

Sarah rolled her eyes. "There's a bookseller up by the Billingsgate. The old boy in there likes me, says I remind him of his daughter." The two of them shared a frown at the implication in those words. "Anyway, last night I was very, very nice to him, so this afternoon I asked him if there was anything he could let me have."

"Sarah, you really shouldn't have, but I'm incredibly grateful, thank you. You've my word I'll try it tonight."

"You're welcome. Maybe you can bring it with you tomorrow and we can read some together?"

"I'll do just that. Billingsgate, eh? You've a pretty wide area."

"Cheeky. Yes, well, when you work alone, you have to be careful on whose patch you're treading."

"Understood. Speaking of, I see there's a chap over there looking this way. You might have your first customer."

"Oh, he's not the first today," she said, glancing over her shoulder at the middle-aged man lurking on the corner, "but I should go."

"You look after yourself, alright?"

"Why, Sinclair, you're not worried about me, are you?"

"Never. Good luck for tonight and I'll see you tomorrow."

Sarah grabbed her shoulders and pressed a kiss to Flora's cheek, shouted a brief *night* then melted into the crowd.

*

Katie arrived home to a sight she never ever thought she would see.

Flora was dozing on the couch, a light snore emanating from her throat. An ordinary enough sight after a hard day. Feet up on the footstool. *Still with those damn boots on, I see.* She ground her back teeth together. Still, a perfectly normal occurrence until one caught sight of the book resting open on her lap.

She picked her way around the sofa, resting her hands along the back as she leant down to kiss the soft skin below Flora's ear.

"Flora Begg, after all these years you still surprise me from time-to-time."

"Mmph, more than just from time-to-time, I'd like to think?" She arched her neck, hoping for a little more of Katie's exquisite attentions.

"'Fraid not, soldier. How long until you're ready to go?"

"Go? Go where?"

"It's Thursday, love, and you did say you'd come. But darling if you really are too tired..." She lowered her body further down the couch until she was able to hug Flora's chest, her own breasts resting on the other woman's shoulder. A delicate blend of tobacco, fruity rum and salt filled her nostrils as she pressed their cheeks together.

"Nope. Nope." Flora kissed the back of Katie's hand. "If I said I'd go, then we'll go. Give me five minutes." She slapped her hands to the couch and bounced to her feet, stopping to give Katie are proper welcome home en-route to the basin.

Ten minutes later, she appeared, washed, and freshly suited just as Katie was checking the clock.

"Not bad." said Katie with a lopsided smile.

Flora sauntered towards her and slipped her arms about her waist. "You got changed too. Are you absolutely sure we need to go out tonight?" She began placing kisses along Katie's neckline.

"Hmm, we really should but play your cards right tonight and you may just have your way when we get home."

"It's a deal." said Flora in the most hard-done-by tone she could muster. Katie simply smacked her on the behind and waltzed out the door, leaving a slack-jawed Flora in her wake.

"Are you coming or not?"

"Yes, dear!"

*

The Thursday Club was already in full swing by the time they got there. Some hijinks on the way had delayed their arrival considerably, having long-since given up on trying to appear like respectable members of society.

As soon as the door closed on Gordon Square, Flora's flat cap was summarily tossed away, and her shirtsleeves bared. The scruffed male wig came off and her hair was let loose.

"Hmm, I can't tell you how glad I am that you decided to grow this out again." said Katie and ruffled her fingers through Flora's jet locks.

"It's this place, making me do strange things!" She wrapped her arm about Katie's waist, grabbed her hand and twirled them into the living room. "I never do this anywhere else." she said and accepted a lit cigar from a random hand.

"Hmm, I love the smell of a cigar on you."

"Kate, Flora! You're just in time!"

"For what?" Katie glanced past Flora. The handsome face of Vanessa Bell appeared through the tobacco mist.

"Eddie's about to give us a reading of his new one.

Hello, dearest. Flora, how's life on the docks? Where on earth are your drinks?"

And just like that, she was off. Katie and Flora made the mistake of looking at each other and fell about laughing as another voice shouted out for the lights to be lowered.

Over in a corner, poor Edward Forster was shaking his head. "No, no, please. It's not fit to be heard."

But eventually the man buckled under the cajoling of the assembled crowd.

"*He educated Maurice, or rather his spirit educated Maurice's spirit, for they themselves became equal. Neither thought 'Am I led; am I leading?' Love had caught him out of triviality and Maurice out of bewilderment in order that two imperfect souls might touch perfection.*"

Flora felt Katie's hand slip into her own, and tuned out much of the reading, focused solely on the sensation of soft fingers that teased the taut, calloused skin of her palm and all went still. Seconds into minutes floated by unmarked. But one final line did register.

"*Did you ever dream you had a friend, Alec? Someone to last your whole life and you his. I suppose such a thing can't really happen outside sleep.*"

Flora and Kate each turned to face the other and knew the truth of it. If Forster was right, then the last thirteen years had been as vanishing smoke. And if it were, so be it.

The moment was broken. The lamps fed gas, and a gramophone cranked. Flora took the opportunity to waltz her about the cramped space while she could before Katie was inevitably drawn into the throng.

The others found Flora a curious creature. She'd notice their inquisitive gazes as she'd float about the shadowy edges of the room, surveying them in her turn. They were not unkind, far from it, but under their scrutiny, she was remembered of the little specimen plates in Bill's office. On the odd occasion, when she bothered to stop and think about it, she supposed she should be grateful. She was the epitome of Bloomsbury. A sexually liberated woman who criss-crossed the border of what it meant to be male and female. She had a beautiful, rather bohemian, lover yet worked one of the roughest jobs in London. But these weren't the kind of people she would ordinarily choose to pass the time with. They were scholars, artists, and freethinkers. Flora was of the earth with a permanent layer of grease under her nails and sweat stains on her shirts.

She's happy. Flora looked on and raised her glass on catching Kate's eye and turned away in search of a refill. She found a decanter and backed into a welcoming darkness. *Thank God, a quiet corner!* She shut the door.

There was a click. A yellowy glow flooded the space.

"Sorry, I didnae ken anyone was in here."

"That's alright." said the willowy figure by the lamp. "I wasn't feeling up to much of a party tonight."

"Me neither."

"You're welcome to sit if you'd like? I'd intended on being alone, but you look as though you require solitude."

"I think I will, thank you." A wooden chair creaked under Flora's weight. "To tell you the truth, this isn't really my kind of crowd. No offence."

"None taken." said the girl.

Flora gave herself a mental smack. *She's your age! Fragile wee thing by the look of her. Needs a couple of decent dinners.*

"Forgive me if it's not my place to ask, but are you alright?"

"Yes, just reflecting. I've been... away recently. Sometimes I question whether they are my crowd, as well. Or, more accurately, do I belong with them?'

"It's important to belong somewhere."

"Do you?"

"I did."

"When?"

Doesn't mince her words, does she? "When I was in the army."

"The army? How on earth-?"

"It's a long story." said Flora. "I joined when I was six-teen. Served in the Sudan, then Africa. I left nearly six years ago, now."

"How fascinating. And you haven't belonged since?"

"At home, with my... with Kate. I belong with her. And I like my work, though it's not the same."

"I imagine nothing would be. What do you do now?"

"I'm a docker."

This time the girl actually looked shocked. "The docks? Isn't that rather arduous?"

"Aye, anything, and everything that comes in, we bring it off. An' it can be tough. Someone kicks it about once or twice a week, but I'm a foreman so the pay's not too bad. And it keeps me busy."

"How can you enjoy taking such risks every day? That sounds terrifying."

"It's a thrill, like the army was, though god-knows, I'd never tell Kate."

"Well. You are quite the most fascinating character, Miss?"

"Flora, Flora Begg."

"Thank you for barging in, Flora. I should like to hear more of your story sometime."

"Thank you for letting me stay after I'd barged in. I should probably get back, though. Wouldn't want to be rude to the hosts, even if it's not my thing."

"I don't think you need worry on that count, Miss Begg. I should likely make an appearance too."

Flora smiled and held the door open for her. She had just stepped over the threshold into the living room when Vanessa wafted her way over.

"Virginia, darling, where on earth have you been?"

Flora frowned. *Virginia? Where the hell've I heard that name before?*

"Flora, where have you just been with Virginia Woolf?" Katie appeared in front of her.

"Woolf, that's it!" Flora clicked her fingers. "Why? Should I know her?"

The rest of the evening passed uneventfully, although Katie had quietly but heavily impressed upon her the significance of a private conversation with Mrs Woolf. By the time she had finished demanding a third recounting of the event, Flora wondered if it would have been easier to have knocked on Buck Pal's door and asked for a blether with the king. *Except he'd have probably been out, and I'd have had to make do with the backstairs maid.* This made her thoughts turn to Sarah. *I hope to god she's safe.*

"Where did you go?" asked Katie, who was curled into Flora's side, her fingers tracing patterns across her chest. "You disappeared for a moment there."

"Just thinking thoughts."

"You looked sad."

"No, love. Never sad."

Flora leaned back and let the now subtle chatter wash over her. Most of what was said at these soirees went over her head, but it was pleasant to be with Kate so openly. Behind her, she was vaguely aware of some auld wife gibbering on about 'not being able to get the help these days.' Flora rolled her eyes and stared up at the ceiling. *Some things never change.*

*

Her headache the following morning was killed off with some honest sweat. Once she got moving. Always a bad idea to go out partying on a work night, but she'd made a promise. It was alright for the posh folks that attended these get-togethers. *None of them've ever done a day's graft in their puff!* Flora thought as she heaved yet another sack of sugar up the ramp.

It was a surprise not to find Sarah wandering about dock but maybe she'd been busy with customers. Men had their fancies at all hours. By lunchtime, she was growing mildly concerned and Sarah's share of sarnies went uneaten.

While shifting a load of barrels fresh in from America with a furrow on her brow, a voice called out.

"Did you start your book yet?"

"Sarah?" Flora peered into the gloom of an archway and saw only a white shift fluttering between the giant wooden struts. "I've been worried about you. What're you doing there, lass? Out ye come."

"No. And stay back. I don't want you seeing me like this."

"Like what? Whate'er's the matter with you?"

"It's nothing. Just, please-"

"Dinnae be daft. Now come on."

"No!"

Flora yanked her into the daylight. Heat rose in her cheeks at the sight before her.

"Who did this to you? Who the bloody hell did this?" She gripped Sarah's arms.

"It doesn't matter, alright? Let me go." Sarah wriggled from Flora's grasp.

"It damn-well does matter to me. No one has the right to lay a finger on you. Understand? No one. Tell me who did it and I'll knock him into next week."

"No, Sinclair, that's just it. I'm not having you pulled in by lily law on account of me. I'm a whore. Things like this happen to whores and if you can't handle that, then-."

"Damn it, I don't give a fuck about the law. You are not a whore."

Sarah stared at her uncomprehendingly. "Of course I am."

"No Sarah. There's a difference between what you do and who you are. Nobody deserves this." Flora reached a fingertip to the purple spongy area beneath her eye.

"It was him."

"Who?"

"The man who's been trying to get me to go work for 'im. Last night his 'persuasion' got a bit rough. Well, I say it was him. He's not the bollocks to do it himself. Sent one of his men round instead. I chased my sister into the coal shed to hide. Black as night, she was this morning."

Flora swallowed. "This morning?"

"Knocked me out. Didn't wake 'til gone ten this morning.

When I did, I, I could feel... I think he took one on the 'house." Sarah flushed and squeezed her knees together. "Poor little blighter was stuck out there until I went and found her. Freezing, she was." She rubbed at her arms where Flora had gripped her. Flora pulled her in close and held her as tight as she dared.

"Who is he, Sarah?"

Sarah eased back and looked Flora dead in the eye. "If I tell you, you must promise me you won't go after him, Sinclair. That man is evil, itself. Now swear it."

Flora gritted her teeth and nodded.

"His name is Brian Dempsey."

"Brian Dempsey? Where have I heard that name?"

Flora broke the embrace and trudged off to a net which held a dozen or more barrels. She ripped away the ropes. Stamped all over the seals in horrid black ink; **Brian Dempsey Esq.**

"You unload half his cargo. He's a powerful man round here. It's not just tarts and illegal booze. He owns half the docklands and what he doesn't, he buys off. You can't go up against this man and live. You just can't."

"Maybe not. But I can damn-well get you away from him."

*

Katie jumped at the thud of the door. She watched

as Flora threw her jacket at the sofa and flopped onto it. "Am I to take it today has been less than optimum?"

"Just what the hell does that mean?"

Katie blinked. "I see our honeymoon from last evening hasn't lasted."

"Sorry."

"It's alright. Though I'd rather you talk to me than bark at me."

"I've something on my mind."

"I can see that. What?"

"What was that friend o' yours last night, saying about she wanted help?"

"What?"

"Kate."

"Mrs Frobisher? She needs a secretary, why?"

"Mrs? She's a man in the house, then?"

"After a fashion, yes. Flora, you're not making any sense."

"She's on Morwell Street?"

"I think so, why?"

"Right." Flora bounced off the couch. "I'll be back soon."

"Flora?!"

*

The light was strange at this time of night. The

lanterns from docked ships, diffused in the fog, cast a spectral glow along the water's edge. At a certain point, the ruckus from the taverns faded into the lapping of water against brick and her footsteps echoed coldly along the slipway.

A tattered white dress appeared through a break in the cloud like a ghost then vanished again as it passed.

"Slow night?"

"No one wants to pay for a girl who looks like this. But then that's why he did it."

"What if you were offered a different life? Would you take it?"

"Don't be thick, of course I would but it's hardly likely to fall in my lap, is it? These things don't just happen. Not to cheap tarts."

"What if I were to tell you it has? What then?'

"What have you been up to?"

"A change of circumstance. For you. For your sister."

"I'm listening."

"A friend of Kate's, a Mrs Frobisher, is looking for a secretary. I've convinced her to give you a chance. You'll have bed and board and a small wage. Not much but enough to keep body and soul thegither. And you'll be away frae here where that bastard Dempsey can't touch you. What do you say?"

"I don't know what to say. You did this for me? But a secretary, I wouldn't know where to... what would I have to do?"

"I've no idea. Take notes? Does it matter? Just give

it a try. She might get to like you then it'll no matter if you mess up."

"I-I don't... thank you. Oh, god, thank you." Sarah threw her arms about Flora's neck.

"That's all I needed to hear, lass. You'll be safe there, that's all that counts. Now, I'll see you home and you can set about packing a bag. In the morning, I'll take you to the Frobisher's."

The walk home passed in relative silence. It took several steps before Flora realised Sarah was no longer walking with her.

"Sarah? What's wrong with ye lass? The colour's drained from you."

Sarah nodded at a figure limping through the fog dead ahead.

"That's Dempsey's man. The one that beat me."

"Christ's sake, are you certain?" Sarah gave her a sharp look. Flora nodded and bundled her into an alleyway. She pushed her up against a wall and assaulted her neck with her lips. It was rougher than she would have ever been with Katie, but she had to make it look good. "Act the part, will you?" She pressed her knee between Sarah's thighs. The girl cried out. Sarah grabbed at Flora's hair, but Flora moved it to her back and hissed as nails bit hard into flesh. Sarah ground herself into Flora's leg until footsteps clomped past and Flora ripped her body away. She stared at the hem of Sarah's shift, still clutched in her hand. The blood pulsing in her fingertips matched by the pounding in her chest. "Come on, let's get you home."

Sarah's mouth hung open, her back pressed into the wall and her breathing laboured. "Will you stay with me?"

Flora's voice, when it eventually came, was harsh and alien to her ears. "Long enough for you to pack, that's all."

The next morning, I marched Sarah and her sister to the Frobisher's. It took some settling. Mrs Frobisher was reluctant to begin with when she clocked sight of them, but she was fond of Katie, and she eventually accepted my word.

I also had some grovelling to do towards Kate after my middle-of-the-night disappearance. And rightly so.

I kept a half-eye on Sarah and her sister for a while and learned that she was doing well for herself. It was many months before I chanced upon her again.

Another party, another chance for Katie to 'net' potential customers. I asked her if she wanted a pole with a big hoop about the end of it. The comment received a far more impolite response than I believed it deserved. The wine flowed, albeit in the far more formal setting of the drawing room of one of her more respectable clients. I wouldn't like to say I was bored, but I had spent more entertaining evenings.

"Sarah! You're looking grand."

"Sinclair!" Sarah wrapped her arms about Flora's neck. "I've missed you, stranger. What brings you here tonight?"

"This is Kate's thing." She jabbed a thumb over her shoulder to where Katie was engrossed in conversation with a group of ladies. Flora smirked. *Holding court as ever.* "Seems if you want women's attention, you waft expensive dresses under their noses and disappear before the husband finds the bill."

"I can't vouch for that, but the Frobishers have been very generous to us. Sinclair, I should say sorry. For the last time I saw you."

"Don't be daft. It was an unfortunate occurrence, nothing more."

"Whatever it was, I didn't behave to you so kindly that night and you were only trying to help. Reckon if it weren't for you, I wouldn't be standing here now."

"Well, you did get me a book, so we'll say we're even."

"Did you ever finish it?"

"I did." Flora grinned. "Had to ask Kate to help me here and there saying as my reading partner abandoned me." She winked. "I'm on to Kidnapped now. Since I have this interest in reading, my darling girl's taken it upon herself to furnish me with my own library."

"Sounds like a special lady. I'd love to meet her."

"I'm sure we can arrange something. Not sure how I'd explain away your presence."

"You never told her about me?"

"Not entirely. She knows I found you a job."

"But you didn't tell her about my-"

"Former employment? No. I'm not always the sharpest knife, Sarah, but I've no death wish either."

"I see your point. But how about we set up a regular reading date? I wouldn't like for you to feel I'd abandoned you for good."

"I'll drink to that. I've missed your company. Lunchtime's gotten very quiet."

"And I-" Sarah's eyes widened. She tugged on Flora's waistcoat. "Th-that's him!" Sarah pointed over her shoulder. "That's Brian Dempsey."

"What?" Her eyes darted about. "Where?"

"There!"

She followed Sarah's finger. "That's not Brian Dempsey, that's Deacon Broderick. I don't claim to like the boy. He was after Katie for a while. He's persistent, but trust me, he's no underworld mastermind."

"I'm telling you, Sinclair, it's him!"

"Alright. Alright. I believe you. What do you want to do?"

"I think I should go. Please, I want to go home. Before he sees me."

"Okay, I'll walk you down the road."

"What about Katie?"

Flora glanced to over to where Kate was now in deep conversation with... Mr Broderick. Her lip twisted in a snarl, but a confrontation would do no good. Not for Kate and certainly not for Sarah. Besides, she trusted her and if the ants crawling up her spine were any indication, she'd have her time to bide.

"She'll be alright for a few minutes."

"You're still so in love with her. Even after all this time?"

The damp pavement scratched under their shoes. Flora had her hands stuffed deep into her trouser pockets. *God, she looks tiny under my coat like that.* She watched Sarah pull the hefty old army serge a touch tighter. "Very much so."

"Am I allowed to be envious?"

"I'd rather you weren't. You're still a youngster. Plenty time for all that."

"You think any decent bloke would want me? I'm hardly an un-plucked petal."

"If he's any sort of real man, then aye, I believe he would."

"I think that's just you. You would have me, wouldn't you?"

"That's a loaded question."

"I know. That's why I asked."

"And it's not one I can answer. Sarah, I've met a lot of girls in your position. And I've never seen them as less than. But you've so much future ahead of you. And I'm settled with my life. I'm content."

"I hope Miss Day realises how lucky she is."

Flora shook her head. "You should feel sorry for her rather than envious. I'm no picnic to live with. That woman puts up with an awful lot." *Burnt carpet springs to mind.*

"I doubt that. Anyway, this is me." Sarah hopped down the first step towards the servant's entrance. "You are some kind of man, Sinclair. I've never known one like you."

Flora chuckled. "No, I'm quite sure you haven't."

Sarah eased the jacket from her shoulders, but Flora met her hands halfway and covered her nimble fingers. "Nah. Keep it. You need it more than I do. I'll let Mrs Frobisher know you took unwell."

"Thank you. My debt to you is only mounting." Sarah pressed a kiss to Flora's cheek. "Goodnight Sinclair."

"Night, Sarah. Sleep sound."

She waited until the lock thunked into place before she turned back down the street but a slender silhouette, illuminated a few streetlamps away, unchanged in thirteen years, halted her in her tracks and she swallowed. For a moment, she wasn't on an upmarket residential street at all, but at the stage door of the Gaiety, a drunken lunatic out cold at her feet.

"I wasn't really in the mood for a party tonight, after all."

"Me neither."

"I couldn't find you." Katie shivered and pressed herself into Flora's body. "Someone said they saw you leave. Where's your coat?"

"Sarah wasn't feeling well."

"It was good of you to walk her home."

"Kate? Are you alright? You seem a bit... I don't know."

Katie nodded against Flora's chest. "Deacon Broderick." Flora stiffened in her arms. "He says he needs to see me. He said he has a proposal which would be to my benefit. I'm not sure what to make of it."

"You don't have to do anything, Kate. Just say the

word and I'll cut him dead. You'll never have to see his face again."

Katie gave her a squeeze. "That's possibly a *slight* overreaction, darling, but I appreciate the thought. Let's just go home. You can cure me of this headache."

"Hmm, happily."

Flora kept Katie close the whole walk home.

*

Flora's Sunday morning constitutional found her heading home with a happy bundle tucked under her arm. Katie was still fast asleep when she'd left. *Why break the habit of a lifetime?* She grinned to herself. *My mission, on the other hand? I will damn-well prove to that woman that I can fry a few sassengers without burning the house to a crisp!*

"Sinky Begg?"

Flora spun on her heel

"It is! It's Corporal bleedin' Begg! How the hell are ya, man?"

"Micklethwaite? Christ!"

The man grabbed her hand with his left, resting a snuffer pole at his shoulder. It was then she noticed the strapping on his other appendage which hung limp at his side.

"Bloody Boers got me. I was invalided out before I got a chance. Got shot up at Magers."

"Damn, I'm sorry to hear that Mick. Heard your lot were did pretty well out there, though."

"Too right. What about you? You still in?"

"Nah, I packed it in about six years ago. Finished up a sergeant. Made it through Africa with a few scrapes. Knee gives me a bit o' gyp now and then but could've been worse. I got back. Plenty didn't."

"You're not wrong. Listen, how's about you and me having a drink sometime? We'll raise a glass to 'em."

"Aye, alright Mick, you're on."

"Fine, tomorrow night. The Red Lion."

"Er, right, Aye. I'll see you there."

Flora's step was lighter all the way home.

I was surprised to find Kate up and about by the time I returned home. I'd hoped to surprise her with a few of those tasty (expensive) sausages from the butcher. Shilling a pound, indeed! But I could see them all hot and sizzling now that I was once again trusted with the grill.

My disappointment grew to dismay when it turned out she'd been quite genuine in her rekindled interest in Broderick.

"Here, get that down yer neck." Mick thumped a pint of stout in front of her. "Your face is tripping' itself all the way into that pot if you're not careful."

"It's nothing, just something on my mind. To absent friends."

"Absent friends." Mick joined her in lifting his pint

and partook of a healthy glug. "Who're you knocking about with nowadays, eh? You married yet? I remember you had a thing for posh birds. What was her name?"

"Kate." Flora smirked. "And aye, she's still my posh bird."

"What, really? You're pulling my leg"

"Nearly fourteen years strong."

"Blow me. Well done, son." Mick gave her a slap on the back. "Kiddies then?"

"No, no wee ones. We're just not blessed that way. But she's got her career and I like my job so otherwise, we're pretty content."

"That's the main thing, I s'pose. Weren't she a turn at some theatre?"

"She gave that up years ago. Got involved with the suffragettes and started a riot. Now she draws up dresses for wealthy women with more money than sense."

Mick let out a bark of laughter. "Your girl started one of them riots? Bloody hell, mate, your life's not been dull, has it?"

Flora joined in his laughter, the heavy beer starting to have its desired effect. "No, can't say as it has."

"Too bad they don't let birds in the army. Them Boers might've given up a bit livelier than they did if they were all like 'er!"

"Another round?"

"Not half." Mick was still howling while Flora disappeared off to the bar.

Several pints and possibly one or two too many

chasers later, the two old comrades lolled back in their chairs like a pair of lead clock weights.

"So, you never did tell me what was wrong with your puss ear-le-err-er-erlar?" He flopped forward onto the table. "S'it women's troubles?"

"Huh? Why-wh-why would I have women'ses troubles? I'm Sinclair."

"No, no, y'see. You. You're a bloke, right? And, and women are, well, women and they are compli- compcat- complicated fings, right?" I mean if women fought like blokes, right? Well, then, they wouldn't be womens."

"Ken what, pal? You are spot on, my friend, spot on."

"Damn right, I am. But see, when womens go acting like womens, blokes like us just don't stand a chance, do they?"

"Right again, son. Wait, what were you saying?"

"You were telling me why you'd such a sour gob on you."

"I've not a sour gob."

"Earlier, man, earlier."

"Ah, love. S'another man, y'ken."

"Your Missus? Nah, why've you not just belted him one, then belted her after then. No woman carries on like that with me."

"Not like that, not like that. S'not Katie."

"You mean you've another girl? Well done lad!"

"No, no, not that either. It's this man. Deacon Broderick, or Brian Dempsey, am not sure which. He's been knocking hoors about. Might be after Katie too."

"Brian Dempsey? Mate, you don't wanna be getting involved with that bastard if you know what's good for you. Keep your Missus well away, away."

*

The door flung open. Katie brushed past without even noticing the man seeking entrance.

"Pleasure to see you again, Miss."

She paused and stared at him. "I'm sorry, I don't-"

"Micklethwaite, Ma'am. We met once upon a time when you were bangin' on the barracks winda'."

"Oh, yes. So, it's you who got Sinclair into such a state last night."

"Erm, I s'pose so. Been feeling a bit delicate myself, this morning."

"Well, you can commiserate together. Good day to you, Mr Micklethwaite."

He wandered through the open doorway and found the figure of Sinclair clutching his head, leaning over the kitchen worktop. "Your good lady ain't so happy with you today."

"Ah, morning Mick. Nah, she's not too fond of drink. Or of me when I'm in drink. That's why I don't do it too often."

"Modern man, eh?"

"Not sure about that but it brings up bad memories for her. Her father, like. Man had a temper. Not fair of me to put her through it. Last night was an overindulgence."

"Decent of you. Which is what brings me here."

"I don't follow you, pal."

"Well, see, oddly enough, I remember a fair bit from last night and I recall you mentioning a certain Brian Dempsey and that your good lady might be in danger of entertaining his company."

"Aye, it's a concern. There's a young lass who used to hang about the docks. He sent one of his heavies to give her a good hiding when she refused to work for him. I see his name on some of the barrels coming off the ships."

"You would do. This boy's major underworld and bent as a figure-eight. Got at least a dozen magistrates in his back pocket. I suggest you keep your separate ways. And tell this girl to do the same. Find another patch."

"Believe me, I'd love to. And don't worry about the lass. I've got her honest work elsewhere but now I've a worry that this Brian Dempsey might be the same Deacon Broderick that's been sniffing about Kate. I'd dismissed him as a bit of a whelp but perhaps that's been my mistake."

"Tell her to keep away until you know more."

"Hmph, Kate doesn't listen to me when she sets her mind to something. In fact, that's where she's off to the now."

"We should do some digging."

"Aye, but where? I've not a clue how to even start such a thing."

"You leave that to me. I've a mate of mine, ex-regiment, left after Africa. He's turned private detective now. Finds people the coppers can't. Has his own connections if you know what I mean?"

"You trust this boy?"

"I do. Lives on the edge of the law but knows what

goes on and he's a good bloke. I reckon he'd do a fellow squaddie a turn."

Flora thought for a minute then handed him a mug of tea. "Alright. You're on."

*

"You see, Miss Day, setting out on one's own needn't be difficult or financially prohibitive if one possesses the right connections." Broderick's pale grey coat swished as he led his topper through a theatrical bow.

"It's certainly impressive, Mr Broderick, but tell me, how do you come to have such a building to give away?"

"Give away?" he said, replacing his hat and raising his black cane with the silver embellishments. "Hardly. To sell to a friend at a competitive price. I'm a businessman, Miss Day. I make investments. And you, my dear, I believe are sound investment."

Flora's always said he was a dandy. More like dandelion. "You are avoiding my question, sir."

"You're right. I should have known better."

Katie swept a hand over a dusty workbench, flinching when a splinter poked through her glove. "And what would you ask of me in payment?"

"A modest fee. And your reacquaintance. I realise that at our last meeting my behaviour was inexcusable and entirely unbecoming of a gentleman. I wish to make amends. Get to know you properly. Mentor you if I may."

"And pray tell, what your wife might think of such an acquaintance?"

"My wife would have very little to say on the subject. She trusts me unreservedly."

Something in his tone tasted sour, but then hadn't she always dreamt of striking out on her own? *It needn't be for long, does it? I can play at his game.*

"Well, Mr Broderick, under such generous terms I am certain we can come to some arrangement." *Please forgive me Flora.*

"Then I believe we have an accord." He offered his hand but, on her grasp, he bent forward and grazed her cheek with his lips. "Excellent. I'll have my solicitor drawn up the papers. Now, how about a drink to celebrate our new association?"

She flinched as the scruff on his jaw scraped her skin. "It's a little early, don't you think?"

"You might be right at that. Very well, I shall just have to buy you the lunch to go with it."

This is such a bad idea. She's going to hit the roof. The image of Flora's reaction turned her stomach, even as she looped her arm through his.

*

The house was empty.

Flora draped her jacket over the back of the couch and glanced at the bottle of amber fire standing sentinel on the sideboard. *Damn thing's winking at me.* But a corresponding throb in her head led her to fill the kettle instead. *I'm getting too old to be spending nights getting half-cut on beer and spirits.* She was about to pour the tea when the front door burst open, and Katie came waltzing into the kitchen.

"Well, hello there my darlingest, dearest darling."

"Er, hello?"

Katie giggled in a way that was strange to Flora's ears as she snaked her arms about her neck and kissed her. It was clumsy, devoid her usual well-crafted skill. Her hands roamed freely over Flora's body, tugging her shirttails loose.

"You're in quite a mood this evening."

"Why? Am I not allowed to expect a little ravishing from my lover when I come home?"

"When you put it like that- have you been drinking?" Flora pulled away, her nose twitching.

"Just the teensiest drop or two. Don't tell me you don't approve, Flora Begg."

"No, it's not that. It's just not like you."

"What's sauce for the goose." Katie prodded her finger into Flora's chest and yanked on her collar.

They staggered towards bedroom, Flora's appetite for food, forgotten. As soon as they landed on the bed, Flora pinned Kate's wrists above her head and pushed a knee between her thighs. "I haven't seen you like this since that night you came with me to sergeant's mess ball."

"Yes, well I had an interesting proposition today, and a celebration is in order. Now come do your duty by your maiden fair, Corporal. You're still wearing far too much clothing."

"That's Sergeant Begg to you, Miss. And what proposition? You were with Broderick today."

"Yes, I was. Does that matter?"

"What sort of proposition?" Katie lifted her face to Flora's, but she moved away. "Kate?"

"Not the sort for you to worry about. Don't you trust me?"

"You? Yes. But him?"

"Darling, for once, will you please accept that I might know what I'm doing."

Put like that, Flora had no choice. *If I push this any further, she'll slip away. I still don't have any real case against the man, either.* And Kate's palm was warm on her breast. "You're right. Just please be careful."

Kate's gaze softened and her kiss this time was tender. "I promise I shall. Flora, can you make love to me? Please."

"That is something you need never ask."

Katie stared at the ceiling. Her every nerve ending had burned as soon as she'd walked in to see Flora standing by the kettle, her rolled up sleeves, the braces which had been slackened to dangle about her thighs. Crazed with her need for Flora's touch, that affirmation of her love. More than that. She needed Flora to possess her. Her business dealings with Deacon, the trip to his lawyer to discuss the drawing up of plans and subsequent alcohol-fuelled afternoon left her both exhilarated and disconcerted. *He is repulsive. But the pretence of going along with his desires... you can't lie to yourself, Kate. You like it.*

She shifted her head to the side. In the darkness, she could just about make out Flora's profile. "I love you, so much. I wish so much that I could bring myself to be truthful. But I'm a coward. I'm not like you, Flora. I can only hope that I never have to tell you. But if it does come to it, I'm begging you now to understand."

Flora stirred and Katie bit her thumb, but the eyes remained shut. She trailed her fingertips along the line of Flora's cheek as the weight of the other woman's arm slid across her hips. She settled closer and tucked her nose next to Flora's.

"Please forgive me."

*

"Begg! Some bloke's here to see you." A gruff voice called above the rude clank of the crane. Flora waved at the older man. Once the crate was safely on the ground she strode up to the quayside and blinked at the sight of Micklethwaite and the suspect-looking individual beside him.

"Sinky, thought I'd bring Garfield by. He's your man."

"Mr Garfield." Flora went to extend her hand but brushed them over her trousers instead. "Sorry. Mucky. I hear you're an old comrade."

"I am. Mick here's told me your story. I reckon I can help. Be truer to say I reckon we can help each other. I've been after Dempsey for years."

"You're certain Deacon Broderick is this same Brian Dempsey of yours?"

"'Fraid so. Mick only gave me the bare bones, but I gather you've an interest in seeing this fella put away."

"Aye. If not for keeping him away from my lass, then for a girl he had beaten up. She recognised him, clear as day."

"Wouldn't be the first time, either. He's not so handy with his fists, himself, but he takes great delight in sending 'is boys out to do his dirty work. Likes young girls especially."

Flora forced her hand to relax. "Is my lass in danger?"

"Hard to say. What's his interest in her?"

Flora stared at him.

"I see. Keep an eye on things for now, I'll do some digging. Now you've given me an alias for him, I'll see what I can find although I wouldn't mind betting it's only one of many. Meantime, this other girl, the one he had beaten, would she talk?"

"Don't know. I'll ask. Although if she says no, that's it. I won't force her. She's been through enough already. We'll have to find another way."

Garfield's jaw stiffened but he nodded. "I'll be in touch."

*

Sarah's surprise when Sinclair turned up on the tradesmen's doorstep the day after, turned to swift disappointment when the true purpose of the visit became clear. To her credit, she'd agreed to help. When he returned the following afternoon with Mick and Garfield, the Frobishers even laid on a tea.

"Mrs Frobisher, I should like to thank you for allowing us the use of your parlour. 'Tis gracious of you."

"Of course, it's no trouble, Mr Begg, though I do wish I were more cognisant of your purpose."

"How much has Sarah told you about where she came from? Of how we met?"

"She has told me the crux of the matter. I am aware of her former employment. I admit, it caused me great concern at first, but over the weeks and months, she and her dear sister have become part of the family."

"I'm glad. She's a good lass. Mr Garfield is a private investigator. He's been working closely with the police on a matter regarding a former... acquaintance. But I must warn you, Mrs Frobisher, Mr Garfield walks in worlds that the police canna be seen to. Are you certain you're prepared to be a part of this?"

Mrs Frobisher and Sarah shared a look. "Quite sure, Mr Begg."

"Alright." Garfield addressed Sarah. "What can you tell us about Brian Dempsey?"

"Man's a brute."

"Can you be a bit more specific?"

"He'd been pestering me for weeks to work in one of his whorehouses. Not keen on single girls working one of his patches. An' I kept refusing. Then he had me beaten. Just bruises. The bloke he sent said I wasn't to be marked. Permanent, like. Not this time. Just enough to see me starve for a few days. If I said no again, it'd be a different story. He wasn't lying. That's when Sinclair found me. The next day he brought me here."

Garfield glanced at Flora for confirmation then turned back to Sarah. "You've had dealings with this man before?"

"Wouldn't call 'em *dealings*. Threats, more like. But I came across his name more than is healthy for anyone."

"How much d'you know about his business on the docks?"

"I've heard from some of the girls who work for him. They get given stuff. Stuff to make 'em quiet or loopy. Comes in at the docks. The girls wait for it every Saturday. Sometimes they get told to give it to the customers. Either from the madame or the men themselves."

"Any idea where it comes from?"

"I can tell you that." said Flora. "His shipments only come from one of two places; New York or Jamaica."

"Then he's importing opioids or cocaine illegally

from across the pond and distributing them through his businesses."

"But those things are legal, aren't they?" said Mick.

"They are, but the trading and importing of them was banned last year. Though actually catching the bastards is damn-nigh impossible. Sorry ma'am." Garfield had the good grace to bow his head at Mrs Frobisher's glower.

"You alright, Mick?" asked Flora.

"Course." He shifted in his seat and ignored everyone's gaze.

"What about this link between Dempsey and Broderick? I mean he must be offsetting these dodgy dealings with whatever his legitimate businesses are. Or visa-versa. Must be some digging to be done there?"

"Don't suppose we could convince your missus to do the digging for us?" asked Garfield but Flora pursed her lips.

"No. No way. I'm already pushing my luck just trying to keep her away from him."

"Just an idea. We'll do it the old-fashioned way."

"Which is?"

"Break into his office."

Outside, Flora grabbed Mick's elbow before he could escape.

"You alright, pal? You seemed a bit nervous in there."

"I'm fine."

"Really? 'Because I'd hate to think you were in any

sort of trouble. Like the kind of trouble that comes off barrels and whore's fingers."

"All fine, Sink. Swear it."

"Good. Because I wouldn't like to believe you'd lie to an old comrade."

He hopped on his toes for a moment or two and ruffled his ginger hair. "Look alright. Alright. I got some stuff from him. Well, not from him. One of his whores. 'Try some of this,' she said. So, I did, only I've been trying it ever since and I can't bloody stop myself. I've tried, Sink, honest I have, but it's the only thing that stops the pain in my arm."

"What stuff, exactly?"

"I dunno. It's white, like a powder or sum-mink, you snorts it, and it makes you feel good. Thing is, I don't remember what happens afterward. I dunno whether I've worked my nuts off or not. You're just sort of, floating."

"Hoi, snap out of it, man." Flora smacked his jaw. "Maybe some good will come of your after dark amusements after all." She said, once he'd managed to re-focus his eyes. "But once this is over, it stops. Understand? I'm damned if I'm going to let a mate of mine fall by the wayside. Agreed?"

"Agreed."

"Good. What's the name of the girl who's been feeding you this stuff?"

"Nell. Gorgeous Nell."

"I'm probably going to regret this, but I want you to go to Nell and find out what you can. Don't let her give you anything until you've found out something useful."

*

"You're home."

Katie turned in her seat. "Of course. Where else would I be?"

"Oh, I just thought you might have been out with your new best pal."

"He's not my 'best' anything. It's purely a business arrangement, nothing more."

"That how he sees it?"

"You're not getting jealous, are you?"

"Does he?"

"Flora, I thought we settled all this last night."

"And you're avoiding my question."

Katie shrugged and turned back to her drawings. "He sees it in whatever way he chooses."

"But you're not encouraging him?" Flora rest her hands on the back of Katie's chair.

"Of course not."

"Kate."

"I'm not. Deacon's always had designs on me, that's true but my designs are strictly in dresses."

"Look me in the eye and say that." She dipped her head next to Katie's, her voice soft. "Look me in the eye and tell me you're not playing dangerous games, Kate."

Kate tilted her face so that her breath tingled Flora's lips. "I am telling you now and once only. I have no interest in Deacon Broderick but for his money and business connections. That's all."

Flora sighed. It still wasn't an answer, but she could tell she was erring perilously close to the edge.

"And what's more, while Deacon may be a bit of a letch, there's nothing dangerous about him. He's merely persistent. A quality I can use to my advantage if I'm clever about it."

And there it was.

"Kate, I may have reason to believe Deacon Broderick is not the man he claims to be."

"I see. And your evidence?"

"Gathering."

"You're gathering evidence on the man poised to springboard my career. This is a new low for you." She pushed on Flora's chest. "Are you really so petty that you would stoop to making such spurious accusations based on nothing but a dislike? A personal grudge because you see me as some sort of property that no one else can have?"

"Property? You weren't acting much like property last night! I took you the way *you* wanted to be taken, you made damn sure of that. Guilted me into it, too. All because I went out for a night."

"That was absolutely *not* what happened!"

"Then what?"

"I-, I felt-... nothing. It doesn't matter now."

"Now you listen to me, Katie Vaughan-"

"No. You listen to me. One of these days you are

going to get it through your thick skull that I only want you. I have only ever wanted you. I just hope I'm still here when you do."

"What the hell's that supposed to mean?"

"It means you're going to drive me insane with your constant doubting. You do it all the time, Flo. You're making me doubt myself."

"I, I never meant..." Flora faltered and gazed about the room.

"Too late. You always have and you'll never change. Now if you'll excuse me, I'm going to wash then I'm going to cook us some dinner. I assume you won't object to that."

Flora could only nod.

"What the hell just happened."

*

Dinner was consumed to the hollow clanks of forks on China. As soon as her plate was cleared, Katie returned to her pencils and Flora went to clean up.

"That doesn't look like one of your usuals." Flora peered over Katie's shoulder, watching the way the candle-light flickered off her lover's nose.

"Because it's not. It's for me."

"You?"

"My house. Or what will be. When I open. I'm stockpiling designs."

"Makes sense. Do you have the clients for them already?"

Katie nodded. "A few. On the quiet."

"That's wise." She stroked tendrils of black hair from the nape of Kate's neck and watched the tiny pinpricks rise from her skin. "You've never really changed, you know that?"

"Haven't I?"

"It's not a bad thing. On the rare occasion I stop to look in the mirror, I find more and more greys that weren't there before. An extra line or two. But you... you're the same woman whose flame-kissed face I fell so much in love within that dressing room at The Gaiety."

"Perhaps I've changed in other ways."

"Aye, perhaps so. You're a woman of industry. Never one to stand by and let things happen. And I'm sorry."

Kate leaned into Flora's hand. "I know. And I love you. I just wish you would trust that and trust my instincts as you do your own."

"That's fair."

Kate twisted her neck and kissed Flora's palm. "Go to bed. I'll be through in a while."

"As you say. Oh, I got a letter this morning from Bill. He's in London next week for some conference or other. The old boy's finally gone and gotten himself married. I don't suppose, I mean, if you'd feel like maybe going out for dinner with them? He is my oldest pal, after all and, I'd like to, well..."

Kate's face softened. "You are silly at times. Of course, I want to."

"Great. I'll send word we'll meet them next week. He's staying at The Rag."

"The what?'

"The Rag. It's the officers club up Mayfair. Suppose he's trying to impress his bride."

"Probably. Night Flo'"

Katie sighed and turned away from Flora's retreating footsteps. Her gaze fell on a scrap of brown leather, a needle poking halfway along a tramline of tan stitching. She picked it up, turning the cloth over in her fingers and jumped when the tip of the needle pierced skin. She shook her hand in the air before taking her thumb between her lips and suckling at a tiny bubble of blood. She stared again at the piece of leather.

"I don't even know what's real anymore. For most of my life, you've barely been real to me at all. I know what you did for me was what you thought was best... but I am so angry with you. How can a mother just give away her child like that? How could mine? Now, all I remember of you is this." With an effort, Katie pulled the sharp sliver of steel through the cloth, squeezing through the thick material. The hiss of smooth metal followed by the scrape of thread.

"I can just about remember sitting by your knee while you sewed. You'd stroke my hair on your lap when your fingers needed rest. You'd stitch until you could barely see anymore. And there was a tune you used to hum. I don't even know what it was. I don't even know whether my memories of you are real or fantasy. But this...this is the one thing I know was true."

She flipped the patch of leather across the table. "Do you know what it's like? To doubt everything you are? To have no idea if your past was something real or something your imagination made up to fill in the gaps? Did you even think? Did you ever wake up in the morning and wonder what the point of you was? Wonder what was so wrong with you? Now that I think about it, I think perhaps you did." She sniffed hard and dug the heels of her palms into her eyes. "God, what am I doing. Maybe I am going mad after all."

Then she dried her eyes and banked the fire.

*

"Why do these places always have to be so bloody hot? Not like anyone keeps their clothes on in 'em."

"Well, I never! 'Allo there, stranger!"

Mick swiped at his forehead and raised his cap in greeting the flamboyant, woolly-haired madame. "Long-time no-see, Bette. How are you, lovely?"

"Don't you *lovely* me, Mickey. You haven't graced us ladies with your company in far too long. Oh, but did you ever look so smart?" Bette smoothed a hand down his shirt. "So, what brings you to my humble establishment this evening?"

"Information."

"Nothing else take your fancy? I'm sure we can find a nice girl for your pleasure... or failing that, mine."

"Just a drink, that's all."

Bette snapped her fingers at a rather well-endowed girl carrying a large jug.

Mick raised his glass, now filled with sweet, crimson libation. The plinky plonk of an out of tune piano rang out from the parlour next door, enough to cover their conversation. "What d'you know about Deacon Broderick?"

Bette stared at him.

"Brian Dempsey."

"Oh, I know very well who you meant. Why you asking, is my question?"

"Mate of mine, an old comrade. His missus might be in danger. Knocked about a local whore too."

"And you fancy yourself as some rescuer of poor damsels? Look, I take good care of my girls, but you know what half of the punters are like. They all get a good beating now and then. Stupid thing probably deserved it. Say I did know something, why'd you come gracing my doorstep?"

"One of the girls two houses down said you might. And it looks like she wasn't wrong, neither."

"I knew him. When he was a nipper. His mum an 'ore, same as me. Good woman, she was. Sweet thing. Favourite among the more refined gentlemen. One night, she made a mistake. Got herself with child. I never could see how such a gentle girl as her could've given birth to a creature like 'im. His father must've been a right bastard, is all I can think. I thank God she didn't live long enough to lay eyes on the monster he became. Monster born as Brian Dempsey."

"So how did Deacon Broderick come about?"

"He worked the docks as a boy. As he got older, of the managers took a liking for him. Took him under his wing, if you like, taught him the ropes. How to keep a business, run books, and a few other... skills. When Dempsey was about, twenty, I think, this manager died under mysterious circumstances. After he changed his will."

"Nice story but that just proves he's a crooked bastard, not how he changed his name and bought up half of London."

"I'm getting there, I'm getting there. Indulge an old madame. The boy picks up where his master left off. Uses a real business to hide his black-market dealings. Starts buying up whorehouses all up the docklands and all around the East End. But the young man always has ideas of grandeur. His supposed father was a gentleman so why shouldn't he be one? So, he buys himself some fancy togs and styles himself a new name. He had the right connections, after all. Supplied half the gents in Mayfair. Charms himself into high society, buys off the ones he can't. He changes his name to Deacon Broderick and finds a wealthy widow woman of passable looks. Enough to get him the urge now and then until he got tired of her and started coming back down the docks. If he treats her the way he treats the girls down here, I feel sorry for the poor woman."

"And you wouldn't have any objections if an associate of mine were to take him down?"

"Be a blessing on us all, Mr Micklethwaite. Blessing on us all."

*

"Wonderful! Just sign here please, Miss Day and the property is officially yours."

It had taken a full week for Caldercruik, of Caldercruik & Banks, to draw up the papers which would tender the docklands warehouse over to her. A whole week of dodging questions and neglecting to tell Flora where she was going, ignoring the devil on her shoulder whispering things like, '*She's not stupid, of course she knows.* But where were those pesky little nagging voices just when she needed them most?

Kate scratched her name on the dotted line.

"Excellent!" Deacon clapped his hands. "Shall we go out and celebrate, my dear?"

"Well done. That's quite the lady you have there, Mr Broderick. And such a pretty thing, too."

"Oh, we're not-"

"You're correct, Mr Caldercruik, quite the lady indeed."

Caldercruik turned his hawkish eyes on her. "I understand, Madame. I assure you, discretion is our very watchword. All of our clients may be confident in that."

"I appreciate that, sir, but truly we are not-"

"My dear girl, you need not be embarrassed." The old man rambled on. "Mr Broderick has been most candid about your association. Now enjoy your success!"

"Yes, come along Katherine, let us find somewhere with a touch of glitz and glamour befitting London's next big couturier. And who knows? Perhaps the world!" He raised his hat in farewell as he led Katie away.

"I'm hardly dressed for anything fancy."

"Nonsense. Every debutante in the Home Counties could appear before us this very instant and you would outshine them all!"

"I think you started celebrating without me, Deacon. I'm hardly in the first flush of youth."

He halted their pace to face her, clasping her hand in both of his, which drew the admiring attention of a nearby elderly couple. "You truly have no idea, do you?"

"What?"

"You are beautiful, Katherine Day. And I count myself fortunate to be cast in the mere rays of your presence."

She bit the inside of her cheek. *I can only imagine what Flora would have to say to that.* "I fear you flatter me far too much, sir." she said, her mouth a taut line. *If only I could have introduced him to Evelyn Grayson.*

"I think not. Now, where shall we go? Mayfair? Selfridges? The Savoy?"

"Really, Deacon, it's not necessary. I'd be more than happy with a quiet coffee somewhere."

"Palm Court it is, then. I shall take you for afternoon tea then if the evening beckons, something a little bubblier. What do you say?"

She hesitated, then slipped her arm through his. "You are a generous man. Thank you."

*

Across town, Flora, Mick, and Garfield sat round a corner table in the smoky Royal Oak. Garfield grunted and slapped at his case files, now stuck on layers of ancient beer.

"That looks like an awful lot of paper with not very much on it." said Flora.

"And you'd be wrong. His accounts make for some interesting reading. He's broke."

"What? That can't be right. The man's loaded. You said yourself, he's got his own wee empire."

"Yeah, but he owes more than he's earning. Too many competitors. What's more, he's been shifting funds from his legitimate businesses to pay off the sharks. The drug imports ain't cutting it. Too many sticky fingers, I reckon."

"There's always bits and bobs go missing from the docks. Most gets written off."

"Which Dempsey can't afford to do no more." said Mick.

"You mean Broderick." said Flora.

"I call bastard, either way." said Mick.

"There's more." said Garfield. "This wife of his, you say you've never met. They got married in Saint Patrick's."

"Alright, they're Catholic, so what?"

"She is, he ain't. Now, she can't shunt the bastard. Or rather, she won't let him shunt her."

"The girls in the brothels certainly had a few nasty things to say about him."

"Hmm. What's the betting his missus wouldn't mind seeing the back o' him?"

"Exactly." Garfield lifted his pint. "I'm willing to bet she'll dish the dirt. He's sold off their house on Russell Square and chucked her in a flat round the less smart back end of Westminster. You having much luck your end?"

Flora shook her head. "I know she's still seeing him. I just don't know how far it's gotten. She was talking about some building or other near here."

"Bloody hell. He's selling off his stock. She hasn't signed anything, has she?"

"Not as far as I know."

"Let's just hope she hasn't. I'd bet my last penny she'd get more an' she bargained for. Right, drink up."

*

Katie raised the China cup to her lips and sipped. She allowed herself a sigh as the butter-smooth, mildly bitter warmth flooded her mouth. *Tastes different to how Flora makes it at home. Flora's tastes earthier, somehow. Like her.*

"Everything alright?"

"Beautiful, thank you. I was just thinking."

"Oh?"

"Nothing important." She replaced her cup and saucer on the table. "About the small things we take so easily for granted without a second thought."

"I couldn't agree more. I imagine such simple elegances are a rare occurrence for you these days."

"I'm sure I don't know what you mean."

"You know perfectly well to what I am referring. You belong in fine settings such as these."

"Do you see me as an ornament?"

"Hardly. You are far more exquisite than any mere bauble, though I confess, you'd look quite wonderful by my fireside."

"And if I said I'm more than happy by my own little fireside?"

"Are you honestly? I've been watching you very closely these last weeks, and I cannot help but note a certain change in your demeanour of late. You should be delighted! You're about to achieve you're every wish, yet I find you worrisome."

"I don't know what it is. Perhaps because I haven't been altogether honest. With Sinclair. He doesn't know the full extent of our involvement."

"I'm certainly not going to complain about that. I don't want him coming after me with a shotgun. And what goes on between two people outside the home is surely none of the other person's business. After all, it isn't a marriage, is it? You're no stranger to scandal, living over the brush, strutting the London stage, inciting riots. Therefore, I'd say you are free to pursue more refined pleasures." He reached across the table for her hand.

"What are you-? That's not what I meant at all. I meant he doesn't know about my buying the warehouse from you."

"Oh, quite so. But can you truly deny this connection between us?"

"Up to a point, no. As good friends."

"Very good friends." He slipped his fingers between hers.

"I can't be that awful, am I? I know! Let's visit your new property. It'll look quite different to you now it's yours."

She plastered a smile across her lips and allowed him to keep his hold on her as the chair was scraped out from under her.

*

The butler looked the three of them up and down, galled at the audacity of such ruffians dirtying his doorbell.

"Yes?" He asked from beneath an extraordinarily hooked nose which plucked back and forth between them like a hungry hen.

"We want a word with Mrs Broderick. She in?"

"Is she expecting you?"

The three of them exchanged looks.

"Who is it, Farclas?"

"Three... gentlemen to see you, madame, though I have yet to determine their business here."

A finely dressed lady, several years senior to any of them, appeared behind the sombre man's shoulder.

"Madame, I really do not think it wise to-"

"Show them in, Farclas."

"Please understand, I didn't know what he truly

was when I married him. Not his circumstances. His... temper."

"S'alright, Mrs Broderick. You wouldn't be the first woman to be caught out by a wrong'un." Garfield scratched at his 5 o'clock shadow. Flora socked him in the gut.

"I apologise for my associate, Madame. He's all the sensitivity of that doorknob there. You were saying?"

"Deacon was still a young man when we met during a debutante ball. I'd recently been widowed, and I suppose I was flattered by the attentions of a handsome youth, especially when surrounded by such beauty. My friends warned me, of course, but Deacon can charm the birds from the trees when he so desires. And he desires much. All the usual things. Money, power... women. Deacon doesn't love. He possesses. And when this is denied him, one must suffer the consequences."

"My fiancée, Kate, has known him for years. How is it we've never met?"

"Mr Begg, I would not allow any woman I cared for to associate with Deacon. And the reason we have never met is simply because we live largely separate lives. Can't seduce his young girls with a wife in-tow."

"How much d'you know about your husband's business affairs?" asked Garfield.

"More than I am supposed to. You imagine I don't know where Deacon comes from? Or about what he truly is? It all came tumbling out eventually. These things always do. Unfortunately, it was too late. Believe me, I would have been free of him years ago if I could have, but my people do not divorce."

"You're Catholic. It'd be a disgrace tae you and your kin."

"I was already a disgrace by marrying him in the first place as far as my family were concerned. But at least I still have the respectability of a married name. If we divorced, I'd lose everything."

"So, you live with it."

"And blind myself to the things I cannot. Whatever I might suffer in his rage is my penance."

Flora stretched forward, placed her fingertips on the woman's hand and dipped her head. "If we're right, we can put this man out of your life for a very long time. It might be difficult for a time, but you'd be free of him. Would you consider helping us?"

"The desk in his study. Take these." She handed Flora a ring, attached to which, were three tiny keys. "He's been in some difficulty lately. Selling off stocks and shares. He sold our home in Bloomsbury and brought us here. He abused my father's good nature until he was forced to cut us off. I heard him over the telephone yesterday saying he has sold off one of his warehouses by the docks, but there was an edge in his voice. Gleeful. I knew that tone. Whoever's bought it has more than they bargained for."

Flora's hackles rose. "Did you hear anything else? Please, it could be important." The shift of light in the other woman's eyes made her innards lurch and Flora forced herself to breathe. "It's Kate, isn't it? You know more than you're saying."

"I know he's been after her for years. On the telephone, he made a comment about 'finally being worth the wait.' I had no idea."

Flora bent over the woman's chair and leaned into her. "Where's this warehouse?"

"I-it's one of the Link Blocks. N-north Quay. Next to the customs office."

"What's wrong, Sink?"

"Bloody woman's with him now." Flora shoved downwards on the chair and tossed the keys to Mick. "And she wouldn't damn-well tell me where the hell she was going. Keep searching, I'm going after them."

*

"You were quite right, Deacon. It does feel different this time." Kate picked her way over the detritus which littered the concrete floor, hands clasped to her lips as she spun on her heel to face him.

Deacon pushed himself from the doorframe, and walked slowly towards her, his mouth twisted in a feral grin. "Are you happy, Katherine?"

"I think so. This really is a beginning, isn't it?"

"Oh yes. A new opening. For both of us. A venture. Together."

"Deacon, I couldn't have done any of this without you. Thanks to you, I have a whole list of potential clients, contractors to turn this place into proper workshop. And I believe Mr Caldercruik will keep my affairs in perfect order. I owe you so much."

"I can't tell you how glad I am to hear you say that." He reached for her and ran his palms up and down her shoulders. "Because there is a small matter we should discuss."

The man's eyes gleamed.

"Deacon, what are you doing?"

"Now, Miss Day, I believe the time has come to discuss your payment. I've held up my end of the deal. Now it's your turn."

"My turn? But I've already-" Katie felt her wrists gripped behind her back and her body hoisted up onto a workbench, her legs forced open about his waist as he dragged her close.

"You paid a cut rate for this building. But my expertise? My connections you've already abused. You didn't think you would get away with just giving me money, did you, you little tease? Now, let's see what you're made of. I think if you can keep that brutish Scot happy you should be well up to the task of pleasing me. Of course, if you're not... I'll consider your debt quite unsatisfied. Right then, open up." He shoved up her skirts, as she wriggled her hands free and pushed at his chest.

"How d-"

"Come now, you're all grown up. You knew what you were doing, tempting me all these weeks. I've known enough whores to recognise your little game. Now are you going to behave before I- oof!" A hard shoulder charged into his side, and he hit the deck.

Flora had gone in low, a straight crack to the ribs. Most satisfying. But she didn't have time to enjoy it for long. Deacon was on her, his hands tight on her neck. *For a mincing fop, he's a decent grip on him!* She got a fist past him, aiming straight for the eye and clocked him a good one before scrambling back to her feet. He stalled. An upturned wig lay on the floor.

"What the- you vile bitch! Now it all makes perfect sense."

"I'm not the one peddling drugs and ruining folk's lives."

"Little side trade."

"Getting your girls to dope up the clients so they dinnae ken what they've paid for and what they haven't. Very clever."

"Well, it keeps the merchandise in better condition for longer. It works in their favour too. Means they get a longer crack at the whip, so to speak, until their usefulness to me reaches an end. And now, I'm afraid, *Mister* Begg, you have proven you know too much. And as for your precious Kate, well, regrettably she will have to answer for your crimes as well."

He took a run at her. She was prepared to block him but at the last moment, she caught the sickening glint of metal, just as it plunged through her upper chest. Steel sliced muscle with a sick snap of bone and costochondral.

Her vision blurred but she heard the scream over Broderick's laughter.

She gritted her teeth and wrenched the knife from her body. She wouldn't have long. The hilt was slippery, but his abhorrence at her blood on his hands gave her a split second. She thrust the blade beneath his ribcage and straight for his heart.

The pair of them collapsed on to the floor.

Another scream then cries of '*Sink!*' to the screech of a policeman's whistle, but it was all sounding very far away.

*

Days passed in a fever. If it were not for the vaguest awareness of Kate's hand, I'd have contentedly sunk into that delirium. In that place, I was aware of nothing. Every so often, her voice would breach the haze, but the words were nonsensical, and I'd twist and contort in my own sweat, the ache in my chest real again. I wanted to stay in that comfortable place of no rancour, no retribution. No heart hurt. I could die happily oblivious. But of course, you know I did not.

"There's an old mill by the stream, Nellie Dean. Where we used to sit and dream, Nellie Dean. And the waters, as the flow, seem to murmur sweet and low-"

"You're my heart's desire, I love you Nellie Dean." Or at least, that's what she'd tried to say.

"Flora!"

Flora grunted as she attempted to hoist herself up, but Katie pressed her back onto the cushions.

"Don't move."

Flora blinked against the sweat coating her eyelids. "Bit rich isn't it, you giving me orders?"

"I understand we have things to discuss but we should at least wait until you're a little more recovered." Kate reached for a washcloth and dabbed it at Flora's forehead. "Close your eyes." Flora hesitated but did as bade and Kate repeated the motion over her eyelids then slipped her fingers behind Flora's head and brought a glass to her lips. "Slowly."

"How long?" Flora asked once her head was back on the pillow.

"Four days. You scared me."

"I scared you? I'm not the one gambling my life away with gangsters."

"Please, can we not?"

"No, we can't. You and your antics nearly got me killed after I warned you-"

"You warned me? Flora, I'm not a child and you don't have ownership over me. You don't know what's best for me. I'm not your wife."

Flora frowned. "No. You're not. But I was right about this. And you wouldn't listen because you were convinced you knew better. And that bastard nearly killed us both."

"I wasn't the one consorting with... with prostitutes! Your friend, Mr Micklethwaite, told me the whole story. Were you ever going to let me in on that little secret?"

"Don't you dare judge those women for what they've had to do to survive."

"Oh, so it's different for them, is it?"

"Don't be ridiculous. You can't compare what you've done. You weren't doing any of this to survive, you did it because it was a quick fix to get what you wanted. And maybe to sting me in the process. But you played with fire, my lass. And if I hadn't loved you so damn much, you'd have gotten burnt as well."

"Loved?"

"Aye. You're as well a stranger to me, Katie Vaughan or Day or..."

"And you don't love me anymore."

"Don't be stupid. What, of anything that's occurred these last weeks would possibly persuade you that I no longer love you? Or at least I love the woman I thought I knew. Kate, you strung a major underworld criminal. Now that takes some bloody acting skills if it wasn't real. Worse still, you didn't trust me. Your ambition put us both in danger. I grant you, I doubt his wife will be too cut up that he's in his box. But I killed for you, Kate. You realise that?"

"I can't talk about this now. You should get some sleep."

Flora rolled over at the knock and Mick's dulcet tones wafted through from the hallway. She covered her chest with the blanket and snatched her wig from the table.

"I'll see myself through, shall I?" The man frowned as he took a seat by Flora's legs. "Blimey, she's never a happy bunny, is she?"

"Hmph, not now, she's not. Words have been had."

"Can't say as I'm surprised."

"Aye, she's not best pleased. But I can't back down. Not this time."

"Quite right, too. So how you feeling, anyway? Glad to see you awake."

"Dunno, in all honesty. Beginning to wish I hadn't woken up at all."

"Ah, don't say that. Look what I brought you." He fished from his pocket a folded card and handed it to her. She slipped her fingers between the edges and opened it up to reveal a long-sided photograph. "You remember that day?"

"I do." Her voice cracked. Staring back at her, were two dozen youthful faces, many of whom were never to see daylight again, disintegrated in African dust. "Where did you get this?"

"That boy there?" He pointed at a young man sitting on the floor with crossed knees in the bottom row.

"Aye, Campbell."

"Well, coincidence is a marvellous thing. He died the other week. I was helping clear his house and clocked sight of the picture. I didn't know he was one of your lot, but I recognised you. Turned out he met a girl down here too and stayed with her. So I wrote his sister and asked if I could take this for an old comrade. Maybe remind you what you once was."

"Thanks, Mick. It's good to see it again."

"Lot of them lads never made it back, I'd wager."

"A fair few, aye."

"Ever miss it?"

"Don't you?"

"Every day."

"There you go, then."

"You know, Garfield could use a man like you. He's offering you a job, once you're fit again, course. Reckons you've a knack for it. Also, he's the one who's squared it away for you an' all. Self-defence, no worries. Secretly, I reckon the cops are grateful. No one's gonna miss that bastard. Least of all his missus. Think you did everyone a favour. Including the judges what were in his pocket."

"That's good of him. Tell him thank you for me. I'll have a think on his offer."

"They raided the building, by the way. Found a dozen barrels of powder and opiates. We reckon he was going to let Kate take the rap for it and come back later to collect. She's in the clear, but afraid she won't get the money back. Oh, and those *clients* he promised her? Whores. Thought he'd get them a freshen up at a cut rate. Attract a better class of punters."

"I owe you one, mate. And you? Are you in the clear?"

"I am. Can't say I'm planning to stop popping down to see Nell anytime soon but a cockstand's all'll be happening there. I'll make sure of that."

"Doctor MacKechnie's looked in." Katie appeared in the doorway.

"Morning, Begg."

"I'll leave you to it. Have a think. You know where to find me. Miss." He tipped his cap to Kate on the way out.

"Y'know, you really need to stop patching me up all the time."

"I think what you *mean* to say is, you need to stop getting into so many scrapes where I have to patch you up."

MacKechnie occupied the place recently vacated by Mick and lifted his medical bag onto his lap.

"True. I'm just grateful you happened to be in London. And that the lads knew where to find you. I don't trust civvy doctors. That's why I make a point of never needing one."

"All part of the service. So, how're you doing?"

"Ach, you know me. Cailleach bhuan. Tha saod orm."

"Neo-fheargach?"

"Chan eil."

"So that's why we're conversing in the Gàidhlig? Because you're fine?"

"Damn it, of course I'm angry. What do you expect?"

"I can only help heal your body, Flora. I canna soothe your soul. If I were you, yes, I'd be angry. I'd be livid. But I'd get over it. Fast."

"That's easy for you to say."

"Aye, it is. But I know wounds. And unless you burn them or stitch them shut, they fester. But I've lectured you enough for one day." He cut away at the bandage covering Flora's chest, dripped water where it had stuck to the damaged flesh. "This'll hurt like the devil."

Flora gritted her teeth.

*

31st December 1913

"Here's cheers, my dear." Sarah passed Flora a glass of champagne.

Flora twisted the flute in front of one of the many candles which adorned the mantlepiece. "Slàinte."

"It's been a hell of a year."

"It has."

"I owe you for all of this. My life, Sinclair. You gave us this."

Flora's lip curled mirthlessly. "Where is wee one tonight, anyway?"

"She's somewhere, running around and driving everyone mad. Could hardly leave her behind on New Year's Eve."

Flora did chuckle at that. "Hogmanay."

"Hogma-what?"

"Hogmanay. That's what we call New Year's Eve in Scotland. *Hug yer mammy* night."

"I can't hug my mammy, but you're the closest thing Maddie and I have had to family, so?"

Flora placed her champagne aside and reached forward, pulling the young woman close. "I'm so glad you came here tonight."

"I've longed to hear you say that Sinclair. Even if you don't mean it the way I wish you would."

Flora pulled back and shoved her hands into her pockets. "Sarah, I-"

"It wouldn't be such a mad idea, would it? You don't look

like you're all that much in love anymore. Why not settle down with us? I'd treat you right, take care of you proper."

"It's not possible, Sarah. It's not possible because, for all our present difficulties, I do still love her. And I'm not interested in anyone else."

"But you aren't happy. I can see it."

"You see right, I won't deny it. But that doesn't mean I'm about to jump into anyone else's bed."

"She won't even marry you! You're blind, Sinclair Begg. A damn blind fool." Sarah left her drink stomped off. She found Katie holding court with a group of beautiful people in glamorous frocks and gripped her arm. "And you're a bloody fool too."

Katie flushed as she glanced at Flora by the fireside and tried her best to ignore the scandalised murmuring behind her back. She gave her a questioning look to which Flora only shook her head.

It was five to midnight, and the party gathered about the mantle clock, glasses charged at the ready. The windows were opened on the off chance of hearing the bells if the wind blew in the right direction. The crowd was all too much. Flora disappeared out the front door and down the stairwell. She inhaled the crisp night air.

She tried to smile at the happy couples and drunken pals that passed by but when the bells bellowed out across London, the street was silent. She went to lift her glass to her lips then remembered she'd left it behind when her hand came up empty.

A coat slipped over her shoulders and a crystal tumbler pushed its way between her fingers.

"I looked round and couldn't find you."

"I needed some air."

"I'm sorry. I should have thought twice about inviting everyone. You've never been one for New Year."

"It's the looking back." Flora took a sip of her whisky and closed her eyes.

"I don't associate you with looking back."

"Only at this time of year. It's the Scot in me."

"Can we not look forward, instead?"

"Can we?"

Kate spread her fingers across Flora's shoulder blades and eased closer until her arms wrapped about the other woman's chest, her cheek pressed to the wool covering Flora's back. "Come back to me, my love. Please? I miss you. So much."

The intoxicating scents of Katie's spiced perfume mixed with malt and dried fruit set Flora's head in a spin. She covered Katie's hands with one of her own. "I want to, Kate. But I'm at a loss as to how." She stepped out of the embrace. "I'm gonna go for a walk." She downed what was left of the whisky and left the glass on a snow-covered step. "I won't be late, I promise."

"Please, Flora-"

Flora held up a hand. "Just give me some time, alright?"

That was the last time I ever laid eyes on Sarah. I often wonder how her hard-fought life turned out. I've no idea whether she stayed with the Frobisher's or found herself the good man and marriage she so craved.

Kate and I carried on as best we could over the coming months but there remained a rift that would not go away. We never kissed except in greeting when there was a risk of a raised eyebrow if we didn't. We barely touched. Dinners were eaten in near silence. And it was my fault. Past a certain point, I could no longer blame Kate. But neither could I shake myself into making things right. For the first time, we just couldn't seem to fix things.

*

26th July 1914

"What's that?"

Flora sat on the couch, her legs stretched out in front of her, a piece of paper cradled in both hands. Once upon a time, she would have stolen up behind her, snaked her arms about Flora's torso and snuggled into her neck. Lately, any time she had tried to get close, Flora would pull away. This fear over which way her lover would jump was both strange and rapidly becoming unbearable.

"It's a letter. From Harris Stockwell. Colonel Stockwell's nephew."

"Not bad news, I hope?"

"Not directly. Whether we want to acknowledge it or not, there is another war coming. Stocker's nephew is heading up one of these new territorial battalions as part of a Highland Division. All northern boys. Never seen a day's action in their puffs. He's offering me a field commission of Lieutenant. No questions asked, that way. And I've decided I'm going."

"You... you what?"

Flora shrugged. "He needs good soldiers. His uncle suggested he write to me. I'm still of fighting age. No reason I shouldn't. I leave tomorrow morning."

"No reason? Flora, how can you say that? You and I aside, you're not even in the reserves anymore. You did your time, you're under no obligation to ever fight again. Didn't you say that Detective Garfield offered you work if you didn't want to return to the docks? Besides, you can't leave so soon. The whole idea is preposterous."

"That's not who I am, Kate. It never was." Flora stood to face her. "I'm a soldier. It's never gone away and now, I need to get something of myself back. The letter arrived three days ago. I already wrote and told him I'd head north, meet him at HQ in Perth."

"You've been sitting on this the last three days? Were you ever going to say anything or were you just planning on leaving me to wake up one morning and find you gone?"

"I'm telling you now. At least, when I was in the army, I knew what I was doing. I knew where my place was and what that meant. It was simple. Like me. Here, I'm lost."

The crack in her voice drew Kate into Flora's body and she grabbed her collar. "Then find it with *me*. Are you forgetting, I saw what you were like when you came back the last time?"

"But I can't, can I? This, this estrangement between us, it's killing us both, Kate. And the army wants me." Flora pushed her hands away.

"*I* want you, damn you. You blame me for what happened, and I accept that, but you won't let me make it right, either. Please just tell me what to do, Flora. What can I do?"

"Nothing. I don't blame you. Alright? I don't. Broderick was a bastard."

"Then what?"

"You convinced that...man, that you wanted him. You had him believing you were his to be taken. All because of your damned ambition. Because it was the quick and easy way to get what you wanted. And now I can't help wondering how good an actress you've really been. I know now why you got so angry with me when I pushed you on it. It's because as wrong as I might have been for the way I went about things, there was a great deal of truth to it."

"I'm going to pretend I didn't hear that because the Flora I love would never say such a vile, cruel thing. It's true. I felt dirty. *He* made me feel dirty. And I regretted every single second of it, even while it was happening. But look how you reacted? How the hell was I ever supposed to come to you? I had no choice but to watch you walk away once before, not knowing if you'd ever come back to me. Don't you *dare* make me do it again!"

"I'll be gone on the first train. Consider my debt paid in full."

The hallway door slammed behind her.

"FLORA!"

I was gone before the sun rose. It was the most stupid thing out of a very, very long list that I'd ever done. But it was already too late to take it back.

17

＊＊＊

"So that's it. Your wife's a crackpot."

It had taken some time and no small amount of pleading to get him to come over. To his credit, Jim had sat patiently throughout her story. Now his face reddened but whether it was the logs snapping in the hearth, or silent fury, Laura couldn't tell. "Please, say something."

"Have I ever really known you?"

"That's a fair question. And the hard truth is, probably not. Not all of me."

"Hardly anything by the sounds of it. I just don't get it. Why?"

"How do you tell your husband that your entire marriage has been based on a lie?"

"You never intended on saying yes to me, did you?"

"No."

"So why?"

"Fear. I was scared of being alone. I was still reeling from everything that happened. Coming home, felt like a different planet. I hit the party scene big style. Every morning was a fresh hangover. Then there you were. White charger and everything. We got on. You made me laugh. You were kind.

But I never intended on loving you. The more time passed, the harder it became to tell you the truth. I won't insult you by trying to pretend I didn't lie to you, that I just omitted truths. You deserve better."

He nodded, his jaw working back and forth. "Does anyone else know?"

"Clara. I hit a low point one night and just blurted out the whole thing. She held me as I cried. We woke up on the floor together. That's when I made the decision to shut my past away. Place it in a box and never look at it again. That was just after you proposed."

Jim blew the air from his lungs with careful measure. "It's not like I don't get it. In a logical way, I can see it. How it all happened. One thing leading to another. But none of this is logical. Do you even want to be married to me anymore? Or to anyone?"

"I understand. And I don't know, is the answer. Marriage never really felt on the cards after Afghanistan. Even before, it was all about career. I never considered playing happy families. But you came close." She placed her hand atop his, but he pulled away and regained his feet.

"Came close? Sounds like you've already made up your mind. Was I ever going to get a say in any of this?"

"I never intended any of this, Jim."

"Laura, you were never going to tell me!"

She sighed. "You're right, again. You're right. I'm a terrible person and a liar and a horrible, horrible wife to you."

"Yep, pretty much."

Despite the situation, they both started laughing.

"Oh god, this is awful, isn't it?"

"Aye. It is. I can't pretend otherwise. Anyway, I'm gonna head back up the road to Geordie's."

"What's his couch like?"

"Not bad. It's comfier than it looks. And his missus cooks a braw stew. Old-fashioned, like."

"And that suits you, doesn't it?"

"It does. Maybe that sounds wrong in this day and age, but that's what I'm looking for."

"I really am sorry, Jim. I made too many assumptions."

"You did. So did I. But I can't deny I'm angry. I'd like to think that at some point over the last however many-"

"Five."

"Five years of marriage, you could have been open with me at least once. Could have trusted me. You trusted your mates more than the man who's shared your bed all this time. I was always honest with you. Brutally, at times maybe. And maybe I've been a bit dense. I'm just a bloke, Laura."

"You're not 'just a bloke.' You never have been. You're one of the good ones."

Laura opened the front door, but he hesitated on the doorstep. "Did you ever love me? At all?"

She bit her lip and he turned away. "Jim, wait. I'm just trying to find the right words."

"It's a yes or no question, Laura."

"I did love you. Part of me still does. Just not in the way you want me to. For a long time, I really did believe I'd fallen for you. But as time went by, you felt more like a brother to me."

"Oh aye, a brother you'd shag at nights when you got the itch, eh? There's a word for that."

"Look, I'm trying to be honest with you but you're not making this any easier."

"Oh, I am sorry. I'm sorry I'm a little bit pissed off that my wife's just told me our entire marriage has been a sham. Sod it, I'm away. Goodnight."

"Night Jim."

He set off on the path back up the Strath to remote Rhilochan. He could have taken the van, of course, but had started out that evening with a feeling he'd be needing the walk by the end. It was a healthy hoof, and he was suitably worn out by the time he made it to Geordie's front room.

"How'd it go, then?"

Jim covered his face with his hands as he dropped onto his boss' sofa. His bed for the night.

"Not so good by the look of you. Had hoped you wouldn't be back the night." Geordie handed him a glass of something suitably smoky. The older man must have been working late as he hadn't bothered removing his lurid orange hi-vis trousers. His matching mud-splattered hard hat tossed on the telephone table. "Sheenagh's already gone up for the night."

"Well, you were overly optimistic. I dunno, pal. I got more than I bargained for. She's got problems. And I could deal with that, I think. But she doesn't want there to be an 'us' anymore."

"You can't mean that, surely?"

"She's not the woman I married." He shrugged. "And I'm not the bloke she really wanted."

"There someone else?"

"Nah." Jim shook his head. "That much, I'm certain of. I don't think she wants anyone."

"She wants a divorce?"

"Guess so." Jim took a long swallow and helped himself to another pour.

"I'd go easy on that stuff, son. Is there no a chance this could all blow over? You know what women are like. Sheenagh threatens me wi' divorce every other week. It's called marriage."

"Laura hasn't threatened me with anything. She's always been fiery. It's what drew me to her in the first place. But this is something different. Apparently, all the signs have been there, I just wasn't seeing them. So I'm told. Is it so wrong to want a marriage like my mum and dad had? Laura didn't have that for long, maybe that's the problem."

"Y'know, I pity you youngsters now, I really do. Things were a lot simpler in my day. Being without Sheenagh... it's unthinkable. Back in the days when I worked on the rigs, she managed the house and brought the bairns up all herself.' I didn't even know how to pay a bill. She amazed me. And ne'er once did I hear her complain. But I'm sure if she had her time again, she'd want more from her life. Folk have changed, son. I wouldn't want to be young now. So, what's it to be?"

When no answer was forthcoming, Geordie tapped him on the shoulder. "I'll leave the sheets on the chair for you. D'you need to take tomorrow off?"

"No. No, work's the best place for me."

"Fair enough. I'll leave you to it, pal. Night son."

*

Morning was greeted with a thud at her slippers as she passed the front door. She bent to lift the thick package and turned it over to find a sender's stamp that read '**Queen's Own Highlanders Collection, Fort George.**'

"That arrived quick."

She shredded through the envelope on her way through to the kitchen but dropped it onto the table when she saw the sheer volume of papers they'd sent.

"Definitely coffee first."

As soon as the heady aroma of ground beans filled her nostrils and the first sip of warm liquid comfort passed her lips, she skimmed the headed notelet paperclipped to the top.

Dear Mrs Donoghue,

Thank you for your enquiry. I have done a thorough search through the battalion diaries, cross-searched with the officer's name and number you provided, and I believe these may be of interest to you. It does seem that your relative had a somewhat meteoric rise through the ranks- a most unusual and fascinating case! I will just mention that certain records regarding your ancestor have several deletions. It is entirely possible that he was involved with matters of a secret nature or that there were some aspects of his position which were required to be kept confidential.

If I can be of any further assistance, please do not hesitate to contact me.

Sincerely,

J.M. Gordon

She raised an eyebrow at his use of the word ancestor.

"You wouldn't mind me pinching you as a relative, would you?" she asked the empty room.

Immediately beneath the notelet were pages and pages of splodgy photocopies scrawled with streams of loopy handwriting.

"Where the hell do I start?"

A picture snagged her attention. It was a squad photograph, the kind she'd been required to pose for before her tour to Afghanistan. Printed along the bottom border were the words; **1/4th Battalion, Seaforth Highlanders, August 1914.**

"How many of you came back, I wonder?'

Something twinged in her stomach, and she closed her eyes. Memories of a half-dozen smiling faces flashed behind her eyelids, the particular feel of an arm wrapped in a camo-jacket pressed to her cheek.

Her eyes skimmed the cheeky, wide-eyed expressions of youth. Boys. Nothing more. Flora, she spotted straight away. Not just because of her officer's uniform with its double pips on each cuff, or because of her obvious age compared to the rest, but because of the eyes which stared straight out from the grey glaze. Laura had come to know that hawk-like stare so well. "It's almost like you can see me too." While the others appeared frozen, a single instant of life captured on a plate, Flora seemed so alive by comparison. "You found where you belonged."

The sergeant to Flora's right looked oddly familiar too. Laura wandered through to the little study room where she'd stored the biscuit tin of pictures and rifled through until she'd found the one she was looking for. *It's that picture I found stuck to the mirror that day when I went daft at Jim for moving things.* She hadn't paid very close attention to it before, but in the kitchen where she could compare the two images side-by-side... "you're the same."

Close-cropped dark hair, overly sincere but with an undeniable twinkle in his eye and brandishing three bold stripes topped by a single crown on his arm. *He's a handsome devil, I'll give him that. I certainly would. Shut up brain, have some respect, for God's sake!*

There was nothing written on the back of the image save for two tiny letters in blue ink, so faded she couldn't make them out.

The next easiest document to make sense of was the one marked, **Record of Service**. "These haven't changed much, thankfully."

There were two of these. The first was a medal card, the type held for every service person on issue of medals. This, she dismissed.

The second was several pages long. "My god, Flora, you were a busy woman."

Date of embarkation; November 1914, landed at Le Havre...

18

6th **August 1914**

"Come in, Begg. I've been looking forward to meeting the man my uncle speaks so highly of. It was he who suggested I write to you in the first place."

"Glad to be here, Sir." said Flora as she accepted his hand, though she did wrinkle her nose. *Boarding school brat.*

"Take a seat Sinclair. I think you should know right off the bat, I am aware of your uniquesituation. I remain somewhat shocked, but my uncle assures me that I am not to allow that to deter me. He tells me you proved your worthiness on more than one occasion and that I couldn't hope to have a better soldier at my side. My uncle, as you know, is not an effusive man by nature and therefore I trust his word on the matter and no more shall be said. I understand Major MacKechnie is also cognisant of the matter and has passed you fit for service. So, no more need be said as long as you maintain the secrecy of your identity. Clear?"

"Thank you, Sir."

"Excellent. You certainly look the part, anyway. I confess, I'm pleased to have such experience under my command. My uncle regularly regaled me with tales of your exploits in the desert. In fact, you will find one or two of your old comrades downstairs. It is my bitter regret that I have not yet seen shots fired in anger, myself. So far, my own service has been a matter of teaching civilians to fire on a static target. I need steady hands at my side to show the younger lads how it's done. As a veteran of the last war, you will already command their respect."

"I don't believe you should be so hard on yourself, Captain. You're not a Stockwell for nothing. You doubt that, even for a second, and the men'll ken it. Should think yourself lucky. You don't know what's coming. Such a thing should make you brave, no' feart."

"And does knowing what's coming make you 'feart,' Lieutenant?"

"No one truly knows what's coming, Sir. If we did, we'd all spend our lives running the opposite way. I can't say I've never had doubts, can't say I've never questioned my actions or those of others. But I believe in duty, as every man should. Your uncle was a great man. He taught me as such."

"I thank you for your candour. You'll find your sergeant-major doing his best in the drill yard and there's a, discreet, tailor expecting you for a fitting this afternoon. We received orders just yesterday to arrive in Bedford for inspection in a little under a week. You have until then. Oh, and, uh, welcome back to the Seaforths, Lieutenant."

"Thank you, Sir. And don't worry, we'll get 'em in shape before the off."

"Come on, come on, step lively, lads!" The sergeant's gruff bawls rattled about the stone quadrangle.

The troop of part-time squaddies slugged at a most unsatisfactory traipse about the perimeter, wooden mock-rifles hanging off their elbows, more like ladies handbags than weapons.

"Not much cop, are they sergeant?"

The burly uniformed figure halted his chugging motions, the ferrule of his dark-wood calliper held mid-air as he turned to face her.

"You've filled out a bit. And an RSM, eh? I remember when you could barely lift a pack on to your back."

"Christ preserve us. Sink?"

"Aye, lad."

Drew Barclay's pace stick clattered on the concrete as he made a grab for her hand and pulled her in for a thump on the back. "God almighty, I swear as I stand here, I can't believe it. You're not jumping back into the line of fire, again?"

"I am, lad. Where the hell else would I be, eh? Can't let you have all the fun, can I? Stockers the Younger up there offered me a commission." she said and held his shoulders.

"And we're gonna need you. They're saying it's gonna be over by Christmas but no sure I believe it myself."

"Old sweats know better."

"Aye. This lot think they're heading off on a jolly."

"Canna say as I blame them. We just need to make sure they're as prepared as we can get them. Rest's up to fate."

"I've seen you change fate, Sink."

"Mebbe. But somehow I reckon this time's going to be different."

30th September 1915

Kate,

  We've been stuck in some god forsaken hellhole called Loos.
Young copped a Tuesday. Whole battalion did. In
all my years as a soldier, I've never seen anything of the like. They
say as it's getting called, was successful but looking around
* We have this land, grey and barren. The*

"This is getting ridiculous." Katie slapped the letter onto the desk and flopped back in her chair.

"Knock, knock?"

"Yes, Mrs Belfridge, what can I do for you?"

Mrs Belfridge was a rather forbidding if genteel lady of Edinburgh. Ever smothered in black crêpe, Katie had been quite terrified of her when the elder woman had turned up on her doorstep demanding a job.

"I came to see if- oh, but you look as though you were in the middle of something. I can come back later."

"No, it's quite alright. It's illegible anyway. I've never had the heart to tell him none of his letters make it through the censors unscathed."

Mrs Belfridge peered at the mottled paper. "May I?" At Kate's nod, she turned the pages over. "Written in pencil. Excellent. Have you a notebook, Miss Day?"

"Yes, why?" she asked, already having opened one of her desk drawers.

"Allow me to let you in on a little trick." Mrs Belfridge proceeded to lay Flora's letter onto the proffered notebook and scrubbed her pencil over the back with great vigour. She repeated the process again until an impression formed. "Letters are censored with ink. It can't remove the indents left by pencil marks. You might not be able to read every word, but you'll get the gist."

"You have hidden depths, Mrs Belfridge. Where on earth did you learn such a technique?"

"My husband, god rest him. He was in the diplomatic service."

"He taught you well. Thank you. A bit of a come down, isn't it? Wife of a diplomat to working for a glorified dressmaker?"

"The come-down, Miss, would have been destitution. Your employment allows me comfortable living and one whereby I can feel in some way useful. I'll come back later about the fabric requests."

"You're very kind, Madame Belfridge."

Belfridge nodded and took her leave.

Katie glanced about the office. She hadn't done much to it since she'd moved in. It still had an intensely 'old man' atmosphere, all dark woods, and decrepit cabinets. But its greatest attraction was the nice bottle-shaped present the previous tenant had left behind in the top drawer. "Never understood what Flora saw in this stuff before." She raised a tipple in front of her nose. "Here's to you."

Somewhere on the Western Front, 14th July 1916

The way the sound echoed among the trees was disconcerting. Her own breath sounded obnoxiously. The woods were an eerie anathema to the pockmarked moonscape of No Man's Land. There was nothing peaceful about the smoke which drifted in the spectral light. She hated it, but it was a necessary evil. She'd given the nod to Barclay and disappeared.

Lifting herself out of her squat, she straightened her kilt and made sure everything was in the correct place. She found a pothole at the wood's edge and shook her hands through the muddy water then dried them on her tunic.

At least where the trees were thinnest, she could keep a weather eye for any disturbance, friendly or otherwise.

Dearest,

I was sorry to hear about Captain Stockwell, I understood you'd grown rather fond of him in your time together, though he sounded nothing like his uncle. I'm sure the Colonel appreciated that the news came from you. I can't think of anyone better.

When I read your letter, I could almost hear your reluctance at taking over command, even if only temporarily. Far too high and mighty for the likes of me, you'd say. Made me smile. I'd say little does these days, but that's defeatist talk, isn't it?

I've abandoned fashion almost entirely for the time-being and turned the workshop over to balaclavas and canvas bags for the boys. Who knows, you might even be wearing one. It'd be funny to think. I've even hired a second-in-command, Mrs Belfridge. God only knows what I'd do without her now. Go to pieces, probably.

I know you don't get much time to write and you've far greater responsibilities now.

Thinking of you always,

K

Flora crumpled the letter and tossed it in the dirt. To the eyes of an outsider, it was a perfectly polite letter. *Aye, from an aunt or a bloody cousin. And now you can't damn-well do anything about it because you're stuck here like the stupid arse ye are.*

Heaving herself to her feet, she retrieved the balled-up paper and made her best attempt at smoothing it back out again. "What did you expect? Damned idiot."

"Quiet today." Private Burns poked his eyes above the parapet, his bayonet sticking up beside him.

"Well, it won't be if you keep doing that, ye great loaf. Get yer heid back down!"

"Sorry."

Private Grant ignored the slip and carried on shining up the rifle bolt in his hands. "You're new here but you'll learn quick. Or get your head blown off, whichever comes first."

The young man paled.

"Only a joke, laddie. Have to keep your spirits up out here."

"I suppose getting blown up is funny?"

Grant shrugged. "You'll be laughing soon enough, boy. When you've passed through enough roads straggled about with bits of man and beast and can't tell which is which anymore. Aye. You'll laugh because you can't find it in you to do anything else, knowing you'll likely be joining them soon. But then, maybe not." He grinned and fished out a tarnished hip flask. "Where are you from, lad?" He handed him a cap full of amber liquid.

Burns stared at it wide-eyed and swallowed in one. Grant laughed at the boy's recoil and offered him another dram.

"Dunfermline."

"Fife? What on earth are ye doing in the Seaforths?"

"I was in Edinburgh on family business when the recruiters came through. Next thing I knew, I'm drummed up to the castle and being sworn in. Mum begged da' not to send me on such an errand in case the army got me. But he did anyway. I couldn't swear to it but I'm sure the old bugger looked smug when I got home and told them I'd got my marching orders."

"Dunno what to say to that, save you're one of us now. Here's tae you, son."

"Cheers."

"Ha! Cheers. Slàinte, boy, slàinte. You're a highlander now. A kilt-wearing, whisky-soaked highlander."

Chagrined, Burns smiled. "Slàinte. Decent bunch, though?"

"The best and am no biased to say so."

"Captain seems a bit funny, though."

"Ho, don't let the RSM hear you say that. Thick as thieves, those two. Came through the Boers together."

"Do I hear my name being taken in vain, Grant?" Barclay's head popped out from a nearby dugout.

"Nah, not at all Sarge. Just telling this one about how you and the captain were in the last lot."

"We were indeed. Damn-sight different to this, though. Like sticks and stones compared to bombs fill't wi' shrapnel. Not to worry, though, Burnsie. We'll look after you. What's that you're boozing?"

"Last o' the whisky my missus sent. Want some?"

"Aye, go on then. Don't tell Captain Begg." he said, accepting the flask Grant rattled in front of his face. He had just the snippet of a second for a quick glug before said Captain stomped through the trench and straight into the officer's dugout. Grant stuffed the illicit drink back into his tunic, but Begg didn't appear to have noticed. Barclay frowned and gave it a second or two before he ducked in after her.

In the candlelit gloom of the interior that stank of dead earth and decomposing wood, Flora had already flung her cap on the desk and christened her mess tin with something spiced by the time Drew joined her.

"Not quite single malt but it does the job." said Flora, sipping at the pour of rationed rum as she slumped back into her chair.

"What happened?"

She glanced at him and unfurled the offending note from home. Drew hesitated but gave it a skim.

"Not any better then?"

"I really tried with the last one. I did."

"You can't fix this with one half-decent letter, Sink."

"I know but what else can I do? It's not like I can just pop round with flowers and a sorry smile."

"Well not you, anyway. You'd probably whip them off a grave."

"Excuse me—"

"Oh, come on. You're not exactly the most romantic, are you?"

"And how would you know, like? Come to that, why is it you've never married, yourself?"

"I don't think that's allowed." Drew took the spare seat and pinched a sip from Flora's tin.

She cast him an exasperated look. "You know what I mean. You're a good bloke. Handsome. Almost as humorous as you think you are."

"We're not discussing me, but since you asked, I'm a soldier."

"Bollocks. Loads of soldiers get married, same as everyone else."

"Alright. I never found the right one."

"And what kind of lass would be the right one, then?"

"One that you'd approve." He stole another glug to which Flora replied with another healthy pour.

"What?"

"You're my oldest comrade, Sink. Took care of me better than any parent, showed me the ropes. You think I could ever settle on anyone who couldn't measure up to your standards? If I was ever to marry, she'd have to be someone you'd be alright with. And I've never found her yet."

"Promise me this, Drew. When we get out of this, you won't wait any longer. Marry the first girl you fall for and don't regret an instant. To hell with my approval."

"I dunno. This isn't Zulus flinging spears or Boers shooting Martini pop guns. But a deal's a deal. Only if you fix things with Kate."

Flora sighed. "What the hell am I going to do?"

"As we've established, I'm no expert. But you've time yet. Keep it simple. As soon as you get some leave, go steal thae floo'ers and say you're sorry. I guarantee she'll have missed you enough to forgive."

"Credit me with some decorum. I'll buy them from the train station."

Drew chuckled and moved to take his leave. "Will that be all, Sir?"

"No. Tell Grant if he's going to drink, either do a better job of hiding it or at least bribe his commanding officer with a wee dram."

Somme, 21st July 1916

There hadn't been enough time to prepare. The morning had been a shower of frantic orders and haphazard emergency ration-packing before a forced march through what was left of Fricourt and its maze of crumbled trenches where occasional arms and feet jutted through the mud walls, then on up to Mametz. The roadsides were packed with begging refugees and all around were stray men of scattered uniforms hiding behind dead eyes. Above, floated the absurdly cheerful shapes of great hulking balloons. The nearest guns were distant enough to allow the zip, zip of the Royal Flying Corp's finest to be heard dipping in and out of the clouds. *Poor sods*, thought Flora, *they've got even worse chances than us.*

On the final approach to Mametz, her eyes began to well up as the acidic vapour of tear gas burned the back of her throat. All around, the land was pockmarked and grey beneath the summer evening's sun.

They arrived at 0300hrs to take over the ludicrously named 'Happy Valley' trench, only to find the earth rocking beneath their feet as the German bombardment attempted to blast them to bits. Though based at the edge of the woodland, the shattering of windows from the nearby ruined village could be heard over the shellfire. The blood oozing from a thousand rotting corpses filled the thick air with a coppery taste and the starbursts illuminating the night sky had a hazy, otherworldly quality.

Time to go.

The entire 51st division moved as one in single files, bolting as fast as they could from shell hole to shell hole across No-Man's Land, a hail of explosions raining down on them from the incessant enemy artillery.

Flora choked on the smoke- her lungs filled with cordite. She hadn't a hope in hell of hearing Tam the Piper over the din, yet he was only a foot or three ahead of her. Finally, they made it to High Wood. Home for as long as they could hold it. Not that there was much chance of getting any real rest until daylight- the continual flares firing above their heads from another nearby attack put pay to that. But though sleep was impossible, many of the boys, dead on their feet, swayed with closed eyes while those who were able, set to digging.

Daylight eventually broke through the smog, though later than it would have back home. Utilising an abandoned periscope, Flora got a better grasp of their surroundings. The landscape was flat, and barren save for the craters. The earth tainted with the effluence of bodies, both human and animal, which had stunk up the fog during the night. Bones crushed into tank treads, many of the metal beasts, themselves, upturned in the thick, brown sludge. Everywhere she looked were the drowned trappings of war.

She snapped the periscope shut and set about ordering the men to begin improving the trench and burrowing funk holes for cover.

"Sergeant!"

"Aye, Captain?" Barclay pushed his way through the trench.

"Take three of your best lads." She leant close to his ear.

"Head back to Fricourt and bring back supplies. I think we could be stuck here a while."

"What makes you think that?"

"Just a feeling. I don't think we're going to get relieved from here as quick as we'd like to hope. Go, be as quick as you can and make sure whoever you take has guts of iron. Alright?"

"As good as done."

"Good man."

It was dark and Drew had still not returned. Flora pressed her eyes to the lip of the periscope for the umpteenth time, but the horizon remained undisturbed. She launched the periscope at the wall of the trench.

"Christ's sake, man, where the fuck are you?"

"Here, Sir! Sergeant Barclay's returned but two of the men are unaccounted for."

"Bring him in, Mr MacKenzie, send up your lamp."

Drew staggered down the slope, sweat lashing from the man's forehead and under his oxters while crimson dripped down his chin, his gait laboursome.

"Hell, lad, what happened to you?"

"Ran into a bit of trouble. Wilson and MacKay, we lost them. We were hard-pressed to carry them back wi' us."

"Damn. But we'd nowhere to give them a proper burial anyway. God rest 'em. What news have you on the supplies?" Flora led him back to the officer's dugout, such as it was, half collapsed in at one end.

"Spoke to the quartermaster. Explained the situation. Said

he'd get food and fuel sent as soon as he could but couldn't say when."

"Aye, a fine story, that. What happened to your leg?"

"Shrapnel, I think. Just a cut, nothing more."

"I see. And that'll be why you're hirpling along there like old Father Time, then? Go and get yourself seen tae, man."

"I'm fine, Cap."

"It wasn't a request. Dressing Station. Now. Drink your tot and go. I'll not have you falling to bits for no good reason."

"As you say." He tipped his tin cup. "They're busy over there the night."

"Aye. Dunno how far but they've been going at it steadily the last few hours. Sky's lit like Bonfire Night."

"You ever wonder what would have happened if they'd succeeded in blowing up auld King James?"

Flora shot him a sardonic look. "You do pick your moments, Drew." She topped up his mug and the two of them stepped back into the night air.

"Nah, but really, you never think what the world would be like if some things hadn't happened? What if Charlie hadn't been beaten back at Culloden? What if Wellington lost Waterloo?"

"What if your mother had said 'not tonight, dear'? I suppose there's something to what you say. I've no doubt in a few years' time, folk'll be asking the same of us. Hell, we'll be asking it of ourselves." Flora glanced at the turf wall where she was leaning and noticed a couple of fingers protruding, a simple gold band on one finger gleamed in the intermittent flares. "Asking what it was all for." She poked them back into the mud. "Now I mean it. Go find a dressing station. And don't bother coming back 'til they say so."

"Aye, Sink. Just so you know, I meant what I said the other day. And I know why we're here. At least you and I, anyway. We're here because we're soldiers. And there's no one I'd rather stand alongside."

"Nor I, Drew. Nor I. On your way past, tell Corporal Higgins to give the lads a rest for the night. I've had them digging in the last couple of hours to keep them busy. I reckon they'll sleep now, even through that racket."

Barclay dipped his head and disappeared down the line.

Night turned to a day of maintaining kit in a bid to stave away the anxious wait. In the face of starving men, having still not received those desperate supplies, Flora asked about for volunteers and ordered them off back in the direction of Mametz with a stack of empty haversacks, under strict instructions not to take 'no' for an answer. One man's throat was so desperately dry, he had raised his face to a drip of water which dangled tauntingly from the edge of the trench, tainted a sick green pus, but she grabbed him by the tunic just in time. "Don't drink that, ye great gowk! Christ!"

The men eventually returned after dark with plentiful supplies, but how long would it last? Yes, her lads would have a good feed now to buoy them up for whatever was to come, but not for the first time did she wonder if they'd simply been forgotten about? Or worse, ignored. The Mametz Road was not one any man or beast wanted to roam and certainly, the men who returned, so victorious, would never speak of what the daylight had revealed.

The few stars which managed to twinkle down through the clouds that night found Flora once again in position at the fire step. Incessant rain drummed on her steel helmet. 'Thanks for blasted headache' she muttered. Although it may also have been the friendly shells supposedly chipping away at the German's defences. Word had finally flowed up the line around late afternoon that the order to attack would come this night. *And they couldn't have picked a better bloody evening!*

"Bombardment's intensifying, Sir." Higgins barked.

"So that's what all that crashing, and clattering was about. Well spotted, Corporal." *The artillery has livened up, though. Can only hope they've done their job.* There was a scramble from behind. The shushing of boots and rifle bolts. *Sister company's formed up at the back of us. Take it we'll be going first then. Course it is.* Flora rolled her eyes. *Here we go again.* "Stand the men to, Mr Higgins, fix those bayonets."

"You heard the officer, lads, step a bit lively."

The hands on her pocket watch struck zero hour and a flurry of high-pitched whistles, already synonymous with the uncertainty of fate, cascaded down the line. Flora braced her lips and breathed air into her very own death knell. *God forgive me for the souls I have just condemned.*

Higgins' shout of *Rach sìos!* met a united cry of *cuidich 'n righ* on the hand-over-fist climb up the trench wall. Flora followed the piper, her pistol raised at shoulder height. *God, I*

*envy them. I miss my rifle. You need something solid gripped in your
two hands for a job like this.*

The going was boggy. Although the shower was already
passing, the rain had done its done and their boots sunk with
each step. The flashes grew more and more blinding the further they trudged. A spray of bullets sprung from an unknown location with the accompanying tell-tale rat-tat of
machine guns. The air was choking with cordite and Flora
could barely see a hand in front of her. The piper had vanished
in the flashing fog and calls for stretcher bearers from somewhere behind made her guts twist.

"Steady lads! Keep the heid!"

Flora whipped her head around.

"Drew, what the fuck are you doing here?"

"Where else would I be?"

It was too late. She was too busy glaring at Barclay to notice the glint of metal rocketing towards them until the last
gasp. "Find cover!"

She bolted.

There was a fox hole a few feet ahead. Diving in headfirst,
her neck twisted awkwardly. It could have been moments or
days before she came to.

I'm breathing.

Dazed, she cried for Drew, but her ears were deaf to her
own voice. Slowly, once the ringing had cleared, she managed
to haul herself to the lip of the crater.

He hadn't made it.

A slice of shell casing had whipped the legs from under

him. She crawled, bodily, to where he lay, disturbingly still. She grabbed his hand and shook him. "Barclay! Up, man!"

"My day's done, Sink." His eyes fluttered and rolled in all manner of direction as he tried to focus on Flora's voice.

"Arse. Should've stayed where I put ye."

"Hmph. Sod that."

"Idiot."

Drew shook his head. "Nowhere else."

Flora nodded and pressed her forehead to his.

"You should go."

"Can't leave a friend, can I? Not like this."

"Duty first. No one gets to stay here forever, Sink. None of us."

"You've never been scared. Even as a snot-nosed kid."

"Because I had you to teach me. Now I get to return the favour."

"I swear, I'm coming back for you. I'm not leaving you out here to get blasted to bits."

"Now who's an arse? Go on. Leave a dying man be. I'll be seeing you again soon enough."

Flora shook her head and squeezed his hand. A cold sweat broke across her back.

Drew's eyes stared emptily skyward. She tilted her lips to his ear. "My laddie. Socair, saighdear." But he was right. She would mourn later. There was a job to be done. Her jaw stiffened and she set her gaze through the smoke and hail towards enemy's trenches.

London, November 1916

"Right Edith, this is your place. Now, most of the shop's been turned over to war work. Bags for gas masks, woollen socks, balaclavas, that kind of thing. One or two of Mrs Day's most trusted seamstresses are continuing with her private commissions but here, the girls are stitching canvas. That all clear?"

"Mrs, eh?" said Edith, taking her place, already stringing thread from bobbin to needle. "I've 'eard funny things about *Mrs* Day. That she's not a Mrs at all."

Madame Belfridge lifted a wooden ruler and smacked it against the desk. Every ear in the work room pricked.

"Mrs Hoplin, you came to us highly recommended, but gossip about one's employer will not be tolerated in this establishment, is that quite understood?"

The middle-aged woman flushed. "Yes, Madame Belfridge. I is only wanting to ensure there was nothing improper going on, that's all. Just an innocent enquiry."

"Get on with your work, ladies."

Belfridge and her long, black skirts swished away, no doubt to admonish some other poor unfortunate, but an eavesdropping figure remained within the shadow of several floor-to-ceiling storage units, ears straining to catch the rest of the chatter. Edith turned to the youngster quietly stitching away beside her.

"What's she like then, this Mrs Day?"

"She's alright. Quiet. Don't see her too much, really."

"What about this husband, then? Ever seen him?"

"He's off in France. Fighting."

"Huh, convenient."

"How d'you mean?"

"Well, I mean, 'aven't you heard the stories? About her being a bit funny, y'know?" She made a nudging motion with her shoulder and winked at her.

"No, I haven't and if you're not careful you'll get yourself into trouble if you carry on. I don't care what folks say. Mrs Day's a kind employer and she pays a good wage and for you to be-... besm-... besmudge her reputation ain't right. Her husband's away like all good men, and us that's left are doing our bit. That's good enough for the rest of us, should be for you an' all."

The eavesdropper's lip curled.

"You're not from round here, are you?" Edith pressed on after a minute or two.

"No." said the girl. "Came down from Lancashire last year."

"Oh. Runaway, are you? Come to seek your fortune, did you? Thought the streets'd be paved with gold, did you?"

"No and it's none of your business, either. Let me ge'rron with my work, even if you're not going to."

"Ooh, bolshy, aren't we?"

"Stop that, you." Another voice chimed in from further along the bench. "Leave the girl alone."

The shadow-lurker had heard enough and sloped off unnoticed.

"Five yards of the red chiffon was all they had, I'm afraid, Mrs Day. Good cloth is hard to come by these days, after all."

"Yes, I understand that Mrs Belfridge, but they promised ten!" Katie pressed her palm to her forehead and screwed her eyes shut.

"Are you quite alright?"

"Yes, I'm fine. Sorry. But anyone who ever said running a business as a single woman was easy, even in this day and age, needs their head examining. One sniff of a skirt and traders run roughshod over you until you may as well declare bankruptcy and pack the whole lot in. We've come so far, but it's never enough, is it?"

"No, it never is." Belfridge agreed, not unkindly. "I was there that night at The Hicks. I saw you carted off in the back of that police wagon, you, and the others. I'm not sure I'd have ever had the courage."

Katie's mouth twisted. "Someday, I'll tell you the truth about that night."

"I look forward to it. In the meantime, I'll have Harry go and *harry* the merchants. Will that be all for now?"

"Yes, that's all, Mrs Belfridge. Thank you."

Katie huffed as she rifled through a large chest of drawers and slammed several bolts of fabric on top of one another. *Why is nothing ever where it's supposed to be?* She wrinkled her nose. *Eurgh, must remember to get Albert to have a look at the drains. That's the last thing I need, all the cloth I have got stinking of sewage or whatever that god-awful stench is!*

A throat cleared behind her.

"Yes, what is it–"

A figure appeared around the doorway and halted. Barely recognisable, but for a tell-tale crinkle about the eye.

Her first instinct was to leap into Flora's arms, but she didn't dare for fear she would fall straight through, her was skin so silvery & taut.

"I've heard of apparitions. But say you're no shade. Say you're truly here? You're alive?"

The figure offered a sad smile. "No, lass. I'm no spook or shadow. Just feel like one." Beneath a top layer of rust, Flora's voice was warm and familiar. Kate eased her arms about the other woman's neck and Flora's breath caught. "I'm sorry Kate, I'm sorry, I'm sorry, I'm sorry. I've been such an idiot."

"Oh god, no, we both were." She pressed her face into Flora's tunic then at once regretted it.

She had only smelled the like of it once before, many years prior when a mouse had died behind a tiny hole in the kitchen. It had taken Flora two weeks and an utterly useless borrowed cat to find it. By the time she pulled it from the wall, its little half-mouldering body had turned green and gloopy.

Katie pulled back and kissed her, but even Flora's mouth tasted strange. Not unpleasant, exactly, but the metallic tinge was alien and she jolted from Flora's mouth.

Flora's brow creased. "You're married?"

Katie's stomach dropped through the floor. "Yes, I'm married."

Flora's entire body shook, and she desperately wanted to be sick. "When?"

"Oh, about sixteen years ago, now. To you, doughnut!"

"Huh?"

"I am Mrs Sinclair Day. Who else would I be married to?"

"I don't know, you've never called yourself *Mrs* before, you never wanted to. You said you weren't my wife."

"I know. But this war's given me a lot to think about. I passed through Waterloo one day last year, just after Loos. I saw the coffins and the poor souls coming off the ambulance trains. Their burned faces and empty gazes. I ran to the ladies and wept at the thought you might be among them. Then I went home and put this on." She held up her hand and sure enough, on her ring finger was a plain yellow band. "It's worthless. An old bit of costume jewellery. But calling myself Mrs Sinclair made me feel closer to you. Like it tied us together somehow. Like, in some small way, it made up for the awful way I behaved before."

"And if something happened to me, you'd be a war widow the same as everyone else." Katie's face fell but Flora tilted her chin. "It's alright, Kate. You were right. If anything ever happened to you, I canna bear the thought, but if it did, my grief would be that of any widow. Without you, I could not go on. Why should our grief be any the less just because the law doesn't acknowledge it? At least, by claiming you're Sinclair's wife, you'll be seen as equal. I can't fault you for that. And by the look on your face earlier, it seems you thought you were a widow."

"No! I... it's just... I can't imagine the things you've seen."

"And neither do I want you to. There are some things words can never convey. Like my love for you. It's never gone away, Kate. Never faltered."

Silence fell between them. For long moments, they simply stared at one another, absorbing the feel of each other's arms.

"Darling, I have some work I really need to finish. Why don't you come through to my office then I'll take you home?"

"Of course." Flora offered her arm. "What's a doughnut?"

"I'll buy you one sometime."

Katie led her back through the workroom, passed the ladies hard at their machines, eyes agog at the kilted officer. Flora tugged on her hand as they passed by the young Lancashire girl from earlier.

"What's your name?"

"Vicky. Well, Victoria really, sir."

"Victoria, I heard what you said earlier. Keep an eye on this one Kate, she's a grand worker." She winked and Vicky flushed. Flora tipped her hat at Blabbermouth beside her.

Katie eyed this little interaction with interest as well as the murmurs which accompanied them. *'Handsome brute too, well I never! Not that I ever doubted it.' 'See, pays you not to go gossiping.'* But she was too distracted to pay them much mind. She pulled Flora into her office, whereupon they each found a corner, Katie at her desk and Flora a chair on which to rest her eyes.

The light was turning grey, and the workroom girls gone by the time Flora jolted herself from sleep by her own snoring and went arse overhead.

Kate decided it was long-since time to take her wife home.

"That's new."

Kate led Flora over to a steaming claw-foot bathtub. She held a mysterious bundle of supplies tucked under her elbow.

These, she placed on the floor. She rose once more and slipped her arms about Flora's waist, pushing her nose into rough khaki.

Flora's hands shook. Her best attempt at unhooking the column of fastenings at the back of Kate's bodice met with mixed success. Kate cupped Flora's face and kissed her thoroughly, then took her hands in a gentle grasp and placed them on her bared chest. Lips tingled under melded breath as Kate removed the final clasp. Heavy breasts tumbled into Flora's palms.

"I've forgotten how you feel."

"You haven't touched me like this in so long."

"I've been such an idiot."

"Sh." Kate threaded her fingers into Flora's hair and kissed her again. "It doesn't matter now." She broke away and dabbled her fingers in the water. "Come on."

Flora's uniform dropped into a dirty puddle alongside Kate's dress.

The scalding water stung as she sat down but the sensation of Kate's mouth on her own was more than enough distraction. She spread her knees as far as the tub would allow to let Kate kneel between them.

"Darling, I need to tend those cuts. You're not supposed to taste like blood."

"What am I supposed to taste like?" Flora's lip nipped as she smiled while Kate reached over the side and popped the top of a tin containing some sort of salve and set it aside.

Kate narrowed her eyes and dipped a cloth in the water then brought it to Flora's mouth.

"Cinnamon. You always tasted of cinnamon."

"Because I liked apple tarts."

"Mm hmm. That was after I domesticated you. I remember when we first met. All I could taste was that god-awful gunpowder."

Flora laughed. "Aye, it was like foostie eggs!"

Kate rolled her eyes and continued dabbing at the tiny splits. "Indeed."

Flora winced when the cloth brushed against a more sensitive spot. "I certainly have made you put up with an awful lot over the years."

"No more than I have, you." She gathered up some of the salve onto her fingers, but Flora jerked her head away.

"Gah! That stinks! What the f- hell's in that?"

"Dear, dear Captain Begg. Your teacher did not do a very good job at moderating your language all those years ago, did she?"

"S'pose not, Miss Vaughan."

"That's Mrs Vaughan-Begg to you, soldier." Kate sighed. "Whatever am I to do with you?"

"I don-mmph!" Kate smudged the salve all over Flora's mouth in one big glob and laughed as she frantically tried to swipe it away with wet arms which only succeeded in turning her entire face into a gooey mess. "Eurgh!"

Once the hilarity died down, Katie turned to lay quiet in Flora's arms. They remained there until the water turned cold.

With the whiff having been cleansed from Flora's body, they finished in a flurry of towels and crawled between sheets cleaner than anything Flora had lain on in over two years. Kate's delicious body slid into hers.

"I have missed you. So very much." Flora's voice was barely above a whisper, much as her caress. "Your skin. The feel of you."

Kate's stomach fluttered beneath Flora's teasing fingertips, and she responded in-kind, but their kisses and touches grew languid. "Need a pair of matchsticks?"

"I'm sorry, love. The spirit's more than willing but the body's not crossing the picket line."

"You're exhausted. And we have an entire week to catch up on lovemaking. Sleep for now."

"Not sure a week's going to be long enough."

"Coming from the woman who can't keep her eyes open."

"Hoi, spriggan. You better believe it."

"Sleep. I'm not going anywhere."

Unfortunately, Kate wasn't the slightest bit tired. She was awake to watch every twist and twitch of Flora's fitful rest. Once, she tried to touch her, but the memory of a similar time, long ago now, flashed in her mind and gave her pause. Her chest tightened. With a huff, she rolled out of bed and left Flora sleeping.

She headed through to the adjoining bathroom and picked up her dress from the floor, pulling a face at the soggy sleeves which she examined, pinched between thumb and forefinger before flinging it into the laundry pile. Then she turned to Flora's uniform.

*

Aaaaahhhhh!

The shriek sent Flora tumbling over the edge of the bed.

Eurgh!

Flora staggered, still very much naked, towards the source of the screams and slapped a hand across her mouth at the sight which greeted her.

Sliding about in the puddles left over from their bath, on her tippy toes and her skinny legs bare, Kate danced back & forth on the tiles, Flora's khaki tunic held aloft.

"What the hell are you doing? You damn-near caused me a heart attack, woman!"

"There're... things! Disgusting things, crawling about in your clothes!"

"Ah. Damn, I thought I'd got a' the wee beasties out. Maybe no. Gie's it here, then."

"You knew?" Kate's whole face convulsed. "Ugh!" Flora took the jacket from her and inspected the seams. "Wait a minute, what's all that black stuff everywhere? Looks like soot." She cast Flora an accusatory glare.

"Aye, well that's how you get the wee beasties out. They hide in all the nooks and joins there so you just run a match along and burn them. See?"

"No! No! Flora, you are not setting anything alight in

this house. I'll wash everything properly. Just, go back to bed please."

"But washing doesn't get rid of them."

"Perhaps not, but it won't hurt either. Now go on, off with you." Kate eyed the heap of uniform on the floor. "Eurgh." She gave a final shiver and bundled everything up into one big sack and dumped in the hallway. *Mrs Pearson, the laundry woman can help me with those. Wee or otherwise, I'm not tackling those... things, myself!*

*

"You are sure it's been alright, you taking this last week off?"

"I am the boss."

"Hmm, I like the sound of that." Flora stroked her fingers under Kate's chin and kissed her.

It was a beautiful crisp morning, and she would have been a liar if she'd said she didn't enjoy the admiring looks they received; Flora, dashing in her uniform with multiple ribbons at her breast, and herself, decked in one of her very latest daywear designs. They cut a debonair couple. Walking hand-in-hand along the gravelled pathways of Hyde Park was a pleasure she had taken too often for granted in the past.

A great boom like thunder exploded and rattled about the trees.

Flora yanked on Kate's hand and hit the deck behind a bench. Her whole body trembled. Her free hand covered her head.

"Flora, what on earth are you doing? Flora!" Kate wrenched her hand loose and groped for Flora's shoulders, but the eyes that met hers were not Flora's. The darks of her pupils almost swallowed the whites whole. She was staring straight at her but there was no recognition of Flora even seeing her. Kate cupped her face, spread her fingers across her cheeks and prayed their warmth would seep through. "Please, see me Flora. See *me*. I'm right here. You're safe, I'm safe. Sweet girl, come back to me."

These words, she repeated until Flora's panic began to thaw. Her eyes darted left and right, left and right, her breathing ragged. She covered Kate's hands with her own and gripped them hard. "I'm sorry. Dunno what happened there."

"It's alright. It was just a noise, that's all. See?" Kate nodded over Flora's shoulder to a group of aging workmen busying about the bandstand and a broken-down cart where several tonne-weight of wooden planks had collapsed. Flora nodded and Kate helped her to her feet.

Fortunately, the clatter with the cart had caused quite the furore among several nannies and governesses on their daily perambulate and so no one had taken much notice. Or, if they had, they'd at least had the decency to not gawk. Kate smoothed her hand up and down Flora's chest and took hold of her hand again. "Do you want to keep going?"

"In a bit. Let's sit for a minute."

They watched the workmen for a while. Flora

smirked at the foreman who was doing his level best to placate the crowd of shaking fists and waving brollies. The tremors eased a little and Kate let her head rest against Flora's shoulder.

"Normality."

"It's nice."

"'Tis. Least for a wee bit. I forgot to tell you, I ran into one of your old heroes."

"You're my hero."

"Besides me." Flora pressed a kiss to her head. "A while ago, I ended up in a hospital at a place called Royaumont. Nothing serious. But while I was there, I bumped into Elsie Inglis. She was giving the place the old once over on her way through and she turned up at my bedside. I said 'hello' for you. Thought you'd like that."

"That's wonderful darling, thank you. Did you meet Dr Ivans?"

"Maybe. There was a high-falutin' looking wifie walking about with her but she didn't say much."

"What were you in there for anyway?"

"Ah, nothing to worry about. Just scrapes."

Kate chose not to answer at first, content to allow the day-to-day sounds of the birds and the distant rumble of wheels bring them both back down to Earth.

"You haven't said much about it since you've been back."

"I'm not sure what to say."

"You mean you don't want me to hear it."

Flora continued to stare at the workmen, now returned to their labours. "It's peaceful here."

"Yes, love. Very peaceful."

*

"I wish you didn't have to go." Kate stretched until her toes squeaked on the wooden bed end.

"Can't honestly say I'm all that keen myself but I dinnae have much choice in the matter."

"I know. It's one of the things I love most about you."

"And the one that causes you the most aggravation." Flora smirked.

"That too. What time do you leave?"

"Midday. I've managed to cadge a lift to the station."

"I want to go with you. To the station."

"If you do that I may never leave."

"And that would be a bad thing?"

Flora shifted her head closer and kissed her. "We have five hours." Flora said, on the chime of the living room clock. "Speaking of, I'm not used to seeing you awake so early. How does it feel?"

"Oi!" Kate jabbed her under the covers.

"Oi? That's hardly very ladylike, Mrs Begg, should I be concerned over the company you're keeping these days?" She laughed as she flipped them over and straddled her lover's hips. She caught the expression that flashed across Kate's features. "Sorry. Shouldn't have said that. Was a poor joke."

Kate shook her head and hooked her fingers over Flora's

shoulders. "It's alright. We can't go tiptoeing around it forever. Never again, darling. I swear that to you right now. I will never again do anything to risk us." She tried a smile. "At least Drew will be glad to see you. I imagine he's missed you a great deal this past week." Flora's expression grew sober, and Kate's stomach sank. "I'm sorry, sweetheart. Were you with him?"

Flora screwed her eyes shut and gave herself a good shake. "When all this is over, I am coming home and never leaving your side again. You have my support, Kate. I realised something the other day. I've never once told you I'm proud of you. I am so very, very proud of you and everything you've achieved. You're a wonder, Katie Vaughan-Begg. I love you."

"I love you too, you stubborn, pig-headed Scot. And you are very silly. You've always told me you were proud of me. The first time you came to see me at The Gaiety."

"That was nearly twenty years ago!"

"Ah, but I remember."

Flora pulled a face and tilted her head from side to side. She sunk back into the pillows and found Katie's hand, stroking the gold band on her wedding finger. "We should have done something while I was home."

"I don't think a church would take us, darling." Kate smirked and twisted her fingers between Flora's.

"No but, I should have made you a promise."

"You already have. And each one, you have already kept a thousand times over."

"Some of them. Can't claim all of 'em. But I meant something more formal."

Kate leant close to her, rubbing her face into the pillow, a coy smile playing about her lips. "Promise me now."

"What would you most have me promise?"

She gave the question all due consideration then tucked her nose to Flora's cheek. "Promise me you will always return to me. That's all I have and will ever ask you again."

"That is one thing I will always do." She pulled their joined fingers to her mouth and kissed Kate's ring. "I swear to you, that I belong to you and no other. Should I never come back to you, know that it was only through death in the attempt. But that will not be for a great many years."

"Good." Kate giggled and pressed her lips to Flora's jaw. "And I vow that for as long as I am on this Earth, no other shall ever have me. I am yours, Flora Begg. Now and forever."

"You may kiss the bride, y'know."

"Oh, I shall, my darling. And I shall not stop until the clock takes you away from me."

January 1919

I used to think the world was dull and grey,
The days went by each in the same old way,
And nothing seemed to matter, and life kept getting flatter,
But everything seems changed and strange today.

I never knew a sunshine could be half so bright

Or the world so fair to view.
I never knew the stars could shine so clear at night
Or that the sky was so tender and blue.

"Pretty song."

"Yes. My friend, Ellaline sent it. It's the latest by Mr Wodehouse. I find I can't stop playing it."

Mrs Belfridge regarded her. Kate still hadn't raised her eyes from the pile of invoices. "It's been over a year, Katherine."

"There's still time."

"He's gone, my dear. And it's awful but you must face it."

"No. This happened last time. When he was in Africa. I hadn't heard anything for months and it was because he was on his way home. In fact, he turned up on my doorstep in the middle of the night." Kate's mouth twisted. "I didn't find him until the morning."

"That isn't what's happened this time. And I think you know that. The war has robbed us of so many good men."

"I know no such thing and nor do you." This time she did look up, her pupils steely. A lesser woman would have withered under that gaze. "Bill said Sinclair was only missing. That means he could still be out there somewhere, desperate to get home."

"He's gone. I'm sorry but that's the truth of it. When it happened to me... when Tom fell on that god forsaken field in Africa, I couldn't accept it any more than you can now. But one has no choice. What would Sinclair say if he knew you'd turned down your big chance because you've chosen to put your life on hold? In his name?"

"He- he would-"

"He would tell you to stop being ridiculous and get on with your life. Go to Paris. Monsieur DuPont is a reasonable man. Tell him the truth. Tell him you've changed your mind. He'll understand."

"But what if he comes back? He comes back and I've gone? He'll think I've abandoned him. Our vows."

"I thought you weren't really married?"

"We weren't." Kate blushed. "Not legally. But last time he came home, we..." She trailed off, no longer able to hold the older woman's eye.

"I think I see, my dear. You made a sacred promise, and you mustn't think I don't understand how difficult this is, but I cannot stand by and watch you wish away these precious years. You honoured the trust between you in life. Now you need to honour his memory as best you can. It's time to move on."

"I'm afraid."

"That's entirely natural and right. You have to learn how to stand on your own."

"I don't know how."

"You'll learn in time. The London workshop is well-enough established and can manage on its own. You're about to start anew. Where better than a city which is also re-building?"

"I don't want to do this. I can't."

"You can and you must. And when enough months

and years pass, it'll hurt a little less. Each day, you'll breathe a tad easier. Then perhaps, someday, you might even be able to let someone else into your heart."

"You never did."

"No. But I live in hope."

19

A few weeks later, the fall of Mhairi's expression the after she opened the door made her break a little inside.

"Please don't shut me out."

"It was just so crazy. We'd been joking around not an hour before. Next thing you know, I'm in *Black Hawk Down*. All these years later, I still can't get my head round it. They were all gone." Laura clicked her fingers. "Just like that."

One recently empty, if begrudged, mug sat on the narrow wine table to the side of her chair. She swallowed, her throat dry in spite of the tea.

"I owe you an apology."

"Aye you do. But what for? For what you said or for not having the balls to come apologise before now?"

"Both. I'm sorry. I've had a lot of time to think this last wee while."

"I'm sure you have. I heard Jim moved in with Geordie up the road."

"Aileen?"

"Who else?"

"Indeed. But I have done a lot of thinking. And I really

need to get this out. I think, deep down, the only thing that any of us really want, is to feel understood. If only by one other person. Even if it's only by a stranger. Being misunderstood. Dismissed. Having someone else sweep everything away like it doesn't matter. It's the most painful thing in the world and all the self-validation crap in the world won't stop the self-doubt. My entire life, I've just been waiting for the axe to fall, waiting for the next hit to land. Always feeling like I'm wrong. Like I'm sitting the wrong way, said the wrong word, breathing the wrong way! Like I'm the most loathsome, unlovable creature put on the planet."

"You've been practicing that for a while, haven't you?"

"Yes. But it's no less true."

Mhairi shrugged. "It's no way to live."

"No, it's not. And I am so tired, Mhairi. You wanted to understand, but I wouldn't let you."

"Well I'm glad you've told me. Little late though."

"You're right. Again. And I'm still sorry. But at least you're talking to me. This thing with Jim...am I wrong not to want to be married anymore?"

"Not if you do the honest thing. The dishonest thing was marrying him in the first place if it wasn't what you really wanted. But that doesn't make you a bad person."

"I just feel like he'll never get it. Why can't he get it? You do."

"Different people have different frames of reference. And he's invested. He can't see it from your side because he's afraid of what he'll find. And, God love him, he can't climb inside your head."

"I don't think he'd want to. No one would. I look at Flora

and Katie and I think, Jim and I could never be those people for each other."

"Maybe. Maybe not. But then, people didn't have time to waste in those days."

Laura held her face so near to the hearth, the fierce heat bit her cheeks and turned them red.

"Why do you do that? It's like you're trying to burn yourself."

Laura sighed. "It helps me feel. It's the scratch of the sun I remember most. Never sweated so much in my puff. That and the stink. And it doesn't matter where you go. It gets into your clothes, your hair. Still smell it now. It's like dung and... and dry. As if you could smell dry."

"It sucks the life from you."

"Exactly. How...?"

"Just a guess. I was thinking of dry white wine. How it evaporates on your tongue and leaves you thirstier than you were before."

"That's a good analogy."

"I know."

"Eating *babies heids and arses* too."

"Now there you've lost me."

"Beef casserole with doughboys. The Yanks wondered what the hell they were serving in the cookhouse, so we told them it was 'babies heids and arses.' Scottish delicacy, don't you know?"

"Please tell me they didn't believe you."

Laura laughed. "I've no idea. It was an old joke. Put me off beef stew for life, though."

Mhairi turned the mug in her hands and thumbed the handle. "What are you gonna do?"

"I don't... alright, that's a lie. I know what I want to do. But I need someone to tell me it's okay."

"You've decided to go it alone."

"Again, how did you-?"

"You wouldn't be asking permission to stay with him."

Laura nodded.

"So, dare I ask, how's the research going? Still delving into the forbidden past?"

Laura's expression shifted. "I am, actually. And... it's helping. Or distracting. Not sure which. Maybe both. I haven't had a chance to tell you, I went to the National Library when I was in Edinburgh and this woman put me onto the museum at Fort George. They've sent me loads."

"When I suggested you might find it a good wee project to fill the time with, I never thought you'd take it so much to heart."

"I didn't either. I've never been one for looking back."

"Maybe there was a reason you came here?"

"You don't believe in all that fate gibber, do you?"

"Why not? Let's face it, you were never going to open up and talk before, were you?"

"I got pushed into seeing some army well-being woman when I got back. Didn't do me a lot of good."

"And did you ever try again?"

"Would it have made any difference if I did?"

"It might. Did for me, anyway."

"What?"

"It was years ago. When Izzy came along, and things went

pear-shaped with Dave. What, get yourself impregnated with the first bloke who's willing then drop him when it gets too hard? I highly doubt granny would have approved."

"I'm sorry. Those things I said in the hospital-"

"Had some truth. You weren't wrong, Laura. At the time, I felt like such a slapper. But with some help, I learned that life isn't as black & white as my upbringing made me believe. I thought I was so worldly; well-travelled, decent education. But where we come from has a greater hold on us that we realise."

"I think I'm beginning to see that."

"Have a cogitate on it, anyhow. There's a world of difference between having a couple of sessions with someone you've been plonked in front of and finding someone you can develop a true and unconditional connection with."

"Isn't that what this is, then?"

"Oh no, I come with many conditions. Many, many conditions. Like not nipping at me through a haze of anaesthetic when I can't fight back."

"That's fair. It's funny... well, not funny, but I found out Flora ended up in Craiglockhart."

"Craiglockhart? Why do I know that name?"

"Didn't you read your war poetry at school?"

"Wilfred Owen."

"And Siegfried Sassoon. It was a shell-shock hospital. They called it 'Dotty Ville.' Heard some mixed things about it during my time at Napier. Anyway, the regimental diary was pretty sparse on detail but a friend of mine managed to find Flora's medical records at the Royal Ed."

"And?"

"And it's pretty awful reading."

20

30th August 1917

Have taken over command of B Coy. 1/6th Batt. Unit has taken bit of a beating. Morale v.low. Previous C.O, Captain Begg last spotted roughly 10yds from line. By request, Cpl Higgins has taken search party for body recovery.

Lt. Hitchens

Perhaps you have smelled death before. Felt the thick, sweet ten-drils push up into your nose and you've no choice but to sniff, for it's better than tasting it whole. But death on an industrial scale is something no mortal can un-see. Un-smell.

I returned a stranger.

Once upon a time I had arrogantly believed there could be no more wars to fight. Surely empire could no-longer justify the ripping apart of another's body & soul in sic a way again. But I'd underes-timated man's hunger for blood & dirt.

Germany will not remain in silent fury forever. There will be more to come. Other battles hard fought. But my day is done and when God grants it, I will rest easy. We each are intent on leaving our mark on this rock. Some manage it. But in time, it is swept away in dust and mud, as all mortals are, and the world turns on as if you never were. So, what then matters are the deeds we commit in favour or foul of others in the short time we are given. A lesson those I served with learned well.

Drew Barclay's shattered bones remain in the earth where he fell at my side. His sacrifice was his legacy. I was dead in heart and mind with no such honour.

Craiglockhart. You may well have heard of it. A hellish place where disturbed men became the damned. Those of us who would not oblige the state by dying quickly enough were moved on to private convalescence when the temporary military hospitals closed.

In 1920 I was brought to Cramond House, a small auxiliary hospital by the Firth of Forth. It was once a country house surrounded by a large estate, converted by the owners in a bid to 'do their bit.'

For a full eighteen months after I was dragged from the Passchendaele quagmire, I remained silent. My body should have ached but I was aware of nothing. One nurse in particular, Nurse Russell, would read by my bedside through long nightshifts but the words made no sense. Her gentle voice barely registered. I haunted my own body like an unwelcome wraith. Behind my eyes, tracked the spectres of my former selves. Of dead men's faces.

Myself, and the others like me are forever indebted to those women who remained diligently at their posts long after the war had ended, and the world went on without us. Left to die in quiet corners. We were a sight, us broken things. But they never flinched.

We did not dare venture beyond the safety of those walls. Society was not prepared for us.

MacKechnie visited as often as he could. It was he who had me brought to Edinburgh. At the end of the war, he was promoted to Lieutenant-Colonel, attached as an advisor to some military council in the capital. My treatment was secured under his direct authority. But even he could not break my condition. Then the strangest thing happened in the Spring of 1919.

I woke up.

Cramond House, July 1920

"Thank you, nurse."

A fresh cup and saucer of tea with two biscuits placed on the side table next to her wheelchair. The teacup trembled only slightly in her fingers now. Progress.

A single keen eye which matched the colour of the surrounding pines swept as far as it could across the waves that tumbled through the estuary. Passing breezes ruffled her hair, now grown a fair length.

"You're welcome, Major."

With the glass doors closed behind her, there were no reflections, no sympathetic looks. Only the gulls and the sea.

A newspaper landed on her lap and Flora grumbled.

"Seen this?"

She huffed and flipped the paper over.

Katherine Day Set to Make Shock London Appearance

"And?"

"D'you not think it's about time you settled this and put the past to bed?"

Bill MacKechnie hiked up his trouser legs and perched himself on the low granite wall beside her.

"What do you think I'm doing here, Bill? She doesn't need this."

"For the love of God, Flora, the woman doesn't even know you're alive! She thinks you died on some god forsaken field."

"And she'd be right!"

"Don't you think she deserves to know the truth?"

"What? That I'm a half-blind cripple? Let her be haunted 'til the end of her days by the sight of *this?*" she jabbed a finger in front of her face. "This is my fault. No one forced me over the parapet that night. My choice. No one else's."

"You were already suffering from shell shock. I should have-"

"It was reckless. Nothing more. Don't go making me out to be any kind of hero. I wanted to be the one to shut him up, that's all. Better let her think me dead."

"Flora, this isn't you. The Flora I knew never cowered from anything. She'd never give up."

"Well, that's your hard bun because this is all that's left." Both fell silent.

"Have you ever stood at the oceans edge, with icy breakers

wrapping about your ankles, and wondered if the tide may catch you and pull you under?"

He'd known bringing this up would turn into an ordeal, but the man was desperate for something to jolt Flora out of her apathy. Anything but this stolid defeatism that had shrouded her the last few years. One single flare of anger might him the tiniest hope that some trace of his oldest friend was still beating in there. "Can't say that I have."

"It's how I've felt ever since that day. I let her down. Let them all down."

"You haven't let anyone down. Yet. But you will now if you stop fighting. You can walk with a stick, yes?"

"Not great."

"Well get practicing. I'm putting you on the next train to London and there's an end to it."

*

Crowds. Everywhere.

Flashes left, right which centre which shot sparks and smoke pluming through the claustrophobic air had her gripping at her chest.

Kate! Kate! What can you tell us about the latest line? Will you be opening in New York this season?

How about you and Mr DuPont, Mrs-?

Journalists yelled over the heaving throng while Flora concentrated on trying to push her way through the bodies jammed in the hall. She glanced up from a brown, woollen shoulder just in time to see her target shuffled off by a gent in grey homburg and matching coat.

"Kate!" She tried. "Kate!"

Mannequins sipping from champagne flutes floated serenely about the room as a living dream through the clamour and for a second, Flora was distracted by the outlandish beauty of what she recognised, could only be one of Katie's creations. Then an arm bolted itself across her midriff.

"Sorry Miss." The voice attached to the arm said in a Cockney rumble. "You can't go any further."

"But I know her."

"Oh, yes, I'm sure you do, Madame. Like every other wishful woman in London."

"Now, look pal-"

"Yes, yes, I know. You was best pals at school, and she'd be frilled to see you again if you could just get say 'allo. Although, must admit, you ain't the usual type." He flicked his eyes up and down and wrinkled a mushy nose.

Flora wrenched herself away and battled back through the crowd, finally finding a good use for her crutch.

Is this what it is to be a full-time woman? Christ. There has to be a back entrance to this place, surely to God.

At the end of the block was an opening.

Damn.

In front of the opening was an iron gate, several feet

high. Flora craned her neck to find the top before the opening of a motorcar door snapped her attention back through the rails. There was only a step or two between the building door and the open car.

Shit!

"Kate!" She scrabbled frantically at the rails, desperate to gain purchase. It was no use. "Katie!"

Kate paused, one foot in the vehicle. Slowly, achingly slowly, her profile tilted into view. That silhouette Flora had spent so many hours picturing. The graceful slope to her nose the full lips, and perfect cheekbones.

Flora stretched out her hand through the bars, her crutch braced between her knees. "Kate, it's me, please."

Kate slid a pair of tinted glasses down the bridge of her nose. "Flora?" She bolted for the gate and slipped her fingers through Flora's before ripping the white satin gloves from her hands, without a care where they landed, and squeezed Flora's fingertips with her own. "This can't be real."

"I hope so, though I scarcely dare believe it. You've barely changed a day. I can't say the same."

"No." Kate took a step back. "You're wearing one of my suits. It's chiffon."

"Aye. It's comfy."

"Your hair's long."

"It is."

"I don't know what to say." Kate stared at the face that, once upon a time, was hers each morning and knew as intimately as her own. But it was changed from almost all recognition. The deep-set scar that slashed from forehead to opposite jaw. The sunken right eye, turned a spectral-white, blanketed in shadow. The crutch that Flora was clearly trying her best not to lean on.

"Me neither."

"Why don't I take you home? At least we can not know what to say, in private."

Flora smirked. "Please."

Kate reached forward again, slipping her hand through the bars to caress the curve of Flora's mouth. "Stay there."

"It's been a while since I was last in London, Kate, but this isn't the way to Bloomsbury."

"Because it's not. I moved."

"So where are we going?"

"I have an apartment in Mayfair. I live mostly in Paris these days, but I like still keeping a home here too."

"Paris." Flora snorted. "Probably looks a bit different to the last time I saw it."

"I imagine so. And when was that, exactly, Flora?"

The driver twisted his neck in the front seat.

"I'll say one thing for your man, there. He's artless." said Flora, loud enough for him to hear and he spun his head back toward the road again.

"Spring 1917. I had a short leave pass. A few of us went boozing, that's all."

"I see. It was a more attractive prospect than returning home."

"It wasn't that kind of leave. None of us were much a fit state to travel."

"Was it after…?"

"Before. But it was in the middle of Arras. Gay Paree might have only been an hour away, but it was far enough from the blasted guns." Flora stared out the windows, watching as the streets got progressively smarter.

"We're here."

*

Flora wandered over to the window and gazed out over the twinkling lights of London. A door clicked behind her.

"Turn around."

Her eyes fell to the floor, but she did as bid.

"I've never seen you afraid before."

"No, I dinnae suppose you have."

"I'm not sure I like it."

"Neither do I, much. But it's the way of it now. I'm not the person you knew."

"So? Where the hell have you been all this time? Not dead, anyway."

"Just about. Or may as well have been."

"I don't follow you."

"No." Flora sighed and tapped at the windowsill. "I was dead, Kate. In mind, at least. I couldn't think, couldn't talk. Up until just a few months ago."

"How? Bill told me you'd died. That you'd never come back from Passchendaele! In fact, I saw him only a few months ago. Why would he-"

"Because I told him not to. I didn't want you seeing me like this. Couldn't stand the thought of the look I'd see on your face. I read the papers. You've done so well for yourself. You were better off. Felt kinder than making you feel obligated to... this."

Kate stared at Flora's cowered form. "You know, I look at you and so much of me wants, needs, to run to you. To hold you tight and never let go. But this other, ugly part, is so damned furious with you. Do you have any idea how many hours I have spent dreaming of this moment like every other war widow? Everyone thinking I'm mad. Only I didn't need to, did I? You've been alive all this time. And now that you're here I want to slap you. How could you do that to me? How *could* you?"

"I'm sorry. I shouldn't have come. I-" Flora moved towards the door.

"Don't you dare." Kate grabbed Flora's arm on her way past and Flora winced. The echo of those words said in rage long ago, still held so much power. "You're never leaving me again, Flora Begg."

"But this is me now. Sinclair's gone. He's served his purpose. This is all that's left."

"You are all I have ever wanted, Flora. Why did you never believe that?" She touched a finger to the other woman's cheek.

"Because I'm not good enough for you. Never was. And certainly not like this."

"For the love of god, I thought we had this dealt with years ago."

"Look at me, Kate. Look at me! Can you think of

anyone who would choose to wake next to sic a creature each morning?'

"Yes. I would. I love you. Damn you for it, but I love you. I always have and I always will. Lord-knows I've tried not to. Tried to put you behind me. For years! But no-matter what I did. However hard I tried. You were still there. In here. Driving me crazy. And yet all this time you were alive. Hiding from me. How dare you do that to me. How *dare* you!"

Flora reached forward and gripped her arms. "You're right and I'm sorry. And I will be sorry until the end of my days. I have no right to ask your forgiveness, but ask it, I must. I can't be without you, Kate. I know I've put you through utter hell but please, let's not end like this. Please. I will beg if I must, for I've no pride left."

The silence drew on too long and Flora loosened her fingers.

"I forgive you."

"Huh?"

"Flora, the things we have done, the suffering we have caused each other over the years. I would still take them all than bear the alternative. You forgave my crimes twice before. In the grand tally of things, I dare say there's enough blame to go around."

"Sounds vaguely familiar."

"Yes. Only it's the wrong way round."

"Maybe so. But for the rest of my life, I'll never forgive my own pig-headedness. I've lost us so much time."

"You have. Just swear to me, no more. I won't do this again. I can't."

"I swear. You have all of me, Kate. What's left of me.

No more army, no more running away to wars that aren't my fight. I'm not going anywhere again, if you'll have me."

"I only have one question. Are you ever going to kiss me, Captain Begg?"

Flora cupped Kate's face in her hands and just barely traced her lips over Kate's. The brief contact tingled, and an answering shiver rippled along her spine. "It's Major now."

Kate wrapped her arms about Flora's neck and pressed her mouth firmly against hers. "Well, Major, I'm not willing to waste any more time. Now, for God's sake, put your hands on me."

Flora fought for breath as their kiss grew in intensity. Hands trailed bodies, searching both the familiar and the new. Kate was still slender and surprisingly firm. Her skin still so soft. Flora cupped a breast in each hand, her thumbs grazing satin-clothed nipples.

"They've somewhat lost their oomph, I'm afraid."

"Dinnae be daft. I've still got one good eye to see with. You're perfect. Always have been." Kate's touch awoke sensations long consigned to memory but when her fingertips slipped beneath the hem of Flora's taffeta shirt, she jumped and pressed Kate's hands away.

"What's wrong?"

Flora looked away. "I'm not as you remember. Under here. I've changed."

"Darling, that doesn't matter. Not to me. Whatever you look like now, do you really imagine I would want you any less?"

"You might."

"Then you do me a disservice. I'm forty-one years old. My body's different too."

"But you haven't been sliced from stem to stern."

"It's just one more scar."

"But it's not though, is it?"

"I'm not going to know unless you show me."

Flora hung her head and didn't protest any further as Kate proceeded to undo her shirt. Despite her best effort, she couldn't disguise either the widening of her eyes or the minor hitch of breath at the sight. Flora went to pull the panels of her shirt closed again but Katie stopped her and pushed them aside.

"You weren't exaggerating, were you. Darling, I can't pretend this isn't a shock. The thought of whatever it was that's twisted your body this way makes me sick inside. But you're beautiful."

"How can you say that?"

Kate pushed the remaining material from Flora's shoulders, letting it to drop to the floor. She took the other woman's face in her hands and waited until her gaze was returned. Then she raised herself on to her tiptoes and kissed the corner of the body-length scar where it began at the corner of Flora's forehead. Inch by inch along the thick ridge to the corner of her jaw, pausing by Flora's generous lips and each closed eyelid on the way. "I can say it because it's true and because I've never stopped loving you."

Her fingers traced flame-like markings which blazed up the sides of Flora's abdomen. "Does it hurt?"

"No. Not hurt. But it feels strange. Like the skin's singing."

"Do you need me to stop?"

"No. Please. Don't stop."

Kate dropped her head, her lips finding the base of Flora's neck where the two collarbones met in the middle and the hardened scar picked up again to continue its path of devastation. Her tongue could even pick out the individual divots where stitches would have once held the torn flesh together. A single streak trickled down her cheek and filled her mouth with the taste of salt.

Flora's head tilted back of its own accord and her fingers wound through Kate's silky curls, releasing them from the tight clasp pinning them back, urging her face closer to where she most longed for the other woman's touch.

Kate reached her hip and nipped at the protruding bone, heady scents rose thick to greet her nostrils. *She's gotten so thin. Fragile. She's never been fragile.* She regained her feet, kissed the frown which appeared on Flora's brow, and guided her backwards to the master bedroom. "Trust me."

Hours later, when the first rays of dawn snuck in through the gaps in the curtains, Katie lay with her head resting on Flora's shoulder. Neither of them were much interested in sleep yet, despite having spent the entire evening exhausting each other. She traced her fingers over the scar tissue on Flora's abdomen, its appearance still raw even though it was now several years old.

"Out with it" Flora chuckled, her voice gravelly. "I still know you Katie Day and I know you've something rattling around that pretty head" she said and dropped a kiss to the aforementioned scalp. Katie hummed in the back of her throat before answering.

"Can you tell me what it was like? I want to know what happened to you out there. What it was that made you run from me."

The question was hardly a surprise. In fact, it was completely expected. She just didn't think they would be having this talk so soon. But then she should have known better. "You pick your times, don't you?"

MacKechnie had said it himself; the woman deserved the truth. Flora had put her through enough. The real story would hurt, yes, but no worse than the torture Katie's own imagination had no-doubt concocted over the years. Then again, would her imagination even be able to come up with such horrors in the first place? After all, Flora wouldn't have. "You sure?"

"Yes" came the reply in a tone which brokered no room for argument. "You're not running this time, Flora Begg."

"Darlin,' I couldn't run anywhere right now." Her legs shifted beneath the covers. "Alright. Passchendaele. Passchendaele happened."

Passchendaele, 23rd September 1917
Poelcappelle, 2200hrs

It was German retribution which had ultimately failed. Three days prior, the 51st Highland Division had captured the enemy trenches at Poelcappelle in the Steenbeek valley. The fighting had been brutal but quick. Now it was tit-for-tat as far as the officers and men of 6th Seaforths were concerned. Their brethren in the 5th battalion had been defeated over a fortnight earlier in a failed attack on a German machine gun post. Now the other side were out for blood.

It happened just as the Highlanders had begun to consolidate their victories in their captured trenches. By the time the Germans launched their counter-offensive at Flora's unit, her men were near dead on their feet but rage over the heavy losses suffered by their comrades over the previous days kept them fighting. An intense barrage of shellfire was levelled at them before a mass of spiked pickelhaubes came in great waves. In the end, it was mass slaughter. The Seaforth's Lewis Gunners unloaded devastating fire in retaliation at the German presumption. It was a Saxon blood bath, short and brutal. By the time the machine guns and artillery ceased their firing, the grounds to the south and east of Malta House were strewn with German corpses.

But that did not mean the noise of grim death had halted.

Flora staggered through the captured section of trench. An incessant wail rose above the reddish smoke. To her left and right, exhausted Highlanders hunched in corners either shivering or rocking back and forth with their hands about their ears. Their own sheer savagery had driven them beyond the limits of human sanity.

The cry was German. A kid, by the sounds of it. Trapped just beyond the line. The usual number of casualties who shouted into the frigid air in the aftermath of battle had either been picked up by stretcher-bearers or else fulfilled their obligation and ran out of blood to leave the living in some semblance of peace. Now all was silent, but this one lad just wouldn't give it up.

Shut up! Cried a Scottish voice.

"Caught up in the wire, I reckon, Sir." Corporal Higgins appeared at Flora's shoulder. She nodded and took another long look down the line at her men. Laddies just like this one, stuck in the mud crying unmistakably for mother and home. Her chest clenched at the sight.

"I can't." She murmured under her breath.

Her face set, she grabbed at a ladder.

"Sir! Where are you going? You can't–"

"Stand down, Higgins. Christ preserve us, I'll cut him free or kill him, whichever comes first."

"But Sir!"

Flora was already up and over, crawling through the mud towards the barbed defences, only half-destroyed by the bombardment.

She found him, suspended in wire, as if he'd been lying in bed when the mattress gave way and all that was left was the frame, holding his limbs aloft.

As she got nearer, she could see that, against all logic, one piece had become wrapped about his throat, half a dozen individual barbs jabbed into his neck, leaving streams of blood to trickle into the earth, too slow to kill him.

Flora stared at his face in the moonlight. To her, he

looked about twelve. "Just a chiel'." She glanced down at his body and at the gaping wound in his torso.

"Ich möchte jetzt nach hause gehen. Bitte? Ich möchte meine familie sehen." His head was tilted so far back he could've barely seen her face, but she gripped his hand.

"I can't understand you, soldier. But I can send you home. That what you want, lad? D'you want to go home?"

His speech was laboured, and another trickle dripped from the corner of his mouth.

"What the hell are you doing, Flora?"

She removed her steel helmet, removed her wig, and bent as far over as she could without becoming entangled herself.

"Mutter."

"That's right, pal. Mutter wants you to come home."

She let go of his hand and removed her revolver from its holster, raised it to just below the man's chin and slipped her finger over the trigger. She assumed the click she heard was only her pulling back the hammer, but she never got the chance to fire. An almighty blast filled the night. Herself and the German boy were flung apart, and it felt as though her every bone shattered. It was strangely euphoric. It made her want to laugh. She barely felt the landing at all. A dozen stars flooded her vision. It was pretty. Like Kate's eyes those precious moments she would hover above her and giggle.

That was how Higgins found her later. Blank eyes staring up at the stars, a smile on her face. Oblivious to the damage the shrapnel had wreaked upon her body.

"So that's my sad story. After the explosion, Higgins took two men out to scout for any remains. They found me and quite reasonably, thought the shell fragment had split me in two. By all naturals laws, it should have. They gathered up my broken body and took me behind the lines. They dug a pit, deep as they dared go and started burying when one of the boys thought they saw me twitch. Higgins told him he was talking daft and kept shovelling but by some miracle, I must've coughed or Higgins thought something wasn't right, and they yanked me out double quick. I was nearly buried alive." She shivered. "Anyway, I ended up in Brandhoek where one of the nurses recognised me and managed to get hold of Bill. You know the rest. Far as I'm aware, Higgins kept my secret. I owe him everything, but I've never been able to find him. What about you?"

Kate blinked. "What about me?"

"Paris? A flat in Mayfair. You're a successful woman in your own right. And still so beautiful. You must have had offers."

"Yes, I've had offers. But none that I accepted."

"Why?"

"What do you mean, 'why'? Are you honestly trying to tell me you're upset at the fact I haven't bedded anyone since you?"

"No. But, well, aye. I wanted you to be happy."

"A fine mess you made of that plan, then, wasn't it?"

Flora gave her a bemused stare.

"When are you ever going to learn? I wasn't ever going be happy with anyone but you and since you were gone,

I just couldn't find the urge to... seek intimacy with anyone else. There, I've said it. That what you wanted to hear?"

"You know it isn't."

"No. What's more I believe you. But I took my vow to you seriously. I meant it with all my heart. I couldn't bring myself to break it. I tried once."

"Oh?"

"Oh, indeed and I'm certainly not going to give you the satisfaction of the telling you the gory details."

"But darling, you satisfy me so well."

"Yes, and you shall have to be content with it." Kate kissed her, a single finger teased the length of Flora's neck and chin. "I learned a great deal about myself after you disappeared. I learned how to stand on my own. I didn't enjoy it, exactly. But I came out of it stronger. For the first time, I felt properly in control of my own affairs. I want you, Flora. I am always going to want you. But I don't need you to carry me anymore."

Flora grinned while it was Kate's turn to bite her lip and close her eyes. She allowed her to stew for a bit and contemplated her next words but Kate got impatient and cracked an eyelid.

"Why are you smiling like a fool?"

"You. You've become the woman you were meant to be. Without any aid from me or anyone else."

"I wouldn't say it's been without *any* aid. I've had people to call on. I couldn't have achieved anything without Mrs Belfridge. The woman's a godsend. But can you be with me on these terms?"

"Daft lass. I couldn't be prouder of you. The real question is, will you have a half-blind cripple?"

Kate pressed a kiss to Flora's chest. "Tonight, and every night from now on, I will send a special prayer of thanks to Corporal Higgins."

For many months, Kate shuttled back and forth between London and Paris. I had no intentions of ever returning to France and so, except for helping her pack and unpack, left her to it. Not that she needed my help. For a woman who went through so many identity changes, from Katie, to Kate, to Katherine Day, Vaughan or Begg, she was exactly who she was meant to be. And I loved all of them.

"Afternoon, Kate."

If she was surprised to see his head poking round her office doorframe, she did an admirable job at hiding it. "What can I do for you Doctor MacKechnie?"

"Rather a cold greeting for an old friend?"

"You're a clever man. You cannot honestly be shocked, surely?"

"S'pose not."

"So, I repeat the question. What can I do for you?"

He hesitated and drew a chair. "May I?" At her consent, he took a seat and perched his elbows on the desk, drawing her attention. "I've resigned. An action that's been overdue for some time now. I attended my final conference and announced my intentions this morning. But that's neither here nor there. I stopped by to see Flora afterwards and I have some concerns." He waited for a reaction. When he received no more than a raised eyebrow, he continued.

"Her health seems to me to be in the decline. She came on in leaps and bounds back in Edinburgh. The progress she made from the state she was in to where she is now is remarkable. But she isn't active enough to keep that progression going. Her body must be kept moving and her mind engaged. I thought seeing you again would be the lift she needed." He reached for her hand. "You have done wonders for yourself. A flat in Mayfair speaks for itself. You've built an empire from nothing. But with the greatest delicacy, I don't believe this is where Flora needs to be."

She stared at him and retracted her hand to lean back in her seat. "You're correct. The truth is, I've been thinking along much the same lines for a while. She won't say it, of course, but I see it. I see how her body becomes more crooked each day. She shakes. Her mind plays tricks on her when she doesn't realise I'm looking. Then if I come up behind her and she hasn't heard me, I practically have to peel her of the ceiling. Sometimes she won't talk to me at all, just sits for hours staring at nothing. When she wakes up beside me sweating and trembling, I can do nothing to soothe her. She coughs. All the time. I don't remember her even catching so much as a sniffle before."

"Though I'm Catholic, I've never been much one for miracles, but 'til the end of my days, I'll never understand how she wasn't blown to bits. It's only to be expected being so close to an explosion would have some sort of lasting effect. I'm afraid, the damage is done."

"She needs to go home. I have been in discussions with Mrs Belfridge here and my head seamstress in Paris. I'm going to take Flora back to Scotland. I'm going to care for her as best I can."

"I'm not sure what to say. I'm grateful. But is that the right thing for you?"

Kate folded her arms. "You're grateful? You forced me to live as a widow for three years and you're grateful?"

"I understand you're angry, bu-"

"Angry? Anger doesn't even begin to describe how I feel. You seem to forget, I have far more insight into the mind of my-. Into Flora's mind than you ever will. You may have shared experiences together which I can only guess at. God-knows, I'd never have had the stomach to live through what the two of you have. But I have shared a bed with that woman for over twenty years. It's me she comes back to, not you. Me who eases her aches of mind and soul. And for two years, you kept her from me. You hid her away in a place where I couldn't reach her. You *lied* to me."

"I admit that the bond you two share is both rare and strong. But you must also come to terms with there being a part of Flora you will never understand. Just as there is a part of me my own wife will never know but Flora does. I promised Flora long ago that if anything were to happen to her, you would never know the truth of it."

"In the event of her death, I might just about have been able to accept that. But in a catatonic state, you could never have known what she wanted. You took it upon yourself to prevent me from being by her side when she needed me the most."

"You wouldn't have been able to help her anyway. In fact, I'd go so far as to say that you seeing her that way could have stopped her getting any better at all."

"Well, we'll never know now. You stole away three precious years from us, and I will never forgive you for it. More than that, you came here, looked me in the eye and expressed your sympathy for my loss!"

"Because Flora *was* lost. To all including herself. And I didn't believe she was ever coming back. When she did, she gave me strict instructions never to tell you. That was her choice, not mine. Until I saw an article in the paper saying you'd be back in the country, and I backed her into a corner."

Kate narrowed her eyes at him. "You love her, don't you?"

"As a dear friend, of course."

"No, it's more than that."

"Even if that were true, what of it?"

Kate perched herself on the edge of her desk. "You know, Flora actually wanted to go and see a specialist."

"Specialist of what?"

"Someone who deals with war wounds. Prosthetics. Not for her, for my sake. She said it couldn't be pleasant, having to look at her every day as she is. I won't try to pretend it wasn't a shock, seeing her that way. At first, I could barely recognise her, and it wasn't just the scars, either. But the closer I looked, the more I saw her. She's still in there."

Kate circled back around her desk and leant forward, looking at him intently. "I couldn't blame anyone for loving her, even if I wanted to. Say you've convinced me. Will you be returning to Scotland?"

"I will."

"Then I've a favour to ask. And you'll do it."

To his bemusement, crossed the office and closed over the bi-fold doors.

*

Kate hated the fact that love, alone, couldn't fix me. I was angry that I couldn't make myself better just for her. But she never looked at me like I was a disappointment, nor never once allowed me even a moment of guilt when I found I couldn't do something, and I loved her all the more for it.

If you had seen the way the boy in the Edinburgh garage's eyes had rolled back in his head at this most fashionable of ladies waltzing in an demanding the most expensive motorcar he had, you'd have laughed too. We rolled out of there with the only Bentley the poor lad had ever seen. He'd only had it a few days.

I didn't even know she could drive.

It wasn't the return I'd imagined but I was ready to come home, the glitz and glamour of the city lights left far behind us.

Strangely, I think Kate felt relieved. The endless dream-chasing was done, and we could both just step back and enjoy what we had fought so hard for. No more fires to douse, no one trying to destroy what we'd built. It was finally over.

The wind whipped sand into their faces from atop the dunes. The sun sparkled off the clear waters and icing sugar scape of Dunnet Bay.

"I don't know what else to say. I'm running out of ways to tell you how grateful I am." Flora turned to Kate and focussed on the mixed aroma of fresh seaweed and the aldehyde-sandalwood of Kate's new perfume. Another French acquisition.

"Stop saying 'thank you.' You owe me nothing, darling."

"That's not true." She shook her head. "I would never have come back if you hadn't brought me here."

Kate slipped her arm through Flora's and rest her cheek against her shoulder. "Tell me."

"We lived just beyond the headland there, see where that lighthouse is? There's an inlet with the world's tiniest harbour. Wee place called Scarfskerry."

"What was it like?"

"Crofter's life. Da' was at the fishing most of the time and left me to run the land. Ours was one o' the few roundabout to survive the clearances. Just, mind you. Wasn't easy."

"You've told me little about him. What made you leave?"

"There was nothing here for me. Never felt settled as other girls did. I couldn't imagine being tied to a man like my father and then, when he did marry, his wife saw me first as an inconvenience and second, a disgrace. She wanted a brood of her own. I was a reminder of... a truth she couldna' handle."

"You've never spoken of your real mother at all."

"She was... an open-hearted lady. I was the first, but I wasn't the last." Flora tilted her face to Kate's. "I canna find it in me to judge her. If there's one thing I've learnt, folk will do the most desperate things to survive. Da' never spoke of her much either way. All I knew was her name was Maggie and it was just her and her old grandmother. That was it."

"I'm grateful to her, and your father, even if he was hard to love at times." Kate gave Flora a squeeze.

"Your father's your father, eh?"

"Exactly. I wish I could have met him. Even just once."

"He was a difficult man. But I regret not being here at the end. I didn't know for sure he was dead 'til the day."

Kate hooked her arm through Flora's and she gave her thigh a squeeze. "I've long-known that a part of you never left this place. Why did you never come back?"

Flora shook her head. "I'd disgraced him enough. He'd have made up some story about where I'd gone. To come back before now would've been too much. For all his faults, I couldna quite bring myself to do that to him. Though now I feel it's been far too long. Anyway, enough of me. What about you?"

"I came to terms with my past a long time ago, my love. When I met the most wonderful woman who also happened to be the very best of men when she needed to be. And I had a mother who did the only thing she could to ensure I had a future. I can't resent her for that. And I enjoyed my time on the stage. It gave me a steppingstone. It gave me you."

Flora absorbed that, then noted the tiny pinpricks which had broken out all over Kate's arms. "Are you cold?"

"Not enough to move."

We stayed on that beach until the sun began to sink below the horizon and our skin prickled beneath our coats. Kate wanted to stay and explore, and I have to admit, Caithness still tugged at something inside me that I had believed long buried. So, a few days were spent trailing along the track roads which ran between the hamlets and farms. We slid across the endless shifting sands and watched the play of shadows across the moors. And I taught Kate how to say KAIT-ness properly.

One day, I took her to Duncansby where the inky Atlantic waters are chased away by the rough white froth of the North Sea. Or rather, she took me, I just directed.

I showed her the stacks which jut up from the ocean floor like giant witch's hats. We rambled over the grass verge and all the way along the cliffside. With a nod to the incumbent sheep, we shut the gate at the far end, Kate having taken to her bare feet for fear the native's 'deposits' might ruin her Parisian heels. I was informed they were far too expensive to be besmirched by dung!

I glanced back at her as I led her to the cliff's edge, right as the bay sweeps in a perfect arc, and I caught her chest hitch at the sight.

The stacks themselves were near-enough black against the gentle waves that lapped at their feet. But it was the way the sun sparkled and seemed to dance about the rocks.

It's a humbling place and the tear which dropped from her eye was between her and the Earth. I did not ask, but took her hand in mine all the same.

I wasn't sure whether to be relieved or upset that few folk remembered the name Flora Begg. My father would have likely stopped mentioning my name after I ran. But I'd made my peace with the place. On leaving, I felt myself fallen between two stones *yet again, just as I had many times in my youth. Something inside told me this would be my last visit.*

"Come away and sit yerselves doon. Bill's out the back but there's tea made."

Helen MacKechnie, a fine wee woman with a bosom which matched her arse, bustled about with a duster before hurrying off through the kitchen. "You'll have to take us as you find us, I'm afraid. By god, the place is in an uproar. Bill! Tidy yourself up, man, there's visitors here!"

Kate and Flora exchanged sly grins and took a seat on opposite sides of the fireplace.

"Did I say, 'welcome to the Highlands'?" Flora asked.

"I like it. I'm sorry I didn't take the chance to meet her before."

"Aye. Really-speaking they married quite late in life."

"How old is Bill now?"

"Oh, pass. A year or two older than us but couldn't say for sure. And she's definitely older than him."

Bill appeared, wiping his hands, and picking at the dirt trapped under his fingernails.

"Here he is, the noble son o' the soil. Never thought of you as a man of the land, Bill. Too mucky."

"Ach, my uncle used to keep a farm. Spent my holidays there as a lad. I've not got anything so grand, just a garden but I enjoy a potter. What brings you by?" He directed his gaze at Kate.

"I decided it was past time Flora went home, so

we've spent a pleasant few days roaming around Caithness. We thought we'd stop off and pay you a visit at Rogart on the way back to Edinburgh."

"Kate wants to move to Scotland, and I must confess, I'm hardly opposed to the idea." Flora stretched her hand across to Kate's knee.

"I see." said Bill. "Whereabouts were you thinking?"

"Somewhere quiet." said Kate. "Edinburgh's very grand but it's too busy. Caithness is beautiful but it's too sparse."

"Well, there's a farmhouse up for grabs just along the road if you'd consider moving here. Locals are friendly with a braw pub stumbling distance."

Kate cast a glance at Flora. Whether she's realised it or not, her eyes had lit up.

"Drink your tea and have a think on it. You can always take a gander at it later. Plenty daylight left." Bill hadn't missed it either. "Settling down at long last, eh?"

"Think it's overdue, don't you?"

The early evening Summer sunshine stretched on as two shadows crunched arm-in-arm up the gravel path in the direction Bill had sent them.

"What was going on back there?"

"How do you mean?"

"I'm only half-blind, Kate. The other half sees just fine."

"Alright. Bill came to see me a few months before we left London. Views were exchanged."

Flora bit down on her first response. "I suppose you had your reasons, and I won't ask what was said, but I hope whatever it was is resolved?"

"It is."

"And that's all I'm getting?"

"Precisely."

Flora's *hmph* died away when Kate pulled her to a stop. "Is this it?"

"I think so."

"Can we go in, d'you reckon?"

"The door's open, I don't see why not."

Together, they stepped over the hillside threshold.

The house was dark and unloved. Cobwebs drooped from every crevice and what remained of the carpets stank something foul.

"Mind your step." Flora lifted Kate's hand as she navigated over one of many rotted beams that had caved in from the ceiling. "Wait 'til I see that bloody Bill. Bet he's having a right laugh."

"I love it!"

"What?" Flora spun on her crutch. "You can't be serious, love. It's falling to bits!"

"Mm, true but that hasn't put me off you, has it?" Kate grabbed Flora's collar, a mischievous glint in her eye. "I am serious. Flora, we could make this place into whatever we wanted. And it's going cheap."

"Aye, well I'd say there's a reason for that. It's surrounding you."

"I mean, we could buy it and have plenty money left over to spend on making it ours."

"Or we spend a bit more and buy a house that willnae fall down about our ears in the middle of the night?" But Flora's resolved withered under the glimmer in Kate's expression. "I'm fighting a losing battle here, aren't I?"

"Yes, my darling, I rather think you are. But I promise, it'll be worth it in the end."

"I trust you."

And she was right. For the first few months, Kate travelled between our new home in Rogart, London, and Paris, setting her affairs in order. The main running of the business was passed over to the ever-reliable Mrs Belfridge who would oversee a further four trusted supervisors. All Kate had to do was sit back and collect the money, although she still kept final approval of all designs.

While she was gone, the renovation of the house, which our new neighbours affectionately took to referring to as 'The Begg Hoose,' gave me a new purpose. It'd been over forty years since I had last laboured in the keeping of a home and I was surprised more than anyone, how quickly I settled into it. The boys of the Strath were a cracking bunch too, and they helped with the bigger jobs.

Kate took to it well. In the main. Apart from providing her share of village amusement when she'd don her heels to feed the chickens.

Her most trying adjustment was in our lack of an inside loo. She wouldn't believe me at first, when I told her usual practice in answering that particular human call was to disappear up the brae ahent the hoose and into the bracken. Then just as I thought she'd accustomed herself, one day there came a shriek wherein I thought every banshee in hell must have prevailed upon us!

I looked out the window and was helpless.

On the hillside was Kate, bare arse flapping to the whole Glen, and both sets of cheeks red as a hoor's lipstick, as she hopped a' tween the rocks.

Not only had she happened across what must have been a very grumpy sprig of gorse which jabbed her behind in protest, but then to add further insult, instead of a dock leaf, in her panic she'd grabbed a clump of stingy nettles.

Poor lass. She'd never have made a soldier.

With the door clunked shut behind her, Kate dropped her hat and gloves on the sideboard and rushed through to the kitchen.

"Darling, that's-. Oh, I say!"

"Like them?"

Kate lifted her hands to her face. At first, Flora cringed and braced herself but the twill tufts at Kate's shoulders took on a suspicious shoogle. Followed by an odd squeak.

"Out with it, come on."

Kate buckled and howled. She laughed so hard that after a few moments, she had to grip her arms about her waist. "I'm sorry, but you must admit, you are a sight!"

Flora looked down at herself. It had taken much ingenuity to get herself perched onto the worktop. First, the counter had needed bolstering up in order to take her weight, so she had gathered up some of the old cupboard doors and better scraps bits of wood to build a pair of horses. Then, she'd used a chair as a step. Her crutch was propped between the counter and the kitchen table with a bucket of paste suspended from the middle. Flora, herself, was caked in more paste than she'd managed to get on the walls.

"They're beautiful, darling. If a tad... squint." Kate broke down again. The skew-whiff tiles were too much.

Flora rolled her eyes. "I admit, I haven't quite placed them in their final positions yet." Which only prompted another round of hilarity.

"I'm sorry, love. It probably doesn't help that you're trying to do it side-on, and there I go laughing at you." She picked her way over the gloopy newspaper covering the floor and wrapped her arms about Flora's neck.

"S'pose it does look a sight mess."

"Just a little, but I love you. And from today onwards, I'll be here to give you a hand."

"It's done, then?"

"It's done. The company keeps my name, but day-to-day running is out of my hands."

"Any regrets?"

"None whatsoever."

"Good. I have something for you."

"Better than squint kitchen tiles?"

"Even better than that."

Flora hopped down from the counter and disappeared down the hallway.

Kate prodded at one drooping square and giggled at

the droplets of glue that slid down the wall. She set about tidying up, dismayed when only some of the newspaper ripped away when she pulled at it, the rest remaining stuck to the lino. Not to mention her velveteen gloves. "Well, it suppose it's all going to have to come up anyway. And you won't really be needing these anymore, will you?"

"I do love this table. Do you think we can save it?" she asked as the sound of Flora's gait drew nearer.

"Aye, 'course. Wee sand and seal it with some varnish. It'll come up a treat. Now, sit ye doon, lass."

Kate frowned but did as bade. Then Flora came to rest beside her, perched on the table. She dangled something in front of Kate's face.

"It's a necklace. Is that Jet? But that's for mourning."

"Not Jet. You remember when we stopped off at Scarfskerry? Well, I picked this up from what was left of the old croft. It's Caithness slate. All the houses are built of it. It's a wee piece of roof tile. I spent a few evenings polishing it but wasn't sure what to do with it. I mentioned it to Big Eck when they all came to help with the roof beams. Turned how his missus does a wee bit jewellery making.

Kate, I made you a vow years ago, only it's taken me far too long to honour. So, I reckon you deserve a new one. This slate kept generations of my family warm and safe. Protected them from the elements, a home and hearth..."

Kate pressed her fingers to Flora's lips. A flicker of understanding passed between them. "It's the first piece of jewellery you've ever given me. Will you put it on for me?"

Flora nodded as Kate turned around. As soon as

the clasp was secured at the back of her neck, Kate raised the fragment of stone to her lips.

"It's never coming off."

When Flora entered the kitchen much later, she was at the sink, hands deep in soapy bubbles. She took hold of her waist and spun her around until Kate's hands soaked her back and she plunged her own into the hot water. "Did we, or did we not have a discussion regarding our kitchen duties? If you will insist on cooking our every meal, then I insist on cleaning. Although, I admit, having you like this is a welcome distraction." Flora presses closer, squeezing Kate between the counter and her own body.

"You looked so content, I thought I'd get on with it."

"Not the point." Flora kissed her while her hands scrubbed at the leftover plates in the sink.

When all the dishes were propped up on the drainer, Flora dried her hands then manoeuvred them to the corner of the worktop and helped Kate hop up. Kate's thighs slid apart out of an instinct all their own, as Flora kissed her way down her body.

It didn't take long. It never did when Flora decided so. The woman who could literally tease the pleasure from her body over several hours, also knew the exact buttons to press for a quick result.

As Kate gathered herself, Flora wrapped one arm wrapped about her waist while the other filled the kettle and set it to boil on the hob.

"I've always said you were the arch multitasker, my love."

"I aim to please."

"And you do."

"Hmm, I'm hardly a prize catch." Flora glanced down at herself. "Most women would have run for the hills."

"Oh, you mean you're no-longer the strapping twenty-one-year-old who could ravish me the entire night then turn up at barracks at silly o'clock and do a full day's work? I'm hardly an April lamb, myself." Kate slipped her fingers beneath Flora's collar and kissed her. They remained in this pleasant haze until Kate began to unbutton Flora's shirt.

"Why, Mrs Begg, what on earth are you up to?"

Kate's *hmm* vibrated against her ear. "Feeling you. I want to touch you because you are mine to touch." Flora allowed the rest of the shirt to be peeled away and Kate's fingertips grazed every bump, every patch of bubbled skin on Flora's torso. "No one has ever made me feel completely safe the way that you do."

"Even now?"

"Even now."

They continued their exploration while Flora reached across and poured the water into the pot and stirred the tea. She even managed to pull the milk out of the fridge, several cupboards along without breaking from Kate's delicate attentions. Then she lifted the two mugs and took them away to the coffee table in the living room.

Kate folded her arms and smirked as Flora moved to the radiogram that ran along the wall beneath the windowsill.

Once it had warmed up, a familiar tune wafted through the air, as comforting as the fire that burned in the hearth.

"I remember this song." Flora stretched out a hand towards her and drew her into a loose embrace. "Up for a little shuffle? Oh, if you were the only girl in the world, Kate..."

"You were always the girl I sang to." said Katie as they slipped into an easy embrace and began swaying to the music. "Then when I started designing, it was always you then too. I used to imagine your reaction to me wearing whatever I was drawing. If I could hear your laugh, I knew it wasn't quite right. If I pictured your eyes glazing over, it was perfect."

It was Flora's turn to chuckle this time but as she pulled back, Kate was frowning. "You alright?"

"Touch of a headache, that's all."

"Come and drink your tea." She led them both to the couch, mildly surprised when Kate pulled her head into her lap and started stroking her fingers over Flora's still bare torso, up to her hairline and back down again.

"Feels nice."

"Are you falling asleep on me?"

"Mm, bed."

"Not yet. I want to stay here just a little longer."

*

It was a few hours later when Flora gradually became aware of Kate's breath tickling her nose.

"Kate?"

Kate stroked her thumb over Flora's cheek. "You used to have little black marks just here."

"Hmm, real catch, wasn't I?" Flora shifted her head on the pillow.

"Oh, indeed you were. Protecting me from all those drunken ruffians."

"It was only once, as I recall. Anyway, I doubt I could protect you from a soggy teabag now."

"This threat of teabags isn't keeping you up at nights, is it?" She felt the curl of Flora's lip against her forehead. "I've always felt safe with you. Think of it. I've lived an entire lifetime in the knowledge that another human being would risk everything to keep me safe. And you've trusted me not to abuse it. Even after..."

"Our brief wobble. We both paid the price."

"I took you for granted. I became reckless."

"Hmph, something no one's ever accused me of."

"I suppose. Not that there's much you need to protect me from now. Except maybe a stray chicken or a runaway goat."

"Or stingy nettles. You'll always be beautiful." She slipped her fingers through Kate's hair. "You know I'm not going to be here forever. These lungs are going to get me at some time or other. I don't want you to be lonely."

"I know, but the way I see it, I'd rather have you for six months, than twenty years with the wrong person."

"I just wish I could've given you a family. I'm afraid, Kate."

"Of what?"

"That there'll be nothing left of us. Nothing to say we were."

Kate sighed and brought her face even closer to Flora's.

"I'd be lying if I said I'd never wondered what a little you would have been like. But I've had more than anyone could ever ask for. I've shared thirty years of wonderful memories with someone I know will love me beyond death. My mother gave me to a chorus line when I was too small to understand what was happening. In time, they gave me to Mr Edwardes. You were the first person I ever gave myself to. Whatever happens, whenever the inevitable comes, know that I am happy, and I have no regrets. Do you think we could do something about those tiles, though?"

"First thing, love."

21

We were happy. This house brought us a peace that neither of us had ever experienced. Kate took care of me here. Helped me to bed in the evenings when my wounds ached. I remember one night the pain was too much for me to make it up the stairs. I made a bed for myself on the sofa. I was just dozing off when two arms wrapped around me from behind. She kept me warm throughout the night. When I'd wake her with my nightmarish thrashings, she never once faltered. Never angered or lost her patience.

In the mornings when I was better again, I'd make tea and put the eggs on to boil.

One morning, she wouldn't wake. I begged her open her eyes, but I had felt that peculiar chill too many times.

She'd died in my arms.

I wept.

Fifty years of unshed tears felt like they'd never stop. I held her for what must have been hours for it was dark again by the time I could bring myself to let go of her.

We'd had exactly six months.

Something just went bang in her brain. It wasn't 'til much later that Bill came clean. She'd been seeing him privately for some time. My darling girl was in pain, and I'd noticed nothing. Bill had been under orders not to let on. I have never been given to such rage.

Then Bill pointed out that perhaps that was my divine penance . And while the man spoke true, I cannot find it in myself to forgive, though perhaps it's not for me to hold myself judge & jury.

You see, Time is only your best pal in youth. As the years pass and the distance between your memories and the events which borne them grow, she 'comes an unforgiving mistress. A vile, cruel, and merciless bitch, she waits until the moment is ripe to exact her price for your mistakes. In my darker moments, I cannot help but wonder if Kate's life was the price of mine. By all-natural law, I should have died on that battlefield. Higgins should have filled the ground until the earth burned in my lungs. I wish he had. Now, I am left to rot in the open air and that damned swan refuses to sing her song for me.

I have never been particularly religious. But three faces stare back at me from the mirror, and I pray god not let me linger.

I never wanted to be the last.

And now I know why I needed to write you, dear reader.

Laura swiped at the tears which streamed freely down her face. The abject pain and loneliness in Flora's final words were a sock to the gut. Coming to this place to read the final part of the letter, as a final pilgrimage almost, had been a conscious decision. "Now I wonder if this was such a great idea."

Hither & thither, her eyes darted. Ears cocked for the slightest crunch of leaf underfoot. With one final glance, she slipped the trowel from her jacket, and jabbed at the base of the headstone. The scrape of metal on sodden earth obscene in the silence of the Kirkyard.

"I think this belongs to you."

She kissed the roll of paper and buried it.

A man appeared out of a shed so with the flat side of the tool, she patted down the disturbed earth, shoved the trowel into her back pocket and regained her feet in one smooth motion. It wasn't that she'd done anything *wrong* exactly, but to the casual onlooker, her behaviour might have looked a tad odd.

He stopped at the other side of the grave and leant on his fork.

"You're the young lady I had on the phone?"

"That's right. I found her, thank you."

"Ah, that's no bother. Didn't have much luck with the other, I'm afraid. Sorry. I asked round for you in case any of the older yins might know what'd happened to her." Grubby hands pushed a tatty grey beanie back from his eyes.

"There's no burial record?"

"Not that I can find. She a long-lost relative of yours, then?"

"Yes. Yes she is. She'll never know it, but she's helped me. In ways I can't really explain."

The man tilted his head. "I see. Well, I'll leave you in peace to visit. Tìoraidh."

"Aye, tìoraidh. And thanks again." Laura turned back to the words on the headstone and traced the letters that made up the name Katherine Vaughan-Begg.

"Well Kate, it's nice to finally meet you. Flora's told me all about you." Laura's bottom lip began to tremble and her knee started to shake so she sat back, propping herself on her elbow. "It's funny. I recognise so much of her within me, but I've grown to love you both. You reinvented yourself so many times until you got it right. I don't understand how you did it, or where you found the courage. You made so many messes, you both did, but you learned to stand on your own in the world. And still managed to love with a whole heart. You're the holy grail of women, Kate. And you were stronger than you ever realised. I wish I could take you Both with me.

I didn't think so at first. At first, you were just an annoyance. Sorry. But I'm gonna miss you two and this place so, so much."

"Thought I might find you here."
"Jesus, Mhairi, you scared me!"
"So, what's she saying to you then?"
"That I've been an utter plank." Laura frowned.
"Ken if the wind changes, ye'll stay that way."
Laura poked out her tongue but chuckled. "I wish I could find Flora, though. Can't help but wonder where she is."
"If you mean her remains, I have something that might interest you"
"What?"

"I was digging over the garden the other day, thought I might plant some veg this year. My spade hit something solid under the bedding by the house. So, I dug away at it. Turns out, I have a coal bunker I knew nothing about."

"You didn't- she wasn't-"

"No, nothing like that. CSI Rogart? That'd keep the village talking for years! But there was an urn. An empty urn."

"So? It could've been anyone's."

"True. But someone glued a cap badge on it." Mhairi handed her a small, blackened object. "Did my best with a brush but-"

"The Seaforths. It still doesn't-"

"I'm living in Bill MacKechnie's house. Mrs Matheson casually dropped it into conversation the other day. Turns out he's a distant uncle."

"Seriously? And you didn't know?"

"It's not so unusual. Round here, *everyone's* related. Hardly something to brag about."

"So, all this time, Flora's been in your house. Or was, at least. I wonder what your auntie thought."

Mhairi snorted. "I think the fact she was in the coal bin kinda says it all."

"S'pose. God, poor Flora. She should've been here. Not disintegrating in some bloody coal bunker."

"Well don't know that she isn't. Maybe Uncle Bill scattered her here afterwards."

"I don't think he did."

"What makes you say that?"

"I don't know. I just think, if she were here, I'd feel it on some level."

Mhairi stared at her. "You feeling okay?"

"I know I sound crazy. I can't explain it. I just don't sense her in this place. Maybe I just can't imagine her being surrounded by dead things. Strange, but reading her letter, having her voice in my head, she's been as real to me as anyone."

"You do seem to have developed a bit of a bond."

"She's an old soldier. And she was reckless, and headstrong. Maybe a bit arrogant." She gave Mhairi a rueful smile. "I don't think she ever considered failure a possibility until it happened. She really believed she was invincible. And I can understand that, to be fair. However many battles she fought through, the things she saw, nothing really seemed to touch her until it was too late. She was the talisman. I think that's why what happened to her was so hard to take."

"Hubris."

"Something I know nothing about, of course."

"Of course." Mhairi rolled her eyes.

"I have this, by the way. I haven't been brave enough to open it yet."

"National Records Office?"

"It's Flora's death certificate. I found the entry online and ordered it blind. I'm not sure I even want to see what's on there. Seems so final."

"She died a long time ago, Laura. You're just scared that one day you'll end up like she did."

"I'm a condemned woman"

"How so?"

"Because I'm standing here with nothing but regret. And I hurt. For us both. All I want is to return to a time that's beyond my reach. I have the world at my feet, and I don't want any of it. After everything, I just wish I could go back. Do things better."

"You married Jim because you were afraid of being on your own. And your experiences have only reinforced that fear. But that doesn't make you doomed."

"Will you open it?"

Mhairi ripped away the paper and concentrated on the looped script obscured by black copier splodges.

"Well?"

"Patience." Mhairi arched an eyebrow. It was a look of schoolteacher disapproval which Laura instantly recognised. "It says... Flora died on the 28th of May 1938."

"Ten years."

"Hmm?"

"Another ten years after she wrote the letter. What was the COD?"

"Heart failure. Witnessed by W. MacKechnie, Army Surgeon, retired."

"She must have been in so much pain. She'd had a falling out with Bill when Katie died and lost touch with her old friends, the ones who weren't already gone. No family. In the letter she was praying for death. Imagine spending the last decade of your life like that."

"Laura, you're not her. You're choosing to face the world on your own terms rather than carry on in an unhealthy relationship. That doesn't have to be so scary. For what it's worth, I think you did the right thing. Trying to keep a marriage going when the two of you wanted such different things would have been cruel to you both. Letting him go, it means you both have a fair shot at being happy."

"I used him."

"You did. But I don't believe you did it out of malice."

"I ruined his life."

"Are you determined to be a martyr? Do you honestly think you're so special that he'll never be able to get over you? He's thirty-five, not dead."

"Cheers pal."

"You're welcome."

"Help me up?"

"Sure, ask the woman on crutches to help you up. So, now the letter's gone. How d'you feel?"

"It's not gone entirely. I made photocopies. One for Dornoch Historylinks and one for the Highlanders Museum as a thank you. And I'm splitting the outfits between them."

"Wow. That's pretty generous. There are museums down south who would pay a fortune for some of Kate's collection."

"I know. But I think she'd be happy. It was Kate who wanted to move here. I think she'd be glad to be remembered this way."

Mhairi pressed on a twig beneath her boot. "Y'know, they picked a fine spot." She scanned the view across Strath Fleet and tucked a wayward blonde curl behind her ear.

"They did. And although I wasn't happy about moving here, I am glad. If nothing else, this place has made me face up to a few things."

Mhairi turned on her single crutch and began the slow dander back up the gravel path. "When do you leave for Harris?"

"Next week."

"And?"

Laura shrugged, hands stuffed into her jeans pockets. "It's time. Beth says she might have a buyer in-mind."

"Oh?"

"Aye, herself. Think she's seen the way wind's blowing. She wants out the NHS quick. Got plans for a right wee cottage industry."

"All change, eh?"

"Ah, good on her. It's time to let go. Ruth agrees."

"Who's Ruth?"

"My therapist. God, that sounds so American."

"Check you out, lady! You feeling empowered? All 'woman, hear me roar'?"

"Don't talk shite."

"Well, you know, if you need a hand, Summer holidays are coming up and Izzy's a dab hand with a paintbrush. I'd let you have her for nothing?"

Laura grinned. "I'd like that. And, hey, if you'd like to come too? Might be nice to have a friendly face."

"I'll consider it." Mhairi tipped her a wink.

Laura returned to the house and dropped her jacket on the hallway table. Jim appeared in the kitchen doorway rubbing his hands over with a tea towel.

"You had any dinner yet?"

"No." She shook her head. "What smells so nice?"

"Just an omelette, nothing fancy. Wondered if you'd like one?"

Poor boy's going to be living off school dinners when I go.

"Thank you. I'm just gonna go sort out a few bits and pieces." She tilted her head in the direction of the study.

"You really like it in there, don't you?" He leaned on the doorway and folded his arms with an easy smile.

"I do. Have you noticed the house feels different lately?"

"Different? In what way?"

"Quieter, somehow. More settled."

"I think you're imagining things. Those ghosties at it again, eh?"

"Hmph, maybe you're right. Or maybe it's just us. I know this has been awful Jim, and it's all my fault, but I do feel more settled now."

"Nothing's ever just one person's fault, Laura. I know I've been making my anger felt, but you're right. We need different things. And for whatever it's worth, I'm sorry if I made things harder."

"Thanks."

"You know you're welcome to take whatever you want. I wouldn't hold anything hostage."

"I appreciate that, but the truth is I've no idea where I'll be a year from now. Whatever I take needs to be something that fits in the pocket of a backpack!"

"I haven't pressed you on anything and I won't but, I would like to know you're safe."

Her lip quirked. "I'll be fine. I promise. First stop Harris and I can guarantee you, nothing's going to happen to me there."

"You sure about that? Last time Mhairi came back with a broken leg."

"Well, that's Mhairi. And no bikes this time, I swear."

"Alright. I'll leave you to say your goodbyes. One super veggie-packed omelette coming right up."

"Veggies? your omelettes are usually just one big gloopy mess of cheese and half-cooked eggs. You're getting better."

"I am. Promise." They shared a smile and Laura turned away. "Can I ask you one last thing?"

"Sure."

"Was it me?"

"Was what you?"

"I mean, did I ever do anything that made you feel like..."

"No, Jim. You're the perfect guy. For the right girl without half as much baggage. This one's on me. Believe that. And keep eating your veggies."

She smiled at him one final time then ducked into the cosy confines of the room she had previously dubbed 'the music room.' She took a seat at the desk and lifted the lid of a black portable gramophone, sat on its own little side table. "Amazing." Laura fingered the coarse remnants of a green and gold HMV label. The tiny terrier with his curious nose.

"That's different." With careful hands, she raised a 78 off the turntable by its edges and squinted at the centre label. "Why have I never noticed you before?" Fortunately, the disc had been protected under the lid and remained relatively dust-free. She pushed her thumb against the needle. *Damn.*

Leaning over the contraption, she fiddled about with a compartment at the back of the turntable and spied a brown paper packet. Inside were a dozen or so needles.

"I haven't done this since I was a kid."

She gave the tonearm a few turns until she felt a good amount of tension, released the brake lever, and let the turntable run. Once she was certain the mechanism was running freely, with delicate precision, she lifted the arm over and placed it on the edge of the record. Resting back in the chair, she allowed the crackly lyrics to wash over her.

> On a day not far away, but oh, how distant it seems,
> I began to shape and plan a golden palace of dreams.
> Gallant, and shining, and splendid,
> It grew, and grew, and grew so beautiful,

> Soaring high, it touched the sky, all bright and new.
> And now, in smoke, it's ended as castles of dreams always do.

1938

> I built it of moonlight and madness.
> Each star was a true lover's one,
> But ruin, and heartache, and sadness,
> Are all that is left of it now.

Bill slammed the front door behind him and popped his head into Flora's study. She was dozing at the desk, the gramophone left to play for its own entertainment... again.

"That damn tune's never off in this house. See you're still wearing that ratty old cardigan as well. I'll go and put the kettle on, shall I? Oh, suit yourself." He stomped off in the direction of the kitchen, still chattering away. Eventually, to the whistle of the kettle, he reappeared with two mugs of tea in-hand. "Christ, Flora, how long's this going to go on for? Flora?"

He dumped the tea on the desk. "Flora! Dammit, woman!" He gave her a shake and pressed his fingers beneath her ear. "Would you really rather die than have to speak to me? Flora!"

'Flora!'

Oh, why must we always be dreaming,
If dreaming can never come true?

Laura's eyes shot open and she regarded the reflection staring back at her in the mirror.

"Have you been here all this time? Or did my imagination just cook you up to make it seem like I've been doing something important the last few months? Atmosphere, I guess. Or wishful thinking."

She plucked the two photographs sticking out of the mirror frame. The first, a dashing young couple posed in front of an ancient wooden rollercoaster with illicit smiles. The second, a handsome chap in uniform with close-cropped hair and the cheekiest glint. She stood and glanced about the room, cradling the images carefully in both hands.

"I'd bring these to you if I knew where to find you. But I've no idea what happened to you. So I'll take them with me. I hope you don't mind. Jim'll only end up throwing them out otherwise.

You said once, in your letter, that the ghosts which truly haunt us aren't things in white sheets but the fragments of what we, ourselves, once were. Tiny pieces of our own soul sheared off and left to float about in the ether like jagged bits of glass; in each one, a different reflection. Now and then, from the corner of our eye, we'll catch a glimpse of something frightening and shy away. Well, I tried burying mine in all the wrong ways. But they grew up from the earth, twisted about my body like a vine and rent me to shards. You're the only one I know who understands that feeling.

Understood.

We've both been shattered. I need to close the door Flora, and I won't look back, but not because I'm running.

Something of you stayed here. It scared me at first. But I've come to understand you. I get the feeling you'd laugh at me for saying this, but you're the person everyone wishes they had on their side. You never ran from anything. Even when maybe you should have. I think it's time we both found some peace. So for the first time in a really, really long time, I have a plan.

I'm grateful to you, Flora. And I promise I won't let you and Katie be forgotten. That's why you left the letter, isn't it? You were afraid that the love you shared would be lost and there'd be nothing left. More than that, you were afraid all memory of Kate would be lost. So I'm going to write it all down. Time can have someone else. I think the world still needs the both of you." Her lip curved in a wan smile. "I'll take my leave of you now, if that's alright." She slipped the postcards into her cardigan and tapped a finger to the gramophone. "Pretty song."

Laura allowed her eyes to linger round the room for one last time, hopeful. But the room remained still. She gave a snort, turned back towards the door then twisted the key in the lock, adding it to the postcards in her pocket.

"Rest easy, Soldier."

THE END

Lightning Source UK Ltd.
Milton Keynes UK
UKHW010028291021
393012UK00001B/24